C000178423

The Elephant & The Polish Question, and Other Stories

with every good
wish —

Helen Lynch.

The Elephant & The Polish Question, and Other Stories

Helen Lynch

Published by bluechrome publishing 2009

2 4 6 8 10 9 7 5 3 1

Copyright © Helen Lynch 2009

Helen Lynch has asserted her right under the Copyright, Designs and Patents Act 1988 to be identified as the author of this work.
This book is sold subject to the condition that it shall not, by way of trade or otherwise, be lent, resold, hired out, or otherwise circulated without the publisher's prior consent in any form of binding or cover other than that in which it is published and without a similar condition including this condition being imposed on the subsequent purchaser.

First published in Great Britain in 2009 by
bluechrome publishing
PO Box 109,
Portishead, Bristol. BS20 7ZJ
www.bluechrome.co.uk

A CIP catalogue record for this book is available from the British Library.

ISBN 978-1906061678

For Ernest Malshinger and Betty Lynch, and for all those who are not seen.

And for Mike and Jenny, my parents, because it mattered after all.

Contents

A VERY Brief Guide to Polish Pronunciation

Although I have on rare occasions altered the spelling of individual Polish words for ease of reading, I have left almost all Polish names and proper nouns in their original form. Tastes vary, but for those who might like some clues as to how to pronounce these or who like to feel they are hearing them fairly accurately in their heads, I am providing a few tips here:

First of all, **w** in Polish is pronounced like **v** in English. So Iwona equals Ivona, Sylwia = Sylvia, wodka = vodka and so on.

J operates like a **y** (as in yellow), so Julia becomes Yulia.

The composite letter **dz** acts like the **dg** in 'budget' in English (or the **g** in 'geranium' and the **j** in 'jump'), so that the name Jadzia virtually rhymes with 'badger' and Wandzia with 'ganja'.

Ci and **cz** make two slightly different **ch** sounds in Polish, but, roughly speaking, Babcia (Granny) can be rendered 'Babcha' and Marczak 'Marchak'.

Similarly, **si** and **sz** roughly equate to **sh**, so that Basia is pronounced 'Basha', and Krysia 'Krisha'.

Rz - as in the word Przedszkole (the Polish for Pre-school or Kindergarten) sounds rather like the **j** in the French word 'je'. Polish is phonetic, and all letters are sounded (-szkole is 'shkol-eh').

I have omitted all Polish accents, and some letters (such as Ł) which don't exist in English. In pronouncing Polish words, the stress falls on the penultimate syllable.

Our Experience Your Satisfaction

The moment the wheels stopped turning on the tarmac came the slow hand-clap of the passengers. No-one stood up. My ears still whirring from the descent and our hurtle along the runway, I looked around the cabin. LOT Airways had decorated their plane with what appeared to be wallpaper in a lilac, floral design, peeling where it met the baggage lockers. The clapping was brief but somehow chilling. Was it derisory, or genuinely relieved, appreciative? I'd never travelled by plane before and wasn't sure what was normal.

The 'applause' petered out with a final smattering of claps.

'Don't worry,' the lady next to me leant over. 'We are just happy to be landing safely on ground.' She gave a motherly smile and her rings flashed as she pushed her glasses back onto the bridge of her nose. 'It is your first time in Poland so you will not understand very much things. LOT Airways is all the time flying this terrible planes what Russians give to us. Very old, very broken planes. No-one fly such planes any more. There are many accidents. Fortunately Polish pilots are best in all world. They were flying even spitfires in War.' She paused to primp her high-lighted blonde hair and loop her finger through the gold chain which had got lost under the scarlet polo neck of her sweater.

I couldn't help trying to work out the age of these pilots - twenty in 1940, so that would make them…nearly seventy? I can't say I found the idea of snowy-haired, septuagenarian pilots terribly reassuring, spitfires or no spitfires.

People were standing up, pulling large items of hand-baggage from lockers and blocking the aisle. My neighbour tugged the lapels of her checked suit-jacket across her bosom and waited. Since she seemed a seasoned air traveller, I made no attempt to get up either. We had exchanged only smiles on the flight, but now she told me that she had been visiting her sister in Nottingham. It had been very difficult for her to get the passport, even with such proper invitation. She managed to combine matronliness with glamour, and to give the impression that she was tough as well as kind.

'Barbara...I am Barbara. You can say Basia,' she introduced herself. 'Why do you want to come here? You must be crazy. It is place of largest suffering on the earth.'

There had been a decisive shift in climate. In London it had been a sunny September day. Here, at the foot of the steps from the plane, soldiers with long, triangular capes held their sub-machine guns diagonally across their bodies while a light sleet blew over them.

The airport seemed to consist of a single, low building. After a very long wait and slow scrutiny of my passport and other paperwork (exempting me from having to change a certain amount of foreign currency for every day of my stay), I signed a document declaring that I had brought precisely £2.50 into the country. I would have to visit the police station in Lodz after two weeks, I was informed, to apply for a visa that would last for the full term of my contract. In the meantime, I was reunited with my suitcases, which no-one showed the least interest in searching, though lines of Polish passengers were waiting with bulging canvas bags to be questioned about their contents. I was released through the sliding door into the main hall, where large numbers of people with hopeful expressions and bunches of flowers jostled behind a cordon.

I had no idea who might have come to meet me, so scanned all the faces in hopes of signs of *their* recognition. At the thinner end of the crowd, individuals waited with placards bearing names of passengers or of companies. I read them all, but none bore any resemblance to my name. I wandered into a clearing and looked around. I had been so busy with the differentness of everything, with noticing how smartly dressed everyone was, with how many were wearing hats and how many of the men had moustaches - and with listening to the language with that total non-comprehension which almost passes over into a kind of fluency - to register the gravity of my situation. I had no Polish currency, as this was to be supplied on my arrival, and no idea how to use a Polish phone. The only people at the airport to speak any English had been the scariest looking officials back at the passport and currency declaration booths. I looked round in the vain hope that Basia might not yet have been swept off in the bouquet waving multitude.

My eye seized on the English words on a poster in the window of a bureau ahead of me, stating baldly: ORBIS Polish Travel Agency OUR EXPERIENCE YOUR SATISFACTION. Would it have seemed less menacing if there had been a comma, I wondered? The bureau was closed anyway. That was why I'd come, wasn't it? To have an experience and to be altered by it, whether I wanted to or not. Would my experience be to the satisfaction of my hosts, or to my own? It was impossible to know.

12

All of which was a distraction from my immediate circumstances. I had no idea what to do next. I wanted to get out of the dislikeable military chill of the place, but kept being drawn into the pleasures of observation: how many fur coats there were, how people seemed to give three kisses on the cheek on greeting, and above all the tantalising qualities of the language. Understanding nothing and understanding everything are more nearly allied to one another than to any state in between. Without even the occasional jagged interruption of recognition in the flow of sound, it feels exactly like a language you know, only in negative. After all, when every single word is equally mysterious, it's somehow easier to imagine being able to comprehend all of them. Babies must feel like that. I felt myself suspended in a condition of total possibility, like a child whose babble can develop in any linguistic direction whatsoever.

The name called over the intercom system was similarly incomprehensible and bore very little relation to my own, but as the message appeared to be in English, I wanted very much to take its advice and head for the Something-Not-Quite-Audible-Bureau. An elderly man in a peaked cap, seeing me spinning gormlessly around, kindly pointed out a row of doors in the wooden partition to the side of the main arrivals hall. I couldn't even say thank you, except in English.

The fair-haired man wearing trousers tucked into boots, to whom I was introduced by the pony-tailed young woman in a blue uniform, smiled a lot but spoke no English. I hadn't caught his name, and didn't know how to ask for it to be repeated. The young woman, who did not seem to be the person who had made the announcement, did not speak English either, and, considering her job done, ushered us out of her office cubicle. The man smiled some more. I smiled too and held out my hand. He instantly took it, flipped it over and kissed it fervently, peering up through his hair trustingly and with more smiles. I pointed at myself:

'Helen - Helena.'

He threw up his hands, nodding, saying something which included the word 'matka', mother, and repeating my name. It was the first Polish word I'd recognised, (since it was contained in Chapter One of *Teach Yourself Polish*, which, in the haste of the whole enterprise was as far as I'd got). It might mean that I had the same name as his mother, which was probably a good thing - or it might mean 'Mother of God, Helena, what are we going to do we don't understand a word?!' Either way, he pointed to his chest and pronounced 'Wladek - Wlad-ek' very slowly.

'Wladek,' I repeated, and nearly held out my hand again. Perhaps to forestall the same impulse himself, he ran his hands through his hair, then, promisingly, picked up my suitcases and nodded for me to follow him. As he stowed them in the boot of a grimy white Lada, I seriously hoped there had not been a mistake. It was all pretty circumstantial. Had

I allowed myself to be collected in place of some long-distance arranged bride?

'Francais?' I tried, as the car pulled away.

He looked non-plussed.

'Deutsch?' He nodded vigorously, beaming, at which point I had to confess, partly in sign language, that I didn't. Not really. As the three or four phrases I could produce in German were grammatically quite convincing and spoken with a passable accent, Wladek refused to believe me. After five or ten minutes of excited German on his part, he subsided and I realised I had already disappointed my first person in this new country.

Windsocks distended in the stiff breeze and silver leaves fluttered on the poplars lining the centre of the dual carriageway. The sky achieved only a marginally lighter gray than the wide road.

'The Instytut phoned. Your train's in about two hours. Wladek has a ticket for you.' Felicity Redclyffe of the British Council was one of those women who always make you feel that you have bounded rather than walked towards them, and that, with the least encouragement, you might become over-excited and muddy her skirt with your paws. There was always the tiniest of gaps before her replies as if allowing time for me to collect myself and calm down.

Wladek had disappeared among bookshelves full of 1950s and 1960s penguin paperbacks. I scanned the spines, some blue, some orange: C.P. Snow, Christopher Fry, John Galsworthy.

'Poles like him,' Felicity commented. 'Friend of Conrad's,' moving swiftly on before this could be deemed the opening of a conversation. 'You can wait here and Wladek can drive you when the time comes. He should be free about then. There's plenty to read.' She smiled briefly, the kind of smile measured exactly to meet requirements but extend no invitations, and went into her office.

No danger of a cup of tea, then, I thought. None of that 'Welcome, my fellow countryman, how about we exchange information of mutual interest and get to know one another?' stuff. This was unfortunate since, after only an hour in the country, I already felt that eagerness at the sight of a compatriot that makes you want to greet them as a friend. I wanted to chat, to ask questions about Poland, about her life here. Felicity did reappear intermittently as I sat on my stool leafing through *The Forsyte Saga* but I understood that my impulses were presumptious and she was manifestly busy.

Surrounded by framed posters of Big Ben and Windsor Castle, feeling completely cut adrift from Britishness, I knew that outside, in the crowded Warsaw street, was another world, which both engaged and excluded me more than anywhere in my life. As for Felicity Redclyffe, I couldn't bear that 'I can take you or leave you' attitude which I ascribed to the British upper middle classes. Especially the middle aged - or pretending to be middle-aged. Felicity couldn't be more than forty. Was she *trying* to be a stereotype? Her tartan hairband and sky blue cashmere sweater gave way to a worsted skirt and beige tights as if she metamorphosed half-way down, in the process of turning into stone. I detested the whole class thing. Thank God I was going to be out of *that* for a while.

It was frustrating to have to wait, eager to put as much distance between myself and Thatcher's Britain as I possibly could. Spending so long in resistance, alienated from everything that is going on, in the end the trick is not to turn into an inverted version of what you oppose. I'd seen it with other people. I didn't want it to happen to me.

There were occasional glimpses of Wladek in the stairwell, or at the end of a stack, but I couldn't blame him for avoiding me, appalled by the absence of a common language. He knew he still had the drive to the station to come.

The platforms at Warszawa Centralna station were underground, shadowed and grey, with pillars painted on one side in dark, aquamarine blue. The slabs of colour, like Mondrian rectangles, gave a modern impression. There were not many prospective passengers, and these stood spaced out and disconnected from one another, united only in staring at my suitcases. The sole exception was an elderly lady in a grey raincoat with slightly dishevelled hair, who shuffled about, intent on her own concerns, at the periphery of my vision. I couldn't see why my luggage should merit such disproportionate scrutiny. The cases were not smart, though their airline labels were still prominent.

It made me nervous, as if I were transporting something everyone else knew about but me. Was I so obviously a foreigner, or was a Pole who'd been to the West also worth gazing at? Did they imagine those cases to be full of contraband, of desirable Western goodies? Worth envying? Worth stealing? Or simply worth staring at hard enough to extract their contents through the canvas by sheer eye-power?

My ears strained after the announcements coming over the tannoy system. I had worked out that the much repeated word 'peron' must mean platform, since 'Per.' and a number appeared on the sign above my head. I thought I could make out some destinations and numbers, but I hoped that Wladek had left me in the right place. Luckily, when a train drew up at my platform, it was clear that the little wooden flaps next to the doors stated where the train was going, and also, upside down, where it had come from, or where it went when travelling in the opposite direction. The second one to arrive had Lodz written on the flaps.

I put my suitcases onto the train and climbed up after them. The step was higher than on a British train. The old lady was behind me and I felt a poke in the ribs. Thinking she might need some help, I turned around. She was half trying to climb onto the train, so I offered her my hand but she didn't take it. She had rolled up her raincoat and was pushing it towards me, speaking all the time. Her eyes were as grey as her hair and her pupils were very small. Was she begging? Was she pleading for something? Under the coat she was tugging my handbag, lifting the flap. I grabbed the straps in both my hands, producing my first ever spontaneous Polish utterance - '*NIE!*' - and fell backwards over my suitcase. The old woman's face seemed to go backwards too, perhaps with the force of my wrenching the bag, and as I tried to stand up, someone slammed the door and the train started. Oh God, had I hurt her?

'Do you succeed to be O.K.?' a small, sweet-scented man with wavy brown hair and a large moustache inquired, taking my elbow. He stowed my suitcases carefully in his compartment and ushered me in after them. 'What a welcome in our country. That is really terrible,' he was saying. 'I introduce myself. I am Marcin,' he kissed my hand, 'and this is my friend Rohan. 'He is from the Iran. From Persia we like to say.' Rohan was darker and plumper, but just as immaculate as Marcin. He wore a crisp shirt, a fringed burgundy scarf and a mustard waistcoat. The paisley-patterned scarf spoke of Noel Coward to me, but was probably a traditional Iranian design. With small gestures of his soft, plump hands, he spoke in English slowly and gently, as if to spare me any of the harsher sounds of my own language.

Marcin was the more bubbly of the two.

'Rohan is my special friend this year in my department,' he explained, 'because I have for many years the interest in the Persian poetry. Do you know about it?' I shook my head. 'I manage to invite him for one year here.'

'And what is bringing you to Poland?' Rohan asked.

'I'm starting a job, at the English Philology Department at the University in Lodz.'

'Ah, we will be your neighbours, so to say,' Marcin put in. 'We will to work in same building but in the upstairs, in Polish Philology. Your rivals, no your poor relations. Mostly it is the rich kids which are studying the English Philology. If I can ask it, how did you to find this job?

'It's a kind of exchange programme with the university where I studied, except that the exchange only goes in one direction.'

'Polish students are not allowed to go to West for study, naturally,' Marcin affirmed. 'Who knows what terrible things they might to learn.' He made a mock-horrified face.

'Every year my university sends two or three graduates or postgraduates over to teach. The scheme has been running for about four years, I think.'

'I think I heard about this one time,' Marcin said.

'I don't really know much about it. I decided to come all in a bit of a hurry really.'

'Why? Are you on run from police?' Rohan suggested.

'Or are you Communist? I heard there are some in West. Did you come to discover our Communist Utopia here in Poland?' Marcin teased.

'No, not at all. I did come to have a bit of a rest from *my* government though. The Western Utopia isn't a lot of fun at the moment.'

In the fields, four women in big, bunchy skirts were bending over rows of beets, pulling at the green leaves and tossing the beets onto a wooden cart. Two wore coloured headscarves, and one stood up to wipe her arm across her forehead. There was a man in a cap and shirtsleeves standing on the cart, while the piebald horse waited, munching and shaking its head.

'Oh no,'said Marcin, 'we are very fond of your Mrs Thatcher here. Fabulous. We hope she will come soon to visit in the Poland.'

'Perhaps when she does you would like to keep her. She's not very popular with a lot of people back home.'

'I met also one time the young English girl in Warsaw. She was strongly not liking this Mrs Thatcher either. Perhaps it is just the young womens are not liking her.' Rohan suggested.

'It's not only young women, I promise you. Anyway, in the West, most people think Gorbachev is wonderful, but in Poland …?'

'No,' Marcin agreed, 'we don't like him. Is better than the ones coming before, but we don't to trust him.'

'And plenty of Russians seem to *really* dislike him. So perhaps the opinions of those closest should count the most, don't you think? Perhaps those people have more knowledge.'

'You know, I will tell to you the funny story. Some years ago, I stay with my friend. He is student organiser in Wroclaw in this moment when all miners is having in your country the strike.'

'You mean when your generous General Jaruzelski sent Polish coal to help the British government defeat …'

'That is right, yes. Well, there was *delegacja* to Polish Miners' Union from Union of Miners in Britain. They was visiting in Wroclaw for one or two weeks, staying in Polish Miners' Club. They were soon arguing very bad. The Polish miners couldn't to believe how these British miners didn't to like Mrs Thatcher. She is very fine woman, they tell to them, very big friend to Poland, very big ally to the President Reagan. There was fighting even on street. The Polish miners were beating the British because they insulted the Mrs Thatcher.'

'Don't you think that's amazing? I mean, I don't assume I know more about Poland than you do.'

'Of course not, you have just arrived, but soon you will… Everyone like to think they know better, to be superior. Anyway, maybe they are right. Maybe the stranger see more clear.'

'I don't think so, maybe a few things, but…'

'So maybe even we are right about your Pani Thatcher,' Marcin patted my arm. He paused a moment. 'You understand, it is difficult for us. So much is lying in T.V. Even the pictures are lying. Everything is to show us how bad is situation elsewhere, especially in the Western countries, in America, South Africa. We saw in recent time many pictures from the South Africa. Surely is not so bad like they say, police and army shooting all those negroes. It must be exaggeration for sure.'

'You mean you would believe that South Africa is governed by happy black people because the official news tells you the opposite?'

'Maybe not exactly. But such a system, this apartheid, surely it is not possible?'

Rohan offered me some *paluszki*, pretzel sticks dusted with crystals of salt. They were delicious.

'*Paluszki* mean little fingers,' he explained. Gazing out of the windows, I noticed the frequency with which we passed long rows of brown wooden cattle trucks, drawn up in sidings or travelling in the opposite direction. I couldn't help a frisson of alarm and the thought 'You'd think they'd change the design.' Whoever 'they' were, the people, with one spontaneous voice? The government by decree? How was it 'their' fault if such cattle trucks had bad associations? Probably they didn't for those who saw them every day. They had been cattle trucks before and they were cattle trucks after. Why alter a perfectly serviceable design? Besides, they might be goods wagons and not cattle trucks at all for all I knew. I was hardly an expert on rail freight, was I? And let's face it - I looked out fondly at an old man and his grandson in their cart, the horse trotting smartly up to the level crossing - no-one's changed the design of *anything* very much.

'I propose the question for you,' Marcin was saying. 'Why is there no AIDS in Poland?'

'I don't know. Isn't there?'

'It is joke, you will see. Why is there not the AIDS in Poland?'

'I don't know. Why is there no AIDS in Poland?'

'Because AIDS is the disease of *twentieth* century.'

I laughed, and they laughed even more.

At Lodz station a man wearing a corduroy jacket with a baggy blue jumper came to meet me. He was stocky, even a bit chubby, half blood-hound puppy, half handsome, overgrown boy, with a rueful smile and a floppy, blond fringe. There was something a bit 'Brideshead' about the hairstyle, and he later admitted that he had spent a semester at Oxford the previous year.

'I am Pawel Czernik,' he said, shaking my hand and then kissing it. 'I am allocated for being your so-called "guide" here in Lodz. First I will show to you your flat. It is not the final flat for you, only the temporary one, I may say, but for some nights. I will drive you in my small Fiat, the so-called "Polish ice-cube."'

We bounced and wove through the streets, dodging cream and red trams and bumping over tram-tracks and cobbles and pot-holes between tall grey buildings whose character I could barely make out, except that they appeared to be 19th century and both ornate and dilapidated. There was something about the random spaces between some of these build-ings and the newer ones, odd patches of ground, serving no apparent purpose and often overgrown, that suggested bombsites.

'My apologies for all of this bumping about,' said Pawel. 'Our city is not famous for the smooth roads. After the War, probably you know it, all Warsaw was destroyed and many other cities. Lodz was not so se-verely damaged, so it was for some time the capital for administering all repairs for other cities, especially Warsaw. Unfortunately, the repairs for *this* city were not coming about.' He gave his trademark apologetic grin. 'It is not so comfortable for you.'

'Oh no, it's fine.' I already found it all entrancing, though a less partial observer might have been forgiven for supposing that the War had ended just a few weeks before.

Pawel left me at the flat, which was on the third floor of a yellow, five-storey building. Before he went, he emptied a mound of crumbling white cheese onto a plate, and deposited half a loaf of dense, grey bread and a large beef tomato. I didn't know then how generous that tomato was.

'With luck, I succeeded to find for you the tomato,' was all he said. 'I can leave for you the small sum of money, some few *zlotys* only, I'm afraid, until you are having the wages. There is also tea in this cupboard. Chinese Dragon Tea. I think you must be tired.'

The furniture was the utility style that I remembered from my great-auntie's house in my childhood, wooden chairs with blue seats and a yel-low, formica-topped table. The gas stove was called DOROTA, or so it said on the oven door. The sofa in the living room was dark red on a plain, toffee-coloured rug. There was a small work table with a grey, 1950s-looking telephone and, in the corner, an enormous Russian T.V.

I went out onto the balcony, but the view was already hazy with dusk and smoke. I was hungry and the cheese, bread and tomato were ex-tremely good. The ceramic electric kettle, glazed with two large blue flowers, didn't work, so I boiled a pan of water for tea, before realising I didn't want it. It was only six o'clock in the evening, but already I felt like sleeping. I could start a letter to Rob tomorrow. There were so many things, so many events and impressions I wanted to tell him about. The phone wasn't connected yet, Pawel had said, but it was in any case impossible to make international calls without reserving them through the operator.

In a single queasy wave it came, missing Rob. I wanted his voice. I wanted his touch. I wanted his body next to mine in this chilly flat. Somehow it surprised me, as if in all the hurried planning, the frantic preparations, the decision that this whole jaunt was a good idea, I'd over-looked the most obvious thing.

It was plain that the sofa ought to pull out into a bed, but I didn't appear to have the knack of it, succeeding only in heaving the whole thing up into the air several times and grazing my arm. The sofa would be fine to sleep on just as it was, so I amassed the three cushions at one end, but could find no bedding. There was no wardrobe in the room.

Later, I would discover that, since Polish living rooms often doubled as bedrooms, there were rarely wardrobes. The bedding was so invariably kept in the space beneath the seat of the sofa - the space I would have discovered had I known how to pull the bed out properly - that it had not occurred to Pawel to mention it. However, it was cold, so I wore another pair of socks and a sweater and cuddled under my coat. Later, I would discover that 'Central Heating' had a whole different meaning here - whether it was turned on or not being centrally determined, in Moscow, some joked - and that the deciding factor was date rather than temperature.

I had an image of Rob sitting at his kitchen table, typing away, painstak-ingly interpreting the asterisks and arrows of the unwieldy manuscript I'd deposited just before I left, the extra half pages attached with paperclips. It was so sweet of him to have offered, and he'd make such a good job of it. He must be nearly finished by now. The bound version of my Mas-ters' dissertation had to be submitted next week.

I would have felt guilty at taking him away from work on his own the-sis, except that I knew, as far as he was concerned, any break from *that* was welcome. In the interests of producing a piece of original research, why on earth had he let himself be persuaded to focus on largely ne-glected poems that no-one would have looked twice at if their author hadn't gone on to do a damned sight better? There was a very good rea-son why these poems were neglected, Rob fumed. He'd already written the whole thing in his head anyway. He'd done the interesting part, worked out all the arguments. He was just finding it incredibly difficult to get down on paper. Nowadays his frustration mostly descended to personal abuse:

20

'Shelley was a tosser,' Rob declared, 'dragging poor old Mary around Europe in whatever state, whether pregnant or postnatal, and the kids too, whether sick or well, shagging whoever he liked!' The punishing schedule had killed off at least two of the babies, and it was a wonder it hadn't finished off the mother as well!

The parts of the thesis I *had* read seemed pretty good but Rob had talked me into the idea that it was a doomed enterprise, only to be completed through gritted teeth and for the sake of honour. Certainly not with the aim of getting an academic job. There weren't any of those.

Rob wasn't the best advert for further study, and, anyway, I wanted to do something else first. When he'd finished, Rob had suggested, he might get a job abroad, in France or Italy, maybe even the States. We could go together and I could study or work there, but in the meantime I grew suddenly restless.

When the Polish job came up unexpectedly, part of the attraction lay in the fact that I didn't seem to have any mental image of Poland. In 1981, I'd lived in a house without a television. I couldn't even conjure up footage of Solidarity and Martial Law, though this lack of preconception did not appear to be widely shared:

'What d'you want to go there for?' Tara was a sociology student and my fellow waitress at Beninos, her opinions always as spiky as her hair. 'All miserable as sin - and nothing in the shops. I worked with a Pole once, at Café Metro - one of those guys who came over after '81. Awful, bigoted little man. Couldn't stand Jewish people, I remember. Kept going on about it.'

'You can't judge by one example,' I protested. 'He probably wasn't typical.'

'It wasn't like anyone had asked him.'

'Well, I still find it hard to believe that there, of all places …'

Did I just imagine that I could smell gas? I felt so snoozy already that I could hardly be bothered to go and check - but then, it seemed a bit ridiculous to die in my sleep simply because I didn't have the energy… I crawled out to the kitchen, and sure enough the gas was on. I turned the knob and went back to the doubtful warmth of my coat.

I dozed but I could still smell gas. I should've opened the window to disperse it fully. The thought of introducing more cold air was not appealing. Could it do me any harm, whatever gas was still wafting about? I really couldn't face getting up again. I'd checked once, for God's sake. This was becoming neurotic, like keeping going to see if you've locked the bathroom door as a kid.

When I was at primary school, my best friend's parents had one of those American comedy sketch records from the fifties. For a couple of months we used to listen to it every day, drinking 'cocktails' we made up from whatever was in the fridge and laughing ourselves silly. I remembered one of the monologues on the subject of flying, the air hostesses so perfect and so intimidatingly beautiful and competent. 'Coffee, tea or milk?' they'd say with a fixed, gleaming smile as the gibbering air passenger tried to point out a fire in the engine visible from his window. A line came back to me in bourbon-drenched, New York tones: 'You'd rather die than make an ass of yourself.'

Even *to* yourself, I thought wearily, wrapping the coat round me and mincing with it into the kitchen. Dorota wasn't like the gas stoves I'd come across before. On the dial, OFF was in the middle. The opposite of ON wasn't OFF, it was ON again, and gas was spewing steadily into the room. I opened all the windows and stood there shivering.

As soon as I woke up, I went out onto the balcony to look at the view, the disparate tower blocks and their coloured balconies caught in the prism of the early morning, the full yellow-green crowns of the lime and horse chestnut trees in between. I could hear the rattle of trams, a far off train, a factory hooter, but nowhere the roar of car engines.

I'd arranged to meet Pawel at the Instytut of English Philology at ten, so I took the map he'd drawn me and wandered across the bridge behind my block towards Narutowicza Street, one of the main thoroughfares. There was a small wooden kiosk selling cabbages, a few plums and bruised yellow apples in crates. Just beyond, near the crossroads, was a triangular warning traffic sign depicting a tractor and a horse and cart. On the corner, three old women in dusty pinafores and floral headscarves were selling small bunches of vegetables tied together, cream from metal churns and bouquets of meadow flowers from jam jars. One had a small pyramid of apples on a green cloth. Smiling at some remark of the others', her face was as wrinkled and brown as an over-ripe russet, but her apples looked a good deal firmer and rosier than those on sale at the wooden stall.

I should get some food to take back to the flat later, but I wanted to keep moving. The main street combined massy, angular 'Communist' architecture with faded nineteenth century grandeur. Trams hurtled by, crammed with more people than would have seemed possible. The blackened edifice opposite me was an early twentieth century structure supported by pillars consisting of the titanic forms of four muscular workers, presumably representing different trades. One had a hammer. There was little doubt that this had always been a heavily industrial city. Facing this on the other side of the road, was the pale, square, modern theatre, with fountains arranged in front.

A man raised his trilby hat to a woman with a brown fur collar that he passed. In general, though, the people appeared dogged and manifestly miserable. Yet in spite of this, and, considering it was all so strange, I felt oddly at home. The sensation was similar to that of forgetting a word but knowing it'll come to you in a moment, or when you can't quite place who somebody reminds you of. It was partly the sense of going back in time, to a past you haven't lived but have inherited. I reminded myself that such nostalgia was unlikely to be shared by those for whom this was everyday reality. As daily existence, no doubt it was not at all romantic, the primary experience simply that of living in a depressed and totalitarian state.

As though to confirm this I entered the supermarket. The shelves contained very little: some bottles of clear liquid that seemed to be vinegar, some small bottles of solidified milk, some of which were bright green. The label said 'kefir', but I couldn't determine whether this were yogurt, sour cream or some other substance? There were also brown paper packets, I presumed of flour or rice, even sugar, with the contents handwritten on them in blue biro.

At the end of the shop was a meat or delicatessen counter. There were lots of meat hooks hanging on the wall behind, but from only one a remnant of smoked sausage dangled. The woman in front of me was buying eggs, which were presented to her in a paper bag, and butter. There were three assistants behind the counter. One picked out the pack of butter, the second cut it in half and wrapped it deftly in brown paper. I was impressed that she produced a perfectly folded parcel without using any kind of tape. The third woman took the money and dealt with the till. The customer seemed to be asking the first woman a series of questions, but the answer she got was always the same: '*Nie ma.*' I took this to mean that the goods requested were not available, but the phrase was uttered each time with such complete indifference, the assistant looking steadfastly and almost scornfully past the woman into the middle distance that I wondered whether I might be mistaken.

I managed to buy a smoked mackerel from the pile on a tray at the end of the counter and went away with my brown paper parcel well pleased with myself. It must be awful to have to deal with such scarcity all the time, yet for me the limited choice, the dim lighting, the 1940s Co-Op feel to the whole place were pleasantly restful.

Feeling ravenous, and realising that I hadn't exactly maximised my options with my single purchase in the supermarket, I ventured into the building next door, which announced itself as a 'Bar Mleczny' or Milk Bar. This was a kind of cafeteria which, true to its name, offered a variety of dairy dishes. I pushed my tray past bowls of butter beans, some pink blancmange, handle-less mugs of steaming milky drinks in several colours and something labelled 'kasza manna' which looked like semolina.

I went for the semolina and carried my tray over to one of the high stools. It *was* a bit grim, I supposed, reminiscent of Orwell's 'Victory gin in chipped mugs' scenario in *1984*. The knives had all had their ends snipped off, though whether to render them undesirable as objects of theft or to prevent stabbing was unclear. Was it a deliberate policy, also, I wondered, to have such dingy lighting in every interior? Never more than a forty watt bulb to be seen. Personally, I found it quite soothing, but perhaps I was already being lulled into a stupor. Were the reasons economic, ideological, or just plain psychological? You could have lifted the morale of everyone at a single stroke, simply by the introduction of a hundred watt bulb! But I guessed that wasn't the desired effect. Even a sixty watt bulb would have made a difference.

Turning into Kosciuszki Boulevard, I recognised Pawel at some distance by his posture and his oversized sweater, leaning against the large stone gatepost in front of the Instytut, his hands in the pockets of his corduroy trousers. He took me up the steps into the building, which was very dark. There was a wooden porter's cabin at the foot of another short flight of stairs, and, ahead, what appeared to be the large, main staircase. Inside the porter's cabin, an elderly man in braces and shirt-sleeves was making himself a glass of tea. Pawel introduced me to Pan Edek, who kissed my hand and made several jokes, at which I smiled as much as I could while he and Pawel laughed.

Pawel led me along a black and white tiled corridor lined with chairs, with ashtrays on tall stands at regular intervals.

'Here is where students are waiting between classes,' he explained. 'Here is Dean's Office,' he pointed to a door in the dark, wooden panelling, 'And library is down there.' He signalled along a lighter corridor. 'We won't to go there just now. The librarian, she is very hot-tempered, and she won't yet be beginning her working. It is best not to disturb,' he grinned. An enormous framed poster of a beefeater, and another, a family shot of the Royal family taken around 1970, which I guessed to be gifts from the British Council, adorned the walls by the library. 'And this is the Sekretariat,' Pawel announced, taking me through a large door with frosted glass. 'This is where everything happen.'

It was indeed a hive of activity, with several secretaries and a number of members of staff gathered around the pigeon-holes. Pawel began introducing me to a bewildering array of colleagues.

'This is Professor Rutkowski.' Small, sandy, bearded man, linguist. I tried to make mental notes. 'This is Michal Ceynowa.' Lanky young man with long hair and a drooping moustache, taught modern drama. 'Unfortunately our head of the department is not here today. She has not been well, and Professor Goljanek, her deputy, he is still in America until the next week ...'

Pani Marysia and Pani Malgosia, the two senior secretaries, kissed my cheeks and patted my arms, exclaimed over me to Pawel and patted me some more. They chivvied Dorota, the junior secretary, until she had brought me a glass of tea with lemon. It was clear I was going to be looked after. It wasn't until I received with gratitude this pleasant and enfolding welcome that I realised the difference from meeting the teaching staff. There had been something else in their eyes, which I occasionally sensed even from Pawel, a fear that they were about to incur some obligation they were unwilling to undertake.

Dorota was a former student, Pawel said, which is why she spoke such excellent English, to which she wasn't admitting at the moment.

'Of course not,' said Dorota, her head on one side. 'I am ashamed - no, I am shy for my English.'

Dorota, in ankle boots and a tight skirt, did not in the least resemble her squat, square and treacherous namesake, my stove. She was very pretty, with loose curls, wide eyes and very arched eyebrows. Her make-up accentuated the last two features, giving her a surprised, knowing, flirty expression.

'Will you come to me for drink?' she asked me. 'Soon, yes?'

'Yes please. I'd love to.'

'Next week, we arrange it, O.K.?'

Pani Malgosia was telling me something.

'She says you are the first,' Pawel translated. 'The others will arrive not until Friday. The other two so-called "Native Speakers" she means. But she says there is something already here you will like to see.'

Pani Malgosia was indicating two large brown paper sacks standing next to her desk, gesturing to Pani Marysia to drag them closer.

'It is most unusual,' Pawel commented. 'They are on time this year. Usually it is at least two months late.'

Pani Malgosia bent over the sacks and presented me with two bars of soap in a plain wrapper, then, with a flourish, two rolls of grey toilet paper, crinkly, almost like crepe paper.

'It is present,' Pawel translated her words. 'From Ministry.' She patted my hands, which were cupping the soap, and balanced the two rolls on top, saying something else, and darting off to fetch some brown paper from her desk drawer, retrieving the items to wrap them in a parcel. She did it so deftly, reminding me of the woman wrapping butter in the supermarket, still smiling. Pani Marysia made suggestions from the sidelines, then pinched my cheek. I tried 'thank you' in Polish, and they went into elaborate gestures of disclaimer.

'A starter pack,' I said to Pawel. 'That's really nice.'

'Oh no,' he said, 'unfortunately it is for whole year. All staff are having such gift.'

I noticed another man standing over by the pigeon-holes surveying the scene, and smiled at him. He wore a dark blue suit, and with his black beard, longish hair and piercing eyes had rather a Rasputin look about him.

'Ah yes,' said Pawel, 'this is Doctor Makarenko.'

'I am very pleased to be meeting with you,' Doctor Makarenko said, kissing my hand. 'I am the Head of Methodology in this Instytut,' he looked up at me from under his impressive eyebrows with a sorrowful and burning gaze which convinced me he was on the brink of imparting some piece of tragic knowledge or arcane wisdom, crucial to my work or my life in Poland. I listened intently as he took my hand again, his eyes brimming with sympathy for the terrible burden he was about to transmit. 'I'm afraid,' he said, 'that I can offer you no advice whatsoever.'

I was back at the flat and it was still only six. I ate the smoked mackerel with bread and the rest of the tomato. I wanted to write to Rob, but there already seemed so much to say that I didn't know where to start. By the time he read it, after the three weeks it would take to reach him, how much else would have happened? Why couldn't he just be here too, to share it, and so I wouldn't have to miss him so horribly?

To avoid the imminent surge of feeling, I went into the living room to try the T.V. The two-prong plug went into the socket, but the socket was hanging from the wall. Unsurprisingly, nothing happened when I tried to switch on. I surveyed the plug again. Night one gassing, night two electrocution, I thought nervously as I shoved the whole socket back into the space in the wall. The set leapt into life with a loud crack that made me start in terror. I sat back on my hands, laughing.

Interspersed with footage of blue-jacketed police with batons holding back crowds of waiting fans, the evening news began with the unmistakable figure of Mrs Thatcher alighting at Warsaw Airport.

All Souls

We had arrived at an awkward time. The raised female voices sank down when Kasper knocked the second time. The domophone at the entrance had not been working, but since Kasper had a key to the outside door we had clumped up the concrete stairs to the third floor landing. There was no light behind the peephole of the door, and for a moment I wished I were outside again, despite the cold.

I didn't know this part of Warsaw at all so it was a good thing Kasper had met me at the tram stop as arranged. Rather, it had been arranged that I should meet *someone* at the tram stop. I was expecting Sylwia, my friend's sister, but, since I didn't know her either, it was no hardship to transfer my responses and expectations when hailed by the tall young man.

I suppose the word for him was 'willowy', given his slender build, his pallor and the impression of toughness without strength that he conveyed. He wore high boots, his dark green raincoat was loose and flowing, and it struck me almost at once that he was dressed like a cavalry officer. Probably this had something to do with the way he pirouetted a little and clicked his heels as he kissed my hand. Sylwia had a class earlier, he informed me, and could not be sure to be here on time. He would please to conduct me, he declared, with his very great pleasure.

The streets of this district were composed mainly of 1920s and '30s buildings of grey or brown stone, three or four storeys high, reconstructed after the war. In between were newer blocks of flats, not much higher. Kasper was a student of history. His study of this subject had taught him many things, he said. His name, for example, 'was name of very famous old Polish nobleman in Eastern borderlands of Lithuania.'

'Was this before or after King Popiel got eaten by the mice?' I asked, trying to show that I was not completely ignorant of Polish history, but prompted in part by his own mouse-like appearance. On the long neck his head seemed small, the more so because his hair was cut so short as to be a mere fuzz. His chin was tiny, his nose thin and small, and the colour of his hair was so truly 'mousey' that it looked grey as well as brown.

He laughed. 'Oh after, after. But many hundreds years ago. It is also name, Kasper Boniewicz, of very known Polish officer in War.'

Polish history was very difficult, he told me. The most difficult. But you could learn many things. About the terrible actions made by other nations of course. Especially in his country. But he liked also to study about old kings and time when Poland was very big, strong.

His face glistened slightly as he bent towards me, explaining this. Even his eyes - pale grey, pinkish a little - were mouse-coloured, I discovered, though not the colour of a mouse's eyes

'I very like,' he said, 'one day Poland will have king again.'

I thought a king was the last thing Poland needed, and I said so, whereupon he lectured me firmly and with some eloquence on the importance of a monarch in Poland. We had one in my country, I observed, and it didn't seem to help much.

'No, no, you are quite wrong, you see - ' and he began to set me straight on the role of the British royal family and the esteem in which its members were held by their subjects.

I got him to move on, to walk that is, for we had come to a standstill, and at least he couldn't lecture while we went forward because of the wind. It wasn't strong so much as dense, a thick wind of grit and dust that seemed to scratch at the dry, bare trees. The solid things - the grey buildings, the paving stones, dead leaves and the bark of trees - appeared to be breaking down before the rasping air, which took their particles and flicked them in our faces. If the process went on long enough, it was possible to imagine that the disintegration of matter would be complete, the tangible forms disappearing as the air condensed. Nothing would be left of the substantial world but such spectral, wind-cast shapes as might curdle for a moment on the whirling currents of air.

The flat was in a modern block between two older ones. Kasper's second knock, as I say, was more effective. A short, dark girl in jeans and a red sweater opened the door and smiled at me.

'Hello. Come, come please.' She backed into the tiny hallway full of coats and boots. 'Have you a good journey?' She bent down and fished about under the hems of the coats, bringing out a pair of slippers for me, looking over my shoulder at Kasper still framed in the doorway.

'Yes thanks. It was very quick, only an hour and a half.' I put on the slippers. 'Are you Sylwia?' We went forward into the main room.

'I am Sylwia,' said a much larger girl, placing teaspoons and brown glass saucers on the table. She was big-boned with a round, flat face that shone a little, like a moon, or a cheese. She wore her light-brown hair in a bob, twenties-style, and low-waisted, black clothes. The way she moved was pleasing, especially her legs in the long woollen skirt. Her hands, setting out the spoons, were luminous like her face.

Her friend in the red sweater was more compact, with a narrow face and more obviously pretty features, strongly defined against her olive skin beneath the black, short hair. Although she appeared, as she was, a young woman in her early twenties, she looked simultaneously as she would when she were much older. She would not change greatly over the years, for she bore already, barely beneath the surface of her skin, her older self, and her gestures conveyed the capability of a more experienced woman, probably her mother.

'I am Iwona,' she said. 'I am living here. My boyfriend, Kasper, already you know.'

So we made our introductions and sat at the table to eat cheesecake and drink glasses of tea. The room was small but light, despite net curtains at the window and the uncompromising cinder-grey sky outside. Beside our table and chairs, a sofa-bed, covered with a blanket, stood on the red, patterned rug. A heavy-fronted dresser of near-blackened wood took up the far wall, with innumerable cupboards and drawers, and glass-doored sections containing ornaments, books and china.

'Are you sure it's not too much trouble for me to stay tonight?' I asked with British politeness, hearing my own words as the faintly incomprehensible bad faith that in this context they must seem. 'I could easily get the train home.'

Kasper indeed looked at me as though I had missed the point, any point.

'Poles are very hospitable' he stated blankly, with a touch of menace.

'No, no, of course,' Sylwia said, 'you want to see Warsaw, Dorota explain to me. You are welcome.' Sylwia's sister, Dorota, was the secretary at the English Institute where I worked in Lodz. 'How do you like Lodz?' she went on. 'It is not such an interesting city for you I think, very dirty, very ugly.'

'Oh, I don't know,' I protested. 'I like it.'

'It is full of workers,' Kasper said, as if that decided it, as if they themselves littered up the place. I had visions of the hapless proletarians in caps and grimy overalls strewn across the tramlines and about the broad streets between the decaying nineteenth-century mansions, as in the aftermath of some nuclear accident.

I glanced towards the books in the cabinet. Most of them concerned Art History. These were hers, Iwona explained, following my gaze. Sylwia, on the other hand, 'studied economy' quite far away from this district, but she was almost all the time here at Iwona's because her room at the hostel she shared with four other girls.

Had they known each other long?

They laughed.

'Oh very long, since secondary school.'

I could tell it was so, for despite their polarities of appearance, and possibly of temperament, they moved like dancers in relation to one another, in their gestures and in the flow of their conversation, the modulation of their voices, reaching out an arm here, stepping back there, as though a single thread drew their limbs. I thought of sisters who have slept from their earliest days in the same bed, shifting position and rolling over, moving through the long course of the night in the symmetry of their sleep.

I wondered what they could have been arguing about before we came. It could not have been anything important since this connection still appeared intact. Kasper was not really participating and contributed only the occasional listless remark as we compared our subjects of study and I spoke a little of my teaching at the Institute. Yet his every gesture, dusting some crumbs, lifting a teaspoon, seemed to attach to itself an unnecessary importance, as if he found the movements of his fingers of extraordinary grace. He stirred his second glass of tea, long after the leaves had settled, and made them whirl. I had the feeling he was trying to dominate us, though he spoke far less than he had on our walk. I tried to ignore him, for I liked the two women very much.

What was Sylwia's class that day? Not economics on a Saturday, *surely?* Iwona jumped up to fetch a book from the dresser. They had both been, they said. There was a series of lectures on Jewish history and culture, and now a group of young people was beginning classes of Jewish dancing. Today was the second lesson.

I braced myself. I had been in the country a mere two months yet already I knew that I had not the stomach for this subject - an inevitable one, I found, arising from nowhere, unsought, among the pleasantest people, like a compulsion, possessing, amid all the denials, a confessional urgency. The presence of a 'Westerner' tended to ensure it, for did not the topic concern the reputation of their country?

It was not at all true, I was regularly assured, that Poland was an anti-Semitic country. No, you had to understand what Jews were like. All Communists were Jews was the explanation. *That* was why Polish people did not like them. And before? Why, Jews were rich, they 'owned all factories,' they 'made Poles work for them'. I did not suppose that Sylwia and Iwona would share the sentiments of the grandmother of one of my students, who'd spat the reason for her hatred: 'Jews are buried sitting up, so on the Day of Judgement they'll be up before us. There! So now you know!' Nor even the unquestioning indifference of most of the young people I taught ('I have nothing against Jews. I have never met one'), accepting the current homogeneity of their country, however achieved, as a self-evidently desirable outcome with no ethical implications for themselves.

As for the War, 'Poles helped Jews in the War', they were taught that in school, and besides, millions of Poles died also, in the camps, like Auschwitz, and elsewhere, yet 'no-one in West' seemed interested in them, only in Jews who 'always pushed themselves forward'. Yes, those pushy Jews, elbowing their way ahead, leaping up on Judgement Day, somehow pipping the Poles at the post, snatching from them their cherished role as most ill-treated and suffering nation on earth. Was that why I had found myself in conversations in which numbers of dead were disputed as if there were some kind of perverse competition, as if a dead Jew somehow cancelled out a dead Pole, as if every Jewish death that was conceded negated or denied the pain of a Polish one?

Iwona was studying me. I must have seemed rather odd. I looked down at the book they had given me. It consisted mostly of photographs, captioned 'Faces of a Vanished World' - long-coated men and bewigged matrons in wedding groups, three bearded men with caps and sidelocks outside their workshop, a panoramic view of the Jewish Market at Bialystok in full haggle, shawled women and peak-capped men perched on barrows or clustered round the best buys. Still, in light of my previous thoughts, I took against the whole thing. The presentation and (from my rudimentary translation) the explanatory notes reminded me of the collections of sepia photographs of particular towns 'as they were' - as if these people had been effaced by the natural passage of time, like bustles or horse-drawn buses, that the world had simply moved on from and outgrown them.

The two girls were waiting for me. I did not want to raise my eyes. I tried to calm my response - yet I could not face their well-meaning inadequacy. In fact, having run the whole gamut of emotions in my head, I felt sour, as if I held them responsible for all they *might* have said. I made some ungenerous comment, I don't remember what.

Iwona and Sylwia frowned, then they smiled. Yes, yes it was true. But Poland wasn't really an anti-Semitic country. It was very sad. Many people don't understand in Poland. They don't like Jews.

'There *are* almost no Jews,' I said. 'Haven't they noticed?'

A small pause.

'But there *is* Jewish dancing. There will be. It will not be dying away.'

I looked at the tablecloth.

'Come, we show you,' Iwona pulled me to my feet. 'I always love the dancing,' she said, glowing, 'since I was little girl - even before I meet my Kasper,' as if it were surprising she should have had any feelings or preferences in that period of pre-history. She looked fondly at him: 'At secondary school we go to the ballroom dancing, me and my Kasper,' (she looked at him again, but his head was turned slightly away from us and

31

he seemed preoccupied with other thoughts), 'later, Sylwia too with us.' Sylwia put her arm to my other shoulder and somehow, between the dark veneer and sparkling glass of the dresser and the jutting sofa, we managed to improvise to some made-up Hebrew-sounding tune (in my case heavily indebted to 'Hava Nagila' and in theirs presumably to some melody from their class, which harmonised surprisingly well) an improbable dance.

Kasper had the decency not to intervene. Perhaps he was sulking, for we had not urged him to join us. He sat silent, watching intently first one of my fellow-dancers then the other. At a certain point he disappeared to the bathroom and we forgot him. Sylwia moved with a heavy grace, her long legs seemed to swivel and slide with ease beneath her skirt, whereas Iwona, being smaller, had to jig up and down more. So we bobbed and whirled, I concentrating hard to follow the steps, laughing as we crashed into the furniture. Despite my reservations, or perhaps because of them, I grew at once so involved in this dance that my eyelids prickled as if I would cry, and I was borne along by waves of love for my two partners.

As though prompted by this drunken behaviour, we lost no time in opening the wine, a redcurrant from Sylwia's uncle's allotment, and a barely alcoholic concoction called Daisy. I produced the present I had brought, some Swiss chocolate from the dollar shop, which we broke into squares on a saucer.

As with any heightened sensation, my ribs were punctured by a sharp longing for Rob, that he could be here, meet these people, see what I was seeing. Or at least be at the end of a 'phone, or waiting for me back in Lodz, rather than a thousand miles away, where even what I might manage to describe by letter he could not read for three or four weeks. That time-lapse between my present, my experience and his, was one of the most unbearable aspects of our separation. And what was *his* experience now? Was he propped up in bed, reading quietly against that familiar wallpaper, after a successful day on his doctoral thesis? Somehow I doubted it. More likely at a party, or down the pub, shrugging off his writer's block with his easy sociability. Who was he talking to now in that engaged, slightly flirtatious tone? Did he yearn for me as keenly as I did him in crowded rooms, as his letters claimed? For the first time I felt the assurance of my own primacy waver. In those situations wouldn't it be hard not to revert to the way of being of the single 'questing' man he had been when he met me? What on earth was I playing at? Had I come away to *test* him - or indeed myself?

'We will have *kolacja* - you know what is *kolacja*? You say 'supper', yes? With *kanapki*, you know, small sandwiches.'

Iwona had been showing me a book of photographs of artefacts from the Czartoryski Collection in Krakow. It was unfortunate, given my reflections, that I 'came to' just as she was pointing out three miniatures,

King Zygmunt Augustus flanked by his wife and his mistress on either side. I could look at some of the other pictures while they prepared the food, Iwona said, leaving it on my lap. I barely took in the Magdalen writing a letter and Saint Lucy holding her eyeballs on a plate, like two peeled lemons, before going to offer to help. The kitchen was so tiny the two girls had to take it in turns to open tins of pickled red pepper, and mushrooms, to slice them incredibly small, and to make up the *kanapki* with slivers of cheese, sausage and pickled gherkin.

Kasper, I felt, lurked. I was used to Polish men affording nothing by way of domestic assistance and in this case it would hardly have been feasible, but at least they usually kept out of the way. Kasper, however, after another visit to the bathroom, hung about among the coats in the hall, where I also had to stand to be passed things from the kitchen to put on the table.

Iwona and I had been transferring plates from the dresser and, as I returned to the kitchen, I saw Sylwia, half-turned, one dripping hand above a pool of peppers and vinegar on the chopping board, just as Kasper brushed the back of two fingers upwards over her breast, pausing as he reached the nipple to crook one finger round it. Clutching a handful of wet peppers, she gave a mesmerised smile into his face. I backed into Iwona coming out of the sitting room, but she went straight to the stove to check the hard-boiled eggs. Had she seen? Did she know?

We ate our *kanapki* with more wine and more tea, the combined effect of which was beginning to make my head pound a little. Sylwia was telling me that the unemployment in Western countries was exaggerated by the Polish government for propaganda purposes, and that, besides, it could not be so bad as the compulsory employment which was the case in Poland.

'A Polish man have to go to the job even if there is nothing to do, even only to drink the tea.'

Kasper seemed to have transmitted to her with his touch something of his own personality, though perhaps it had been there all along and I was only now registering it, for in retrospect she had been consistently more decided in her opinions than Iwona.

I agreed it was very difficult with propaganda to work out what the actual truth might be, especially if you had no other information, but that the truth is not always automatically the opposite of the official lies, that indeed there was unemployment in the West, a lot of it, and that many people found it very hard …

Kasper and Sylwia looked ready to take issue with this, but Iwona changed the subject: tomorrow would be All Souls' Day, did I know it? When all people light candles for their dead ones. Kasper gave her a sour look.

'It is not like in West, where cemeteries are strongly neglecting,' he put in relentlessly.

It was true, Iwona blushed apologetically, they had seen pictures on T.V. It was very sad.

It certainly *was* true, I conceded readily, at least in Britain. Many cemeteries and churchyards were not so well cared for and we did not have the tradition of going all together to visit graves on a special day to put flowers and spend time with the dead, which seemed like such a good idea.

The atmosphere improved at once and Kasper lost interest in the conversation.

Would I like to go to see these ceremonies, the two girls asked? Unfortunately they had to return on quite early train to Bialystok, to their families, for this important day. It was long journey but they could explain me the way to their church. It was in Zoliborz, Popieluszko church, had I heard about it?

Sylwia produced a picture of the priest, tucked in another book, to show me. She took it, she said, a year before he died. I had seen other photos of Popieluszko, so to speak 'official' unofficial shots that circulated with the sanction of the Church, but those had all been edited or selected, 'purified' to stress the priest's otherworldly qualities, as befitted one en route to the status of saint. This image, however, struck me as both unauthorised and earlier. The man looked more uncomfortable but nicer, less handsome and less fey, squatting on some steps in front of a store cupboard, probably in his vestry.

'Yes,' I said, 'I would be very glad to see it. Tomorrow, yes?'

****

Sylwia and I lay on a folded quilt with our heads underneath the table. When I woke it was still dark. Iwona's shape in the web of darkness gleamed slowly white on the sofa-bed - not motionless as I at first thought, but throwing itself backwards over and over. I was truly frightened, still in that state of leaden body and half-dream of first waking, when you cannot lift a hand to save yourself and the scream in your head will not rise to your lips. I stared unbelieving at the wishbone of her chin, tipped back and skewed at an incomprehensible angle to her neck. A fit, I thought, as though reasonably - the white of the sheet, the forearm forming greyly from her night-dress sleeve, her throat flung back over the end of the bed. The darkness clutched and curdled in uneven places, the shapes would not resolve. Until at last the sheet covering Iwona's body gave way in my understanding to Kasper, his cropped head bent low behind her ear, slamming himself forward and falling back like a half-stunned bird against a pane.

It was not sound that had woken me, I felt sure - in fact my hearing seemed only belatedly to register the muffled but undoubted rustles and creaks from the sofa-bed. No, it was the extraordinary intensity that hummed and shuddered and realigned the particles of that dark air over all the objects of the room. I turned protectively to Sylwia - she *must not* see - but she lay with folded hands like a lady carved on a tomb, untroubled by my side.

How disturbing, how violent and inexplicable the act seemed. Is this how a child would feel waking up in their parents' room? Was it just *Kasper's* lovemaking that would have struck me this way? Graceless and brutal, somehow distasteful, like everything else about him. Or was I unconsciously afraid of sex itself, frigid, as the boy had said when I was fifteen and wouldn't let him put his hand down my bra at the pictures? I'd thought it was because I didn't want him to find the tissue paper filling out the right cup in an attempt to even up the size.

I'd certainly made up for it since, if the evidence of those first weeks and months with Rob was anything to go by, that summer of our mutual obsession. Yet even then, had I not felt faintly alarmed, in the grip of an infatuation over which I had no control, forever seeking to arrive at an account of our relationship, 'trying to get your mind round rather than your leg over,' as Rob teasingly complained?

It was easy for him: he claimed to have fallen in love with me the moment we met - whereas I experienced him more as a kind of biological nemesis in that first encounter, overwhelmed by an attraction my brain had barely caught up with enough to register. It had never happened that way round with me before. There had always been friendship first, the slow, dawning indispensability of the other person. I had no idea how Rob would have appeared to me if I hadn't been spending all my time in his single bed. What if my attachment were to 'it' rather than to him? In those early days, on the rare occasions when I was upright, walking around, it seemed that the entire centre of my body had melted, that my pelvis had somehow dissolved such that it could not support me in this unnatural stance, and my whole physical being conspired to render me horizontal once more.

When I told him, Rob thought this was all very funny, and brought me some wine and some toast, and made me put down the book I was supposed to be studying, and started to kiss me again. It was at least three in the afternoon because the ice-cream van trundled down the street outside, tinkling its four-bar tune. We always laughed and called it "our tune", pretending we meant it as a joke.

Now, lying in the dark on Iwona's floor, I went looking for him, through the night, across the thousand miles and in the bedroom window. There he was, curled up in bed, smelling of himself asleep, brown forearms crossed, hugging one pillow, another half over his face, and

Manfred, our cat, draped like a halo round the back of his head, his favourite position. How we loved that cat, with his ginger and white fur and his extra-large ears. He had been our child, our first living creature together. Like a little old childless couple with our gingerbread boy, we were so proud of his exploits and achievements, loving to talk about him to ourselves and to others, detailing, discovering aspects of his character. Our first baby. Perhaps we should have a real one. It was blindingly obvious.

I felt suddenly afraid, as if returning unannounced. What if the pictures I had so cosily created were false? What if he were in that very bed doing... what *they* were doing... with someone else? I blacked out the image, but a sour liquid stung the back of my throat. Was it *that* I was watching by proxy here? Don't be so superstitious, so stupid - I was glad to chastise myself, squashing the thought, and thereby overlaying the other scene that had come so easily into my head, as boldly delineated as if I had seen it.

All had gone still on the sofa. Would they have gone straight to sleep or be lying, awake and aware? Now that I no longer felt it, I realised that I had been faintly indignant, wanting them to know what they'd 'subjected' me to. In the event, my ears straining, imagining their listening stillness in the dark, I played dead for all I was worth. After all, I reasoned, in a one-room flat, where Sylwia must countless times have stayed, she must be used to Kasper and Iwona's nocturnal activities. It couldn't be the first time - maybe this was even meant to be the last. Had this regular proximity contributed to a desire on Sylwia's part to take her friend's place? Or had Kasper begun sometimes to visit *her* instead? I tried to ward off this line of speculation, but there was no need, for I found I had exhausted my curiosity. I did not want to be awake. I did not want to be there.

I must have dozed, because it was morning. Kasper was gone. Sylwia was stepping round me, laying the table. Iwona emerged from the bathroom wearing a towelling robe, a towel wrapped in a turban round her head. She was smiling faintly, her lips compressed. Was it triumph? Or suffering? I couldn't tell. Was it a reconciliation I had seen last night, or a parting fling? Could Kasper simply not make up his mind, or did he intend to string both of them along? I put on the dressing gown Sylwia gave me. Iwona set out some rolls in a small basket. We began to pare cheese and slice sausage for breakfast.

******

The wind had dropped completely. There was a dab of frost in the centre of each paving stone and the breath of passers-by fizzled on the air as I walked through Zoliborz. White sheets splodged with the red letters of

Solidarnosc hung openly over the railings of the church. At the gate, a glass case displayed photographs of Lech Walesa and Vice-President Bush shaking hands by a black limousine, laughing and joking together on a balcony, Bush's eyes and mouth wide open towards the crowd. Two other snaps featured an elderly couple with pain-pinched faces, whom the caption identified as Popieluszko's parents. In one the mother clasped Bush's hands, in the other she was embraced by Walesa.

People in stout coats and boots, the men in caps, the women in knitted hats, streamed into the churchyard. Younger people wore the latest, machine-knitted ski-hats in turquoise or bright pink. Children were ushered forward, cupping their candles in small glass beakers in their gloved hands. Popieluszko's monument was gleaming black granite flat on the grass. The smaller children were helped to place their glass beakers on the concrete slabs in front of it, to light the candles and to cross themselves.

A few not-too-secret policemen hung around just too long doing just too little. That was the point anyway, that people should know they were there. One or two of these men clearly enjoyed that - but at the same time they were afraid. They knew they dared not do anything that might offend the people in this place on this day.

Those who had relatives buried in the cemetery had brought flowers to arrange. There were green metal benches in the aisles next to some graves, and the older women sat down, pulling children onto their knees, offering advice while their daughters fussed over the flowers, chatting, like little family parties with the dead. What a lovely way to do it, I thought, as flowers and candles mushroomed on the level slabs. I watched one family greet another, tending the grave next-door, but most appeared so thoroughly preoccupied with their own grave as to totally ignore the neighbouring family if they did not otherwise know them. Wouldn't they see each other here every year? Would this not amount to an acquaintance? And what if someone were left out altogether? I could see one bare grave from where I stood. Since the dead were more likely to have a family member *emigrate* than move to another city, most were probably well catered for.

At once I felt excluded. However much I came to love this place and the people in it, my love would remain unrequited, because incomprehensible. I had the wrong nationality, and in this country, which for a hundred years at a stretch did not exist on the map but only in the hearts of its people, of people with the right blood, this was an insuperable barrier. 'You must be crazy to come to this awful place', people delighted in telling me. For them, loving Poland was an inherited affliction, it could not be contracted by an outsider. I might have friends, might feel and receive affection, but I would never be allowed to care about this place and its outcomes. I knew with certainty that were I to die here no-one

37

would come for me. Even the family of the adjacent dead would not spare a candle for my untended grave.

I looked round. They were still stolidly queuing before Popieluszko's grave. It ought to have been uplifting, these people honouring the man murdered by their oppressors, testifying that what he died for believing, they also believed. Yet the atmosphere was of a grim and slightly cynical defiance, tinged with self-loathing and at some level humiliation. The Solidarity banners, after all, were *permitted*. It is hard for those who perceive themselves as powerless to believe that the enemy they fear has no choice, has conceded to them out of fear of what *they* may do. No, 'they', the oppressors, permit because it suits them, because it is a trick, or a sop or some other ruse: the people are part of 'their' plan, not the other way round.

The unsmiling people holding bouquets for their own dead continued to come through the gates. Though they seemed so self-absorbed in their little family groups, at the same time I had the impression that they were somehow collectively viewing themselves from the outside. It occurred to me that this day, as with almost everything Polish people did, was for them an expression of *national* identity: 'We look after our cemeteries,' their every gesture said. 'We commemorate our dead. We have a proper sense of things. For we are Poles, and this is what *we* do'.

If I were a member of the Communist administration, I thought, and witnessed the scene I was seeing now, I would despair. For this force was unvanquishable, and in a single moment I saw how it would be. It was hard to imagine the people in this cemetery, with their dignified cynicism, their resentful apathy, rising up in concerted political action – yet this could change in a flash. Still, even before this, the Communists would be lost, for the leaders too, before all else, were Poles, and, whatever their ideological convictions, could not sustain themselves detested by almost all of their countrymen. As time went on, they would be unable to stare at their own faces in the mirror in the morning: the heavy pall of Polish loathing that hung low in the air of the whole place, unremitting, all the time, would crush them. For they would experience it as the one thing they could not bear, a denial of their own Polishness. Since the end of Stalinist times, they had played the nationalist card whenever they could, had tried to convince the populace that they could have their own, Polish form of Communism. Unfortunately, the people did not appear to believe that Communism was Polish at all. The authorities would make concessions, desperately strive to reinstate themselves in the unwavering eyes of their compatriots – but they would not succeed. Slowly, almost without realising, they would give up. Ultimately they would be hated out of existence.

Embedded in the wall of the church itself was a plaque bearing the inscription Auschwitz. Beneath it a spreading patch of glass beakers enclosing their swimming flames leached from the base of the wall. There were other plaques, evenly spaced, for the other camps. I looked at the two candles I had brought, and slipped one onto the only bare slab I could see among the ballooning bouquets of those all around. I read the name, Arkadiusz Hordynski, thought how fine, how resonant it was, even as I stepped back, troubled already at what I had done. What if his family came later and found the intrusive flame, an interloper's false and unwanted remembrance? The world dissolved behind my self-pitying tears. I placed my other candle, arbitrarily, before the plaque for Treblinka, which as yet was comparatively bare, and fought my way out against the flow of the swelling, grim-faced crowds.

****

When I caught the train to Lodz that afternoon it was almost dark. Soon the flat fields, the sheds and orchards, the horse-carts and people with bicycles waiting at crossings were sucked into blackness, and I began to see, in the villages and small towns we clattered through, beyond fields and on hillsides, the geometric shapes of the cemeteries pricked out in thousands of tiny points of light. Around statues in town squares as we pulled into stations, dozens of coloured glass beakers refracted their wobbly light and wreaths tied with patriotic ribbon poked out of the crevices above wall plaques. As the train groaned out again, in the distance across the muffled black spaces hung the low patches of flame, like diminutive forest fires, and we fled towards the city, home to a million souls and their remembered dead.

The Hut that had Beer

We arrived at four o'clock on Christmas morning, standing on the platform, feeling the slap inside us as the icy air met the warmth of the vodka we had drunk on the train. On the adjacent platform a black steam engine was working itself up to depart, amassing a fog of steam, yellow against the snow. The town before us seemed exactly as had been promised, a magical place, the snow-crusted eaves of the wooden houses almost touching the ground and the overlapping roofs receding like a miniature mountain range towards the first of the real Tatras, which loomed over someone's garden fence at the end of the street. Men in fur hats were ferrying people away from the station in sleighs to the sound of whips and bells and hooves crunching on snow. The glow of their cigarettes jiggled in the darkness in front of them and the heavy moon gleamed above us like the polished carp scale given me to put in my purse for luck.

'Oh, you are going to Zakopane. How lucky. You will love it there,' had been the invariable response of colleagues and students on hearing of our trip. 'It is real Polish mountains.'

It was clear that this place of so many childhood winter holidays held an unassailable position within both personal and national mythology. If they had to acknowledge the public unfriendliness of their countrymen, they could at least assert that in the mountains everything was different, and that 'Highlanders *always* say "hello" to everyone they meet.' Not that their love of the natives of this region required these members of the intelligentsia to revise their opinion of peasants as drunken and ignorant, for the Highlanders of the Tatras were apparently a special category, indeed were not peasants at all, as was explained on several occasions. No, they were the descendants of generations of aristocratic political dissidents exiled to the area under the various occupying powers of Poland's history.

'And before War all artists and poets were coming there, especially when dying of the T.B. It was very exciting, you can imagine,' one of my students had told me.

'Well, where do we go?' Harriet asked, following our various expressions of delight at the scene before us.

'It is at the end of the street. We can walk, if you can carry your packs,' Aneta told us.

Aneta was one of Harriet's students, and her particular friend. She was very shy with the rest of us, with that particular kind of shyness which does not imply admiration for the qualities of others, simply the inability to express contempt. She had frizzy brown hair and a round face that gave the impression of crumpling towards the centre, almost as though someone had punched her, and therefore I could never quite dispel the sense that her shyness and smileyness were to ward off further blows. It didn't help that I knew she was probably party to Harriet's reservations about me - whatever they might be - and that Harriet and I were not such good friends as we should have been. Harriet somehow held me at arm's length and closed off all my attempts at greater intimacy, as though everything I said or did confirmed her worst suspicions. I couldn't work out whether her objections were moral (she was a firm Christian) or personal, or both.

Anyhow, Harriet clearly felt comfortable with Drew, the other 'Native Speaker' at the Instytut, and in Aneta's unthreatening presence, in a way she didn't in mine - though since Rob's arrival ten days ago I'd ceased to be bothered by any of that. Certainly, we'd all been getting on very well during the long train journey. Through the fug of vodka in the carriage, we'd taken turns to pick out samples from Rob's Polish phrase book - 'Can you direct me to a dentist? My tooth is in need of attention' and 'Thank you, but I've done enough dancing for tonight' - laughing ourselves silly. Rob was here and everything was all right, that simplest of equations, just as I'd been certain it would be. I leant against him as we walked up the snowy street in the dark. Drew, Aneta and Harriet moved ahead and the stars hung so low as to seem almost audible.

We were not alone: small groups of young people bearing rucksacks and skis were tramping up the street ahead of and behind us. The Dom Turysty was an ornate, wooden building, a 1920s version of an imperial hunting lodge in design, backing into the forest on the edge of the town. There were assorted heaps of bulging rucksacks in the main hallway, with skis propped like the frames of teepees over them. We were given our keys by a smiling old woman - a room for the two men and another for the three women, an arrangement we soon swapped around to our satisfaction. Didn't she want to see our documentation?

'Oh, tomorrow, tomorrow,' she waved us away.

We had never been anywhere so informal before - it being one of the main principles of a Communist country never to let anyone go any-where or do anything without the maximum amount of fuss and the greatest number of authorisation papers displaying stamps and multiple signatures.

It was in the morning that our problems began. Rob's papers did not satisfy the heavy-jowled official at the desk. Rob was a visitor from a 'K.K.' - a *Kapitalisticzny Kraj* (Capitalist Country) - as were Drew, Harriet and I, though our employment by the Polish Ministry of Education gave us special status, effectively wiping out this stain on our characters. Or-dinarily, Western tourists in Poland were required to change ten pounds sterling at the official exchange rate for every day of their stay. Rob's documents from the Instytut, declaring that he was an invited speaker and therefore a sort of temporary lecturer, were supposed to exempt him from this. If he did not change that amount forthwith, and furthermore pay an entirely different, higher rate for his stay in their establishment, he would have to leave, the man announced. Aneta remonstrated with him. It would depend - we saw him look at her meaningfully. Aneta appeared stressed. Her face grew pink. After our initial consternation we stood back a little to let Aneta handle things. She soon relayed the situation: a bottle of vodka should do it.

'Say we want to see the *Kierownik*, the Manager,' I suggested.

'*He'll* only want a bigger bribe,' returned Aneta.

'I don't think so because you can see he doesn't like that idea,' I indi-cated the man, who was pretending to be engrossed in his paperwork and unconcerned about us, but who had clearly reacted to the word *kierownik*.

Aneta was both embarrassed at our treatment and also resentful that we wouldn't play the game. We could afford it, after all. It wasn't that excessive.

'There's nothing to stop him asking for more tomorrow,' Harriet pointed out.

Rob and I took what we considered a principled stand:

'We're not going to reward him for doing what he should do anyway. The papers *are* in order - and he knows it.' Ten pounds a day for Rob's twenty-day stay in Poland would be two hundred pounds; we hadn't got anything like that amount.

'He'll never believe *that* - we're foreigners,' said Harriet.

'Perhaps he'll learn something then,' I put in, piously, while Aneta looked as if she didn't believe it either.

'It's only a bottle of vodka, for fuck's sake,' said Drew. When I looked across at the man's face, though, I knew that to pay him the bribe would be a collusion in cynicism that I just couldn't stomach, morally *or* politically, and I was sure Rob felt the same.

Aneta went back to represent our stand, embarrassed at having to do it but doing it doggedly and very well. I was uncomfortably aware that we had put her in an awkward position, while Harriet managed to convey that we were being insufficiently sensitive to this. It was pretty obvious that she and Drew were contemplating buying the vodka regardless - though they couldn't very well do this - and Rob and I reflected bitterly that some folk wouldn't recognize a moral dilemma if it jumped up and bit them.

In the midst of this disunity, the official at the desk went so far as to concede that he would not throw us all out until first thing the following morning. At Aneta's request, we retired to our rooms so the negotiations could continue in the man's office. I was glad to go, as I was experiencing low stabbing pains, a bit like period pains but somehow sharper and more specific. Must be because I'm late, I thought.

In the event, poor Aneta spent half her morning before she could rejoin us to announce what sounded like victory. We were permitted to stay till Monday - in effect two more nights - but Aneta assured us that this was merely a face-saver and that we would have no further trouble.

Later that day Rob and I nipped into Pewex, the dollar shop, and bought her some Swiss chocolate, wondering even as we did so whether it was quite the right thing to do.

'Oh,' she said, taking it and twisting her mouth in that characteristic way she had. 'Is that *my* bribe?'

'No,' we protested, 'It's a present. A *real* present, to say thank you.' Aneta's expression implied that she was unconvinced by this explanation. She looked pinker and more closed off than ever. But she *had* done something, and we *were* grateful. Why did everything have to be distorted?

Frustrated by the delay, we were all the more eager to explore the fairy-tale town, wandering up and down the main thoroughfares looking at the wood and leather craft, the sheepskin rugs, the brightly glazed plates and embroidered linen. There were folk costumes on sale, as well as dolls wearing diminutive versions of the same. There were trestle tables under awnings displaying traditional patterned socks, hats, mittens and cardigans. There were wooden huts, their windows strung with multicoloured stars and snowflakes made of dyed straw and framed by winking Christmas lights, reflecting pink and green off the garish snow. These grottoes were stuffed to the ceilings with every conceivable sort of 'folkloristic items,' as Aneta termed them: trunks painted with flowers and cockerels, carved wooden horsemen in traditional Mummers outfits - the Tartar in his turban on a wobbling puppet horse - and brightly painted whistles shaped like birds and horses.

The off-duty drivers of the horse-drawn sleighs shuffled about the streets in their long red jackets, embroidered trousers and fur caps, smoking and laughing. Down at the bottom of the main street, by the taxi rank nearest the Pewex shop, the taxi drivers stood around bartering petrol coupons or arranging other deals in their sheepskin coats and ostentatious leather jackets. Always a conspicuous group, and even more so here than back in Lodz, we immediately christened them 'the Coats.' At one point we spied the two groups of drivers, each in their distinctive uniforms, clearly clinching a mega-deal of some kind. They scattered instantly at the approach of a member of the *Milicja* - but Drew swore he saw the policeman wink at one of the last 'Coats' to depart.

And constantly, as we strolled around, we heard in our ears, from an undefined source among our fellow-pedestrians on the crowded pavement, the whisper in English:

'You change money? I buy dollars with you, O.K?'

We were beginning to find the discrepancy between the myth of this mountain idyll and its corrupt reality quite amusing, the more so because it was apparent that since our arrival had come the beginnings of a real thaw, the fairytale magic and illusion draining out of the place with the fast blackening snow. We soon discovered that all transactions had to be conducted through Aneta or our 'K.K.' status was liable to have an embarrassingly inflationary effect on the price of any articles we attempted to purchase, or cause an unfortunate diminution in the arithmetical powers of those seeking to calculate our change.

Aneta's face became pinched with mortification. She resented us, her charges, as though we were a conspiracy to reveal such unsavoury aspects of her country to her. We, on the other hand, actually didn't mind. Despite all the cheating, we liked the people we had dealings with: direct, hard-bitten but genuinely friendly, and above all cheerful. It was nothing personal and, as far as they were concerned, well worth a try.

And yet there was another and increasingly more serious deficiency: there was no beer. We were used to the sudden disappearance or absence of certain commodities for no apparent reason. A month before there had suddenly been no cheese to be found in all of Lodz, where it had previously been abundant, and items like meat and vodka were usually scarce, at least in the shops. I don't know why beer suddenly seemed so utterly indispensable to our enjoyment, or why the refrain of shop assistants and waitresses - '*Piwo? Nie ma.*' ('Beer? Isn't any.') - so dispirited us that we went on inquiring in place after place long after the message should have got across and Aneta had lost patience with us.

45

As the snow disappeared from the lower slopes, the streets began to fill with disappointed skiers at a loose end and in need of refreshment. It wasn't just that Mountain Beer was famous and not easy to get elsewhere in Poland, but that it seemed the beverage best suited to the open-air communality of the place. We could see them in the streets, the men of the town, with hunched shoulders and disgruntled faces, scuffing at the hardened slush at the kerbside as they waited for God knows what. All their heartiness was gone, and though the queues formed outside Monopolowy, the state alcohol store, and beside a wooden kiosk on the edge of town, waiting to get in the vodka for the private celebrations of Saint Sylvester only a few days away, still there was no beer.

So we drank coffee and ate *ambrozja* ice-cream with sweet sultanas in the sallow, art deco interior of the Café Europejska, where a pianist of extraordinary emaciation played pre-war jazz. The pianist's lank hair gyrated on the seventies lapels of his brown suit as his fingers conjured from the keys all the subversive freshness that music had possessed when people heard it for the first time. They were dangerous sounds he whipped up, and for him and his audience that was exactly what they signified. Even so, we resolved that next day we would head out of town.

Thus we sat under the canvas awning of the horse-drawn wagon, grinning at our fellow tourists, elbows and thighs squashed together on the way up the mountain to Morskie Oko, the frozen lake of the Sea's Eye. Every so often the driver would stop the cart and jump down to shovel the horse's green and steaming dung deftly over the side of the mountain. When he did this he stuck his lighted cigarette behind his ear dangerously close to the raised fur earflaps of his cap.

There was certainly no shortage of snow up here as we joined the straggle of day-trippers strung out inconsequentially against the white landscape, labouring towards the lake through snow-laden pines and the bright stillness of the day. The vast frozen disc and encircling mountains seemed locked in a relationship of mesmerised reciprocity. In Summer the water must reflect the peaks back to themselves, and now, in Winter, the hunched, unperturbed forms stared down, contemplating its solidity.

We took the bus on our way back, skiers jammed into the body of the vehicle like a phalanx of ancient warriors with furry woollen helmets and a bizarre kind of hooked spear strapped to their backs. The driver steered with his knees and apparent unconcern, freeing his hands to check tickets, as we raced around the hairpin bends on the icy roads towards the valleys.

Somewhat to our relief, we had to change buses and were deposited in the middle of nowhere halfway down a mountainside. There was only one other person at the stop, and he stood well away from us. Nonetheless he cast frequent glances in our direction as we stood clapping our gloved hands together and swinging our arms, laughing and joking in English. I began to think the looks signified disapproval until he suddenly beckoned to Aneta, who went over to him.

'He says there is beer,' she announced, coming back.

'There is? How do we get to it?'

It involved two more buses and another stop even more remote than the last. As instructed, we left the road and headed into the ring of mountains over the untouched snow.

'Are you sure…?' began Drew, just as we came upon the track and the deep, fresh tyre marks. We followed this spoor for about half a mile until we spotted a large silver tanker dragging itself towards us - and, just beyond, a small, wooden hut, barely bigger than a garden shed.

Even from outside, it was clear that the joint was jumping, pulsating with interior energy like something in a cartoon. Inside was gathered a greater concentration of people than seemed physically possible, some wedged around trestle tables, many more shoehorned into every available space between. Puddles of melted snow from many boots collected on the floor and the waitresses squeezed their way between the packed bodies balancing trays of beer above their heads. There were shouts and sounds of hilarity.

We nudged our way in, greeted with friendly claps on the back and calls to the waitress to attend to us at once, accompanied by a lot of banter about the slack service: We'd been here all of a minute. Couldn't she see that the travellers needed *beer*? There was a jocularity which we realised instantly had been the quality we most missed in our daily lives. This was not the intense, melancholic, manic partying of students and dissident intellectuals that we were used to, with painstaking platefuls of open sandwiches, cigarettes and flavoured vodka from parents and relatives. It was perfectly straightforward: here was beer and here was happiness - simple as that - and here *we* were, in the middle of nowhere among the sheltering mountains.

'The thing about Poland,' Rob was holding forth under the agreeably warming influence of the beer, 'is that the simplest actions have the character of an escapade, and things are usual here that would never be believed anywhere else.' He took another gulp. 'Life has this kind of normalised, *hallucinatory* quality. '

Several hours later, perched on a pile of logs on a horse-drawn sledge, cadging a lift back to the bus-stop, we watched the glowing peaks gently advance and recede, backlit by the moon as it grew dark.

The afterglow of the hut that had beer sustained us for the next two days. Yet Saint Sylwester was coming and again we wanted *company*. We felt a desperation to be among people, not to drink vodka alone in our room but to celebrate the arrival of the new year as some kind of shared and social act. It didn't seem too much to ask. It was as we were scanning the menu in the window of the Restauracja Gajda, promising Bear Schnitzel and Bison Burgers, that we spotted the poster. This advertised a 'St Sylwester Disco Dance Party' at ten o'clock the following evening in a nearby hotel, tickets available at the door. Somewhat to Aneta's pitying amusement, we immediately began to look forward to this prospect to a ridiculous degree. What if we couldn't get tickets? We'd have to go really early. This being Poland, everyone would have the same idea. Then we'd have to go really *really* early.

In the meantime, though, we realised we were running out of money - especially if we were to afford this extra expense. Daringly, we decided to attempt to acquire some without the aid of Aneta, who had gone back to the Dom Turysty to reserve a phone call to her mother. We tried the two banks, at opposite ends of the town, but they were both shut. As we trudged the slushy pavements between the two, Harriet and Drew bet how many times we'd be asked if we wanted to change money on the way.

It wasn't until we were returning up the main street that we acknowledged that not *once* had we heard that familiar passing hiss: 'You change money?' This struck us at first as disconcerting, then as downright *bizarre*. We squelched on, scanning our fellow pedestrians with an odd sensation: how do you look for something that's normally just *there*? What about the 'Coats'? At the taxi rank a mere two cars were waiting, their drivers reading their papers demurely behind their wheels, as though congregating and wheeler-dealing were the last activities it would ever occur to them to engage in.

'There's only one thing for it,' Rob said.

'It'll have to be Pewex,' Drew agreed, squaring up. He girded himself, pulling up the collar of his trench-coat. Both tugged their caps forward meaningfully and assumed a-man's-gotta-do expressions which made Harriet and I laugh, and set off. There were sure to be some 'characters' hanging around the dollar shop: people always needed to change money there.

Harriet and I sat ourselves down on a nearby wall and kept an eye out as Rob and Drew sauntered down the road, the short and the tall, looking more suspicious than anyone we had seen all day. A spivvier pair it would be hard to conceive

The Pewex shop stood on its own on a small side-street leading off the main thoroughfare.

'Have they gone in?' I asked Harriet, who had a better view.

'I think so - there are too many people behind them to see.'

The shop appeared to be packed. We were trying to spot any loitering 'coatie' types in the vicinity when six blue *Milicja* vans and two police cars roared past. Screeching their brakes and spraying the grey, hard-packed, leftover snow at the kerbside, they parked at strategic points all around the Pewex building. There were policemen everywhere, white truncheons drawn: a dozen had gone in and immediately barred the door, while others ringed the shop with linked arms.

Harriet and I looked at each other in disbelief, unsure whether to laugh. Had Drew and Rob's attempt been so crass as to call down this response so swiftly? We went as close as we dared to the police cordon to peer through the window. All the customers had been herded into the centre of the shop. A woman was standing on a step-ladder holding a cash box, a *milicja* man talking to her from the foot of the steps. We hunted among the sea of hats and caps, but as both Drew and Rob were wearing Polish caps we were unable to distinguish them. Drew's stature would ordinarily have marked him out, but we presumed he was having the sense to be inconspicuous. Had they been in the middle of their transaction when the police burst in, or had they completed it? Was someone standing in that shop - where the *milicja* appeared at that very moment to be embarking on individual and seemingly random searches - with a pocketful of illegally exchanged pounds?

Then we saw them, just before they spotted us, swallowing nervously, looking paler, guiltier and just a hundred times more *shady* than anyone else in the place. They grinned at us - managing to look shiftier than ever - and Drew mouthed 'What the *fuck...?*' We retreated before we drew attention to them, or induced them to draw attention to themselves. The other customers resembled an implausible, housewives'-choice conglomeration of innocent-looking and upstanding citizens in comparison to these two caricature criminals What if one of those fur-collared *milicja* men felt like arresting someone for the sake of a bribe ...?

'I know who *I'd* arrest,' said Harriet as we drew back. 'They look *so* dodgy.'

So much for trying to manage things without Aneta. Three hours later, when the doors were finally unbarred, releasing Drew, Rob and the crowd of blameless individuals who had shared their incarceration, we learnt that they had not even begun to effect their mission when the raid occurred. Money had been stolen from the cash-box, apparently, though the police had not in the end arrested anyone.

'What I don't get,' said Drew, looking at the people beginning to disperse into the empty street, where still not a 'Coat' lurked nor a wheeler-dealer loitered, 'is how everyone in this town *knew*.'

In the hotel foyer, people were passing their coats across the marble counter to the cloakroom attendant, a tall, scrawny man with hair sprouting from nowhere else on his head but behind his ears.

'That's it, tuck the scarves in the sleeves. I don't want to have to be doing that, do I? Number 92 - that's it, there you go. Oh, *and* a hat - I might have known.'

Up some red-carpeted stairs to the right, well cordoned-off, dancing and dining were underway for the guests of the hotel and - to judge from a small placard in English - a Swedish business delegation and their wives. To the left, down some more steps promising 'The Cellar Bar', a queue was beginning to form. This lower part of the foyer had a stone floor and arched windows. A table was set up in front of the studded, wooden door leading to the cellar.

'A bit much that you have to come to a dungeon to have a drink with other people round here,' Drew remarked. We'd arrived almost an hour early - but, predictably, others had had the same idea. We joined the queue as quickly as we could.

'Oh God,' I said, 'I hope we get in.'

A heavy man, in the crimson jacket and small tasselled hat of the establishment's uniform, came to the table carrying a cash box and a roll of tickets. He sat down, rubbed his hands and flashed several gold teeth at the assembled company as he opened the cash box. All semblance of a line at once evaporated. I'd never been claustrophobic but I didn't feel comfortable in this crush. People were shoving forward, arms outstretched over one another's shoulders, waving wads of notes in which the dull green of dollar bills was uppermost, seeking to attract attention by calling out in accented English. The man's balding head glistened and the flesh round the gold band on his finger bulged as he took the bribes hand over fist. The hat even resembled a fez, so that he looked like a caricature of Ottoman corruption, charging for a peep at the *seraglio*.

'Hey, how about it, fella? Take a look over here' called the girl next to me, in a high-necked ski-jacket. She had a rainbow-coloured, woollen ear-band and a ponytail. Her accent was mainly American, with the teeth to match: Does your mouth become that shape simply from continuously forming words with an American accent? I wondered. Or is it American orthodontics that produces that distinctive fullness and gleam? Though Polish, she lived in Sweden, she told me when we exchanged a few words, but she'd spent time in the States as a kid. She couldn't much be bothered with this dive.

As possibly the only native speakers of English in the queue, we were curiously mute. Since we didn't have dollars, only zlotys borrowed from Aneta and the pounds we had not managed to change, which - whether from principle or paralysis - we were not waving in anybody's face, we were clearly going nowhere fast.

'Nye then,' Drew shouldered his way forward, then smoothed his best upper-class English accent over his usual Belfast drawl: 'Since there appears to be some kind of queuing system in operation here, don't you think you should at least take the bribes in order?'

We covered our mouths to hide our laughter, nonetheless guilty of wondering whether the 'authentic' tones of the World Service would have any clout at all that might redound to our benefit. The man at the table turned away, squirting words out the corner of his mouth.

'What did he say?'

'Piss off, wise-guy, I think,' I said.

The man turned back:

'Got any dollars?' Harriet translated. 'No? Then piss off out of here.'

At a certain point, having taken enough bribes and allocated the requisite number of tickets, he slammed the cashbox shut and gave a grin of evident malice at the disappointed remnant.

We stood around disconsolately for a few minutes with the other unfortunates. Evidently we did not disperse swiftly enough, for two men in crimson jackets appeared, one holding what I took to be a canister of spray snow. I didn't know you could get that here, I thought, and within seconds my eyes were smarting, and everyone around me was choking and gagging. Drew and another man tried unsuccessfully to open the window and we all spilled out onto the snow, cursing between coughs and rubbing our eyes.

'They tear-gassed the queue,' Rob said in disbelief. 'I saw those blokes - they deliberately tear-gassed the queue.'

'The bastards,' I said, adding in my head indignantly 'and I might be *pregnant.*' The thought was at once completely new and completely self-evident. 'Tear-gassing pregnant women. God, they'd sue your ass for that in America!' I started laughing, the kind of laughter that might not stop until you cry … Luckily Drew brought me up short:

'We've left our coats in there. We'll have to go back in.'

We couldn't help looking longingly at the red-carpeted staircase leading to the hotel guests' party upstairs as we crept back into the foyer. Descending the stairs, a man with a sandy moustache, a white tuxedo and what I presupposed was a supercilious air saw us and, without warning, extended his index finger, raised the tasselled cordon and admitted us. We ducked underneath, gabbling our thanks, and galloped up the stairs, anxious to get out of sight of the hotel staff as quickly as possible.

The dance-floor was full, the long gowns swishing to a Viennese waltz. The band was one of those that plays seemingly without effort, the drummer nodding over his sticks with each lazy beat, as if in the process of dozing off. If we could get across to one of the tables on the far side, we might find a place to squeeze in unnoticed.

We started to move into the crush just as a couple of crimson-jacketed men appeared behind the columns at the top of the stairs, combing the room with their eyes. We inched forward through the dancers, looking edgily over our shoulders. The couple in front of us separated. The man took my arms, while the woman whipped off Rob's cap - which he had inexplicably omitted to remove - and began to waltz us deeper into the centre of the dance-floor. The band seemed to have taken a tonic for they launched seamlessly into a frantic polka. I glimpsed Aneta being whirled past at the edge of my peripheral vision.

Several dances later saw all five of us washed up, more or less simultaneously, at the other side of the dance-floor. Across the heads of the dancers, the hotel's henchmen appeared to have gone. Probably there was no eagerness to make an unpleasant scene in front of the Swedish delegation, though no-one we had yet encountered appeared to be Swedish. Drew spotted a space at the back of one table near a window and we squeezed ourselves in. The waiter was there in an instant, winked at us and took an order for a bottle of red wine. Aneta was flushed, less thrilled than mortified: this wasn't a situation she'd ever have got herself into alone. She knew where breaking the rules could end, and what's more whom it would end up most serious *for*. We, on the other hand, felt exhilarated by our madcap extremity, plotting our escape out the casement window and down a nearby tree in the event of our pursuers' return.

Our neighbour at the table, a stout, blond Silesian called Aloysiusz, insisted on paying for our wine, 'in friendship, in friendship', pointing out sweetly to the waiter that he had brought us the most expensive bottle in the house and *still* tried to overcharge us. Rob nudged me. The accordian player on the dais was standing staring fixedly towards the stairs, quivering like a pointer. He looked across meaningfully at us.

'I think it's time for more dancing,' Drew observed. 'I mean, like *nye*.' There were two bouncer-looking types and two policemen at the head of the stairs. I gave Aloysiusz my hand, while his sister-in-law - I think she was - took charge of Drew and shepherded us all towards the parquet dance floor. The effect of the presence of the two *milicja* men was extraordinary. At once we became part of a mass conspiracy. People who might well have rewarded us with a stony stare had we nodded to them in the street yielded to the automatic reflex to shelter the fugitive and to spite the authorities if possible into the bargain. The bouncers and policemen circled the dance-floor, scanning, scowling, pointing and periodically conferring. I never kept the same partner for a whole dance, doubling back, passed from hand to hand in mid-twirl. As I neared the band, the drummer gave the thumbs up and shouted '*dziesiec minut*' - ten minutes - confirming that he too recognised the triumph if we could make it till midnight. I became preoccupied with trying to master the tango, which I'd never danced before - but the dance created too many gaps and therefore points of access for the 'enemy', so the vigilant accordion-player led a swift return to the successful polka formula.

'*Panstwa…*' Ladies and Gentlemen… 'It is almost midnight.'

The dancers formed three concentric circles, with us all at different points in the middle one.

'In your country you do this, yes?' The man next to me crossed his arms as if in a strait-jacket. I was momentarily bewildered, then inspiration struck:

'*Tak, tak*, yes, like this.' As everyone seemed to be looking at us expectantly, the four of us belted out Auld Lang Syne as loudly and as tunefully as we could. It felt more like a seranade to *new* acquaintance and a fitting tribute. Enough people had a rough idea of the tune to provide a very passable bagpipe drone to back us up, and the accordion-player joined in half-way through - but I could see that the policemen had lost patience: they were going in…

'*Teraz to* …' I yelled. Now this … '*Raz, dwa* …' One, two … I launched into the middle, dragging my circle with me, like a demented primary school teacher, and we lurched into the centre and out again to another chorus. The sight of one of the policemen making intermittent, tentative lunges and having to drop back as the outer circle cantered backwards towards him, with manifest satisfaction at his forced retreat, was to be one of the most joyous memories of the evening. There was the briefest hiatus before the accordion-player announced the hour and the drummer beat out the chimes on his cymbals. Embracing and cheek-kissing broke out all around. We kissed our neighbours and wished Happy New Year for all we were worth.

'God bless America,' said someone to me kindly.

Someone else shouted out: '*No, spiewaj, Dariusz!*' Well, sing, Darius. He had a richly gorgeous bass voice and the first low, beautiful notes dripped from his mouth. Without further prompting those around us joined him. Dropping arms, they stood and sang the Chorus of the Hebrew Slaves from *Nabucco*, as they did at every performance of the opera in protest at their own oppression. At least one of the bouncers knew the words - I could tell by the way he followed the lines with his eyebrows - and sure enough, the next moment his lips were moving. When they finished we clapped furiously:

'*Bis, bis*,' I cried, cheekily - and out of sheer bravado they gave another, final rendition, linking arms once more and swaying from side to side. We joined in as best we could, in our most heartfelt manner. At the end, the bouncers and the two policemen walked into the centre of the ring without difficulty and apprehended us. Instinctively, we moved forward as they approached - I suppose not to implicate or make things difficult for anyone else. Yet the people clapped us as though we had indeed stepped forward to receive our merited applause.

'It's a fair cop,' said Drew in English as the policeman took his elbow. 'I've always wanted to say that.'

'No thank you, I've done enough dancing for tonight,' Rob felt emboldened to risk his Polish and the joke as 'his' policeman reached for his arm. The people nearest laughed. The rhythm had changed to the slow hand-clap of derision for the authorities that went on as we were escorted down the stairs, to the *szatnia* to collect our coats and ejected into the snow.

To Aneta's annoyance, as we headed back along the street to the Dom Turysty - 'Don't you know how serious that was, or might have been?' - we were unable to stop laughing all the way.

New Era, New Perspective

'They said they'd get them here for Christmas.'

'What are we queuing for then? I thought it was coffee.' The young man tugged his navy blue hat further down over his ears.

'Lemons. Cuban lemons. They wanted them here by Christmas. You know, like they always do. Fill the shops.' The woman in the stout grey coat and red knitted hat looked well padded against the gritty wind. She had turned to talk to the young man while keeping her thickly lined boots planted solidly, pointing in the direction of the queue. The line stretched towards the darkened doors of the low, blue, supermarket building about twenty hats, coats and pairs of hunched shoulders away. 'Must've got held up,' she added.

'You're telling me,' the elderly woman in a headscarf in front of her joined in. 'Here by Christmas? They've barely made it for Carnival.' Her two hands clutched the ring-handle of the empty cloth bag in front of her which she raised and lowered for emphasis.

'My neighbour said it would be coffee,' the young man said. 'It's coffee I need. For the doctor. My wife's expecting, you see. Lemons are no good to me. It's got to be coffee. Doctors always get coffee. I want her treated right, her and the baby. It's our first baby.'

The queue did not follow the building round - this had been disallowed some time ago as placing too much pressure on the glass panes - but instead stuck straight out from the doors, and the wind in consequence cut right across it. The caps, hats and headscarves of the people sank lower into the collars of their coats and jackets. More hands were folded under arms or went into pockets. A couple of people stamped their feet, making the ice particles on the frosty asphalt crackle. A haze of breath rose like the steam from the manhole cover in which several pigeons were pacing not far away.

It was impossible to see anything going on inside the building. The windows were blocked by pyramids of tins and by a pink and red bird and flower design painted onto the glass. The front of the queue obscured the doors, which according to the time of day should have been open long before. Perhaps extra time was needed to unload the lemons at the back.

'My neighbour always knows where to get everything,' the young man confided. 'Toilet rolls, soap, she's a marvel. She always knows someone. She's never been wrong before. You can't believe anything these days, but her rumours are always the best ones. Perhaps we've offended her. I know we didn't forget her name-day - Pani Ela, it's easy to remember that one. My wife's mother is Ela too, so we went to hers first. Do you think that was it?'

'Oh I shouldn't think so. I'm sure she wouldn't expect - she'd understand - family is ...'

'She's so tired, Majka, my wife, she can't remember everything. What with working and cooking and cleaning. We've only been married a few months and she's still learning. We were very lucky to get the flat transferred to my name after my parents died. I mean the Association could easily have given it to a bigger family. They'd have been well within their rights. But the Chairman knew my Dad - it was all so sudden - and he knew me and Majka ... well, he knew we might ... It's just a two-roomer but we really...'

'How many square metres?'

'Forty.'

'In Marysinska?'

'No, Czarnieckiego.'

'Oh that's not so bad. My son lives in a flat of nearly seventy square metres, but of course he's been very successful. He's building his own house out at Zgierz, but it's a terrible job to get materials. He thought it would be just perfect for the children growing up, but the boys are 14 and 11 already. They were just toddlers when he started. My daughter lives with us, and her husband - he's in Germany at the moment. He says the pregnant women are three times bigger there and no-one stands up for them on the bus.'

'She isn't very big, my Majka, and she hardly eats anything, even now - she never has - and she says she's fine. She keeps telling me she feels fine. She hasn't had to go into hospital once so far. There've been no complications. That's quite unusual, isn't it?'

'In this day and age, yes, yes it is. There's so much pollution', the headscarved old woman rejoined the conversation. 'The babies are born early, and then...'

'Majka walks everywhere you see - she must be breathing all the time - she won't touch the tram, after what happened to my parents.'

'They're not satisfied with poisoning us from the inside out, they have to do it from the outside in at the same time - it's a pincer movement'. A short man in a black cap and jacket lit another Wiarus cigarette, working

56

his moustache as he drew on it to get it started. He offered one to the young man, who accepted.

'Your parents ...?' the woman in the red hat inquired, 'had an accident? In a tram?'

'Not the collision on Defenders of Stalingrad?' the old woman put in. 'That was terrible. My cousin was coming out of the watchmakers. He saw it.'

'No, no,' the young man said. 'It wasn't that one. That was reported. It wasn't in the centre of town, but on the way to Teofilow, near the tractor plant.'

'Not that one with the cable, the cable smashing down? Oh God, I heard about that', the moustached man said. 'It was reported, but only once, on the radio. I was having my break, but by evening they'd pulled it. It never made the T.V. news at all, I remember.'

'There weren't so many casualties after all,' another woman put in, 'not like that smash-up on Zgierska. That was really bad.'

'It was the third one in a month,' the young man offered apologetically. 'Pani Ela always said that was it. Just one too many.' He sighed.

'Why did they report it at all then?' the man in the cap demanded. 'There's no consistency. That's what drives you mad.'

'I think there were some implications ... you know, about the cable. I don't know. It always seemed like there were implications - '

'Ah, implications,' several nodded, and the small man seemed about to speak when the woman in the red hat cut across him:

'You certainly can't do anything safely these days. Not the most harmless things. Just going about your ordinary business.'

Everyone agreed it was terrible.

'Have you not a few dollars tucked away somewhere?' the red-hatted woman tried to make it up to the young man. 'You could get your Majka that dried Western milk from Pewex - my daughter never drank anything else when she was pregnant. You know our milk isn't pasteurised. Get her some of that Western milk, and perhaps a bit of chopped ham, that'd be best.'

'And try to get fresh vegetables - you know, from a good source. These carrots and cabbages you buy on the stalls, where are they grown? Next to some highway probably. They are full of lead. In some peasant's garden next to a chemical plant. It's no joke. I only ate vegetables from my uncle when I was expecting my Adas,' this from a woman in a mustard-checked coat who was standing behind the young man.

The queue had not neglected to grow while these revelations and pronouncements went on. It now turned a corner, following a low wall, to avoid blocking the way by which the two small Fiats in the parking spaces might nose their way onto the road, though the petrol rationing made this unlikely. The cold, whitish light caught the chipped asphalt and reflected its veined colours, glinting the greys and greens up into the air, rebounding off the coloured screens on the balconies of the blocks of flats. The people near the front were getting restless. There had been a couple of cautious thumps on the doors.

A bus drew into the turning circle on the opposite side of the larger road some distance away. The driver switched off the engine. Several people climbed on, the sounds of their boots clanking on the metal steps reached the people in the queue. Some people hurrying from the flats towards the bus looked doubtfully at the queue as they passed, and quite a number joined it. Others went on, looking back frequently.

Beyond the wire fences behind the bus, the allotments were a bit bedraggled by this time - it was almost February - and the small huts appeared shrunken under the icy mist. One or two people gazed out from the bus at a small yard of black mud and piled planks. Bright green moss grew on the pitch roof of a shed where five white doves were sitting. They all took flight at once, then returned, arranging themselves like symbols on a playing card. They were so white and the moss was so green against the black mud and the black roof, the discoloured shed and the grey sky, seen through hexagons of wire mesh and grainy bus windows.

'That's the best way, to keep out of hospital, until the end of course,' the mustard-coated woman was advising, tucking her brown hair back under her fluffy hat from which it had escaped on one side.

'... if she *does* go in, I'm so worried, all the gifts for the nurses ...' the young man had turned to her, almost desperately.

'How far on is your wife?' the grey-coated woman in front of him recalled him. 'You have to give something to the doctor at the very beginning. That's an absolute priority.'

'That's right, keep him sweet,' the headscarved old woman agreed. 'Probably she's *needed* to go to hospital, but her doctor won't have referred her.'

The man in the black jacket scratched the greying hair at the back of his cap. 'It's unlikely she's gone this far without any difficulties at all. Did it not strike you as a bit suspicious?'

'Aye, I'd say so.'

'Well, I suppose...' the young man looked from face to face. 'I just thought ... I mean, she says she feels fine. Don't fret, Janusz, she says. You always fret. I'm fine, really. That's what she says. She keeps saying it.'

'You have to get it all ready beforehand,' the grey-coated woman soothed him, 'so she can take it with her when she goes in'.

'You can't just go marching in there like Saint Nicholas with a sackful of goodies,' the older man started to laugh.

'Oh but of course,' the mustard-coated woman chipped in. 'There's no way you'll be allowed in there'

'They don't have men in there,' the old lady told him. 'There's the germs to think about . . . people coming in, it wouldn't be safe, not at all it wouldn't.'

'Won't I see the baby then, Majka and the baby, when it's born?'

'Of course not. Everyone knows that, surely? Look, where's she going - to have it I mean? The Jordana?'

'Well we did think perhaps the Polish Mother would be finished in time, but it seems . . .'

'For your grandchildren maybe, son' the man broke in. 'No, so it'll be the Jordana then - well, you go to the car park underneath the maternity ward and you wait and she'll shout to you out the window what you've got, girl or boy. Simple as that.'

'Don't bank on it. You make quite sure you get what she says, love. When my little Michal was born my husband didn't hear right - I'd got another woman to shout for me, I wasn't supposed to move - so off he went down the Agawa, all his friends commiserating with him, telling him a second girl wasn't so bad, and me lying there all the time knowing nothing about it.'

The doves took off in a cloud. On the downward arc of their flight they fell in with some brown pigeons, and all rose for a second circuit through the chalky air. The sky was pink, turning faintly blue above the shoe factory, where the women were coming out onto the roof for a cigarette. The women gathered in groups of three or four, dark in their flowered overalls against the white slabs of the ventilation shaft behind them. Three crowded onto the single bench, one perched on the arm, her left leg lightly swinging as she held her cigarette between her lips with a hairgrip to get the last puffs. Her husband didn't like women to smoke so she had to catch up in her work-breaks. One group was laughing - 'No, no, Pani Paulinka, he *can't* have done' - the voices sailed down from the roof in the same diagonal plane as the pigeons and doves, on what was by now their third trajectory, sheering down towards the line of waiting people.

On the side of the nearest block of flats, a man dangled on a platform lowered from the roof. He was painting with a wide roller, slowly working down the side of the building, but it looked rather as though he was peeling off a grey layer to reveal the snowy underside than putting on a new coat of white paint. Underneath the zig-zagging rows of ten-storey blocks, several smaller houses remained where the old road had gone. Turkeys scratched in the dirt of one garden, while an elderly man repeatedly bent to dip his brush in the pot as he painted the trunks of his fruit trees white to protect them from parasites. The bandaged trees stood with their arms out above him as if he were fitting them for clothes.

In front of the flats an old man was scything last Autumn's dead grass. A group of children with satchels strapped to their backs, well wrapped up and wearing fur caps with ear flaps or hats with long dangling pom-poms, left the water-pump where they'd been fooling around to jump the scythe as it came round. There were problems heating the schools, so children in this district were taught in one of three 'sittings' each day. This must be the second one.

'It's dreadful,' one elderly woman in the queue was saying to her friend. 'So confusing. My son's children, well they live with his mother-in-law, and she, poor woman, has to deal with Jacek off school so much of the day as well as little Ola. You can imagine what it's like.'

Across the road from the dustbins, one of the iron-framed billboards specially erected for the referendum last year displayed in triplicate its latest poster. *New Era, New Perspective*, it stated, sporting an enigmatic, coloured design presumably intended to suggest eyes. No-one registered its message or its gaze.

The man on the platform, lower now, went on with his un-painting.

Szkola Muzyczna

I'd never noticed before how clumsy men are, how they lumber at you, their dangling arms seeming to rotate in the sockets of their shoulder bones, without the least notion of moving aside on the pavement. It struck me when I was out hunting for food in the daytime. Their heads seemed to be situated to the rear of their bodies, the unzipped jackets and taut, ill-tucked checked shirts came at me, even as I dodged them, all but toppling off the kerb, as hands and elbows menaced my very navel.

I was touchy about that area of course, because of the baby, but, even so, surely I wasn't imagining it. Were Polish men worse than others in this respect? Or did women all the time, everywhere, unconsciously get out of the way, shift for themselves not to be mown down by the great unseeing creatures? Had I, all my life, done that? I'd simply no idea - but I knew there was something deeply wrong now. They should be getting out of *my* way. In the battle of the bellies, how dared they assume that their flabby protuberances took precedence over my tautly majestic bulge? I was the one with the precious burden thrust out before me. Admittedly this was as yet quite small and concealed under my coat - but couldn't they tell? Were they so unobservant? Of course they were. Oblivious oafs. Men!

Was it some hormonal side-effect of my condition that had turned me overnight into such an indiscriminate man-hater? Or was this some animal urge necessary to protect my young against the cruising males of the pride? It didn't matter that many Polish men were fairly small and wiry, not big and scary at all. I differentiated only insofar as it enabled me to calculate how much aggression would be needed to see them off. I had the docile-looking ones down as merely gormless and stupid. Some of the smaller specimens were mean and rat-like, while the larger ones, the more obvious and extrovert striders along the centre of the pavement, were thugs and completely vile. Almost regardless of size or demeanour, I didn't trust them: I feared them and they had better not mess

with me. Yet, since they were not a bunch of marauding lions but a series
of men getting to or from work, or off to buy something, as I was, and
in all probability unused to registering the feelings of women passed in
the street, the only one burning up in the glare of that lioness fury was
myself.

Still, the energy generated by this impotent outrage powered me on. In
the breaks between classes, I would tramp the uneven pavements the
length of Piotrkowska Street, searching at odd corners between the
grand buildings for the low, wooden vegetable stalls, where sometimes
there were carrots and, lately, a rumour of radishes. Otherwise, white
cabbage, apples and potatoes were the only fare. It was a good thing my
cravings of the early weeks had been for potatoes. Potatoes and company: the earliest sign of this unlooked-for pregnancy, a sudden tendency
to turn up at my friends' doors clutching a 2-kilo bag of tatties, which I'd
insist on boiling up in their skins and eating at once doused in butter.
Looking up from my plate at my bewildered hosts I'd inquire with a full
mouth, 'are you sure you don't want some?'

Just as well I hadn't longed for oranges or bananas. You could only
buy those for dollars from the Pewex shop. Was it through excess of
some kind of scruple or simple lack of sense that I hadn't brought any
hard currency back from my brief trip home? Not wanting to be the rich
foreigner? No-one believed me anyway, foreigners and dollars being an
inseparable concept here.

That day, after two hours' march, I was returning home in triumph
with a kilo of carrots.

'Hello.' It was Agata, one of my fourth-year students. 'You have been
shopping. It is very boring for you, I think.'

'Not at all. Look - I got some carrots.'

'You cannot eat them you know.'

'Why on earth not?'

'They are full of - what is it, from cars?'

'Lead?'

'Yes, lead. These vegetables for buying in city, they are grown by some
workers near road. They are not good. We are having all vegetables from
uncle in village.'

'I see.'

'You have milk too?'

'Yes.

'You must not drink such milk. Only powdered milk is good, from
Pewex - Western milk, you know, you pay for in dollars.'

'I don't have any dollars. Surely you can't tell me most people don't
drink this milk? I can boil it, can't I?'

'Boil it, yes. But it is not good. Only Western milk.'

I gazed beyond the trams shouldering past one another in the centre of the broad avenue, and up towards the Great Theatre, and took several deep breaths. The wide vista, a legacy of the city's years under Russian administration during the Partitions of the nineteenth century, calmed me.

It would be easier, I thought, if there were more *variety*, if people didn't always tend to say exactly the same things, over and over, even using the same phrases. The effect was cumulative. I might shrug off the remarks of the first person, recover from those of the second, actively resist the third - but by the *tenth* …

'Are you going to the tram at Plac Wolnosci (Freedom Square)?' Agata inquired.

'Yes, but I'm going to go through Moniuszko Park - it's not the quickest way,' I hinted.

'I too. I will come,' asserted Agata cheerfully.

The city was generously endowed with parks, I thought, as we crossed the bridge over the ornamental lake. Agata having scotched my pleasure in my haul of food, we seemed to have run out of things to say.

'You have many trees,' I commented, unwisely. 'I mean, considering it's a city, lots of beautiful, mature trees.'

'Yes, but they are very sick', returned Agata promptly.

I almost burst out laughing at such an archetypal Anglo-Polish exchange: any positive observation immediately quashed, any upturn in the emotional tone at once batted down. Why did I never learn? I suppose because maintaining some measure of morale was necessary to my survival, just as averring that all was not right with the world, their world, indeed everything was *wrong* with it, was necessary to theirs.

'They look alright to me,' I persisted, taking almost malicious pleasure in pressing the button, testing my thesis yet again. I gestured at the broad trunks.

'Oh no, they are dying,' Agata assured me. In the absence of leaves, this was bound to be a moot point. They *had* to be dying: anything less was an implicit compliment to the hated government of the country. I'd have been the same. Were Agata to come to Britain and marvel at the wealth and wonderfulness of the place, would I not be desperately insisting that there were people just around the corner sleeping in cardboard boxes under the railway bridge?

I gave Agata the slip, claiming that I had reserved a 'phone call and had to go home in case it came through.

'Oh of course, you have 'phone,' said Agata, reminding me of my privilege. 'They always give to foreigners - you know, for bugging.' It was a real gift, I thought, managing to imply that I was in receipt of unfair advantages and in the same breath making quite sure that I should not enjoy them.

I hadn't booked a call. Rising through the ten floors of my building in the rickety lift, I regretted my forbearance. The reflection in the mirror on the back wall of the lift showed my face, tired and clammy, the glow of pregnancy unable to project beyond the pores of my skin. I told myself it did no good to keep hearing his voice, only made me incoherent with grief, which he could not but interpret as reproach.

I dumped my bag in the hallway of my flat, took a tin of fish out of the kitchen cupboard, tried absent-mindedly and unsuccessfully to decipher the Cyrillic lettering that ran around its rim and put on a pan of water to boil. I'd better do the potatoes straight away. If I sat down I wouldn't be able to move. According to the T.V. news, egg production was up and a record number of tractors had rolled off the Ursus assembly line. Elsewhere, I had heard rumours of trouble at the Ursus plant, and of something going on in Gdansk, but nobody knew for sure. How *would* you know? The screen showed a sea of white eggs undulating serenely on their conveyor belts while women in white gloves and net hats made occasional minor adjustments to their position on the tray.

I ate my supper with the door to the balcony open. From far below, squeals of children punctured the dark. I pictured the dozens of high-rise blocks around mine, thought of all the lighted windows, all the families clearing up after their meal, of children soon to be called in for *Dobranocka*, the bedtime programme with the little animated bear, of my long evening by myself. The place had the atmosphere of a giant campsite, with children playing late at night around the water pumps.

For some reason I went over to the 'phone. I had the sense that it was humming, and realised as I picked up the receiver that it had been knocked a little off the hook. Two women were having a desultory conversation - not on a 'phone line, it wasn't a crossed line - but in a room together somewhere, a bored-sounding exchange that I just caught the end of.

It had always seemed to me that, provided the population believed themselves to be under surveillance by the authorities, only a minimal quantity need actually be performed. Did they listen to all my conversations, or just some of them? Was it always the same people, or were they on shifts? Did they actually understand English, or was their regular attendance on my emotional outpourings, the long sob-filled pauses and Rob's inadequate comfortings, merely a bureaucratic requirement? It would serve them right to have to hear me blubbing away. I hoped it embarrassed them - though I suspected they were beyond embarrassment.

A couple of weeks ago I'd had such a strong sense of being overheard that I'd actually stopped sniffling in order to say in Polish: 'Will whoever is listening please go away? I'm not crying for your benefit, and I'd rather do so without an audience, thank you.' This had been followed by a series of strange clicks, not as though the listener had been shamed into logging off but rather was trying to find out what faulty connection had betrayed their presence. In fact, they'd done me a favour, as I felt somewhat pleased with myself for having come up with those Polish phrases on the spot and with the tone I thought I'd managed to strike, and cheered up considerably. I'd even succeeded in getting in the 'for your benefit' formulation picked up at my last Polish lesson - always a source of particular satisfaction for any language learner. Explaining the outburst to Rob even provided the opportunity for me to pontificate further in English - hoping now that they *could* understand, revelling in the sense that they had to listen and could not reply:

'What kind of person makes their living from listening to other people's 'phone calls for a discredited regime?'

'Do you think the dis... the what you just said bit was a good idea?'

'Why not? They *are* discredited.'

Now I was staring at the 'phone on the floor of my hall. How was I supposed to deal with my growing and (I hoped) hormonally-induced persecution complex if they insisted on bugging my 'phone?

'This is 52-75-94,' I spoke into the receiver. 'Nothing interesting for you on this line tonight.' I slammed it down. No crying show this evening, I went on, to myself, rehearsing the Polish words. Why could I never hold it together when I spoke to Rob, however positively I started off? I could feel his discomfort, his disappointment in me. After all, we'd *agreed* I would finish my contract. It was only a few more months. He had so much work to do before then, and I hadn't wanted to duck out of my time here half-way through. I wasn't miserable - or I wasn't *only* miserable - yet the moment I heard the timbre of his voice I invariably dissolved into a puddle of yearning and woe. I was a thousand miles from him and I was carrying his child. I seemed to be made of tears.

The T.V. was showing an American drama dubbed into Polish, all the parts, male and female, being read by a single actor. I sometimes watched these productions, as it was often possible to catch the English before the Polish overlay came in over the top, and was therefore quite a good way to pick up more Polish. Tonight, though, I switched off, put on the 'Your Favourite Chopin' cassette and went to run a bath.

Mine was a sit-up bath, which I really liked as the best way to have water right up to my chin. In the back of my mind I wondered vaguely whether perhaps I shouldn't have the water quite so scaldingly hot as I actually preferred it. Could such temperatures affect the baby - gin and hot baths and all that? And what about the odd yellowish colour of the water? I didn't want to have to worry about these things. Did being pregnant always entail such a mass of anxieties? Was this just the beginning of a lifetime of insupportable parental responsibility? Was the tortured look I had sometimes seen on the faces of parents not simply due to lack of sleep after all? In fact, why didn't they look worse? How could they even walk straight, under the appalling burden of responsibility? Why were they not rolling on their bellies howling in the dust?

The E minor Prelude pervaded the flat with the steam from the bath. It seemed at once unbearably Polish, unbearably beautiful and unbearably sad. I turned off the tap, stroking the baby inside me. Just for the sound and the sadness of it I found myself saying:

'Where's your daddy, eh? Where's Daddy gone?'

It was a bad idea. Still stroking, I stumbled over to the armchair and, as usual, started to cry.

****

On Tuesdays and Saturdays I caught a different bus, the eighty-eight from Marysinska Street. These were the days of my music practice and I had to be up early. At the Great Theatre I got down, turning away from the wide avenue, the fountains in the theatre square, and dived into the side streets.

Here the buildings were high and close together over the narrow roadway, the bulging balustrades and ornate wrought-iron balconies of the once-grand houses loomed above the tiny shop-fronts. The darkened stonework was blotched and flaking, formerly pink or pale blue stucco dimmed with grime. The intricate patterns carved around the windows had been nibbled into incoherence and the looped, beribboned sashes inscribed on the facades were smudged into indistinctness, ground into the grubby surface of the masonry.

Heaps of coal, dusted with frost, lay on the uneven pavements and pigeons strutted in the clouds of steam that rose from vents above the underground hot water pipes. Two flags - one red, one red and white - hung from the porch of School Number 39, and two more in front of the House of Youth on the corner. Clamped around every lamp-post, a brace with protruding spokes extended four small flags - two each of the red and the red and white - for the coming anniversary.

Through a barred basement window level with my ankles I could see part of a woman's body, in a flowered overall, her reddened hands twisting the long bristles around the head of a broom. A grey fox with red glass eyes lay curled in the furrier's window with its paws on its tail. The pen-mender's displayed a semicircle of fountain pens, like so many exclamation marks, on a piece of purple felt. The doors and grilles and window frames were thickly painted in dark green, muddy brown or mustard yellow. They really *are* different, I thought, the colours of other places and of other times - and these seemed to evoke both at once. Through the dusty glass I glimpsed a man in a blue beret behind a half-drawn, tobacco-coloured curtain, bent over his sewing machine, turning the wheel towards him with his left hand and guiding the material with his right.

I ducked through the doorway into the dark cakeshop. There was a short queue and the two assistants were busy levering their knives in the flat, square cakes as if they were cheeses, sliding the sliced portions onto the scales with a thud that raised an icing sugar cloud. As they wrapped the pieces deftly in grey paper, I eyed the poppy-seed cakes, the curd cheese cakes, the yeast cakes with raisins and the round *babkas* under an avalanche of sugar. I'd never really worked out the weights, so when my turn came I bought my usual pair of moist, dark brown doughnuts from the pyramid on the counter and ate them going down the street. Now the baby would not be hungry. I could never rid myself of the idea that when I was peckish, the baby must be ravenous, that whenever my stomach rumbled, the child was clamouring, desperate for its next meal.

I had reached the entrance to the Music School, an immense, studded, wooden door, painted dark brown, like the portal of a prison or an ogre's castle. It did not open, except for a small portion in the right-hand corner, specially designed for intrepid mortal visitors. Inside, to the left, another door led into the building itself, while straight ahead, through the massive stone archway, lay an enclosed courtyard. Lacey hems of net curtains - grey, with the sunlight on them - blew out through the open windows of the building over the cobbled yard. A Bach Two-Part Invention, some Mozart, the inevitable Chopin, Moniuszko's songs: the notes pattered down onto the rusty bins, as if the curtains were tablecloths and the sounds being shaken from them like crumbs out of the windows. On their bandy legs, the portly, brown iron dustbins were shaped like cradles for giant babies.

I had to go through the inner door to show my pass to the *portierka*, a terrifying old woman, who peered at the faded mauve type on the pass and hesitated, each time a little longer, as if *this* time she would not permit me to get away with it. She would squint suspiciously at the queer foreign name on the pass, then at me, then at the pass again, conveying a distaste almost amounting to disbelief that such named individuals should exist - let alone that she should have to encounter them.

My pass had been negotiated for me through the Instytut where I worked, and, since I could not decipher the official phrases inscribed on that thin sheet of paper beyond the days and hours assigned me, I felt the pass did not so much authorise as *require* me to spend the allotted time in room 43. Nor did I dare to leave before the specified three-hour span was up, and being therefore, so to speak, a prisoner in that room, I practised as I had never practised before.

Having demanded to see my legitimation card as well, the *portierka* released me into the black and white marble-floored hallway. I relaxed enough to trail my hand along the white ironwork of the banister as I climbed the spiral staircase. It was one of the mysterious enchantments of the place that I never saw a soul - though muted music came from the locked rooms and odd fortissimo phrases escaped to wreathe beneath the patterns on the circular ceiling and among the droplets of the chandelier. Only once, I'd seen a dark-haired woman - a mother or a teacher - slightly stooped above a child, the woman's hand flat between the boy's shoulder blades, steering him round a dark corner. I fingered the contours of the key in my pocket as I crept along the unlit corridor to my room.

There was relief the moment the lock on the door clicked and the room enclosed me. Not that it was a cosy, enfolding sort of room. It was big and light, the brown tiled chimney-stove in the corner belting out so much heat that the long windows were flung permanently open over the courtyard, with the grubby lace curtains billowing out after them. The grand piano stood in the centre of a greenish carpet so thin as to seem held together only by the pellets of grey fluff that coated its surface. The walls were painted pale lemon yellow from the ceiling until halfway down, a baked-clay brown below. Two washed-out prints, of the kind sold at the seaside, hung on the walls - one a trio of kittens, the other a large-eyed girl caressing a pigeon. In a green plastic potholder nailed to a wall-stand, a limp and unidentifiable plant struggled on in its pebbly soil.

I loved that room as if I had been born in it, with what I imagined must be a patriotic fervour. When I was dead, like Chopin, they could bury my heart here - probably in the plant pot. What is more, I *knew* I loved it, experienced the full significance of that place, not in retrospect, not as something to be nostalgic about in later times, like a child who doesn't appreciate the womb in which it swims so happily, but *then and there*.

I set to work on some chromatic scales but had to stop almost at once because of the great rush in my belly. The first run of the scale and the baby seemed to burst forth with such abandon that it made me laugh:

'Do you like that, little one? Do you like that?'

That joy of the child the moment the notes came always caught me, even though it happened every time. It didn't feel like *me* being joyful - though the feeling delighted me - it was quite distinct. How wonderful to feel another's joy inside your very self. Fingers drumming, the semitones regular and rising, the scales now sounded like step after step of accumulated joy, the arpeggios like leaps of joy reaching higher and higher.

I placed the Mozart sonata on the stand, open at the first movement. No-one had ever shown me *how* to practise, I realised. As a child, practice was just something you did - or were supposed to do - between les-

68

sons. Now, though, I took the parts I could not play, found the places where I always faltered, practising them slowly, then faster, then with the metronome, until my fingers *knew*. At last I had outgrown the childish desire to play the piece always from the beginning, expecting a miracle. I had lost, too, that pride which prevented me from pencilling more than a few fingerings on the score, (as though someone might see, and think... *what?*). Why not number *any* note I needed to in order to play correctly and with the same finger each time? Otherwise it was like a circus trainer teaching several seals in his troupe the same trick and never telling them until they were in the ring which performer he wanted to execute it. There *was* no recording angel looking over my shoulder - there was only the metronome pulsing, and the child, to be my judge. I still could not play the whole of the first movement at full pace, but I could at least manage it, at the slightly slower tempo I had chosen, all at the *same* speed.

Hearing the clicking of the metronome and my fingers' conformity, the notes raining out, *in time, in time,* the shapes of the phrases and beauty of the music forming independently of me, I felt exalted and breathless. The child, which had been still for a while, swooped within me, and with the last three chords, surged upwards so powerfully that I had to stop for a moment to press my hand to my belly and sat for a while dreaming. Turning the page, I began to pick out the second movement for the first time.

Out in the street, it was barely ten. The watch-makers and glovers, the oculists and pen-menders, the tailors and furriers and makers of slippers, the hatters and cobblers, the threaders of brushes, behind their felt curtains, down back courts and in basements, had opened their doors ready for customers and gone back to their work. My steps were light as I crossed the street to peer through basement grilles or examine glass cases, mounted at eye-level on the corners of buildings, displaying samples of workmanship to entice shoppers to entrances concealed down nearby alleyways. On the glass shelves, next to some babies' linen caps edged with braid, a sunrise of gloves with fingers outstretched, two pairs of shoes, or an embroidered pillowcase, were the small blue cards bearing name and profession in white writing.

I crossed back again, steps eager and purposeful, yet feeling completely free, as if I were willing chaff, a piece of paper blown along the street from one of the bins. Which to enter first? I had never loved *things* so much as the objects I bought here, presents for friends, for relatives, for the baby - who already had more embroidered caps and brightly coloured bibs than it could ever decently wear. Each time, I could not resist. Had I come to Communist Eastern Europe to discover materialism at last? Back home, there was so much 'stuff' - yet I had no desire for *any* of it. My niece would be having her first birthday - I could get her some of those lovely slippers.

Occasionally I would run into one or another of my students:

'You are looking in our shops? It must be very boring for you. You don't see anything to buy.' they would state, commiserating with me.

I might protest, but they were unconvinced: 'This is Communism,' they would say. 'We have money but there is nothing to buy.'

'And in the West,' I would complete the truism, 'there is plenty in the shops but we cannot afford to buy it.'

These were not 'Communist' shops anyway, but the small, family-run businesses that the government permitted as long as they stayed small. Yet without the Communist time-warp no doubt they would not be here.

I could hardly wait to get away, to dart down the steps and pull aside the heavy blanket, weighted with its leather hem, and see the shelves of fur-trimmed carpet slippers. An old man's veiny hand would lift another curtain and his drooping moustached face peer from the workshop at the back. Then he would come through, and smile, wiping his hands on his apron, and ask what I wished for.

The earlier sullen light had lifted and the buildings of blue or grey or rose-brown stone glowed a little, lapped in their uneven tidemark of grime. The dirt had rubbed its way into the pitted surfaces, arranging itself in darker patches and shadows, flakes of dingy stucco detaching themselves like old scabs behind the crumbling colonnades. It was all absolutely falling to bits, I thought joyfully, raising my face to the implied softness of the stone as though to receive the same murky rinse from the gritty air. Over and over in my head the phrase kept coming: 'I have never been so happy in my life.'

Later I would go to my favourite gloomy café, where the waitress always knew to bring *two* bowls of *bigos*, one after the other, with my lemon tea. There I could prepare lessons, or read, or watch the people come and go, eavesdropping on conversations I was beginning to understand, breathing in the smell of cabbage and apples, mushrooms and sausage. Around two or three, as it grew dark, I would ride home on the eighty-eight, watching the sheet of darkness lower over the jumbled allotments, lulled by the knowledge that my stop was also the terminus, that the engine would stop but my body and senses feel as though they were still travelling long before I had to get to my feet and step down into the dark.

** * * * *

The day it happened began badly, despite being a Tuesday. I could not take the eighty-eight because I had to drop off a book at the Instytut for a colleague. Still, I had managed to get up early enough not to be late for my practice.

I had been playing only a few minutes when there came a burst of rapping on the door. The noise was so sudden, so loud and so severe that my heart nearly fell out of my ribcage, and continued pounding madly against it as I went to the door. No-one had ever disturbed me in that room before.

A woman stood there, a middle-aged woman with dyed black hair that sprang back stiffly from her forehead, wearing an olive cardigan. She began to speak rapidly at once, making sharp, chopping gestures with her hands, a series of ricocheting statements and questions with no pause for an answer, not one word of which I could understand. The inexplicable torrent of sounds and the ferocity with which they were delivered, the furious working of the heavy creases in the walnut skin of the woman's face which seemed by its own action to generate them, so flustered me that I could not comprehend even single and perfectly simple words, much less piece together the import of a sentence. It was as if the peculiar sensation of being shouted at in a foreign language - in which emotional impact so far precedes understanding of semantic content - occasioned some kind of self-protective mental shutdown, and though words were flying past my ears it was barely an auditory experience at all. I took every one as a blow directly in the centre of my being, staring at her face, the face of a demagogue on a screen with the sound turned off.

I tried to say that I did not follow, to please speak slowly, fumbling unsuccessfully for my pass on the lid of the piano. Perceiving my incomprehension, the woman advanced into the room, her words coming faster and louder. Something about a lesson, I grasped, a lesson now, in this room. I must get out. As I backed away I realised there was someone behind her in the corridor, a tall lad of about seventeen, looking at the floor.

'*Jestem Angielka* ... (I am English),' I stuttered. '*Mam* (I have) ... *mam* ... *mam* ...' I looked towards the piano again, gesturing hopelessly, desperate for my written authorisation, for something this person would understand - but the woman had not even paused for breath. I must get out at once. I had no right to be here. At last locating the pass at one end of the keyboard, I pointed to the limp piece of paper with its faded violet print, my pass with its hours and days, my right of possession. I picked it up, held it out, as I did so seeing it suddenly for what it was: a floppy, ineffectual scrap, bereft of power.

At this piece of impertinence the unknown teacher exploded in a stream of invective still more intense than before, plucking at the green and gold brooch at her throat as if she would choke on her own rage. She began driving me backwards before her, prodding at me with one finger, thrusting her face into mine:

'Something about times, something about the Music School, about the Director... that it wasn't my business to... what? ... that I ought to... missed that verb...' I didn't follow the rest.

'It is not necessary... *Pani* is not nice...not polite...' Nothing strong enough, nothing to save my shattered dignity would come to me. Weakly, I picked up my books, my metronome, the key:

'Leave that!' the woman snapped. The first complete sentence of the exchange that I had understood perfectly, but with which I was somehow unable to comply. No hand of mine could relinquish that key.

'Klucz!' she screamed. *'Klucz!'*

She snatched it from my hand, the serrated edge scraped my thumb as it went from me. I looked at the youth who had now followed her a little way into the room. He was looking at me too. If he had appeared even sheepish I could have borne it. Any sympathy, the least hint of fellow feeling might have redeemed something, yet there was none, and at that moment my humiliation was complete. I found it hard to believe she could be much fun as a teacher, but he watched the rout of the stupid foreign woman and betrayed nothing at all, as if this were yet another lesson in how things should be done that he absorbed without question. From somewhere in the battered heart of myself I found it - perhaps my child did it for me, for it was certainly a childish inspiration - the one thing I *could* say which we would *all* understand. I turned to my accuser:

'*Baba Yaga,*' I said - and fled.

Out in the street, they pounded through my head, the rational-sounding grammatical phrases, all the things I should have said. Too late. They wouldn't have made any difference, but I seemed unable to stop my brain generating them anyway, crowding in on one another, elbowing for space. I was racing along the pavement, oblivious to my surroundings. My belly felt taut and uncomfortable, I realised with a twinge of panic, and forced myself to slow down. That was what was so unbearable about the place, I thought: most of the time people like that woman would have been terrorising you about having the right bits of paper, demanding you produce them, threatening to disbelieve them and so forth. Yet when it came to it, the exercise of arbitrary power could come in over the top and bureaucratic rectitude counted for nothing at all. That was what Poles lived with every day of their lives, that knowledge.

Yet still I accused myself: how could I have given it up, my room? Why had I not died in its defence? The sense of loss washed through me. I would go back to the Director of the Music School. I would take a friend as translator and make sure I got an explanation, even an apology. Perhaps I would get both, but I knew that nothing would give me back that room as it had been, my place of safety, inviolate.

The pigeons bunched together around a sudden spurt of steam from the manhole cover on the corner, their grey bodies jostling unproductively like my thoughts. A woman in a green overall started to shovel one of the heaps of coal through an open trapdoor into the cellar with a wooden shovel.

New Era ....

By now the queue stretched almost to the buildings opposite. A young woman in a bright turquoise ski jacket and a pink beret was waiting outside the door of the Student's Hostel watching the unmoving line. She was thinking how your expectations are shaped by what you're used to, how by now there should have been snowdrops and primroses and crocuses easing you into Spring, helping you to pace yourself. Her friend Aneta had assured her that here 'nothing really happens until May, then everything happens at once.' Harriet was beginning to think she couldn't wait. The trees on the allotments did not even have buds yet and the grass was brown and winter-dead.

'Drew! Where have you been?'

'Trying to help Patrice explain to that old hag, the Portierka, that his friend won't murder anyone, even though he *is* black too, if he's allowed to come upstairs to our room for a glass of tea.'

'Did she let him?'

'No way. He just went up anyway in the end, with her threatening to call the police, and Patrice laughing fit to burst and her crossing herself. Then she gave me hell over my Legitimacja, claiming I haven't kept it in a good enough condition and she can't read it, before she let me go.'

'Did she call the police?'

'I don't think so. She forgot about it - or she was satisfied once she'd given me a hard time.'

'She's not the one who told him Africans can't count up to more than five?'

'No, that's the 'nice' one. She *was* offering to help him arrange his train ticket to Warsaw, after all.' Patrice, son of the exiled Zairean foreign minister and studying for a PhD in Economics, had erupted in uncontrollable giggling:

'No wonder the economy of my country is in such a mess. This explain everything!' He slapped first one thigh then the other.

'Patrice is a saint,' said Harriet grimly.

'No, just racially superior,' said Drew. 'I'd have wanted to kneecap her for that.' He tried to pull up the collar of his trench-coat, but realised it was already up.

'A bit parky, I'd say,' said Harriet. 'Isn't that Pawel in the queue, next to the lady in the angora hat? At least I think that fluffy stuff's angora.'

'Don't look at me. I've no idea.'

'About angora or Pawel?'

'It *is* him. We could ask him about fixing up the Polish lessons.'

They went forward. Pawel was just in the process of joining the queue, poking an umbrella into his leather satchel and fiddling with the buckle. He exchanged a few words with the lady in front of him, whom it transpired had a leopard-skin collar to her coat as well as an angora hat.

'Hi, Pawel,' Harriet accosted him. 'Going to the Instytut?'

'I'm not. I'm going to join this queue, I must admit.'

'Hello, Miss Harriet.' A face peeping round the leopard-skin shoulder ahead of them turned out to be that of one of Harriet's private students. Stasiek was sandy-haired with very light eyelashes. As he was extremely shy, he often preferred to communicate through jokes. He tried one now:

'What has two hundred legs, moves at one centimetre per hour and eats cabbage?'

'Don't know,' Harriet told him.

'Polish meat queue,' Stasiek guffawed, the soft baby-hair of his fringe quivering. He worked as a manager at the shoe factory. In fact it was he who had explained to Harriet the system for obtaining new shoes.

'You stand in the line of shoe department in Centrum departmental store. You will see there are some few shoes, not many, on those shelves behind counter. Don't to try buying shoes you like or shoes on your size, only the ones you think will be most popular - you know what I mean? Point to pair of shoes and ask to the assistant for them. She might somewhat to argue with you, but use own judgement of yours, unless you are thinking she really likes you. In this situation her advice may to be worth something. Often, though, the assistant give simply to each person pair of shoes without any single choice about it. Take shoes out-side and look a little around you. You will soon see all people trading shoes they have bought and you can to find the pair that you will like and will not to injure your feet.'

Stasiek's English was often inspired on such topics, Harriet noted, whereas he was frequently unable to string together a single sentence on the subjects suggested by the textbook. Perhaps this was because Polish practices were simply an extension of an absurdist sense of humour and liberated his self-expression like the other jokes. Stasiek had a cousin in

New York, and, if conditions for importing ever improved, hoped to make use of this connection to reinvent himself as a businessman.

The woman in the angora hat had turned to face Pawel with an expectant expression. She had a benign, slightly bronzed face, with comfortable lines, and her hair was tinted the same rich brown as the spots on her collar. Pawel hastily introduced her as his Aunt Bozena, who could speak English. Bozena nodded energetically, but Harriet wanted to get to the point with Pawel about restarting the Polish lessons and so introduced Stasiek, who began telling Bozena a complicated joke about Lenin in Polish.

Only the usual and vaguest of commitments had been extracted from Pawel when Aunt Bozena made the announcement in English, beaming:

'Lenin was Jew.'

Harriet at first thought she was translating Stasiek's joke for them, but Aunt Bozena repeated her assertion as though setting up a topic for conversation. 'Lenin was Jew.'

'Ach, you Poles always say everyone you don't like is Jewish,' said Drew tetchily.

'Well, Marx was Jew.'

'I know, Auntie, but Lenin was Marx's son only in the loosest sense, a metaphorical one, you know.'

'And Satanist.'

'Who? Lenin?' Drew queried.

'No, Marx. My daughter lent to me book published by underground, by Russian philosophe. His name Marczenko, and he showed that Marx was Satanist, that he wrote poems to Satan, in London.'

'In the British Library?' put in Harriet.

'Yes, in this library. There was photograph, and the number to show place where he sat, to write this poems. You could see desk where he was sitting and writing to Satan, to praise him.'

Pawel and Drew between them managed the objection that Marx was an Atheist, but Aunt Bozena was not deterred.

'I know Marx was atheist; I think maybe he is Satanist too. When he was old, Marczenko say, he dressed in robes, you know, on his head like Jew. He was very big Jew.'

'And Satanist,' Drew smirked.

'Satanist too, yes.'

'And what about this philosopher?' Harriet tried.

'Marczenko? I don't know. I don't know if he is very strong philosophe. I hear he is very strong nationalist, Russian nationalist.'

'Perhaps he didn't like Jews either.'

'But one time when I am in Sweitzland with my husband for conference of chemical biologs we are meeting with Sweitzish philosophe - he is writing very much about Marx -and I ask him what about Marczenko.

He say he is serious philosophe. He don't very like him. For him he is too much Russian, Russian, all the time Russian. I ask him about opinion of Marczenko.'

'That Marx was a Satanist?'

'Yes, and he say he don't know. He say it is very interesting. He don't have any opinion to this subject.'

'It would be necessary to see the poems in their context...' Pawel ventured.

'The poems were printed. Word Satan is very often in them, in this poems. I don't know. I think maybe he is Satanist. Maybe is true, maybe not.'

The queue ahead of them appeared temporarily silenced, as though pondering.

It was Drew who provoked it:

'And Lenin?'

'Lenin was Jew,' persisted Aunt Bozena stoutly.

'Not a Satanist?'

'Maybe too.'

'Trotsky was Jewish,' someone conceded, 'Leon Bronstein or whatever - but Vladimir Ilych...what is it ...Ulyanov?'

'Ulyanov, yes.'

'It sounds pretty Russian, doesn't it?'

'But my Babcia saw him - I didn't tell to you - she saw Lenin, yes. Babcia family live near Wilno. Cousin my Babcia get married with very big Commissar, Lenin friend. She invite my Babcia to wedding, to Moscow. She have some pictures, religious pictures, you know. She want give to my Babcia. She cannot keep them more when she marry big Commissar. My Babcia very religious woman. She don't want go to Moscow, but she want take this pictures, to help cousin, you know. So Babcia go to Moscow, and at wedding party she sitting this close to Lenin, like you standing close to me now. He very big friend this Commissar marry her cousin. She *saw* him.'

'Yes?'

'Yes, and he is Jew. Lenin is Jew.'

'How does she know?'

'I told you, she *saw* him.'

The bus waiting at the turning circle on the other side of the road was revving for longer than usual, apparently without effect. It did not pull away as expected and a quantity of dark smoke burgeoned below one of the wheel arches. The driver got down to inspect it, soon joined by two of the passengers, who looked doubtful. A relief bus would have to be summoned. In the meantime it seemed that those in the bus were unsure whether to get off or not. Several finally made their way over to the queue and joined it. They had been in two minds before anyway and this had decided things. A few others stood around the door of the bus to smoke, but most remained sitting, looking out of the windows.

Pomnik

In the Sekretariat of the Instytut, Pani Marysia and Pani Malgosia were trying on hats. It was almost two-thirty and time to be getting ready to go home. Pani Malgosia pushed her feet into her padded boots and stood in front of the long mirror beside the door. She pulled her sweater over her broad hips and tilted the turquoise mohair beret on her tight, plum-coloured curls, straightening her back and twisting from side to side to get a better view.

'I don't know, girls,' she said, turning away from the mirror and pointing one booted toe behind to look back at her reflection over her shoulder.

'What about the scarf?' Pani Marysia suggested, unlooping it from the coat-rack. Pani Malgosia draped the floral scarf over her shoulders, holding it by its two pointed ends, and surveyed the effect on the whole of this addition of black, pink and green. She tutted. No, it didn't really go with the scarf.

Pani Marysia shook her head in careful concurrence.

'With a different lipstick perhaps…'

Pani Malgosia dived for her bag and rummaged, producing a stick of frosted pink between a triumphant thumb and forefinger. Pani Marysia sucked in her own crimson lips, the action helping her to imagine the possible results of an alteration of colour or density on the mouth of Pani Malgosia. Dorota, the third and youngest secretary, arched her eyebrows ready to proffer her own opinion:

'No, no, Pani Malgosia, the rust-red is more stylish, it goes with your hair.'

'What about the hat, then? Maybe that was better after all,' though she was loath to take off the other one still, and continued to take peeks in the mirror.

'The red hat I like,' murmured Pani Malgosia, 'but this one, I don't think it works. I paid dollars for the wool, too, and Pani Karolinka had it ready in under a week. She's always so good.'

'How many?' Pani Marysia inquired.

'Dollars?' asked Pani Malgosia - she couldn't resist repeating and thereby stressing the currency. 'Oh, two and a half.'

Dorota whistled. It was just the right sum to excite admiration, but still a very satisfactory bargain - and the wool had been beautiful. The hat was too, but what was the use if it didn't work...?

'What do you think, Pani Helenka?' she entreated. I was perched on a table next to the kettle and the tray of plates and tea glasses, the crumbs from all the cakes they had been given and shared out that day, swinging my legs.

'I think the turquoise one is lovely,' I said, 'even better than the red one, much more dramatic.'

'Dramatyczna? Dramatyczna...' Pani Malgosia turned it over, unsure whether it was entirely complimentary, deciding it was - though she felt prompted to embark on a re-evaluation of her red hat, which, in fairness to Pani Marysia - who was due her turn at the mirror and was even now gently easing over her ears a green angora dome - she could not do.

'Good afternoon, dear ladies,' carolled the man in the black suit, dusting chalk from his pocket-flaps, as he entered by the main door. He was balding and his face was so deathly white it made the white ring of his remaining hair seem a speckled, dirty grey.

'Oh, Professor Deregowski.' Pani Malgosia and Pani Marysia turned round to greet him, exclaiming over his arrival with such exaggerated simpers that I wondered whether they were making fun of him. He was slightly stooped, his head receding into his neck, and his neck into his shoulders like that of a tortoise, which gave the impression that movement must be painful. Even so, he went round to each of us in turn, standing to attention and kissing our hands.

'In honour of this most special of special days,' he announced, waving his hand at the demolished cakes, 'I hope you ladies will be so kind as to permit me', he took his glasses from his inside pocket and began wiping them on a cloth, 'to read you a short poem composed...', he drew out a folded sheet from his jacket with the mauve fingertips of his dead-white hand, 'in celebration of *women.*'

We murmured our appreciation as he cleared his throat.

'As you know,' he began, 'I am not a poet - indeed, for many years of my life I would not even have dreamed of holding the fortunate position I do today, blessed with the task of educating our youth and transmitting to them the glories of literature, albeit in another language. No, I started out, as you may be aware, as no more than a humble toymaker...'

Ah, so *this* was he. I had never actually seen him before, despite having taught now for some months at the Instytut, and I gathered he had been ill. I knew him only from the folklore of my students, for whom 'no more than a humble toymaker' was a catchphrase guaranteed to send them into fits of giggles.

'Now, in our country, where we have been so fortunate, so blessed…'
He paused a second as though he had lost his thread, or as though temporarily overwhelmed by the beneficence of his homeland's recent fate. 'Where women helped to rebuild our stricken cities, drive tractors on our farms, bring in the harvest to feed our hungry, plan towns and construct bridges, hold the highest positions - I may mention in this connection our own dear Professor Bulska, guiding and protecting our department like a true mother, and our Professors Jablonska-Tomaszczyk and Kujawinska-Ballaban, who adorn each faculty meeting with their views so sensible and so prettily expressed …'

The poem itself, in very similar vein, was not short, and it was hard to tell how far he had proceeded when the side door from Professor Bulska's office opened. She kept her hand on the door handle but did not enter, deep in conversation with her deputy, Professor Goljanek (known to we 'native speakers' in the Instytut as 'Gucci' Goljanek for his love of Western sartorial styles), who was stroking his goatee in time with her words. At the same moment, the main door opened, nudging Professor Deregowski, Pani Marysia and Pani Malgosia back into the room as Mirek came in. He paused in the doorway, raising one leg and balancing his weathered satchel on his knee as he stowed a sheaf of papers in it, swivelling his head to speak over his shoulder to the figure behind him. The stranger in the hallway wore a grey overcoat and a fedora hat, his burgundy scarf flung across his chin and over his shoulder Toulouse-Lautrec-poster fashion.

I was always glad to see Mirek, one of the few of my colleagues with whom I felt on good terms and at ease. I knew that Mirek had been active in Solidarity in '81 and was in all probability still involved in the Underground. He often seemed to be sounding me out, to be on the verge of telling me something important that never quite materialised. Maybe I imagined it - it was so difficult to read signals across cultures, like the time when he told me he felt odd having political discussions with a woman, never having done so before, and I thought he was joking. Still, despite our momentary confusions, I liked him, a gentle, ironic person, with two little daughters I had practised my very first Polish on.

The man in the hallway also paused on the threshold, but in his case the purpose of the gesture - standing just a few seconds too long in the doorway, shrouded in his overcoat and his own charisma like Valentino in his cloak - seemed to be to allow the focus of those present to realign itself on him. At once I determined *not* to give him my attention - though he did look vaguely familiar. Vanity is so off-putting, I thought, and besides, when confronted with people who *expect* to be looked at, I've found I can't add my gaze and meet that expectation. Perhaps out of sheer contrariness, or, by withholding admission of their power keeping some for myself. For they invariably notice the one person who *isn't* looking at them. Yet aside from the embarrassment at the prospect of being so predictable myself, I felt a kind of embarrassment also on his behalf.

He had taken off his hat and held it in his hand. He must have been going on fifty, his face craggy and handsome, not East European looking, though perhaps in honour of this visit he had a 'dissident haircut', short on top and longish about the ears, and his overcoat was a designer version of the Russian army greatcoat.

Mirek was introducing him, the 'well-known poet from England', to Deregowski, who bowed low over his hand while he emitted a string of effusions about poetry in general, his own poor efforts in that line, and how he had this very minute been sharing a few paltry verses with these delightful ladies.

Professors Bulska and Goljanek had joined them, and Mirek retrieved the well-known poet's hand in order to place it in theirs. A few polite words were exchanged. The days had long gone when they could get really excited about any 'poet from England', however illustrious. The cultural gravy trains of Western Europe brought someone or other almost every week to read his work, meet other poets, playwrights etc, and take a peep at their benighted country. Goljanek and Bulska saved their social graces for really useful contacts from the States, who were much rarer, and left the others to junior members of the department. Poor Pawel Czernik, the most junior of all, had been obliged to take trips with such visitors to Krakow and then to Auschwitz three times last month. 'They always say they want to see it, once in their life,' he moaned. 'I wish *I* had only seen it once. Every time I feel the railway train getting nearer I want to run away.'

I saw the visitor look over their heads to run a practised eye over the other women in the room, saw the swift processing of the lifelong appraiser of women discount the two older ones, register Dorota as a possibility, but too dolled-up for his taste. I kept my face turned away, busily hunting for something in my bag. I could afford to be unconcerned about his evaluation and in any case knew what it would be - for was I not young and pregnant and radiantly beautiful?

A few more pleasantries were exchanged. Goljanek in a silky-looking black polo neck under a lime-green, faintly shimmery jacket, still stroked his beard occasionally. He wore his usual slimy half-smile and he spoke in a way that made every utterance sound like an insinuation. He always seemed to approach me when I was cornered - say between a table and the office pigeonholes, too close, speaking in his too-soft voice so I had to lean forward to hear him.

In our naivety, the other native speakers and I had always assumed that 'old Gucci,' with his love of Western clothing, his interest in Walker Percy and relatively frequent trips to the States, was the least likely party-man imaginable. Though unpleasant, he was a world away from some of the obvious old apparatcheks on the staff. Nonetheless, one day he had decidedly unsettled me one day by repeating to me in conversation a rather indiscreet remark I had made in one of my Conversation classes, about which he had no right to have known. It had always seemed to me that the oft-repeated assertion that there was 'an informer in every class', whether or not it was true, did its work as long as everyone believed it. So I had always tried to battle against the temptation to self-censorship and to say exactly what I thought on every occasion. Perhaps I overdid it.

It must be odd for Professor Bulska, with her history of Solidarity affiliation, working with him, I thought, looking across at her. She was smiling her usual careful smile, blinking behind her glasses and pushing her lank hair behind her ears. Her face seemed more raddled than it should for her age and her small round chin quivered when she spoke. It was a kind face, though it withheld such a lot. She was reputed to be an excellent teacher and I knew the students liked and respected her. Her support in '81, when students at the Instytut had been the first in the country to go on strike, still earned her affection among the present generation, and she taught American literature, which gave her added cachet in their eyes.

This made it all the harder that I barely knew her, and sensed on her part a definite intention that this distance should remain. Probably she was simply a rather formal person, and I was a mere 'native speaker'. I surmised that she thought that an unmarried pregnant woman on the staff set a bad example to the students, several of whom were currently in the same condition. That very week I had heard that one of my third year students was as far advanced as I was, though in her case, completely invisibly so.

In retrospect I recalled that Monika had developed a strange habit of hanging her head when spoken to. The usual procedure in such cases was a speedy wedding and for the couple to move in with the bride's parents. At a wedding I had recently attended, not only was the bride heavily pregnant, but so were all three bridesmaids, of which I was one. On reflection, Monika did not seem to have a ring. Did Bulska think I had started a trend? I resolved to speak to Monika. Had she been too ashamed to talk even to *me,* pulling out of next year's exchange scheme to London with some feeble explanation? I should have been more observant, should have guessed.

Mirek was doing the rounds: Pani Malgosia, Marysia, Dorota - Terry Matheson. I stood up and smiled, ready for my introduction. Terry's eyes lit up as I knew they would. At that moment Drew and Harriet showed up, and the three of us chatted away with the visitor with that freedom you automatically assume with one of your countrymen after living abroad for a while. Terry was in any case very easy company, and though he clearly liked to hold court he could also draw people out and enjoy them. This was always with the half-smile of appraisal and appreciation, but the latter made the former quite tolerable, and there is seldom anything too annoying about such flattering attention. For once, even Rob wouldn't have been able to tease me for not noticing when I was being flirted with. There've been times, chatting away to someone in the moments before he pounces, either verbally or otherwise, in a way he clearly feels authorised by me to do, when all that's gone through my head is: 'Isn't this an enjoyable conversation? What a nice, friendly man!'

Terry, on the other hand, was such an obviously predatory person that I felt paradoxically safe and relaxed in his company - though being four months pregnant may help in these situations. Perhaps, just as some claim there are drunks and drinking men, one should distinguish between womanisers and ladies' men, I reflected generously.

Mirek looked at us gratefully and took the opportunity to go and check the facilities in the seminar room where the guest would be speaking, while we caught up on the latest from Britain and answered Terry's questions about life in Poland and the different happenstances by which we had each wound up here.

The small seminar room was packed when we arrived. Terry had brought with him a video of himself reading his latest extended work. Was he planning to show this instead of or as well as reading a selection of poems himself, Mirek wanted to know? Terry wrinkled his nose. He'd been planning to deposit it in the office as a parting gift.

'Give them the choice. Nothing like a bit of democracy,' he said sourly.

Mirek explained to the students that Terry would leave the video anyway, so they could have the real live poet now and the video some other time - two for the price of one. The students rejected cake tomorrow and voted for the video. A video of any description was too glamorous an object to resist, but the decision did seem a little insulting. Mirek gulped apologetically. I couldn't tell if he was really sorry, as this was one of his regular mannerisms. Terry had just been informing Harriet and myself of a recent review in which he'd been hailed as the only contemporary poet in the true Miltonic tradition. Whatever the original insecurities which may have required Terry Matheson's ego to grow to its current impressive size, it was apparent that in its fully fledged form it was definitely of the robust rather than the sensitive variety.

Though evidently miffed, then, the poet took it all in good part and sat in a chair to one side of the T.V. set, such that his real face was next to the one on the screen. His screen face was earnest and declamatory, his real one amused. He was reading a long, controversial state-of-the-nation poem, standing up in a pub with a pint in his hand. I felt immedi-

86

ately homesick for that pub, for those people sitting around the copper-topped tables on that swirly-patterned carpet. Terry Matheson looked as if he quite fancied being there right now too.

It wasn't simply that this was poetry and the words declaimed were in my language, their play and every nuance I could follow. I had often loved the earnest depressiveness and surreal gaiety of the Poles, but suddenly I longed for that ironic, self-deprecating but absolutely straight *unseriousness* I ascribed to my countrymen. I recalled seeing a tiny clip on Polish T.V. - I think it was of some British football hooligans being deported from West Germany. The cameraman trying to film them as they went into court was advised by one to 'do yourself a favour, mate, and fuck off.' It was that 'do yourself a favour' which so completely charmed me, struck me as a model of native wit and directness, even good nature. I must have a serious case of 'tesknota' as the Poles call this nostalgia for home if some 'Orrible Skin'ead - probably even an NF one, for all I knew - could produce this effect. God knows, if we even prefer our own Nazis to everyone else's, there really *isn't* much hope for us.

Back in the Sekretariat afterwards, I saw Terry talking to Mirek, looking across to me, apparently insisting on something. I knew Mirek had planned to take his guest to a production of a famous Polish play at the theatre in Jaracza Street, before going on to meet a local dissident poet. Terry had already asked whether I'd be willing to join them, though for some reason I had the impression Mirek might not be too pleased about that. Terry put his thickly overcoated arm around me:

'You're coming with us,' he said. 'Get your coat on.' It was so much like 'Get your coat, you've pulled' I almost laughed out loud.

'I can't stay long,' I said, 'I have to eat.'

'Don't worry, I'll see you right.'

The action of the play was set in the uprising of the 1830s. There were lots of young men in blue jackets and red and white stripy trousers. Parts of it were comic and there was plenty of gleeful exclamation and leaping about. For the visiting poet, though, this meant two and a half hours of largely incomprehensible visual activity. I felt faintly annoyed on his behalf: why should a language-merchant like himself have this inflicted on him, just because it happened to be a classic of Polish culture? Mirek was far too gripped himself to explain very much. I could just about follow some parts and tried to help Terry out, but he was undoubtedly restless. He put his arm round me:

'Are you comfy? These seats are a bit hard on the bum.'

Personally, I was quite enjoying the liveliness of the scene, the meaningful, barely understood utterances flying back and forth between the actors, and the sensation of sitting in the warm with someone who appeared to care about my welfare. It didn't matter to me if he was a big-shot, or a poet, or whether he took me seriously. Nor that he was a predator, or a well-off London-based writer still banging on about his Northern working-class roots. It was easy to sneer, as Drew had done, at how removed was this man's current life from the clogs and flat caps he still wanted to lay claim to, but I didn't think he was a sham. There was something authentic in his concern, in its straightforwardness, that reminded me of my Uncle Don, who was a train driver, and my Uncle Vic who drove a bread van. Sure, Terry fancied himself something rotten. But so what? I didn't care because he was kind to me, because he extended to me that unmediated, avuncular, ordinary man's concern.

Where was he, the baby's father, he'd wanted to know as we'd waited for the tram to the theatre? Well, it didn't seem right to him. He should be here with you at a time like this. I'd said airy things about a thesis to finish and being able to take care of myself, but I was glad someone had the shotgun out for Rob, old nowhere-to-be-seen Babyfather, because in my heart so did I. Where *was* the thoughtless bugger? He should be here. Dead right, our Terry lad. Don't give me your fancy modern ways of living, my lass, his demeanour said. Suddenly I had seen my situation for what it was, a piece of massively indulgent, middle-class insouciance on my part, and of reckless negligence on Rob's, leaving me to plough my own furrow in an Eastern Europe of questionable stability and erratic food provision. It felt cosy as well as bleak to see it like that, at least while enveloped in the glow of this temporary protection.

'Well I don't know what that young man is thinking of,' Terry resumed, as we took our coats and went outside after the play had finished, 'leaving you to struggle on over here by yourself. Are you managing to eat properly, get all the right vitamins and so on?'

I assured him that I was, with all the loving and unwanted detail of the true obsessive. He was amused. 'You make sure you do. When did you last eat?'

'Properly? At about 12.35'

'Sure it wasn't 12.37?'

'But I had a fair bit of cake, you know, because of Women's Day.'

'Quite right. All women should celebrate their femininity and their great occasions with cake! You need something more nutritious.'

Mirek came out of the theatre cloakroom. We started to walk down the road.

'I'll gladly go to the poet's house,' Terry announced, 'but this lady has to eat. Is there somewhere on the way? What about that place?'

'It's a workers bar,' Mirek was apologetic. 'We really should hurry to Zbyszek's.'

Terry raised an eyebrow. Mirek began to excuse himself: 'You think I am snob, right? But you have to understand that in West you don't have workers such as ours are, drunk and ignorant, you...'

I had heard this claim so many times before that I couldn't resist, though I knew my intervention would do nothing for my relations with Mirek:

'You have to understand, Terry,' I said teasingly, 'that in Britain we have a better *class* of worker...' Mirek glowered.

'The lady has to eat,' the poet insisted. Mirek glared at me and fidgeted.

'I think probably Alishka - I mean Alicja, Zbyszek's wife, can give her something. I'll ask her. Their flat it's just beyond the corner.'

'Good. We won't embarrass her by turning up with such an ultimatum all together. You go round and check it's O.K. and we'll wait here.'

'Slut!' said Mirek's eyes to me, seeming to view the whole episode as a shameless piece of flirtation on my part. He was happy to defer in general to the famous poet, but he was not pleased at being sent off like a messenger boy to carry out the chivalric whims occasioned by some no-count woman. How dared I monopolise this man, who was here to serve an important cultural and political role, which I couldn't be expected to understand? Bolstered by Terry's attention, I felt defiant, but nonetheless uncomfortable.

'I only need a sandwich or something. I don't want to make this woman ...'

I couldn't help remembering my first visit to Mirek's flat, sitting across the desk from him in his 'office', clearly also the bedroom. His wife had arrived home a little after us and had not come through, although she'd sent their six year-old daughter with two glasses of tea. I could hear her banging plates about in the kitchen, and felt awkward that Mirek plainly felt no need that we should be introduced. It was rather as if I were a mistress she knew about but had to tolerate, or at the very least the representative of a cosmopolitan, intellectual life which he was parading but from which she was excluded. I had been in the country only a week. I had no idea whether this was normal.

So we had sat there, chatting pleasantly about politics in Poland and in Britain and various literary topics while the two children trolled in and out. The youngest, Agatka, had actually managed to engage me in conversation about her doll, helped by the fact that she was only three, and therefore my linguistic inferiority was not as vast as it would otherwise have been. To judge from the sound effects, the invisible wife fed them and bathed them and put them to bed, while I soaked up the waves of her imagined resentment, feeling more and more uncomfortable, and Mirek pooh-poohed my suggestions that I ought to be going home.

It was when she called Mirek's name and he disappeared, returning with two bowls of cucumber soup, that I resolved to end my collusion with this denigration, which by now in my mind had assumed the proportions of almost ritual humiliation. Finishing the soup, I insisted I had to leave and headed for the kitchen, shaking the hand of Mirek's wife in a ridiculous, formal way, attempting a 'proper' introduction - whatever that might be - seeking to thank her for the soup, to compliment her on her lovely children, to say I hoped to meet her again - to none of which my Polish was remotely equal. She remained by the stove, and did not look me in the eye. Sullenly? Shyly? I bobbed and smiled.

'How did you meet?'

'As students,' Mirek had said shortly on the way back to the tram-stop.

'Did your wife, I mean Danuta - it is Danuta, isn't it? - study English Philology as well?'

'No, Engineering.' Was this brevity meant to indicate incompatibility and subsequent marital distress or simple lack of interest, a taking for granted? Perhaps they just didn't get on that well. Did Mirek have affairs? Or was that how a wife was treated, an invisible provider, her abilities and aspirations a topic unworthy of conversation? Yet I'd been surprised already at how many women seemed, as a matter of course, to have what would in Britain have been considered high-powered jobs.

'Hang on a minute, I've just remembered. Pani Malgosia told me your wife designed bridges! Is that right?'

'She just now returned to her job,' Mirek said shortly, 'now that Agatka is three and can go to the Pre-School.' With some coaxing, he explained that a mother's job was kept for her for three years, the first eighteen months on full pay, with half-pay thereafter. I knew Mirek wouldn't want to hear that three years' maternity leave was not to be sneezed at. The Communist system could not possibly have anything to recommend it. Moved by sisterly resentment, I was unable to resist this opportunity to annoy him, so I told him anyway.

A few minutes only and Mirek was back, ushering us down a nearby sidestreet to a flaking grey door in the old artisan's quarter. Alicja, in tight leggings and a man's baggy blue shirt came downstairs at once to hug me and take my arm, filling my ears with promises of omelettes and salad - salad! I could call her Alushka or Alunia. Of course it wasn't any trouble - was she not a woman and a mother?! She wore a blue and yellow bandanna around curly hair dyed butter-blonde, heavy, actressy make-up and very small slippers. She looked like a cross between a retired Russian ballerina and a paradoxically maternal Tiny Tears, with her full cheeks and button blue eyes. We shouldn't have sent Mirek to ask if it was O.K. Of course it was. When was my baby due? She was the first person in so long to treat my pregnancy as a joyful event, not a burden and a trouble and cause for anxiety. I almost cried, shocked to be reminded of that perspective, and to recall that it had once been my own.

This was the first 'unconventional' interior I had entered in Poland. For a start, it had no dresser, no glass display cabinets. There were bare floorboards, painted the same forget-me-not blue as Alicja's bandanna, and no rugs on the floor. A kind of mattress wrapped in a bedspread and strewn with multicoloured cushions stood in for the usual foldaway sofa-bed. Above all, the place was messy, Alicja's prints drying on the table, clothes dangling damply from the ceiling over our heads, canvas and frames stacked against the walls and knee-high pillars of books and papers on the floor. Zbyszek was a tall, rangy man with an untidy beard and a bushy ponytail, his faded jeans tight like hose on his skinny legs, making his feet look even bigger in their leather slippers. We sat on stools and cushions around a low table while he read one of his poems, a political soliloquy written in the persona of his typewriter.

From a dark corner where she had been secreted on a heap of cushions, colouring, a little girl of around six crept over to join us. This was their daughter, Pola. Zbyszek introduced her, as she stood unsteadily against the table on one spindly leg like a stork against a chimney-stack, scratching the saggy bit of her tights behind one knee with a tiny slippered foot. Her tow-coloured top-knot quivered, either with embarrassment or her insistence on brazening it out, forcing herself not to retreat. She wore a bright red and black neck-kerchief, and a skimpy denim skirt. I realised as I looked at her how seldom back home in 'the West', I any longer saw little girls in last year's too-short skirt, or children in hand-me-downs that didn't quite fit. Yet when I was a child, barely more than a decade ago, after all, it had been common to try to get one more season's wear out of a garment you'd really outgrown.

I asked about her name: it wasn't one I'd come across before. Didn't it mean 'field'? What was it short for? For Apollonia, Alicja explained. They'd always liked the name, long before their daughter was born - though it was very old-fashioned and unpopular:

'We thought this would be a little wild to name a child this way,' she said. 'Our parents would be very angry. We were young then and not very daring. So we named our cat by this name, for practice. It is very good, truly, to name pet for practice for your child name later on. You can see how you like the sound to call it every day.' We all laughed with her at this idea. 'And Zbyszek is poet,' she went on, 'Apollo, you know, so it seemed very suitably for us. We think maybe for a boy, Apolloniusz, but we always think in our heart we will have girl - and, after all, each one of my husband's Muses - you say Muses, yes? - is always female.' She laughed again. 'Unfortunately this cat died - it was destroyed in an accident with tram…'

'This seemed like not very good sign,' Zbyszek put in, 'and we were a little bit afraid.'

'But when our Pola is born her face it is very wrinkled and her hair it is sandy and it seem she have same face, lines on her face they are very reminding our cat - and when I think that I can tell priest at baptism that I give my daughter this name because I believe she is reincarnated my unfortunately slaughtered cat, how he will be shock, I cannot resist!'

This led on to inquiries about Terry's family, the information that his eldest daughter was about to marry the son of a bishop occasioning some confusion and much hilarity until it became clear that Anglican clergy were not required to be celibate. I caught another glare from Mirek - what did he hold me responsible for *now*? I guessed that in his eyes I had lowered the tone, somehow feminised the whole occasion, domesticated *his* poet. Zbyszek, though, looked quite happy to be 'feminised', skipping off to the kitchen intermittently to help Alicja with whatever she was rustling up out there, though she wouldn't hear of *me* moving a muscle.

So I stayed while Mirek steered the conversation rather doggedly back onto more suitable topics: the modern art exhibition, the Ernsts seen in the Museum that afternoon. I was feeling the strain of having to be up to the occasion, without having the sense that either Mirek or the famous West-European poet were quite getting everything they wanted from it. As for me, I wanted my omelette.

Was that it for me from now on? No desires beyond the need to satisfy my child? Mirek had turned to asking earnest questions about methods of composition, getting Terry to hold forth, slightly wearily I thought. However, as the subject became himself more than or indistinguishably from his poetry, he warmed to his theme. As he spoke about some scene or event he had turned into a poem, it was almost alarming to witness life refracted through the lens of someone's ego in this way. To hear him was to see it actually in the process of being refracted, almost to see it bend. Was creativity, was art really only possible in this way? Why couldn't I countenance that? Were we women trained out of such depths of solipsism, taught from an early age to be horrified at this in ourselves? What if I ever - sorry what if *I* ever - wanted to create anything? I wasn't at all sure my ego was big enough, or only intermittently.

I'd forgotten Zbyszek, of course, who was another kettle of fish altogether. He put my omelette on the table in front of me, moist and chick-yellow (slightly tasteless thought) lounging on a bed of the greenest, scrunchiest-looking lettuce I'd seen in a long time.

That was the temptation for women, I saw suddenly, to be the *subject* of art. The sense that I had with Terry that I *was* my predicament, a case of beautiful, abandoned fecundity in the snowy, industrial wastes ... After all, it was very pleasant to see oneself like this, at least part of the time, the only recourse what must seem the tedious, incomprehensible whine 'but you don't take me *seriously*......' Of course I do, the poet would object, mystified. I represent you far better than you could ever represent yourself. There you are, objectified, immortalised, iconic. What more do you want? What do you mean it's not *you*? So what? It's art. It's better than you.

That very week a student in my literature class, a clever, outspoken young woman, who in another culture would almost certainly have been a feminist, had stated baldly:

'But without men there would be no culture. Women do not make culture.'

The class, of both sexes, had agreed with her. Yet surely there were lots of Polish women writers …

On Friday afternoons I gave a 'private lesson' in English Conversation to a group of lecturers and professors of various subjects. Despite being professors or heads of department of subjects like Economics and Chemistry, the women often prefaced their remarks with an apology, made claims to be heard on grounds of their intuition rather than their knowledge. When the men gave class papers in English on their hobbies, or whatever topic I'd set them, everyone listened respectfully, but whenever one of the women presented a talk, the men chatted throughout. I'd had to scold them, which they found very funny.

'Are you a feminist?' they joked. 'You can't be one. You are too nice and too pretty. We heard there are many feminists in Western countries. Tell us what is a feminist like?'

'It is reaction to Sovietical style of thinking,' my friend Roza explained after. '"Women to the Tractors", it was slogan after War. We in Poland are not liking this attitudes. We can to have all jobs, yes, but we wish to be like the rich womens from society of before the war, to be feminine, to look pretty, not so much to work.'

I had barely put down my fork when the little girl tugged at my elbow, pushing her drawing onto the table in front of me. I was glad of the excuse to speak Polish, especially kids' Polish.

'That's beautiful,' I said.

'It's for you,' she replied. 'Madam can keep it.'

'It's really lovely. Can you tell me what it is?' There were several detailed shapes, carefully coloured in green, pink and yellow crayon, arranged at different points on the paper.

Pola crooked her forefinger in the kerchief at her throat, twisting it from side to side as she made her answer. 'Those are flowerbeds,' she said a little scornfully.

'Oh of course, they're very pretty - very symmetrical - in patterns you know, like a park.'

'It *is* a park,' she announced.

'And what is this, in the middle?' I pointed to a tall structure.

'Pomnik,' she declared simply. I raked my synapses in a futile search for the word, so annoyingly familiar yet so elusive. 'Pomnik', she repeated, standing up suddenly very tall, her straggly top-knot quivering proudly. Of course - a statue.

'Madam knows, it's for Women's Day. That's why it's for you, a present.' Still standing like the little statue in her picture, hands by her sides, she began to recite the official Women's Day anthem she had learned in school. I could barely grasp one or two words per line but I fixed my eyes on the thin little lips earnestly forming the words and knew I could never listen attentively enough to repay her for the vision she made and the honour she was doing me, this small female person with the ramrod arms so valiantly parroting her sincerity. How right that we should sing of women, so great and so worthy of praise! May each one of us indeed live for a hundred years, as the anthem says, ornaments of our state and pride of every heart. I watched her performance, the mother of all those tear-blurred nativity plays and nursery concerts of the rest of my life. It was all absolutely true.

When she finished her parents smiled on her and we all clapped.

We had finally seen Terry off on the train to Vienna, where he was to join his wife, a famous soprano, who was performing there. Like all Polish long-distance trains, it had left at some ungodly hour.

'Time to reclaim my conjugal rights,' he'd said, with his best salacious pout.

Mirek and I were consuming tea and doughnuts in the station café. I still felt some hostility from Mirek, though his face wore the same sardonic expression it usually did. I felt the urge to excuse myself somehow, already obscurely ashamed of the whole episode, like the beginnings of a hangover. I resented this in turn: why shouldn't I be able to enjoy the afterglow of that comfortable and pleasurable sensation of being the object of somebody's interest? Something else suddenly occurred to me. To be up in time this morning, we had all stayed over at the Lumumby Student Hostel, where Harriet had her room and Terry was accommodated on the top floor in one of the more luxurious guest suites. Did Mirek think I had not in fact spent the night on Harriet's sofa?

I tried to pre-empt him, to throw him off by saying the very thing I suspected him of thinking:

'Guess you think I got in pretty quick there.'

I saw in his startled eyes that I had hit the spot, and he made no attempt to disclaim it, but then unfortunately I also caught a glimpse of myself through his eyes: a tarty little cow who had monopolised his poet by appealing to his baser instincts.

'You asked me last week about some activities of the Underground,' he said, and I thought he was changing the subject. 'Naturally I could have told you. You know of course why we don't trust foreigners, because it is well known that many of them work for the Polish police.' He looked hard at me.

'How convenient for the Polish police that you all believe that,' I said, as evenly as I could. He continued looking stonily at me, the floozy police informer. I wondered where my sense of humour had gone. I felt ashamed, then angry with him for making me feel it. Women: whores and betrayers all. 'Never mind,' I said bitterly, 'it's not Women's Day for another whole fucking year!'

Mirek pursed his mouth: 'No-one likes it when women swear,' he observed primly.

Marczak the Dwarf

Marczak the Dwarf travelled in his green cart along Wschodnia Street. His mother was on her bicycle just ahead. She really was quite old now, he thought, noticing her hesitate at the traffic lights before Revolution of 1905 Street. The olive, pink-sprigged headscarf swivelled round accusingly. Like a mind-reader she was, you could never dwell on her unobserved. Yet the wrinkles of her face, like those of the dusty brown stockings stuck out beneath her faded pinny, were many, definite and hopeless. Nestled in the scarf her face looked like that of a marmoset he had seen in a nature magazine - a very shrewd, bad-tempered marmoset. She kept her eye on him until he almost drew level and the lights changed.

The street was crowded with trams and even one or two small cars, but Marczak's little pony found its way. People looked out at them from the tram, dismally, pressed together, their arms jumbled up hanging onto the rails. It was hot without sunshine. Heat pressed down onto the dust that hung above the pavements, kneading it downwards through the electric wires slung across the street. The light shone on the great buildings that rose up from the dirty street, brightening them higher up, enlivening the grey facades, or picking out the biscuit-coloured stone. Down below it was hard to breathe. It was as if the year had missed out Spring and headed straight for Summer, neglecting to inform the sun of the change in schedule.

I first set eyes on Marczak then, in his blue cap. I came into the street just in time to see him turn the corner into Kilinskiego Street. All morning I'd felt like a prisoner in my high-rise tower, spellbound by the promise of a telephone call that didn't come. For no reason at all I decided to follow him, taking brisk strides. I felt liberated without my coat on this suddenly sweltering day, the first after the long months of Winter. It was such a relief to be uncovered at last, to let my round belly stick out before me proudly under the thin, green, floral material of the smock I'd recently bought. Now that I was clearly and visibly pregnant, there would be no more vodka-pickled men lurching into me, slurring their suggestions into my ear. People would offer me their seat on the tram - provided of course I didn't do anything unorthodox, like wear trousers. I would conform, if that's what it took, and I would reap the fruits: a person to be respected. I had even lost my fear of men bumping into me as they barged along. My belly was bigger than any of theirs now and a proposition in its own right.

For the first time, too, there were other pregnant tummies burgeoning on the street: the pregnant women, like a flock returned from migration, suddenly to be seen everywhere. The colours of their dresses in the long-drab streets lifted my spirits, though, unlike me, these women carried coats over their arms, just in case: a Pole never believes in good weather.

They might have a point, I thought, as black clouds seethed over the rooftops of the buildings ahead of me, bouncing the colours of the street into the extra brightness that precedes a storm. I was puffing now. The heat was oppressive, the air choking. I had lost the dwarf and his cart, and so settled for wandering aimlessly and at a slower pace down the nearest side-street.

To no-one's surprise, it rained: a few sheering streaks to start with, and then it poured. I was tempted simply to let it drench me, that warm, relieving rain, but a diminutive old woman, powering herself along at a forty-five degree angle, saw me, a coatless creature, smock clinging to my bulge and straggly hair to my cheek:

'What are you thinking of?' She hissed as she passed. 'You will be ill.' Naturally, being a British person of my class and generation, I believed that any link between getting cold and catching a cold was a Victorian notion unworthy of consideration.

'Huh,' tutted another, coming upon me from behind. 'Where is your coat? You won't think it's so funny when you're ill.'

That's what Babcias are for, I reflected benignly, to contradict the liberated impulses of young women. They were only doing their job, after all - and I *did* have a baby to consider. So I ducked into a doorway and looked across the street at the glistening green leaves and scarlet petals of the early geraniums against the dark wrought-iron of the balconies.

A portly, balding man wearing only his underpants came out onto the balcony opposite, lighting a cigarette. He leant on the railing and smoked meditatively, sheltered by the balcony above him, as the rain fell diagonally before his face. There was another bare-chested man wearing a towel just a few balconies along, and another in the next building but on a higher floor, again in underpants, with a cap and drooping moustache. I watched them watching the rain, drawing in their cheeks and exhaling slowly, and felt the rehabilitation of men in my soul complete.

'A truly Lawrentian scene', I knew Rob would say when I told him, and I would agree with him because I loved him, and because it was sort of true - as though that defined it, as though that really caught the peace and loveliness of the vision of the rain falling on the unwashed buildings and the smoking, reflective men and the slanting rain, rinsing the eyes of all of us clear. I wondered then what it meant to get more like another person, over years, to start to think like a person who isn't you - especially if they don't think like you at all. It could be wonderfully liberating - who, after all, wants to rattle around inside their own consciousness, their own skull like a rat in a cage? But which parts would wither and which come alive? If so much were subsumed, would I like what remained? I was angry with Rob for the remark he had not made, rather as you can hold people responsible, however unjustly, for their behaviour in your dreams, because it was so in character, and also because it was the kind of comment made only by a person who was not there - and Rob's quality of being not there wasn't his most endearing one at present. Was it all an illusion, this future with him? If it weren't for the baby, would I even want to find out?

I noticed a third Babcia, half-concealed in the doorway of the furrier's, eyeing me with a gleam which declared that she might well not confine herself to caustic comments in passing. Before the rain eased and she could make her move, I fled in the direction of my favourite café. Inside, I let the miasma of sausage and cabbage and apple envelop me, mingling with the steam rising from my clothes in the warm room - and it was from there that I saw the cart jolting over the cobbles into a courtyard almost directly opposite. So I finished my meal and entered the alleyway, past the glass case with its display of fountain pens and the neat, blue, printed card - Tadeusz Marczak: Penmender - down the steps and through the dark curtain.

I don't know what I saw when I first looked into the face of Marczak the Dwarf. Wisdom? Kindness? A lot of patience. He seemed in his fifties, but his hair was somewhere between fair and white so it was hard to tell, and he had that very soft, honey-brown skin that doesn't age at an ordinary rate. I only know that when I saw him I felt safe, completely safe from everything that might harm me. I had no idea what I was going to say to him - I had no fountain pen for him to mend. Perhaps I could ask whether he *sold* them also. Marczak rubbed his hands on his blue overalls, his thick fingers marbled with ink. He stepped up onto a ledge behind his counter to make himself tall enough to see over:

'Can I help you?'

He saw from my face that he could, that my presence had little to do with an interest in pens. Always a gallant man, perhaps he could not fail to respond to the still-soggy damsel in distress before him. What else he saw I couldn't tell, but I never from that moment lost the sense that he knew me, and that how I was and what I did were all right with him.

I don't recall much of what we discussed that first time, just that he plugged in his ceramic kettle decorated with brown flowers and made me

99

a glass of tea. He showed me his tools and all the components of a fountain pen.

'It is not so skilful as being a watchmaker or a jeweller,' Marczak explained, 'but I started late, and I like it. I like pens better than watches, or jewels.' He laughed. 'I do my job so that people can write beautiful letters to each other, beautiful poetry.'

I told him about my own not-so-beautiful compositions for Rob, my obsessional lists of tinned fish and vegetables to prove I was eating properly. I told him all of it.

'You need to worry less,' he told me. 'It is easy to say it, I know. You are too practical.'

Yet I found that, with him, I wasn't worried at all. The sensation had simply vanished, like a low-level toothache you've had so long you're no longer aware of it until you suddenly notice it's gone.

After that I went whenever I had free time to the little downstairs room with the faded blue lino and the pale light spilling from a small window above the sink. I read in preparation for classes or marked my students' composition exercises. It was restful but at the same time instructive to watch someone work with such precision. Marczak even made his own nibs. I tied myself in knots trying to explain the English expression 'his nibs' - the kind of crazy linguistic enterprise you only undertake when caught up in an ecstasy of communication with another person. Marczak spoke German but no English, so we conversed in Polish, though he didn't talk a great deal while working, only during his fifteen-minute breaks, which he took at two-hourly intervals. At around 11.30 he ate what he called '*drugie sniadanie*' - 'second breakfast'. I couldn't fail to notice that he brought far more bread and cheese and sausage than he needed, and also that there seemed to be an astonishing variety of pickled vegetables from his allotment that he just wanted me to try or that he was just trying to finish off so he could reuse the jars. I took to the practice of 'second breakfast' most willingly.

Marczak was one of those people who make you feel better at once. He was not compulsively cheerful; nor did he make me feel I was being corrected when his observations were consistently more upbeat than my own. He relieved me of the pressure to be more cheerful than those around me, yet he never gave the impression that he found me a misery. Suffering detained him but it did not overcome him, and this appeared to be a facet of the reliability he showed in all things.

'My name is Tadeusz Marczak,' he had said when he first introduced himself. 'People call me Marczak the Dwarf.' I resolved that whatever 'people' did, I would be different. He was already such a warm, solid and real person to me that I had a squeamish distaste for the notion that he should be referred to as if he were a character from a fairytale. Perhaps I felt some discomfort at the fact that he had some such talismanic significance for me which I would not have liked to articulate. I had known him such a short time yet he embodied my wish for - indeed the very possibility of - a long and happy life. The comfort and ease I felt in his company spoke to me of the promise that domestic harmony and contentment might be possible. I felt with him as I imagined you might after being happily married for forty years. Even so, I pretty soon lost my conviction that, unlike the others, I would be the one to call him Tadeusz or even, if it wasn't too presumptuous, Tadzio: I saw it for what it was, an attempt to distinguish myself and curry favour - needlessly. Marczak was his name and he was proud to be a dwarf.

'It has some kind of grandeur to me, the title,' he said, laughing a little, 'like Alexander the Great.' And though he told me that several times during his childhood, and only by the cunning and stubbornness of his mother, had he avoided being put into institutions, he insisted that 'dwarves are very important in Polish culture, in stories and songs. They are....'

'Cute?' I suggested.

'No, no, not cute. They are heroic. More importantly, they are everywhere - like mushrooms.'

I told him about political correctness and the term 'vertically challenged'. He laughed for about ten minutes. He had the face of a joyous country boy of about twenty when he laughed, the look of a lad who spent all his days in fields.

'It is a civilised country, America,' he said. 'Or it is completely crazy. The Russians are crazy too. What a world we shall have!'

I got up to make him another pot of tea. At first he used to protest when I did this, that I was the guest, that I should sit still and so on, but I insisted. I liked to do it and I savoured the unaccustomed sensation. I knew I was playing at being the little wifey, that I was practising, trying out a role I'd never been remotely tempted by, to see how I liked it. I wondered whether the easy companionship I felt with Marczak, the familiarity but still the desire to provide was really how it would be with anyone else.

'No, no, I'll do it. You are working.'

'You are making something too,' he pointed out, 'and you should sit down more often.'

I changed the subject by asking him about his mother.

'My mother is sick. She became ill the next day after I met you. She fell down, but it was not an accident because she was angry about something and she fell. Then she got flu. She is getting better, but she is crazy that she cannot work. All her life she has never stopped working, but this time I made her stop, me and the doctor.'

'What does she do, for her work I mean?'

'She collects things. It has always been her work in one way or another, but now she does it for Uniontex, the big textile firm, for recycling, usually old products, cloth, rags and such, but sometimes machinery, or parts of machinery. That is why I go out for her with the cart. She likes this work, and in Poland the joke is that when you retire you get a job. She would not like to be one of these cloakroom Babcias giving out peg numbers and toilet paper in a café. I can imagine how she'd do it!' He hiccupped with laughter at the thought.

It had always been just the two of them, and somehow it was clear that Marczak did not wish to elaborate much on the question of his father.

'He had no desire to know me,' was his only comment, 'and therefore I do not see why I should want to know him. My mother always said that the name of a man who leaves a woman when she is pregnant should be used only as a swearword, and since she did not wish to use a father's name as an obscenity before his son she has never told me what it was. She swears by a whole array of saints on a regular basis so I could guess it was any one of them. Saint Ignatius seems to get a particular battering when she is especially angry, so my money would be on him.' Just for a second it crossed my mind that, despite my explanations, Marczak might somehow be under the impression that mine was a similar situation - which it really wasn't - and I felt uncomfortable. Or was it *his* discomfort I could feel?

Yet Marczak was already chuckling over some article in the paper about a prominent bishop whose background closely resembled his own, from the same Northern district and raised in poverty by a single mother, struggling to avoid institutionalisation for polio. Marczak looked up from the photograph of the round, priestly face of the man currently, and unusually, managing to enjoy the rapid preferment of both Church and Party with a droll expression:

'There but for the grace of God ...,' he said.

Once I asked him where he had lived as a child.

'We lived in the same street as we do now - Wolborska Street. It was a Jewish street in those days and most of our neighbours were Jewish. Luckily for me, my mother was very friendly with the mother of my best friend, Solomon. Through their family it was even arranged for me to go on trips with the Jewish Bund for city children to visit the country. We went to a village near Wloclawek. Solek and I rode on a haycart. It was wonderful'

'Did you go to school together?'

'I did not go to any school most of the time. I was supposed to attend a Special School because people with my condition were considered by the educational authorities to be mentally subnormal. There was another school I could have gone to in the neighbouring district. Mama let them fight it out, just stirring the pot occasionally, and meanwhile I went no-where. I was a lot of help to her. My mother always thought school was over-rated as a means for gaining wisdom - or gaining anything for that matter, but Solek repeated all his lessons with me. I know rather more of the Torah than I get to use very often but I am grateful for all of it. He was very patient because he liked better to run about. He had many friends his own age but he always had time for the ones younger than himself. He used to make games for them on the street. The younger boys waited every day for him to come home from school, because he came out half an hour later than them.'

Marczak saw my face. 'Yes, Solek was 'his nibs' for me - right?'

'That's right. "The bee's knees,"' I said, translating directly into Polish.

'Ah, the knees of the bee!' He laughed delightedly, 'the knees of the bee! Just so, the knees....'

One day when the baby was junketing about, creating bulges and undula-tions beneath the material of my dress as if I were secreting a sackful of writhing kittens, I called to him:

'Hey, look.' I wanted him to feel the movement, to plant his hands there. Had I not seen the tenderness with which those hands touched every other object?

'Only a husband should do that,' he said, somewhat primly I thought.

'Well I don't have one of those, do I? Oh come on, Marczak, you're the perfect husband - in fact you're every woman's ideal husband: you're kind to me, make me feel beautiful, feed me cake and soothe my worries - and you make no demands whatsoever! I mean you don't boss me about or expect me to bring you your slippers,' I added hastily to avoid the sexual implication of my words, which suddenly struck me as rather too near the knuckle. 'Do you exist at all or are you a complete female fantasy?'

'Yes, we diminutive husbands are very much in demand. That's why Snow White had seven of us!'

'There you go then'.

'Yet even seven did not equal one handsome prince.'

'But everyone knows the Dwarves are much more fun and much more real than the Prince. You don't like the story for the prince - every story has one of those, they're ten a penny - it's the Dwarves that count. That's why the title is *Snow White and the Seven Dwarves.*'

'Unfortunately in Polish it is just *Snow White*'.

'Well, that's censorship...' We looked at each other and started to laugh. 'I can't believe I'm discussing *Snow White* with... with you - it's bizarre.'

'This is the famous surrealism of Polish life - it is very contagious. I brought it up, remember. I am interested in my mythic stature. It is so much greater than my actual one.' We began to laugh again.

Perhaps because I hadn't got to meet her, I often quizzed him about his mother.

'My mother is not from here. She came to Lodz in the 1930s because she had a distant relative who could find her a job. Her family is from Kashubia, you know the lake region near Gdansk. It has round, soft hills and deep lakes from old glaciers - some are five miles deep. They call it the Polish Switzerland.

During the War, when all the textile factories here had to make army uniforms for the Germans, my mother managed to get back to Gdansk - Danzig it was then. She thought it would be easier for us - Foerster, the Gauleiter of the district there, was supposed to be less zealous in some respects, and it would be possible to hide me where no-one knew us and with family in the country nearby.'

'Did you have to hide?'

'No, no - in fact my mother worked as a housekeeper for a German family in the suburb of Oliwa. Foerster himself lived only three streets away.' Marczak chuckled: 'He was our neighbour'.

'A German family...?' I queried.

'Of course, they preferred to have a Kashub servant than a Polish one. Kashubs have their own language; it sounds closer to German. People still say it - the Kashubs are too German for the Poles and too Polish for the Germans.'

'Do you speak Kashub with your mother?'

'No, Polish - well, with some Kashubian words. It is a mixture. I didn't think about it before. We have our own language, like mother and son.' He laughed again. 'No, really, I didn't think about it.'

'What happened after the War? Did you come back here then?'

'The Germans had to leave. They went on trains and some on ships to Germany. My mother's employer, Herr Halbmann, had always said, when he was giving me my lessons, that in Germany there were special schools for people like me, the best in the world, where I would be treated well and given a full and proper education. He was very sure of this, but I have wondered since whether Herr Halbmann really knew so much about Germany since he had never lived there, nor his family for many generations before him. The Halbmanns would have taken me and my mother, but she wanted to stay. There would be empty houses, lots to 'collect'- and besides her family was not far away in Kartuzy. I re-member I was excited. I wanted to go to the country - but it wasn't to be. Three Russians soldiers came to the house and raped my mother.'

I blinked at the unfamiliar Polish word, double-checking. I didn't know what to say. Why? I almost said. How do you ask *why* someone was raped, as though there might be circumstances in which it might be somehow normal, expected or justifiable? Yet I knew that at the end of the War Russian soldiers had raped *German* women as a matter of course. Marczak apparently read my mind:

'She seemed German to them. Or she annoyed them somehow, when they came to the house. She is good at annoying people. Even me.' He seemed to run out of words.

'You were...O.K? I mean, you weren't there when ...'

'I was in the garden,' he said, 'looking for a hedgehog that used to come there.' Then he added, with the first flicker of malice I'd seen in him, though it wasn't clear at whom it was directed, perhaps even himself: 'I am short but I am not deaf.'

So they had come back to Lodz, to their familiar and barely recognisable street, and obtained a flat near their old one.

'My mother was happy. The flat was a bigger one. She believed all those rumours about Jewish treasure hidden in the walls and under the floor. My mother says those who discount rumours never find anything in life. Some Jews who had survived the war came back to streets in the district, but none came to ours. Solek died in the Underground, not in the camps. He was only what you call a teenager, but he was very strong and very intelligent. I'm sure he was a good fighter. The boys who used to wait for him, jumping out the way of the splashes they made with the water pump outside his building, none of them came any more.'

It didn't seem right for people to have to carry so much history, even if to them it seemed a fair enough exchange for being alive.

'I go to clean the Jewish cemetery,' he told me on another occasion. 'It is my Saturday job,' he grinned, 'except that if I were a good Jew I wouldn't work on a Saturday.'

'I didn't know there was one.'

'It is quite hidden, and people don't mention it.'

'Is it ...is it where the Ghetto was?'

'You say your flat is in one of those streets behind Marysinska. Where you live, child, that is where the Ghetto was. Under your flat. There was a ghetto there specially for children.'

Since he'd made me cry, he was obliged to put his arms round me. Given his height and my breadth it was a good thing I was sitting down. He smelt sweetly, like jam, as he rubbed my shoulder-blades. What we grieved for was beyond consolation, yet it was odd to find that being hugged by someone more diminutive than oneself, rather than being small and enfolded, could be so comforting.

'I will take you there to the cemetery, but before that I will show you my special garden, my allotment.'

We went that Sunday. I was in a bad mood when I met Marczak at the tram stop because people kept staring at my shoes. They were my mother's shoes, in fact, the first and only package I had been sent which had not mysteriously disappeared. I'd mentioned in a letter that I was having trouble finding new shoes, and my feet were getting a bit swollen, so she had kindly despatched an old pair of hers, since we took the same size. I didn't like them particularly, though they were very comfortable. It was the little gold bar across the toe which I didn't go for, considering the feature middle-aged, but which seemed to fascinate passers-by and mark out my footwear as Western and exotic. Since everyone knew, or thought they knew, where every available item came from, those shoes signalled access to a privileged source, and I had undoubtedly obtained something I had no right to: hence the mixture of hostility and envy in those glares. In cultures where the orthodoxy is very clear, people have no compunction about staring fixedly in public at any deviants, as I'd had reason to discover before - wearing a man's cap, or an ethnic-looking scarf, or a pair of dungarees. Yet this was not purely punitive behaviour of this kind. A Polish woman would probably have worn those shoes with pride, correctly reading the compliment contained in the element of jealousy and admiration in those eyes, whereas I simply felt affronted and ground down by that repeated unwavering gaze.

We alighted from the tram next to a forest of jumbled allotments, the trunks of the fruit trees painted white against parasites and the branches of cherry blossom soughing and bending over the bent backs of people hoeing between neat rows of potatoes and celeriac and dill. At one end of Marczak's plot stood a little, wooden hut of rinsed-out green. He'd let wild poppies and chamomile grow up round the doorway, and he'd taken the tiles of some broken chimney-stove - blue-and-white and blue-and-green tiles - and propped them all around the base of the wall and along the window sill. I thought it a bit much for Marczak to dwell in a ginger-bread house, but I found it lovely.

Inside there were paintbrushes in chipped glass jars, pots, tools, a broom and a small stepladder, everything lower down than you might expect - or rather not, by now. He gave me some twigs of cherry blossom to put in a jar. It was a warm day, and aside from some mild weeding, we sat underneath the plum tree and watched the shadows move up and down the trunk and the birds traverse so many garden worlds with each short flight. I realised then that I was more than half in love with Marczak the Dwarf. Drinking our tea in front of his hut, we must have resembled one of those ancient married couples captured by some Victorian cleric-turned-photographer outside their cottage door.

Perhaps on the strength of this, I pushed a little to be allowed to meet his mother, and the next Sunday I followed Marczak into the long, brown hallway. The waxy, tobacco-coloured walls and flaking, wrought-iron banisters were immediately restful on the eye after the hard, bright light outside. In the sole patch of dusty sunlight at the far end, a prostrate, yellowish dog raised his leg behind his ear but found he could not be bothered to scratch. We went up the stairs, each one with a dip in the middle, the grain of the wood worn smooth, so that its whorls shone like polished pools. They were quite slippery to walk on, and I was wearing my mother's shoes again, despite all my resolutions. In this sticky weather they really were the only comfortable option, but their soles now turned out to be as devoid of grip as the stairs.

'Mama, this is Pani Helena'. We had entered a room of mustard, green and brown in extraordinary quantities. Every available surface appeared to be shrouded in multiple layers of dingy cloth of various textures and patterns - tablecloths, bedcovers, antimacassars, never just one of anything - yet the effect of their combination was rather to deaden than to evoke colour.

'Helena is my sister's name,' announced the old woman in the corner, seated on a wicker chair which was draped in several throws. I thought how little of Marczak's sensibility or taste as I had known them in his workshop or his little garden were in that room. 'It is a name only for old women. *She* is not old.'

'I told you, Mamusia. I told you she was a *young* lady.'

'She should be old,' she persisted. 'Then she'd know how it is.' Her eyes resumed their lizard look of complete self-absorption.

I decided against going closer and sat down on the sofa facing her. It was then that she saw my shoes.

'Jew!' she screamed. 'Gold on your shoes - Jew!'

'She doesn't mean it,' Marczak explained. 'She gets upset. All our neighbours in this street were Jewish - before the War.'

'*She* gets upset,' I said, shaking a bit, feeling the adrenaline begin to flood unevenly through my body at the force of her detestation, which seemed to strike most powerfully at about knee-height. Perhaps hatred travels close to the ground, or she really was aiming for my shoes. She lurched to her feet unsteadily and started screaming, the words erupting in such a torrent I had no hope of following them.

'She sounds like she means it to me,' I said.

'No, no, she doesn't mean it.' He went towards her. 'Mama, Mama - *Mamusia*.' Marczak raised his hands to drive down her battling forearms. Holding her hands he pulled down her arms, arranging them against her sides, like someone adjusting a draught excluder, wedging it gently against the bottom of a door. Then he tugged on her hands once more until her knees bent and she sat on the bed, quiet. She did not speak again while he made her a glass of tea and left to accompany me downstairs. No, it was fine, I assured him. I wasn't offended. It was my fault for insisting on meeting her. I was O.K. I didn't need him to walk me to the tram.

I didn't see Marczak again. It wasn't intentional. Perhaps I hadn't meant it when I said I wasn't offended - though I wasn't, with him, of course - or that I felt on behalf of those missing millions I didn't have the right *not* to be offended. I needed time to recover from the awful suspicion that this ferocity, which could strike out of nowhere, this was real, while Marczak, with all his wisdom and kindness and complexity, was only a palliative, an illusion.

Also, I remembered my room at the Music School. I had been back since, resumed my diligent practice, but it was never the same. Was I to be driven with curses from my every haven, cut off from every source of my peace in this trying country? A bit melodramatic, perhaps, but that seemed the only mode in which to express what I felt. Was this recurrent pattern due to the structure of *my* psyche or that of the place? I feared the former. Apart from anything else, I was fast developing an allergy to being screamed at by older women.

That's what Poland did to you, I reflected, turned you into a connoisseur of rejection - though I suspected I might have been one of those already. I fully intended to call on Marczak. I thought he was probably upset too and I didn't want him to misunderstand - not that I understood anything too well myself. I left it a week.

Events in my pregnancy and in the country overtook me and I had to leave unexpectedly. I wrote to him from England, and sent him some pictures, but as he never replied I could not believe he got them - the post being as it was. Years later, when I was living in Gdansk, I took the train to Lodz. There was a photographer's studio where Marczak's workshop had been.

'Old Mrs Marczak?' Her former neighbours informed me. She had gone to Gdansk, to her brother, and her son had gone with her.

In the streets of Oliwa, where I now lived in one of those old German houses, where the sun glittered on the tangled sunflowers and dahlias in the gardens and the mattresses hung out of the windows to air, I wondered if he might be near. We had a hedgehog in the garden, and always, when I walked in the old districts of the town, or as my daughter dawdled on her tricycle on the way to market, I pretended not to hope for a glimpse of green cart.

New . . .

A fuzz of butterflies over the long grass of the allotments, dust hovering as if itself generating the hum of summer above the carefully planted pinks and jessamines. Poppies, cornflowers and chamomile resonate in the verges - and along the tree branches and telegraph wires, rows of swifts too sated to hunt for insects any more.

There were fewer people in the queue now. It was warm but those waiting in line nonetheless retained their light jackets. A crocodile of Pre-School children passed by on the pavement in front of the allotments. Each child had a wrist looped through a long woollen rope, which was held at one end by the teacher and at the other by her assistant. They were going to visit the Fire Station. Later on, after their nap and their afternoon snack, the musicians from the *Filharmonia* would come and play to them. The children and the Helper-Ladies called them the '*Artyści*'. Today the tuba player would be coming, which they liked best of all. Now Pani Beata was getting them to sing their favourite song about dwarves:

'*My jestesmy krasnoludki, hop sa sa, hop sa sa*
Pod grzybkami nasze budki, hop sa sa, hop sa sa.'
'We are the dwarves, under the mushrooms are our houses...'

The children wore woollen tights and lace-up boots as well as sunhats, for they were outside after all and you never knew when there might be a wind.

'*Jemy mrowki, zabie lapki, oj tak tak, oj tak tak,*
A na glowie krasnie czapki, to nasz znak, to nasz znak.'
'We eat ants and feet of frogs, oh yes, yes.
On our heads are red hats, that's our sign, that's our sign.'

The people in the queue cast benign glances on their nation's youth. An elderly man took up the dwarf song. It was he same one he had sung at *his* Pre-School in Wilno before the deportations. Pani Beata got all the children to wave. After they'd passed, someone leant over a pushchair and recited a sing-song little rhyme to the child:

'*Byl kotek na plotek I mruga*

Piekna ta piosenka nie dluga.'
'There was a cat sat on the fence and blinked.
It's pretty, this song, and not a long one.'

As it was Saturday, there were a number of young people taking their turn standing in for their older relatives. It had never turned into the kind of queue, like those for domestic appliances or furniture, where three to five days was the norm and positions in the line were inscribed on a list, so that you only had to turn up for an hour or so each day and sign your name in order to keep your place. Usually, with queues like this one, older members of the family did most of the standing, as their working hours were more flexible. Most people could still remember what they were hoping to find. They certainly weren't queuing for lemons any more. Some of the students near the front were clapping and chanting, and one or two rattled the door. On the whitewashed wall that sheltered the dustbins nearby, the inefficiently erased graffiti still showed: 'You have the Winter, Ours will be the Spring.'

There was more banging on the door. Conversations went on in the queue, quietly and desultorily. It didn't seem to be the content or even the tenor of what was said that effected any change. Some of the students sang for a while. There was some tutting at their high spirits - and at their tendency to sit on the ground, which was clearly unhealthy - but very little dissent from the view that the doors had remained shut long enough. Perhaps it was simply build-up of unconscious pressure, for no-one in particular, or even collectively, had really leant on the doors that much. In the event, whether the doors had been forced or gave way was unclear. The people streamed into the supermarket, rediscovering their anger as they went.

Inside it was even darker than they remembered - and in truth they had not seen that interior for so long they could barely recall it with any great accuracy. Most of the staff seemed not to be there, though one or two, as this was not a 'working Saturday', had been exercising their rights as members of the public and formed part of the queue. In fact, this not being a 'working Saturday', the supermarket should never have been open at all, even in the normal course of things, so what had they all been thinking of? Everything was indeed topsy- turvy...

The meat counter at the back appeared exactly as it had always done: a lone white sausage curled up on a tray, a slab of lard, a large brown cube of fresh yeast, two or three smoked mackerel in a crate. There was even less on the shelves. A young shop assistant was packing the last of the brown paper bags of flour and semolina into a green plastic crate. The retreating back of an older woman and a man, carrying similar crates could be glimpsed disappearing into the storage area at the rear. Only the last pyramids of tins, which had for so long blocked the view from outside the window, and a shelf of bottles of clear vinegar remained.

When Martial Law was declared in 1981, aside from the tanks on the street corners, the uninterrupted military music on the radio and newsreaders in uniform on the television, what seemed most to signify the country's condition was the fact that the authorities had apparently ordered the shelves of the state supermarkets to be stuffed full of nothing but vinegar. People often referred to it among themselves, knowing what it signified, or stressing it to outsiders, to those who had not lived through it. It was a kind of hardship everyone could understand - even though they had not in fact had to exist on vinegar during those awful days. It was shorthand for that pole-axing of the collective psyche of December 13th, a cipher for the real suffering, which for most people was not primarily physical at all,

The human psyche, it seems, needs to represent its psychological traumas in terms of physical deprivation, as though that's the only sort that counts. Perhaps, to our evolutionary selves, psychological damage still has the character of a luxury. Referring to our oldest and most elemental pains, translating states of the soul into literal threats to survival, is the only way we can express what matters most to us. Thus a woman who flees her house after finding her husband in bed with her step-sister will insist: 'I had nowhere to go. I had absolutely nowhere to go.' Years later she will tell the story of how she paced the streets, lighting at last on a pub where she could be sure no-one knew her, lifting her drink and fishing a cigarette from her bag with a shaking hand, deciding which of her friends she could face asking for a bed: 'I was literally homeless, you know. I didn't even know where I was going to sleep that night.'

The teenager who spent a whole weekend in the empty flat of a friend, not daring to go out in case she missed the promised phone call that inexplicably never came, will impress upon her listeners: 'there was virtually no food in the place. I ate dry cornflakes for *three days!*' Only near-starvation can adequately represent the emotional enormity of that fruitless vigil, only the possibility of death from hunger is large enough to contain in displaced form the disappointed love, the hurt, her sense of what she had invested and was willing to endure. Though Poles are far too resourceful to have been reduced to actual malnutrition by the mere absence of foodstuffs in the shops, how else can they convey that complete horror and powerlessness? Those who had the country in their grip said to them: 'You thought you were worth something. You thought you could - but you couldn't.' The rows of clear liquid on the shelves crowed: 'We've got you now.'

So in the blue supermarket that summer day those shelves of vinegar not yet stowed away were an affront. The memory enraged people. One woman shouted at the shop-girl, and several others at the retreating male back. The employees didn't put up much of a defence. Only the older woman returned and blustered a bit - but she was the kind of battleaxe that would have defended anything against anyone - and in the midst of this the pyramid of tins containing green beans, the labels peeling where they'd stood in the sun, went over, with a noise like somebody dropping a piano down a flight of stairs. Above the din, some thought they could hear the sound of ZOMO vans pulling into the buses' turning circle opposite, others that they imagined it. The soft gravel would make a different sound than that, one or two opined, as someone else shushed them to listen more intently.

Over the allotments the air was cooler now, and the swifts, joined by a few swallows, were in the air and back on the job of catching insects. It's said that swifts can sleep while flying, but if so why did they need to sit down most of the afternoon? In the little yard next to the bus-stop the white fantailed doves turned their backs and spread their tails in the late sun, arranged in their preferred formation - like a five of spades in negative - on the pitch roof of the moribund shed.

Unscheduled Flight

The sun was shining outside, fuzzy through the wire mesh on the windows. I glanced over my shoulder. In a chipped enamel bowl on the floor by the door, a blob of cotton wool floated in bloodied water like a cloud. I shut my eyes again quickly. I heard the knot of women behind me giggling and could make out Grazyna's voice boasting to the others about the chocolate bar she had smuggled in under the very nose of old Adamczyk, the doctor. Grazyna and at least two of the other women were diabetic. I had found that out talking to them last night.

'Boy, am I looking forward to that chocolate! Aren't you all jealous, girls? Perhaps I'll share it if you're nice to me. Tonight, when the shifts change. I'm going to have one treat at least before the baby comes.'

That would be on Monday. I'd learnt this also during the same exchange. How did she know, I'd asked? They all knew, they'd said. When the doctors came back after the weekend the caesareans would start.

'Of course, I knew from the beginning I could not have my baby naturally,' Stasia had told me, chewing at the end of her thick plait, 'because of my eyesight.'

'Your *eyesight?*' I'd thought I must have misunderstood.

'Well, you know, I am more than minus two dioptres and so the doctor said I would be sure to detach my retina during labour, with the pushing. Everyone knows it.'

'But you don't even wear glasses.'

'Well, my Bolek doesn't like them, but I have them somewhere. One of my eyes is minus two point five, you know.'

Both of mine were at least that.

'In my country, in Britain, this is not true,' I had said stoutly. 'My eyes are minus three,' I'd hazarded the guess, 'and there they will let me have my baby naturally. One hundred percent,' I'd added for emphasis. 'Even wearing my contact lenses.' It wasn't like me to be asserting the superiority of Western European practices. I usually spent my time trying to resist or undermine the assumption that everything was automatically better 'in the West.'

In this case, though, either the contact lens touch was too much or matters of health did not fall into the same category as practically everything else about their country, for they had given me looks that plainly indicated that 'in Britain' we were a bunch of reckless idiots, and changed the subject. I'd felt queasy. It wasn't clear that I was going to go on to have a baby at all, naturally or otherwise. Me, who back at the beginning used to read the 'Birth' chapters of my pregnancy books and cry with joyful anticipation.

Under the sheets, I crooked my arm beneath my belly, stroking with my other hand, softly, miserably. I knew she would not kick - just as I suddenly knew she was a she - though I felt she was still there, holding on. Yet even as I sensed it, I no longer trusted myself in this perception, or in anything else. We were separated, she within me. I no longer knew how to talk to her. I had let her down and she could not tell me what I needed to know.

My right shoulder ground awkwardly into the thin mattress against the raised head of the bed. Shouldn't it be my feet that were raised, surely? I didn't know how to operate the cranking mechanism on the bed and was in no doubt as to the response I would get from the nurse if I suggested doing so. The pills I had taken were wearing off. I hadn't wanted to take them, yet had been terrified not to. Now I feared they would forget to give me my dose - perhaps the tablets really were all that kept the baby in - even as I felt my body craving them, already dependent on them. Why didn't that nurse *come?* I manoeuvred myself onto my back. My heart was racing and my insides were jittery, a continual fluttering, as if there were a crazed moth behind my ribs.

I looked over towards Grazyna and her friends, but they were exchanging secrets in a round-shouldered huddle on the two beds furthest from me. They'd been friendly enough last night, but now I sensed they wanted none of me (though, to be fair, I had been dozing most of the morning). For my part, they might as well have been bent over a cauldron of chicken feet, stirring with a cleft stick to determine the sex or fortune of one of their unborn children. I was through with unreciprocated tolerance and cultural relativism, with my own pathetic attempts at objectivity. I recoiled from their ignorance and superstition and all their dark otherness as if they exuded a miasma that would itself harm my child. This was my own superstition, I realised, though the knowledge alleviated the sensation not at all. I wanted to be out of there more powerfully than I had ever wanted anything in my life.

****

It had started on Friday night, when Pawel had rung to say there was a problem about the ticket home. There were no flights available for at least the next six weeks, he told me, still with that touch of triumph with which Poles always announce bad news, or any fact which confirms that the world (or more specifically Poland) is as they've always claimed, not a place where you can do what you like or get what you need just because you happen to want to (as foreigners persist in thinking). He had queued for several hours at the travel agent, he reminded me. I needn't think anything was straightforward.

It was very kind of him, and I really *did* appreciate his efforts, I said, but I was perfectly willing to queue myself. Wasn't a pregnant woman allowed to go to the front of the line? We had already abandoned an earlier plan for me to travel by train, with a couchette reservation so that I could lie down for some of the journey, because this had proved 'not possible.' He wouldn't hear of me queuing myself. No, he would go again, but he wouldn't do it tomorrow. Did I think he had every day free to stand in line?

There wasn't much blood to start with, but it was the brightest, reddest blood that I had ever seen. At that moment I felt that my entire being froze, in disbelief, in horror, as if my whole organism had instantly congealed - in contrast to that glistening blood, which looked as though it never would congeal - and had never really started to move again.

Crying, trying not to cry, rubbing my hardened belly, I stumbled into bed. Each time I got up in the night, and still in the morning, there was a little more. I fled from my block of flats and walked the half-mile to Pawel's.

There was no place for me in the hospital that day. Maybe tomorrow. Pawel seemed awkward, putting down the receiver, even as he gave his usual baggy-jumpered shrug. His wife was in the kitchen, banging dishes about. She seemed to be avoiding the living-room, where we were, and the tall, spiky figure, long legs accentuated by black tights under a short denim skirt, strode meaningfully from kitchen to bathroom and back again. Zusia's copper-dyed hair was scraped back into a jutting ponytail and her face, in profile on the curving neck, resembled a skull. Soon she called Pawel from the room.

I didn't want to leave. In fact I dreaded above all to be where I had first seen that slick of glistening blood on the dingy grey toilet paper.

'Please,' I begged him, as he sloped back into the room, 'please can I stay here awhile?' I was eager to pre-empt any other proposition, which I sensed was imminent. 'I'm just scared to be by myself. I'm scared to be at home.'

Pawel went pink, jiggling his hands in his pockets beneath the floppy jumper, his choice of words only confirming my surmise that he had received his instructions.

'We are just going out, apparently.'

'I can't go home,' I said. 'If I could just lie down on your sofa, I'm sure I'd feel better.'

When the front door banged, I lay in the hollow flat, trying to have no thoughts. I knew from Pawel that Zusia had lost a child, or rather that there had not been a child inside her, only a cluster of cancerous cells. Was that why she could not bear to see me? It had not occurred to me until now that perhaps she could not have further children. Had the doctors here - always, it seemed, more drastic in their pronouncements - advised her not to? Or when they took out that never-to-be baby, had they also removed her womb and with it all possibility?

When Pawel returned, alone, some hours later, I telephoned Roza, who drove me at once to the hospital.

'They never take anyone seriously who calls by 'phone,' she said. 'Maybe you will not need a bed anyway.'

She clicked along the concrete floor of the hospital in her stilettos, a light stole thrown about her shoulders, holding herself like Zsa Zsa Gabor. Her baby-doll make-up belied her nearly fifty years and she dealt with the young man in the receptionists' cubicle with the assurance of a femme fatale. A professor of Economics, Roza and several colleagues made up my 'private lesson' in English Conversation on Friday afternoons. It often seemed odd to be instructing people several decades older than myself. Now I held onto her arm like a daughter, unable to speak from gratitude. I didn't care how she did it. I felt I had exchanged the uselessness and dithering of men for the competence of experienced women. She guided me by the elbow, through the corridors to the doctor's room.

He was a short man with cropped hair and a gold tooth. He wore a round-necked overall, like a dentist, but he reminded me most of the driver of the tram I caught in the mornings. His name was Doctor Bujak - Irek - he told me. He apologised for speaking no English and hoped that I would understand his Polish. It took me a moment to identify the complete absence of condescension, social or intellectual, that made him unlike any British doctor I had ever met. He knew at once what I required, holding my hand while a nurse fetched a foetal heart monitor.

'There, listen. Your child is alive, it is happy. Relax now and listen for as long as you want.'

For ten minutes or more - until I was embarrassed to take up his time, to be monopolising the machine - I let that crackling, slooshing sound, with the deafening beats of that tiny heart galloping across it, wash over me, unable to say the words or make any sign that might cause it to stop. Each time he caught my eye, Bujak grinned still wider, like someone who'd laid on a treat for me and wanted to be sure I was really enjoying it.

116

'We will try to find out what is the matter,' he said, 'but your baby - listen how strong. Go upstairs now and rest.' He had never let go of my hand.

I was not so lucky with my second doctor, on the ward. Dr Adamczyk had no qualms about the inadequacy of his English:

'We find out what you problem,' he averred in ominously loud tones before examining me. 'Probably you lose child. You must rest for following months, you hear? In bed, in this hospital, then, if baby not die, you rest at home. Never sexual intercourses, you hear me? You understand what is sexual intercourses? Very dangerous for baby, understand it?'

I panicked completely. 'How long?' I cried, as though his answer might tell me how serious the situation was, as if he wasn't already shouting 'baby... die' and 'lose child' in my face. My question must have given the impression that I was the kind of woman who could not contemplate so much as a week without sexual satisfaction, even for the sake of her unborn child, but I was powerless to alter it, merely switching language to repeat 'how long?' in Polish instead. As if I had any intention or any prospect of having 'sexual intercourses.' As if my baby's father were not a thousand miles away across half a dozen countries and beyond the sea.

'You shut up,' the doctor said. 'Always questions. You shut up.'

I could tell myself that he meant 'be quiet' or even 'calm down,' making allowance as I habitually did for the problem of translation, but the language did its work, as it always does, regardless of extenuating circumstances. Tears were getting in my mouth as I went outside to Roza, to be steered to a nurse who issued me with some slippers and a bed.

***** **

The nurse shoved a plate containing mashed potato and a small rectangle of meat in a grey sauce onto my bedside cabinet. She was about forty, with straggly, unsuccessfully bleached hair. The hairgrip meant to pin it back from her face dangled above one eye. I watched her as she shuffled in her clogs among the beds, pouring *kompot* into plastic beakers, not responding to Grazyna's jokes about putting some vodka in it. There had been a picture in the Florence Nightingale book I'd read as a child of what nurses were like before the advent of the Lady of the Lamp and her companions. The illustration showed a slovenly red-nosed creature wearing an uncaring expression and a dirty shawl, carrying a jug among the unkempt straw pallets of the wounded. This was she, before my eyes, the same heavy-lidded, resentful gaze, the bluish complexion and the red, pinched nose. For my baby, I thought, I must ask her about the tablets, I must have courage. I dreaded hearing my own voice with its foreign inflexion float weakly out into the air of the ward. No successful outcome could be brought about by such a voice.

'Prosze Pani?' I ventured. 'Moje tabletki, czy to…?'

'Nie ma,' she snapped ('there aren't any'), that favourite riposte of shop assistants which I'd heard so many times among the empty shelves.

'Nie ma?' I felt the panic rising. They'd started me on a course of drugs without enough supplies to continue. They were capable of anything. She didn't look at me, and wouldn't have said more, but I pestered her. They'd run out. The orderly hadn't brought up any more. I'd have to wait. Did I think I was so special? What was she supposed to do when no-one brought up the drugs on time? Did I think it was straightforward?

I subsided at once, and brought my plate onto my lap obediently. I couldn't eat it - I must, for the baby, but I couldn't. A tear dropped onto the coagulated grey sauce and stayed there, making no impression at all. I forced myself to chew the meal, piece by piece, counting in my head like a child made to eat its dinner. There wasn't a salad, not even a pickled one, and this was summer.

All those months through the long winter I'd scouted around for food, walking miles to find a stall that had carrots or radishes, once or twice splurging a day's wages on a tomato. Contrary to the assumptions of my acquaintance, I had no dollars with which to buy bananas or oranges, tinned ham or fruit juice from Pewex, the hard currency shop. Though the shelves of the supermarkets were largely bare, the larders and refrigerators of my friends were inexplicably full, but, unlike them, I had no network of relatives and friends who could get hold of this and that for me, no uncle in the country to pass me the occasional joint of ham, no granny who grew beans on her allotment.

Still, I had managed to vary my diet from the inevitable potatoes, cabbage, apples and tinned fish, which, after all, were not themselves lacking in nutrients.I boiled the milk as I was instructed. I had bread and cheese and eggs. There was no meat to be seen in the shops, so my ration coupon was useless, but I had discovered that if I didn't mind spending most of my wages (which of course I didn't) I could eat one meal a day in a café or restaurant, where cutlet, schnitzel or sausage were often to be had. Surely, in the annals of human history, a child-bearing woman who eats meat once a day is doing pretty well?

'Oh no,' said my friends and students and colleagues, 'this meat in cafés, especially in workers' cafés, is very bad. Probably you get from it some diseases. And the milk,' they went on, 'you say you boil it, but it is not enough. The milk in our country is very dangerous.'

I tried to ignore their dire predictions. I knew that an optimistic demeanour or positive observations inevitably provoked this response, being such an affront to their own sense of reality. My role as a foreigner

118

was to be convinced that Poland was an awful place: that nothing in it (except occasionally the character of its people) was to be praised or even tolerated, that the air they breathed, the food they ate somehow poisoned them in the same way that the regime poisoned all aspects of their existence. Despite my attempts to rationalise it, this mood was infectious and I was often anxious. Nonetheless, I was proud of my achievement, writing down every morsel, compiling little daily menus in my letters home:

'Your child and I did very well today,' I'd write to Rob. 'As well as the *bukiet* (bouquet of pickled vegetables) I mentioned, I found a lovely gloomy place like a dance-hall in one of the backstreets behind Jaracza which has delicious liver - not just on the menu but actually available. It's quite cheap so I will be able to afford to go there quite often. So you needn't worry about us.

Tuesday
1 cup hot milk
2 hard-boiled eggs
bread

1 *paczek* (doughnut)

watrobka (liver!)
potatoes
bukiet (including carrot and leeks)
tea (with lemon)

some tinned Russian fish a bit like sardines
potatoes

kiszona kapusta (sauerkraut)

Won't the baby be brainy with all this fish...?'

'Only three more weeks,' I'd written in my last letter, 'until I touch your sweet face and never go anywhere any more.'

I hadn't yet had his reply. If I could just get to him, if I could only be where he was, everything would be all right. I tried to focus on his face. I blamed him, but I couldn't afford to remember that now.

Of course I did remember. Immediately the scene came into my head: the day he had 'sent me back.' We were sitting at opposite ends of his single bed, eating toast from the plate between us. I'd gone over to Britain during the semester break to see him and to have my pregnancy confirmed. Rob claimed to be delighted, as I was, with the 'unexpected

Christmas present' that had resulted from his trip over to see me two months before. I was wavering. For the first time I raised the possibility that I might not return to Poland. I might stay - with him. I thought pregnancy was straightforward and wonderful, a matter of blooming and growth, effortless and inevitable, culminating in birth and baby and the joyful future. I had no doubt I could handle it, even in cold and Communist Eastern Europe - but we had made this baby together and suddenly I felt glued to him by some hormonal adhesive. I wanted to be near him while the baby grew. I didn't want to be alone and far away.

He was brisk and upbeat, as if he was consigning me to another term at some boarding school, like the one he had so hated himself. I could hear the desperation. He had his thesis to finish. He *must* finish. A pregnant girlfriend moping around the place - *his* place - wasn't part of the plan. The suggestion seemed to trigger an autonomy-panic, a territory-panic, all kinds of male impulses which I didn't share and didn't understand.

His grant had run out a year ago. He was on the dole. His girlfriend was pregnant. He must get his qualification and get a job so that he could support this sudden family. I didn't care about any of that. I just wanted *him*. I accused him of giving me a lot of 'stiff-upper-lip and duty' rubbish.

Even so, part of me wanted to fulfil my contract, my obligation, not to let people down. I hadn't gone to boarding school, but I'd read all those school stories as a child, imbibed that upper-middle-class British morality. Part of me felt that I would be running away. After all, it would be an experience, something to tell our child about when it grew up.

So I had been packed off with my trunk and my hockey stick, back to behind the Iron Curtain and beyond the Berlin Wall to the doubtless character-building discomforts of the East. Not that Professor Bulska, my immediate boss at the Instytut of English Philology, appeared to appreciate my decision. In the interview in which I had explained my condition and that I would complete my contract for this year but not renew it, she said she hoped I realised that I would not get any special treatment. Of course not, I said. I hadn't expected any. Why would I need it?

I had always wanted to get on with Professor Bulska, admiring her for her political past and because the students spoke so warmly of her. Yet even before the pregnancy she had seemed indifferent, and subsequently merely exuded in my direction a thin trickle of disapproval and faint dislike. Perhaps she thought that I set the students a bad example - though, in the absence of available contraception, several of them seemed quite capable of becoming pregnant without any reference to a 'role model'. At least three students in the department had preceded me in the condition and, as the custom was, had duly married their boyfriends and, in the absence of available flats, moved in with one or other set of parents. I wondered whether the fact that I showed no sign of getting married was the problem, some discernible lack of shame at my predicament. Or that my crime was simply to be *cheerful* about it, as if being pregnant was just one of the things you could do, a decadent Westerner, making self-indulgent 'life choices.' Without consequences, without suffering.

****

There were consequences now. I looked around the ward. No-one had moved the bowl of blood yet. I made myself look at it. It wasn't mine. Whose was it? The swab of cotton wool had sunk. They had prevailed. That tragic vision which I had resisted and analysed, which I hadn't shared, had made itself reality. I hadn't thought it could. I'd gambled with the life of my baby - how dared I? - trusted everything to my feeble strength. I'd been mad to think I was so resourceful. I'd known things were not easy but I had thought that they were not impossible.

'No, no,' they'd declared, my friends and students and colleagues. 'You must be crazy to carry this baby in Poland. Probably it will die, or have some deformities - you know, in its body or maybe its mental part.'

'Surely Polish women have babies all the time . . .'

'Yes, but they are very sick. Usually they are born before the time, you know. And they have many problems.'

Of course Polish women had babies all the time, but they had not, as I had done, *chosen* to nourish their offspring in Poland, were not, as I was, that fabulous and fortunate creature, a Western European, who could have been pregnant in 'paradise'. My decision was not just in poor taste, it was an insult, a denial of everything they knew to be true, as if Poland were a normal place, as if it were just like anywhere else.

It was clear to me now. Without meaning to, those around me had set out to punish me for my sanguine assumptions, collectively willing on me the confirmation of their convictions. I had pointed out on many occasions that the main threat to the baby's health was that I might jump out of my tenth-floor window after conversations such as these. Yet often the same person would return the next day announcing that they had spoken to their wife or friend, who was 'very worried' about me, and replay the whole thing again. Was it usual to talk to pregnant women about the inevitability of death, deformity or mental handicap for their babies, I wondered? Did my foreignness, my association with the fairy-tale land of Western Europe render me so unreal that I might be supposed not to have the normal emotions in the face of such utterances?

Yet things *had* been getting better: Roza had been inviting me home for supper after class on Fridays. I seemed finally to have found ways to communicate what I needed, and the mother of Jola, one of my students, was cooking huge meals for me each Sunday:

'Eat, eat,' Stenia would say, pushing yet another delicacy before me. '*Witaminki*, you know, *witaminki*.' Tomorrow would be Sunday. Jola and Stenia would wonder where on earth I'd got to. Like most people, they had no 'phone.

This turn of events - with Stenia taking personal responsibility for my producing the healthiest baby in Europe, East or West - had coincided with a marked improvement in the political atmosphere of the country as a whole. It had almost begun to appear that other things *were* possible. Could it really be only a week ago that we had stood - Pawel, Marcin (from Polish Philology), Mirek (specialist in modern poetry), four of my students and I - in the sombre hallway of the Instytut, waiting for a runner from the Law Faculty, where the students were already on strike? At his signal, we were to move into the street ready to form part of the demonstration that would march along Piotrkowska. Everything depended on whether the workers from the Uniontex factory would come out in support. Secret negotiations were underway between student representatives and workers' leaders, for if the students carried out this action alone there was little doubt that it would be suppressed in the customary manner.

Mirek twisted his mouth to make a wry face:

'In '81 our students were first on strike, in whole Poland...'

Pawel stepped from foot to foot, smiled ruefully and shrugged:

'Some went already to the Law Faculty, I know - but well, you know, we are ready, even though we are not so many. Somebody has to make the start - some others will join with us later perhaps.'

There had certainly been plenty of students, from Polish Philology as well as from English, crammed into the seminar room for the hastily convened political meeting two days before, sitting along the window sills and on the floor in front of the benches right up to the legs of the table where the student organisers sat. Were those two days long enough for the rumours to do their work? Since people believed nothing that came from an official source, the authorities had not been slow to make use of the network of rumours that ran through the population. People relied on rumours so much in everyday life and for all subversive information that they were inclined to be far more credulous about rumours (especially if they confirmed their worst suspicions) and far less cynical than they were about anything else:

'The Solidarity leaders don't care about us anymore,' one of my students told me earnestly. 'You know, the leaders from '81. They all started some private businesses so now they have plenty of money and don't care about what happens with us. We try to make strikes but they don't worry about us. They will not help us.'

'Who told you this?'

'It is rumour. Everybody know it.'

The rumour had already gone round that the Warsaw students, who had gone on strike a few days before, were sitting drinking beer on the grass in the sun behind their barricades - a bunch of irresponsible loafers, not serious at all.

Marcin and I went down the steps and looked out into the unnaturally quiet street, full of the air of something happening somewhere, not here, and of people watching, of dozens of pairs of eyes on the door of the building and the far off end of the street. I didn't think most of the students had simply taken advantage of the strike as a day off and gone home. Not a curtain twitched in the buildings across the street but people were there, waiting to see what would happen to determine what they would do. I gazed along the street to where the tram wires dropped over the horizon in the dusty haze above the tracks, listening for shouts, for sirens.

'This doesn't seem altogether wise,' said a voice in my head, with classic British understatement. I would be careful, I would be sensible, I'd told myself. I knew the riot police, the ZOMO, showed no deference to pregnant women. I had heard about Halina W., a tram driver and Solidarity activist in '81, who had been beaten up so badly - four ZOMO officers deliberately kicking her repeatedly in the stomach - that she had not only lost the child she was carrying but had been unable to bear children since. Yet I believed in the efficacy of the good, that if you did the right thing, in good faith, you were rewarded with a good outcome. Tell that to Halina. I used to have a taste for dilemmas but I knew I had not resolved this one. How could I face my child if I could not tell her that I had been willing to risk everything alongside those struggling for their emancipation? Willing to do what? To lose her? To have no child to tell anything at all? Would it not effect the child's life - even if never spoken - that before her birth her mother had lacked courage? Not half as much as being dead, as never being born. I would march, but I would try to stay out of trouble, I repeated, hedging my bets. I was there, in the hallway, with Marcin, Mirek and Pawel, with Danuta, Tomek, Beata and Janusz, but I was afraid.

In the event, a curly-headed young man panted up the steps from the basement entrance and told us hoarsely to disperse. The police had gone in at the Law Faculty. It wasn't clear yet about the workers at Uniontex. The talks needed more time. Disperse was a bit of a strong word for eight people, Mirek joked with the runner. Not very glorious perhaps, but it had felt like a beginning.

******

Kasia surveyed the ward and made a faint *moue* of disgust. She had heard from Pawel, she said, and got in her car as soon as she could. Kasia was one of my fifth-year students, a kind person, thoughtful, and rather frank. Her father, a former scientist, had made a fortune in business by selling the ultrasound gel he had helped to formulate - and which he now manufactured in an outbuilding in the back garden of the detached house he had built himself - to the very hospitals that had once employed him. The Communists allowed this, for he employed only two helpers, and now that he was exporting to Sweden, his enterprise brought much-valued hard currency into the country. The family was not new to privilege - which had simply been suspended for a couple of generations - as they came from old aristocratic stock. Their surname bespoke a feudal past, Kasia's father assured me, though they didn't care about all that now. The name was mentioned in Sienkiewicz's famous novel, *Knights* - did I know it? - and by a very funny coincidence, just four years ago they had been camping by the lakes, only to discover in the tent next-door some descendants of the Radziwill family, to the great amusement and delight of the rest of the campsite's inhabitants.

'I'll bet,' I thought, but Kasia's father had the same honesty and sweetness of temperament as his daughter, and it was hard to be cynical about him. Since Kasia's wealth freed her from the obligation to feel herself *economically* badly off under Communism, she was therefore able to think more clearly about her objections to it. I had often found her company a relief because she could acknowledge enjoying some aspects of her existence. Still, as she took in the ward, I had the distinct impression that, with her father's medical connections, these were not conditions in which she could imagine finding herself.

She asked how I was feeling, then pulled out a white folder from her holdall.

'It is my Masters Thesis,' she explained. 'I show it already to Professor Maksymiuk - you know, it is linguistic thesis - but he say before I submit this works I should to get a native speaker to check it, for grammar and the spelling and so. I know this is not good time perhaps' - she waved a hand at our surroundings with a small laugh - 'but you know, you can't go anywhere, so I thought perhaps you wouldn't mind to do it. I will come back for getting it tomorrow.' She gave another tinkling laugh and her eyes danced, not with embarrassment at the request but simply as part of the charm that would lead to my acceding to it. With a final wave at the door, hand up by her cheek, she was gone.

I looked at the sheaf of typed pages. Was I mad? Did I just *imagine* that I was a real woman with a threatened miscarriage? No, clearly I was a 'native speaker' - temporarily immobilised it was true, but who therefore might as well make herself useful by correcting Kasia's thesis on

God knows what riveting aspect of linguistics! No, I couldn't go anywhere else because I was in a hospital where my baby might die!

I turned the papers over. I wasn't being reasonable. How could I help my baby if I kept being so easily upset? Perhaps Kasia had done me a favour. It might take my mind off things. I inserted a couple of missing articles in the first paragraph before I sensed the familiar trickle, stuck my hand underneath the sheets and brought up the fresh blood on my fingers.

I panicked, leaping out of bed and running down the corridor after the nurse, holding the stained hand in front of me like Lady Macbeth.

'What are you doing?' the nurse yelled, waving away my hand, and glaring incomprehensibly down at the floor. 'Are you crazy? Get back to bed at once. Look at your feet, look at them. You will be ill. How dare you be out of bed? You have no slippers!'

****

It was the middle of the night. Stasia rolled from her back onto her side and stopped snoring. Now all I could hear was the newborn babies crying their thin cries from the nursery at the end of the corridor. The sound was unbearable and I knew it would go on for at least another half hour, because the nurses would only begin feeding at the designated time by the clock. I knew I had a fever - that was the reason the doctor had given for not discharging me, now that the drugs were supposed to have stabilised my condition. If it weren't for that, he would have sent me home, in the care of Roza, as long as I promised to spend the next three months in bed, but my temperature was much too high. He didn't like the look of it at all.

I knew that I was not thinking clearly, but, surveying the darkened ward, I was certain that I'd never be able to as long as I remained there. I did not know whether the 'complication' I had was serious or not. In some other, barely imaginable, parallel life, a British doctor might very well tell me to take it easy for a few days, monitor the situation, explain the possible causes in my language, reassure me that, while not exactly common, such occurrences were not necessarily anything to worry about. In my mind, I conjured him, my fantasy British GP, hearing the detached but explicatory tones I craved, a little cool perhaps, but rational, favouring me with the odd statistic, a man I might not particularly like but one whose facts I could digest, whose cultural signals I could read, who would not drench me with his Slavic despair.

Perhaps they kept such a person in the British Consulate in Warsaw for the consular officials and their faded expatriate wives (immediately envisaged in pastel frocks and floppy hats). Even as I contemplated running away to Warsaw to seek him out, I knew it was ridiculous. It wouldn't happen.

Once, this would have been the baby's most active hour. We used to play a game: I'd put my hand somewhere on my belly, and press slightly, and she'd kick it; then somewhere else, the other side, kick again, the bulge against my hand. I remembered how, after a few weeks of this routine, one day I placed my hand at the top of my belly below my ribs and the kick had come right down at the bottom. I tried again nearer the bottom - a foot, or an elbow, jutted out at the top as far away as possible from my hand. And so it went on. My God, a joke, I marvelled. Already, a joke. It was hard not to picture the curled up form shaking with a cartoon snigger each time, a teehee speech bubble floating in the amniotic fluid. I knew this was probably too 'anthropomorphic' or something - but how could that be since the baby was a person? I could sense from her the wonder and delight of a new game. How early we learn that no sooner do you have a game than you have the possibility of its opposite, or that once you have fully grasped the rules, you can change them. Why could I not learn from my child that you can alter the game?

Now she was sluggish, but stirring nonetheless, more than she had since I'd been in the hospital. I stroked her rhythmically downwards and got the answering kick. I felt her presence as if she'd walked into the room. It was she and I again. I almost laughed.

'Are you with me, kid?' I asked, mock cowboy-style, out of the corner of my mouth, the parody a kind of self-protection against disappointment. And, conceiving the idea as I spoke the words: 'Are we outta here?'

Two kicks and a definite elbow.

Where the hell were my clothes? I put on whatever I could over my nightie, and left the rest behind. The nurses were on a smoking break, trying to get an extra one in before having to feed the newborns. If I went now I wouldn't bump into them coming up the stairs - though I'd have to watch out for them by the outside door. I put my two hands around the base of my belly as though physically holding the baby in and crept past the bed ends into the corridor.

In the unlit car park a figure was standing beside a lone Fiat, looking up at the first floor windows, hands cupped at his mouth. A woman in a dressing gown was at the window which had been jammed partially open. It must be the ward along from ours, the Maternity Ward. I could hear the excitable cadences of her voice wavering up and down: 'No, Lukasz... no, that's right' was all I could make out. Though he was nearer, I couldn't hear his words at all. I remembered one of the women at the Friday 'private lesson' explaining how, since fathers were not allowed in the hospital, women would shout the news of the birth and the sex of the child out of the windows to their anxious husbands waiting below.

The dark was dissolving into a murky dawn. A string of lighted windows rattled along the main road: one of the night trams. I half thought of catching it, but I didn't fancy the jolting motion, or having to run to the stop. It wasn't really very wise, what I was doing, came the understatement in my head. I laughed at it. No, but I was crazy-wise and that was good enough. I recognised the number of the tram and knew which way it went. The dark ahead was fizzling on my face and I realised it was a light summer rain. Never taking my hands off my child, I began to follow the tram tracks down the pot-holed road.

****

I'd thought it would be 'British subject in trouble - just leave it to us,' but instead the man I spoke to on the 'phone at the Consulate said 'Why should we help you?' I had to ring British Airways, he informed me, and they would tell me what, if anything, was available. I'd already explained my situation and could not comprehend that it was not obvious why they should help me.

'Because I'm a human being and I might be losing my baby,' I enunciated very clearly, as if English were not his first language. He didn't reply. 'I'm bleeding,' I added, hearing at once how much more melodramatic that sounded in English than Polish. Bloody marvellous. Poles can't believe that I have any real emotions because I'm not Polish and now the Brits can't relate to them because they don't have any themselves. There were circumstances in which this might have been funny.

There was a pause. I thought he'd gone away.

'Wait five minutes, then ring. I'll 'phone them first,' his voice came back over the line. 'My wife had a similar thing when she was expecting our second,' he added, as if by way of apology, though whether for his weakness or his previous callousness I could not be sure.

I rang British Airways.

'Is that Miss Leary?' the clipped female tones inquired. 'Would you like to fly today or tomorrow?'

After that, things moved fast. Ewa, a colleague from the Instytut whom I barely knew, tipped off by Roza, procured for me two packets of the drugs I had been taking at the hospital, enough to get me home.

'You will need a doctor's certificate,' she told me. Apparently British Airways, terrified that hordes of female aliens will board their 'planes and give premature birth in an endeavour to secure for their offspring automatic British citizenship (a B.A. 'plane is British territory), forbid travel to women over six months pregnant - a full month's gestation earlier than other airlines. Ewa could arrange this, however, since she knew a doctor willing to 'help with such paperwork':

'You will have to pay him a small bribe, but it is not much - only 2,000 zlotys - and after you have bribed him he will do what he has promised. You don't have to worry. He is an honest man.'

I was relieved enough to smile at this new definition of moral probity. I had been hooked into the network of capable women - whom I had more than an inkling ran this society - and I knew now that I would be saved. I heard in the mouths of those around me the verb 'zalatwic' - to fix, to wangle, to arrange - and I was certain that all that they assured me would be done. I thought of all the months I had spent resisting, of protesting that things weren't so bad, that I could manage, that I was managing. Now that I had succumbed, now that I was clearly and recognisably in a Polish condition, namely *crisis* - 'kryzys,' how many times had I heard that word? - now that my spirit was indeed broken, I could at last tap into those limitless resources, which before had been largely denied to me. I was finally in alignment with this place, with its culture and its ethos and, no longer struggling against the current, it would bear me with it and all things - even my own liberation from it - would become possible.

The doctor came, a tousled man in his forties. I explained what I needed, how many weeks pregnant I was, the fact that the doctor who had confirmed my pregnancy in Britain had doubted the accuracy of the conception date I'd given him and had therefore recorded the gestation as further advanced, which was why... He raised his hands:

'Stop, stop,' he said. 'It does not matter. How pregnant would Madam like to be?'

******

I was lying on the sofa with my feet up on cushions to make them higher than my head when Roza and Jon walked through the door. I had completely forgotten about Jon's visit, remembering only just in time for Roza to be able to pick him up from the station. She had evidently briefed him on my situation, and for someone who has travelled for thirty-six hours by boat and train only to have his anticipated stay with a good friend and fascinating Eastern European holiday radically redefined, he was remarkably unruffled. Jon had become a born-again Christian in the two years since we'd shared a student house - a conversion that had followed hard on his desertion by his long-term girlfriend, who had married and had a child within months of their separation - so perhaps he took it all as part of God's plan.

Kasia arrived to say that she had successfully communicated a message to her cousin in Warsaw, from whence it was possible to dial international numbers *direct* (rather than having to reserve an international call twenty-four hours in advance). This should give Rob time to get down to London to meet me. Jon would stay in my flat, but Roza and Kasia would undertake to show him round, invite him for meals, show him a famous art gallery and an equally well-known vodka bar in the city, drive him to see the Corpus Christi Parade at Lowicz, if they had saved or could '*zalatwic*' enough petrol.

Roza heated up some soup she had brought, while from my reclining position I instructed Jon in packing my belongings: one bag for me to take tomorrow, a suitcase that *he* would bring back with him next week. Drew and Harriet, my two fellow 'native speakers' from the Instytut dropped by, promising to cover the exams I would be unable to mark or invigilate, to return books to the library, to settle my 'phone bill and to post my remaining books in packages of two or three back to Britain.

In the midst of these frantic preparations, the 'phone rang.

'Hello, I am Elzbieta Rutkowska, the wife of Professor Rutkowski, you remember me?'

'Yes, I do...'

'I wonder if you could help me, do for me a favour, so to say. I hear you know Roger Woodward of the British Council.'

'I've met him once - but, Elzbieta, I have to tell you I am having some problems with my pregnancy, with the baby...'

'You see I promised the daughter of my friend. She is wanting very much to go on this English Summer School in Cambridge, but her mother told to me there are now no more places. If you could speak to Roger Woodward, perhaps he could help her.'

'I hardly know him. I'm trying to tell you I am leaving tomorrow, on a 'plane, I am very afraid about my baby. I was in hospital two days. I am bleeding, do you understand?'

'But I promised my friend. She is very good in English her daughter. If you could just 'phone very quick to Roger Woodward - or did you say you are going to Warsaw to the 'plane...?'

To hell with English: '*Powiadzialam ze krwawe - rozumiesz?* (I said I'm bleeding - understand?) and hung up. I felt dizzy. I felt bad for being so rude. I felt I had probably made a mistake in the way I'd conjugated the verb 'to bleed.' Could I really care about that? My God, was there no end to it? Would my mind never stop racing? I felt like ringing her back and shouting at her in ungrammatical Polish some more.

'Who was that?' Jon asked.

The 'phone rang again. It was the secretary from the Instytut. Professor Bulska wondered whether I might want the Rektor's official car and Krzysztof the driver to take me to Warsaw, to the airport. Official car? I'd vaguely heard of its existence, but I knew the belated scramblings of a guilty conscience when I heard them.

'No, thank you,' I said. 'It's all arranged. I am getting the train in the morning.'

I derived a faintly vindictive pleasure at not letting them so easily off the hook, but by now it cost little to make a decision which had more to do with instinct and survival than morality. I knew who my friends were. Good flowed only from the good. The Rektor's official car bore the mark of Cain. It was sure to break down or get lost. I could not afford to take my chances with those who spent so much time insisting on the difficulties and hardships of their lives that in some sense they no longer believed in them and required talismans like myself and my disasters to make them real.

I looked at Roza making tea, Kasia and Jon sorting books into piles. These people who surrounded me now - whom I loved beyond measure, who could achieve anything they wanted - would get me home.

Jon was explaining that the boringness of his fellow Christians, their apparent incompleteness and unsatisfactoriness as people, though it had put him off at first, now struck him as a sign that they were onto something. Having to spend so much time and to share a faith with people with whom he had so little else in common must be the task God had set him. I felt hot from the soup and the tea. My temperature still wasn't normal. I went out onto my balcony for the last time. A flock of brown pigeons wheeled in an upward arc across a powdery sky which turned dirty pink where it met the horizon's cloud.

A group of women in headscarves and flowery overalls, workers from the last shift, were smoking on the roof of the shoe factory two streets away. Ten floors below me, in the yard of one of the older houses in the district, sandwiched between the tower blocks, I looked down on the turkeys scratching among the apple trees and the black and white dog lying in the dust watching them. My heart contracted with love for it, this scruffy, ill-assorted, polluted place - not the land of lakes and forests and Chopin, nor yet of self-proclaimed hospitality and indomitable spirit - but this, which its inhabitants did not love, or did not know they loved.

It was early, but I went to bed and woke in the night and found the fever gone. My head was clear and I was suddenly afraid. I crawled in to Jon on the sofa, and he let me sleep while he prayed over me to a God in whom I was all too willing to believe.

****

The station at Kaliska, a fine nineteenth-century building with a curved glass ceiling, had been demolished six months before. Diesel smoke hung over the heaps of rubble like an early morning haze. Travellers had to step along a series of planks over the mud and sand to reach the platforms and the waiting trains. Though no buildings remained, some of the old underpasses were intact and, as the time for departure drew near, more people poured out of these holes in the ground, heaving themselves up on the wrought-iron balustrades.

I sat back in my seat, alone in the carriage but for an old woman with a black chicken in a basket and a soldier reading a magazine. Sunlight prickled through the gritty air. I waved again at my friends on the platform, holding up the mauve knitted baby-slippers with the orange pompoms I'd been given, to show I kept them as a good luck charm. This last part the baby and I must undertake alone, but I felt exhilarated, that minute by minute I was committing an act of unbelievable heroism, completely invisible to the outside world. For I knew now that I held her in, by a combination of my own volition and the attainment of an exact pitch of transcendence that I could hear as if it were a note in my head.

Passing through the city, I glimpsed at the end of a street the high gates of the Uniontex factory, strung across with a looped blue and white cordon, partly blocked by the rear end of a police car. There was no sign of any activity: no people, no Zomo vans, but from the roof a white sheet bearing the word STRAJK in splodgy black paint hung down, one corner half-folded back on itself by the wind.

Wearing baggy clothes and a complicated scarf arrangement to reduce the prominence of my bump, I made it through exit control and onto the plane - though the young soldier queried my exit visa and threatened to send me back. He was a conscript and my look of despair seemed to unnerve him.

'Please,' I whispered. 'I am pregnant. Please?'

He had to call his superior, he said, but when no-one answered his summons, he relented and let me through. More soldiers stood on the tarmac behind the low airport building. I recalled the soldiers holding machine guns and wearing long, triangular, winter capes at the foot of the steps of the plane when I'd had my first view of the country nine months before.

On the 'plane I felt sick, stroking my belly unceasingly. I could not let my concentration slip for a moment, though by now it was unclear whether I was talking the baby through this experience or she me, giving desultory and, to my mind, sorrowful kicks from time to time. Apart from this constant communion, I had to exert all my effort to resist what was by now a compulsion, to visit the toilet cubicle and check for blood.

At the baggage claim at Heathrow he introduced himself as Jim, security guard at the British Embassy, the man I'd spoken to on the 'phone.

'I wondered if it was you, love. Are you all right? You do look ever so peaky, and back there I thought you were going to be sick.'

Not some high-up consular official at all, as I'd supposed, had effected my escape. I was so busy thanking him and receiving his concern and good wishes, that I was among the last people to move towards the reception area. It no longer mattered. Somewhere out there, Rob's face was waiting, scanning those who came through the doors, but we had already made it to safety, she and I.

* * * * * * *

Dr Ferguson twittered as he felt my stomach to ascertain the position of the baby, ostensibly to put me at my ease but rather more obviously to cover his own nervousness. I wished he would shut up - and if he gave that edgy giggle of his one more time...

'Hmm,' he'd murmured indifferently when I'd shown him the drugs I'd been given in Poland. 'These are normally for asthma. Can't think why they'd have given you these.'

'Perhaps they increase the amount of oxygen going to the baby,' I suggested.

He needn't be so blasé about it, I thought. They have thirty-nine million Poles to practise on; presumably they're not completely without medical experience.

'Well,' he said, once I'd got down from the bed, opening his hands expansively as I sat across the desk from him, 'the bleeding is not too severe at the moment - possibly the placenta has become somewhat detached. The placenta moves up the wall of the womb around this time to make way for the baby's head to engage ready for the birth. If the placenta is not too badly dislocated - there was nothing to indicate this on the ultrasound scan but it's hard to tell at this stage - then the bleeding shouldn't get any worse. If you have an increase in the amount of blood or a change in its colour or consistency then you can assume that miscarriage is beginning - but at the moment there really isn't any way of telling one way or the other.'

'So if I miscarry, you'll know I'm having a miscarriage?'

He didn't hear the danger in my voice.

'Yes, that's right.'

'And if my baby dies you'll know that something seriously detrimental to its health is happening?'

He giggled a little awkwardly. 'Either you'll miscarry or you won't - there isn't much to be done about it.'

This was my language, my country. Suddenly I was liberated from all considerations of grammar and, seemingly, of etiquette, from deference to doctors or the British reluctance to make a fuss. I didn't actually grab Dr Ferguson by his necktie, knot it round my fist at his throat and haul him across his desk, but I felt as if I did. I stood up and leant over the desk, pushing my face into his, eyeballing him as he shrank in his chair:

'Listen,' I said. 'I came a thousand miles for this, for good old British common sense, for the unalarmist, matter-of-fact approach, to have my mind set at ease. Over there,' I waved my hand in the direction of Eastern Europe, 'they told me my baby was a gonner if I didn't take drugs or if I stirred from my bed until the birth. I came because I thought - I hoped - that probably wasn't true.' I was yelling the words now. 'But at least those bastard doctors who told me every five minutes that I was going to lose my baby thought it was a BIG DEAL.'

Dr Ferguson was not heroic in the face of displays of female emotion. I could see his mind frantically rummaging for the least scrap from his recent refresher course that might help him in this situation. His eyes darted after the elusive information: don't antagonise the distressed person by seeming to contradict, use phrases that seem to validate their emotion...

I glared at him with disgust. It wasn't coming, was it? The right phrase? At least Poles, with their damned tragic vision, *believed* in tragedy, in waste and horror and grief. They believed that people fought for hopeless causes and were killed, that people were taken from their houses and shot, that entire populations could be loaded onto trains and murdered or made to live far from where they had grown up, forced for generations to speak languages other than their own. They thought life was cruel - or surreal or meaningless or absurd - but they thought it mattered that it was so. They didn't find things 'a bit sad' or 'rather unfortunate' and neither, I discovered, did I.

'I understand how you must be feeling...' Ferguson ventured at last, but I cut him off.

'What if I go to bed? What if I don't move between now and September?'

Ah, bed-rest, that old chestnut. A 'rather old-fashioned remedy', he averred. Doctors used to prescribe it as a panacea for all problems in pregnancy but that really wasn't the thinking nowadays. I'd flipped a switch and he was back in his stride:

'There really isn't any clinical evidence that it makes any difference to the outcome one way or the other...'

'Don't you dare tell me nothing I can do makes a difference,' I menaced him. 'I can get her and me a thousand miles - don't you *dare* tell me that!'

There's no clinical evidence for a lot of things. There's no clinical evidence that the political situation of thirty-nine million people can be transmitted by their collective psyche to another person and thereby bring on a miscarriage. I had a sudden vision of pregnant women going into separate white-walled cubicles in each of which sits a waiting Pole, to determine the gynaecological effects of such exposure. Elsewhere a 'control' group of women would have to be locked up singly with representatives of another nationality - Czechs, for example. Better still, there would have to be a third group, some nationality not oppressed by Communism. The idea was so ludicrous that, when I heard Ferguson's giggle, I assumed for a moment that he was laughing at the same scene, until I realised that the giggle was my own.

I had proved myself a hysterical woman, and I knew what would happen if I kept on laughing. Ferguson sniggered in what was meant to be a sympathetic way about 'hormones' and how they sometimes 'give you gyp,' as the tears splooshed onto my hands shoving the leaflets he had given me into my bag. I marshalled what was left of my dignity and swept belly-first out of the room.

POSTSCRIPT

I went home and to bed. Two weeks later the bleeding stopped, and two months after that I gave birth to a healthy daughter. We called her Konstancja, in recognition of the quality which I still reckoned had saved her life, and of the country which had so fully evoked it.

I watch her, lying in her Moses basket by the fireplace, our little Koshka, sucking gently on the air in her sleep, the full, perfect curve of her cheek that almost obscures the tiny nose and the soft, working lips, the answering shadow on the mattress. Rob is in the kitchen. I can smell the warm butter and onions as he begins to cook. I write a second letter to Jola and Stenia, telling them about our lovely daughter as she sleeps. I wrote soon after my return, to explain what had become of me since my 'disappearance', to thank them for the *witaminki*, for their kindness, for everything. I don't know whether they received this communication - the radio speaks of strikes as an everyday occurrence now, so disruption is to be expected - yet I would hate them to think that I just took their *witaminki* and ran, that I have simply returned to my paradisal Western 'normality' and forgotten them while their country faces the struggles of its own rebirth.

In the event, neither letter ever reaches them. As a Polish émigré friend delights in telling us, the envelopes, with their Western stamps, were probably thought to contain dollars and therefore stolen.

The next day I receive a letter from Poland, from Professor Bulska, asking whether I have a textbook belonging to the Instytut which has not been returned to the library.

'You understand it is important for us,' she writes. 'Unlike in Western countries, we cannot replace them so easily, so please return this book if you still have it, or send the amount in dollars.'

She does not mention the baby.

The Clockmaster of Danzig

They summoned the clockmaker from Torun, the elders and burgermeisters of the great city, and ordered him to make for them a clock of such passing beauty its like might not be found along all the trade routes of the world.

With care he scratched each ochre scruple into the face of parchment-coloured stone; with love he wrote the figures and minute calculations, row upon row in the clay-red writing - until the face was almost filled with precise reckonings and you might know not just of days, weeks, months, years, but of the ebb and flow of tides, the wax and wane of the moon, of the sun's portion and the calendar's saints. Above this he fashioned the main clock face in azure blue with stars of gold, and set it round about with bulls and scales, fishes and waterbearers, to show the workings of the heavens in their slow revolutions. The hastening minutes he pricked out in sharp gold rays, each close upon another, while before them swung with heavy grace the great forked bar, charting the sun within the zodiacal sphere. Amid greater and lesser stars, the sun within that trancing arc was shown, and above that visage curled the dragon, Titmoth, who was before good and evil were, when the universe was shards and golden dust.

As the clockmaster worked his adoration swelled with the scope of his undertaking. For this clock was his whole understanding, and not his only. And though the minutes pass so quick, the vast unchanging patterns of the firmament are slow to unfold. As he scored each mark, he ached towards that utmost precision wherewith he might inscribe the characters to chime with that unseen geometry of the cosmos and the Maker, might synchronise his tiny scratches upon the face of time with the movements of that great etching hand. In such a language a man might speak with God, and voice the mystery of the shifting and eternal heavens. Could this be humility, or its opposite? His sore eyes wept upon the marks he made. Many times his fingers would not bear the weight of his tiny, poised instruments.

Yet at last it was done. The clock stood in the cathedral to the glory of God. The town elders were well pleased and paid him most handsomely; and that his work might not adorn a city less great than their own and thus glorify it beyond its worth, they blinded him, and sent him back to Torun, whence he came.

The years passed and the great city prospered. The grain in its garners was as the sands of the desert heaped up in dunes. The rats in its warehouses were the fattest in Europe. In the Long Market, eyes were dazzled with the glare of the sun reflecting from so many glass windows. The town councillors commissioned a painting for the ceiling of the Great Chamber of the Town Hall, requiring the services of a respected Dutch painter. The eminent Dutchman duly came. Through his humble eyes, he said, this work would serve to reflect to the statesmen seated below an adequate sense of their own puissance and the city's just pride.

For the unveiling of the finished work, all the foremost citizens were gathered. The representation, the artist explained, celebrated the unity of the city with the arc of heaven (here shown as a rainbow) and with the economic system of the kingdom as a whole. *Celesti ingimur arcu*, the painted writing declared, somewhere to the right of the walled city, which was raised upon a triumphal arch, its many towers bathed in light within its fortifications. From out the clouds the brawny arm of God (here identified by Hebrew inscription) gripped tight in its fist the Town Hall's winged spire. Below, the city's merchants stood in groups, hard-bargaining and sober-clad, while Mercury paced between; and round about, an ornamental garden of avenues and fountains and statuary stretched far away to the Vistula, heavy with shipping, and the forests of the central plain. The Dutchman was deemed to have done well, and received several private commissions in a similar vein.

The clockmaster dwelt in Torun, or so it seems, for when emissaries were sent there to search for him he was found. All was not well with the great clock in the cathedral. The town elders were concerned. Nothing would content them but that he should leave the small, walled town on the Vistula and come to them once more.

The clockmaster went to work with care, feeling with his fingers, removing here and there a wheel, a rod, filing this piece and that. And he mangled the bloody hands, there where they met behind the great clock face. And he broke the great clock so that it never struck again. And from the topmost dais - beneath which ranged the signs of the universe in their wondering arc - he leapt to his death upon the hard stone floor.

Your foot is always upon a grave, even as you gaze into the stilled face of time.

Thank You From The Mountain

It wasn't how he'd expected to spend St Sylwester, smelly brown water seeping up his shirtsleeve even though he'd rolled it up to the shoulder. Nothing down the dank hole in the floor into which he'd plunged his arm appeared to be shifting. He hoped the miraculous 'spirala' which Janina kept promising, and which Bogdan had gone to a farm further up the mountain to fetch, would live up to expectations.

He heard Janina clump up the ladder from the barn to see how he was getting on. She wore a blue flowery overall, on top of trousers tucked into boots. The barn, containing three sheep and two shaggy brown cows, was part of the house, just the next door along from the sitting room, under the slope of the roof. For a mother of five with an unreliable husband and a potential flood on her hands, Janina looked remarkably unstressed, Jon thought. She was probably unstressable generally. She didn't have a single grey hair.

Now her hands rested on the dusty knees of her trousers as she bent over him. Her dark hair flopped forward over her glasses but he thought her eyes were mischievous:

'It will be O.K.,' she told him for the umpteenth time, 'when the *spirala* comes.' At least he thought that's what she said, for the noun 'spirala' had by now assumed such disproportionate significance in his limited linguistic world, it had a tendency to wipe out the phonemes around it, even those he did understand.

Jon attempted a rueful sort of grin and let his breath out in what he hoped was a game manner. It was hard to tell whether your body language was doing what you wanted it to whilst lying on the floor with one arm distended down a stinking hole. Where *was* Bogdan?

Janina gave a grin back, one in which amusement at the situation - at *his* situation - rather outweighed anxiety about the threatened flooding of her home. The rich, Western foreigner with his arm down a hole in her hallway. How are the mighty fallen! He was only a lad, he sensed her thinking, only five or six years older than her own eldest, Hania - and not a very handy lad at that.

Janina was asking him something else, which he could not follow. She seemed to be half-entreating and half-laughing at him as she embarked on more sign language. Could he still feel the obstruction? Janina pushed the hair out of her eyes and they both laughed as Jon tried unsuccessfully to use his free arm to brush the damp hair from his forehead, then to blow it out the way, until Janina came to his assistance. Her hand was cool and smelt pleasantly of vegetable peelings.

It was only half an hour off midnight. Jon continued to grope about down the hole, more for form than effect. There was almost no point in being annoyed with Franek: Janina's small and feckless husband had not returned from Zakopane, the nearest town, where he'd headed that afternoon, purportedly to leave a last consignment of his hand-made leather boxes at Cepelia, the State Folk-Art shop. The bars of that resort on this holiday eve of the New Year had, not unexpectedly, proved too much for him to resist. Everyone else was over at the farmhouse of Janina's sister next door. The grandmother and great-grandmother would be presiding over yet more chopping of vegetables into infinitesimally small pieces for the salads, such as he'd seen the army of women produce in Janina's kitchen earlier.

Iwona would be among them. He didn't fail to notice the small flip in his stomach as he thought it. Surely he wasn't getting interested in a woman again like *that*, not after Marguerite and the catalogue of disasters, or rather the series of non-events that had followed. He hoped he would get to have a proper conversation with Iwona at the party later - if he ever *got* to the party.

Like himself, Iwona was a paying guest at the mountain farmhouse. Roza, his hostess back in Lodz, had insisted that he visit the mountains on this, his second visit to her country, and in her motherly but unobtrusive way had arranged everything. Grandmotherly, she'd insisted with a giggle, applying another layer of mascara and adjusting the fringes of her silk shawl before the mirror, for she had celebrated her fiftieth birthday that very week. Jon had been happy to acquiesce, having no particular plans except the desire to see more of the place he'd had such tantalising and bizarre glimpses of a few months before. He'd made no plans, partly out of superstition, being simply glad 'they' had 'let him in' again. Given the recent political turmoil, he would not have been at all surprised to have had his request for a visa refused.

'Yes, you can thank me already,' Roza had replied to his protestations of gratitude. 'I know you will love it there. It is real mountains. In Polish, when we say thank you for something in advance, we say *"dziekuje z gory"* - it means "thank you from the mountain."'

Now that he was halfway up a mountain with his arm down a hole, Jon wasn't so sure that the authenticity of mountain life was its best feature. Franek had built the house with his own hands, and the craftsmanship was spectacular. Franek, it was clear, was an artist. There were intricate carved cornices, every wooden plank of the walls had been beautifully planed by hand and, packed between the planks, were little balls of crushed wood-shavings to act as insulation. Yet no single part of the building was actually finished: there was no handle on the door, or the wood-shaving balls ran out halfway up a wall showing threads of sky - and there were recurrent problems with the plumbing, of which the present difficulty was an example.

Franek was not entirely convincing as a farmer either - though Jon had seen him only yesterday steering his tractor an uneven course up the sloping field behind the house dragging a sledge of fencing posts across the snow. He concentrated, for as long as his concentration would allow, on the exquisite leatherwork from which he derived his primary income. It seemed that Janina did the bulk of the farmwork, with the help of Bogdan and another son, Witek, and, together with Hania and little Marta, ran the guest-house side as well. The house had four large rooms upstairs. Perhaps the family used them out of season, but certainly at the moment, even though only three were occupied, all five children and their parents slept in a room on the opposite side of the sitting room to the barn.

Given the makeshift nature of the establishment, perhaps it was no accident that Janina's guests were mostly sent to take their meals at her sister Genya's house a few hundred yards away across the field. It was as if the two households - one decorous and exemplary, the other feckless and makeshift - were meant to be foils to one another. For at Genya's an overwhelming sense of order and tradition emanated from the dark old furniture, the spotless table-linen, the inherited second-best crockery. Nourishing meals issued from her kitchen at predictable and regular intervals, served by her two elder daughters - who looked demure even if they were not - sensible, round-faced, fair-haired girls, in contrast to Janina's dark and ragged brood. At five, even Kuba, her youngest, already had something 'fly' about him, Jon had thought that morning, watching the boy trail in with a coil of barbed wire he'd picked up on the dump down by the stream, black eyes darting under his fringe as he assessed his opportunities, or his chances of not getting a row, taking in the unattended cake on the dresser.

At Genya's the stove never went out. Nor would she have possessed, as Janina did, a device for boiling a single cup of water rather than making a whole pot of tea. Genya tucked the wisps of her blond-grey hair into her bun as she squatted before the range, drawing out the tray with her oven-gloved hand. Her husband, Alban, was one of the palest men

Jon had ever seen, huge, fair, solid and silent, with a sweet smile such as you might expect to see only on a little girl. Indeed, three year-old Ola's smile was identical, except for its extreme cheekiness, which could not be entirely attributed to overexposure to cousin Kuba. There was no doubt as to Alban's competence as a farmer, since he was at work in the fields every hour God gave. Jon, whose affection was secretly for the renegede branch, considered it no coincidence that Babcia and Pra-Babcia, the grandmother and great-grandmother, presided over this orderly house to a far greater extent, though they didn't live there either - at least not all the time. Jon had not worked out where they did live. Babcia apparently roamed vast distances selling the traditional knitwear she made.

It was at one of these meals at Genya's that Jon had met Iwona. She'd come from Warsaw, he gathered, with her sister, Renata, and two young men with sticking out ears and plaintive-sounding religious convictions. At least that was as much as Jon could tell, and for some reason he immediately christened them 'the wazzocks' in his head. He preferred to assume they were Renata's friends rather than Iwona's, partly because of their eager-eyed immaturity, and partly because, like Renata, they were students of engineering. Iwona had the air of a chaperone, a spinster aunt, he couldn't help thinking, in relation to them. She couldn't be much older than he was himself - perhaps a year or two at most. Still, he'd noted as a warning sign the fact that the proprietorial stance towards Iwona that he'd detected in the taller 'wazzock', Tomasz, had instantly aroused his dislike. Tomasz had taken it upon himself to correct her English in their conversation the other evening - in both cases substituting a phrase more grammatically inaccurate than Iwona's original - in a way that was presumably supposed to be endearing. Moreover, she had let him, in a manner which Jon hoped spoke more of her tolerance and good nature than of her taste. Her small, rounded hands, with their definite palm-lines, moved to smooth back her dark hair. He'd found himself watching the way she shook it after pulling on another sweater to go outside into the cold.

'It is the *spirala*,' Janina crowed. Jon withdrew his arm from the hole to receive the sacramental object from Bogdan. The *spirala* was indeed amazing, a thin, tightly wound coil, like a slender spring almost four feet long. Jon waved it about, made it undulate, then took both ends and flexed the implement as though limbering up. Janina and Bogdan laughed. He was getting quite good at this kind of joke - in the absence of the possibilities of any other. In no time he'd be feeling a positive wit in his new non-language. It was funny how you became a different kind of person in another language, or when you had barely a language at all.

He felt for a moment as he had as a little boy hearing his Grandad describe him as a bit of a wag.

Another quarter of an hour he laboured. It felt totally different manipulating something so far away, in the absence of much sensory evidence more like an act of faith, as if it must surely work - but the drain remained resolutely blocked. He was glad the others hadn't stayed long to watch, but that didn't prevent him from feeling abandoned. Then Polish words came pattering over his shoulder, and Janina was there, pointing to her watch and miming arm-washing movements.

'Is party,' ventured Bogdan behind her, in the first English Jon had ever heard him use. Even his mother whipped round in astonishment.

Jon changed his shirt quickly and washed his hands in the unfinished bathroom among the baskets of unironed clothes. Though the smeared brown arms streaked with soapsuds were his own, he thought of Iwona as he looked at them. This was getting beyond a joke. She had a tiny split in her top lip, he remembered. To be attracted to someone was one thing, to find them a sympathetic person whose subdued spirit seemed to indicate emotional depth - though he barely knew her and there was no reason why sadness should automatically denote emotional depth - even to love them a little, but to be 'in' love…? The difference of that little word, 'in,' was like the difference that tiny split made to her top lip, and to how it made him feel.

Despite being clearly such a capable person, he thought, Iwona didn't in the least resemble any of the series of drab, reduced, managing sort of women he had deliberately sought out after Marguerite, women from the Christian circles he'd then begun to frequent, women whose trimness was really primness. That was what he'd wanted, two carapaces scraping together in an illusion of connection. It had been clear even to him that he had done this in order to punish himself, to let himself know that this was what he was, what he deserved. He hadn't really bothered to ask himself whether he was what *they'd* deserved. And while he'd appeared decisive in those relationships - and he'd shocked his female friends with the detached way he'd spoken of those women - in fact he had been passive to the last degree, with that inertia which had so tortured him after Marguerite's departure.

Why had he not put up a fight, letting her go with some bullshit to himself about 'if you truly love someone you have to let them go'? Where did it say that in his precious scriptures, he would like to know? Because he hadn't wanted to see that she *would* go, whatever had been going on with this Martin. He had let her off the hook - or let her feel that he didn't really want her? All he knew was that inertia enveloped him as in a dream he'd had around that time, where a miniscule version of himself struggled in a whirling tub of candyfloss, ridiculous even in that. For months it was as if he'd been coshed on the side of the head and lay, visible to himself, while his upright body made limited, parodic movements that couldn't have convinced anyone. He was shouting from the bottom of a well- shaft even to make his voice come out at normal volume. It was when he had discovered that his punitive urges extended to the women as well, that in subtle psychological ways he made *them* feel inadequate, that he pulled out of the whole enterprise, despising himself the more, and opted for the respected Christian route of total celibacy.

'Well of course it is a kind of castration,' one of his more secular women friends (who clearly considered this policy a cop-out) had told him, 'her going off and having someone else's baby and all.' Thanks. Was that what it was? Did that explain his choice of the no-sex-before-marriage brigade in the first place, fumbling about and never quite acknowledging what had happened was real? He could never have imagined any such reticence on the part of Marguerite. Marguerite had been his first lover, and *she* certainly didn't mess around in that respect.

He met Hania carrying a box of glasses on the stairs. Her eyes were brightened by the glitter in her hair, which she'd swept up into a fluffed out top-knot to one side of her head supported by three sparkly combs. He offered to carry the glasses for her but she just took him to the kitchen and gave him some others and together they went across the rutted field to Genya's. Since Hania's main mode was coquettish teasing, which was difficult in the dark without language, they went in silence.

There were at least ten women in Genya's small kitchen, in which he was welcome only in so far as he had something to deposit. Iwona was in the far corner, scraping vegetable peelings from a chopping board into the bucket with a small knife. She managed to give him one of her smiles. She smiled like a person who isn't any longer used to having the upper part of her face dislodged by the creases a broad smile makes. Jon succeeded in comforting himself with the idea that he must therefore have provoked one of her fuller offerings. Babcia was adding just a few final pieces of celeriac to her 'Everlasting Zurek' on the stove. He'd heard her explain to Iwona the principle of having this soup forever on the simmer just the other day. Iwona had translated for him, which was kind, he'd thought, as most women here seemed to assume absolutely that, as a man, he was interested in eating not cooking. In fact he liked to cook. Curries mostly.

The table was crammed with the most beautifully prepared food he had ever seen: spiralling slices of pink ham, red tomatoes and diced onions sprinkled with green *pietrushka*, the flat-leaved parsley, eggs sitting snugly yellow in mayonnaise dusted with paprika, cucumber in sour cream and dill, and big bowls of carrot, pea and grated celeriac salad. The display of dishes already looked perfect to Jon, but various women were still fiddling about with them. It really paid off, all this effort, Jon thought, though it would drive him mad to do this himself.

He'd seen it a lot since he came to Poland, this loving attention to detail, the ability to be totally absorbed in the moment. He was beginning to really admire it. When he'd bought a wickerwork toy pram for his god-daughter, while he was still in Lodz, the woman in the shop had spent half an hour wrapping it perfectly in a dozen sheets of grey paper before she would let him take it out into the light drizzle. It was a little girl's toy and must be protected. Being almost at the end of her ball of string, she had painstakingly divided what remained into four thin strands with a pair of scissors. Jon himself had been divided whether to hug her or strangle her by the time she'd finished, but every part of the pram had been covered. Iwona had this quality. She'd been brought up to have it. He couldn't imagine Marguerite submitting to that for an instant.

There was much wiping of hands on aprons, hurriedly untied, the women jostling to squeeze the last dish on the table and to get out of the kitchen, the perfectly coloured and arranged food abandoned on the table. The large T.V. that was always left on in the corner of the sitting room announced the hour with loud chimes. There was raucous cheering from the children who'd bubbled over from the next room, and at once he was being kissed and wished good health and prosperity. Janina ruffled his hair when he gave her a piece of coal he'd picked up to offer by way of a poor cultural exchange. He bent double to kiss Babcia's soft cheek and Pra-Babcia's whiskery one, as well as a couple of other elderly ladies he didn't recognise. Not one had removed her floral headscarf. They pinched his cheek and made jokes about him to one another which sent them into fits of shrieking laughter.

Two glasses of Russian champagne were pressed into his hands. He could see Iwona, to his annoyance beyond the shoulders of both Wazzocks, and though he got to shake Tomasz's hand and to kiss Renata, somehow Iwona still eluded him. Just at this point Franek, prodigal returnee from the fleshpots of Zakopane, sidled up to him, his drooping black moustache working in a fit of earnest friendliness. He liked Franek a lot, and normally he would have loved to hear him talk with real passion about his leather-work as he was doing now, or at least judging from the signs he was making and the richly decorated boxes on the dresser he was showing him. Yet over his shoulder he could sift each syllable of Iwona's, uttered in her slightly gravely voice, from among the melee of other voices and the pop music from the T.V.

Suddenly Franek was indicating a large tome on the bottom shelf of the dresser - a big book: '*duza ksiazka*', he asserted. Jon nodded his recognition. Franek picked it up lovingly, slowing down his Polish:

'Bible. This is Bible. You have Bible - in England?'

He couldn't be much of a born-again Christian, Jon realised, as he found this question extremely funny. 'Yes, you Papist idolaters, and what's more *we* read it - *ourselves.*' That was the proper response of an evangelical Christian, was it not? Yet he found himself wanting to giggle at such a ludicrous idea, to Franek's evident puzzlement. He assured him we did have the Bible in England.

'The same one?' Franek persisted, opening it and showing him the pictures. It was a modern, illustrated version and the two of them embarked on a whirlwind tour through the Old Testament, identifying characters by pointing and pronouncing their names in the two languages - fortunately often similar enough to be recogniseable - repeating them until they were certain of their identity, relishing the similarity and the difference of the words simultaneously.

There just had to be some sense to the world, Jon reflected. You had to pray; you had to give that stuff to somebody - it was a bit of a downer if there was no-one there. Most people pray to their best selves, someone had told him once. Was that all it was? Or was that so very little? It was his own need - he could see that. He had no faith, or very little of it, he suspected. It was more important to love other people, as he loved Franek and Franek was loving him now. As so often on this subject, the banality of his own thoughts depressed him. Franek had brought out a small leather box with two close-fitting lids. It was decorated with inlaid silverwork. For a desk, he was explaining, to go on his desk:

'I give it to you,' embracing Jon.

Janina came up, teasing Franek about his drunken generosity and the rubbish he was no doubt talking. Jon shouldn't listen to him, she said, but it was clear that she in no way undervalued the gift. Franek grabbed her and tried to claim a kiss which she made much of not giving him, in the end pulling his head down by tugging his moustache and kissing the top of his head: All the best - Happy New Year. He must be a truly exasperating husband, Jon thought. Was it possible to bear that without disappointment? Was it possible to have no illusions and still be that fond of him? Was it made easier by the fact there was no choice?

Jon raved about the gift as much as such gestures and single epithets as 'beautiful' and 'good' and 'thank you' would allow. Janina bore Franek away as if he were liable to make a nuisance of himself, and Jon felt at liberty to go and seek out Iwona, who'd disappeared. She certainly wasn't hanging around. Fair enough. Why should someone be ready for you just because you were ready for them?

She wasn't around the food, but he made the mistake of sticking his head too far into the kitchen. Genya's elder daughter and Babcia filled his plate for him, made sure he tasted everything, threatening to be personally offended if he didn't try particular dishes, and plying him with more champagne. He had almost got away at the very moment the tray of chicken breasts and paprika came out of the oven. Two older women accosted him: 'Eat, eat, you're thin as a bird.'

He staggered out through the side pantry. Three pairs of eyes fixed him at once. Marta, Ola and Kuba were taking it in turns to dip their arms into the pitcher of bilberry *kompot*, their own bilberry eyes jumping with naughtiness they could see he was not going to put a stop to. Kuba had the face and eyes of a pine marten under his flopping black fringe. He had Franek's shifty look as well as his propitiatory charm. Ola, Genya's youngest, was curly and fair, most resembling a child from an old Pears soap advert or an Edwardian chocolate box, except that she was extremely grubby. They hauled up their fistfuls of bilberries and stuffed them into their mouths, giggling and spouting bilberries at the same time. Marta, a little older and more aware that even in the lax atmosphere of this night they might still get a row, paused with her purple elbows half out of the pitcher. There were footsteps in the passage from the kitchen. Babcia?! They ran away through the door ahead of him with loud shrieks and dripping arms.

The adjoining alcove was occupied by Hania and her friends, mostly on cushions, listening to music from a ghetto-blaster in the corner. Jacek, Hania's boyfriend, perched on the arm of her chair. Someone came in to tell him Janina wanted his help moving something:

'*Tesciowa wola*' (mother-in-law calls), one of the other girls said. Everyone laughed, as Jacek got up and sloped off with mock resignation. His family farmed at Bukowina about four kilometres away. Jon found it suddenly hugely comforting to think of a community in which you simply grew up, spent your life with the first person of your generation with whom you had the least affinity, and had more children who did the same. Hania was flushed, her round face shining. She was knitting on circular needles, unthinking as she threw her interjections into the conversation. The two other girls present were also knitting.

Waylaid at several points, it was past three the next time Jon looked at his watch. He thought he'd looked in every room. Had that slimeball Tomasz spirited her away somewhere? He hadn't seen Renata for a while either. He crunched back across the snow to Janina's. The ridge above him wore a headdress of firs, the moon flaring behind their black feathery tops with such brightness he could hardly breathe as he looked at it. Perhaps it was the cold. Moreover it seemed that the trees emitted a thin but blaring sound directly into his nervous system.

He tripped over Bogdan among the coats by the back door, sprawled with his head against his elbow, like a figure at a crime scene. It may have been his imagination, but the stagnant pool in the centre of the hallway seemed to have reduced slightly. On the stairs he all but fell over three drunken and sleeping ten year-olds, two near the foot and one at the corner. He crept past, knocking their last half glass of champagne onto the mat.

Recalling the one room he hadn't tried, he came back down again and found her at last, with Renata and both Wazzocks in the room full of beds. This was where the whole family still slept, despite the spacious house, in five single beds and a 'tapczan' - a fold-out sofa - one bed along each wall and two in the centre. The group sat in the far corner and next to Iwona was not the most accessible or obvious place for him to join it, but Jon had done with messing around and sat pointedly beside her anyway.

The topic of conversation was clearly the imminent Round Table Talks between the Jaruzelski government and Solidarity, and much too engaging for them to transfer to English, as they would normally have tried to do at his arrival. Iwona nonetheless turned and smiled her acknowledgement of his presence. Last time he had been in the country had been at the beginning of the strikes six months ago. The current atmosphere of tense expectation was quite different:

'Ah they will talk and talk. Nothing will come of it,' he had been assured numerous times.

'They say that not to be disappointed,' Roza had confided.

Now the discussion on the two dovetailed beds in the corner was all of what Michnik had said, and how Kuron and Geremek had conducted themselves during their fleeting appearances on the news - each of the young speakers revelling in the oddity of seeing these people on television at all, without quite acknowledging this as the source of their satisfaction. Iwona was suggesting something about Zbigniew Bujak, and, though he couldn't tell what she'd actually said, Jon was glad that Roza had made sure that he at least knew who these people were.

There was a slight pause, but to his surprise the conversation did not switch to English, ending abruptly as Renata announced her intention of going in search of more supplies of Russian champagne from Genya's. She would need to be accompanied by both men for this she insisted. Was she afraid of the dark? Did she plan to bring back a *crateload*? Tomasz grumbled but complied. Even to Jon, this seemed a bit contrived - as no doubt Tomasz feared, ambling after Renata with a poor grace. That must be a great thing about sisters. He couldn't ever imagine asking either of his brothers to do that for him.

'I tell her I want chance to know you,' Iwona answered the unspoken question with her usual simplicity, folding those definite hands of hers in her lap.

He felt himself almost start back, like a calf approaching the electric wire at the mere sound of the hum. Those quiet, drab girls with the controlling natures he had for so long homed in on, one after the other he had forced on them the challenge of *making* him fall in love with them. It

146

had been their task to *make* him happy, to render their companionship satisfactory, in short to fail. He couldn't bear the thought he might do that to Iwona, sitting there waiting for him to say something, to his eyes so trustingly.

In fact Iwona was at that very moment conscious that, since Kasper, it wasn't that she no longer trusted men, but that she mistrusted herself. She wondered what she was doing here, making a play for this foreigner, not wanting to seem to be chasing him for all the reasons one might pursue a Westerner. He was a foreigner and therefore glamorous, yet he seemed to her so lost. She doubted her motives and her judgement on both counts. Yet she thought she could still recognise kindness, even in the rather distant form in which it emanated from Jon.

He felt he must repay her for the supreme effort of assertion she had made - quite a feat for someone as reticent as herself - ask her something about herself, tell her something about himself. He'd never asked her about her work, for instance, or regaled her with tales of his multiplicity of dead-end jobs. He'd better get on with it. The silence was becoming awkward and she looked so lonely.

'Why are you sad?'

'I'm not sad,' she countered.

'I don't mean now. I mean all the time.' What a fool! Why on earth had he said that? Of all things? It was enough to make any woman run a mile. It would have made *him* run a mile. It wasn't right anyway - she didn't come across as *sad*, as a misery. Just her spirits were overlaid somehow.

'My boyfriend, he left me. He have the... what is it?... the affair with my friend.'

'My girlfriend left me to have a baby with another man. She's very sweet, the baby,' he traced a shape with his fingers in the air, which in his mind was the delicate little groove down the back of baby Rosie's neck. 'Martin, her husband, he's very nice, very clever and caring, and dark and hairy. He's very... he's not... me. Everything about him is not me.'

'Are you not clever then? You are not very hairy, I see, but aren't you the caring man also?'

'I am, but not like that. *He's* what she wanted.' It didn't hurt as much to say it as it had for months, for years, to know it, to feel it. All those times when there didn't seem to be enough oxygen in the air for him to breathe.

'You should meet my friend, Sylwia. She is extraordinary person.'

Just for a second, he saw how he would hold her face as he kissed her, and knew even as he thought it that he had squandered the moment. Cursed by self-consciousness, he told himself. He'd envisaged the action and now would be unable to execute it - not for a while anyway. They'd lapsed into silence again, under the weight of so much to say. Iwona found herself wondering - it seemed at first inconsequentially - about her grandmother. Would she reach the end of her own life with the sense her grandmother had that, whatever had befallen, she had done everything as she must? She exuded such continuity somehow, sitting there, Jon thought, suddenly certain: There *were* women you could love your whole life and who would repay you in kind. None of which alleviated the unbearable burden of silence which he knew it was his task to break…

'Ho hum,' he mused in desperation. She looked far more startled than the remark warranted. 'What is it? Did I say something wrong?' Now she appeared merely confused.

'I thought you said *kocham*,' she admitted finally.

'I said what?'

'*Kocham*. It means…,' she looked embarrassed, 'I love you'.

'You love…? Oh, you mean… it means… you… you thought I said…oh…no, I just said ho hum.'

'What does it mean ho hum?'

'It means nothing. I said it because we weren't saying anything.'

'I smell the blood of the Englishman.'

'You what… oh… right.'

'We don't very well understand the other.'

'I wish I *had* said it.'

'What?'

'You know.'

This wasn't exactly the sparkling conversation he'd hoped for. And at this point the Wazzocks bounded in, a fraction ahead of Renata, as though she'd been unable any longer physically to restrain them. They were followed a moment later by Franek, being led to bed by Janina. He was clutching the leather box he had presented to Jon:

'You leave my gift,' Franek accused him tearfully. 'You don't like it.'

'No!' Jon was horrified. 'I just forgot it. Tell him, Iwona. I like it very much.'

'You don't like it,' Franek repeated. Janina tutted at him, but did not appear to detract from his reproach.

'I didn't mean to leave it. I must have drunk too much champagne.' Iwona dutifully translated his words. This wasn't too good, having to plead drunkenness through the intermediary of the woman he'd been hoping to seduce, or at least impress a little. 'Look, I left my camera at Genya's too, I think. It doesn't mean I don't value my camera.' Jon was quite pleased with this logical point, and hoped that the indisputable value of Western gadgetry would assist his case. Franek, however, continued to display operatically injured feelings. 'I'm sorry,' Jon tried. 'It was a mistake.' What was it with this culture that you had to be wrong-footed like this all the time? So much generosity - why did they need to feel hard done-by as well? He'd noticed before that all his Polish acquaintances were much happier giving than receiving. The minute he gave them a present they were edgy until they'd given him another, bigger one back. Yes, they liked to be in credit - but now, in this further complication, they apparently had to believe their offering spurned and unappreciated to boot.

It had happened two days ago, he now remembered, when he had succumbed to the knitwear-sellers in Zakopane and bought a tiny pair of socks to take back for Baby Rosie. Did *they* not have socks that were good enough for him? Babcia and Pra-Babcia had wanted to know. Evidently a tightly knit community in every sense, the sock-selling syndicate of Babcias had wasted no time in spinning the yarn of his treachery far and wide. Naturally the news had got back to his accusers well before the evening meal. They had any number of beautiful socks for this baby of his, and lovely little cardigans. He had only to ask. Why had he not asked? Did he not like their handiwork? Even Genya had joined in until he'd felt thoroughly guilty, conscious that he'd committed a crime against their livelihood, their aesthetic, their skill and their hospitality all at once.

Janina had plumped Franek down on one of the beds and removed his shoes - but her wifely devotion went no further and she left him to it and went back to Genya's with a resigned laugh. The Wazzocks had reclaimed Iwona, seemingly without a struggle. All at once Jon did feel drunk - and lost and hopeless. Iwona was Polish too, after all, and probably viewed matters similarly. In her eyes he was no doubt an ingrate and all-round bad-guy - and as for that ridiculous conversation earlier.... He had definitely and decisively blown it. He didn't remember how he got upstairs to bed.

All night he pursued Iwona, through a series of hectic dreams, losing her every time in the random scene-shifts between increasingly improbable locations. He woke exhausted. It was nearly eleven. There were sounds of stirring from Janina's kitchen below. Iwona's party would be leaving later that day. He went downstairs, leaden and reduced from his hangover and the absence of hope. The drain in the hallway, he noticed ironically, was completely clear.

Janina was feeding pieces of chopped up crate into the stove in an attempt to resurrect the fire, while Kuba scurried about purloining the most lethal-looking bits - those sporting the largest number of jagged splinters and protruding nails - for his den outside. Iwona, Renata and the Wazzocks were sipping tea with an air of some fragility. Iwona filled him an enamel cup, set it on the edge of the stove, placed the element in it and plugged in the socket. Jon didn't know what to say, apart from thank you, and found himself staring at the looped element as it began to glow red.

'We are going again to Warsaw,' Iwona informed him. 'If you like you can change your ticket for the train. You can continue riding past Lodz and come with us. Renata and me, we will like to show you around. Renata is staying with me in my flat for some days, but we have another mattress. We can give this to you.'

Jon's brain leapt into action only enough to register that Renata and her companions appeared to be oblivious to this exchange, and to accomplish the thought that he could surely get a message to Roza about his delayed return through her office at the Economics Institute. He looked unbelieving at Iwona's smiling face:

'Thank you,' he said. 'I'm sure I will enjoy that very much. Thank you from the mountain.'

On the Revolutions of the Heavenly Spheres

Jesien - Autumn

'When you are among the crows,' Marzena advised me, 'you must croak as they do.'

The proverb furnished scant consolation for my latest public savaging at the hands of a gaggle of Babcias on my way home.

It had started the very first day we arrived in the town. We came out of our flat in the Assistants' Hostel and stood in the sunshine. Rob was persuading Koshka into her pushchair, while I popped back indoors to deposit our coats. It was a warm September day and we'd only end up carrying them. Two women appeared to be shouting at us from the other side of the street, but this seemed unlikely and we set off for the tram-stop. At once the ladies careered across the road with little regard for their personal safety and descended upon us, gesticulating. We were still unsure of our offence, until their pointing and shrill admonishment made it clear: between the bottom of our daughter's woollen trousers and the top of her socks was a gap of maybe half an inch.

So the nightmare began. Rob and I soon took to referring to any area of exposed flesh on a child as 'Babcia bait'. When I die, I shall see advancing towards me a headscarved old woman, one finger raised, mouth working furiously, uttering a stream of accusations no less unnerving as they become more intelligible, that icon of condemnatory justice, a Polish Babcia. I was fast coming round to the view that Poland specialised in all forms of persecution and that the ante-natal variety might turn out to have been a mere taster.

Certain codes - probably instituted and most definitely enforced by Babcias - govern life in Poland, particularly as regards children. At the beginning of September, irrespective of temperature, the woollen hats go on. These are to be worn by all children, including teenagers, at least until the end of May when they will be exchanged for sun-hats. A sustained heat-wave in June might finally remove the woollen tights (worn by boys under their trousers as well as girls) and lace-up ankle-boots. Poles mistrust good weather as they do all manifestations of benevolent fortune.

There are two things all Poles appear to know effortlessly at all times: the number of metres comprising any room or flat, and the number of degrees of that day's temperature. At first I was slow to realise that this seemingly mystical ability to cite degrees Celsius derived from the simple fact that everyone had a thermometer on their balcony and bothered to consult it each morning. The function of this knowledge was always to prove that the day was colder than it felt, and if this failed there was always the proviso 'ah, but there's a wind.' In short, there was no such thing as a hot day until temperatures reached such dizzy heights that the situation became dangerous and it was necessary to cover up children for the opposite reason.

No doubt the fact that Poland can get seriously cold during 'our wicked winter', as the Polish nursery rhyme has it, has indelibly printed on the collective psyche that cold temperatures can kill. No doubt the British tendency to go around in T-shirts the minute it's not actually raining is similarly culturally determined. The fact that I used to be sent to school, as were many British children, with bare legs turning white then red then blue in December probably has an equally fascinating social and ideological history. Cultural conditioning or not, constantly trying to make a two year-old wear significantly more clothing than they physically feel the need for is hard work - especially if you secretly agree with them.

Consequently, I engaged in a power struggle with my child, with all the unpleasantness but none of the conviction required, and *still* fell foul of the Babcia-brigade on every excursion. And the penalties for non-compliance with these codes is severe. You will be pointed and stared at, not once but wherever you go *all* day. Women will talk loudly about 'that poor child,' how it 'will be ill this very night,' 'what kind of mother' and so forth. The offending mother is meant to hear these remarks, to feel the heat of these glares, which are not susceptible to returned looks or rueful smiles. It is not pleasant to be stared and pointed at by people who will not drop their eyes, yet to them it is their right to do so, for *you* are in the *wrong*, you are committing an outrage, the child has been allowed to take off her hat, what *are* you thinking of? The whole society would endorse them, they feel - and you feel it too.

This in itself is enough to make you wish you'd never got up in the morning, yet this is, so to speak, the *soft* policeman. In the course of a 'bad day' - one on which you have unwittingly transgressed - you must contend with women of middle age and older, who will simply harangue you in the street:

'What are you doing, it's *cold*? Put her gloves back on!'

'Can't you see her on those steps?'

'What on earth are you doing letting her climb that wall?'

'She's on the slide. Take her off! She'll fall!'

The first sentence in Polish Koshka ever uttered was in self-defence, as an irate Babcia tried to pluck her from the steps of a slide:

'*Nie spadnę!* I *won't* fall.

The aggression injected into their admonitory phrases is in proportion to your deviance, which they experience as both appalling and incomprehensible. The punch of bad feeling packed by the average Polish granny - stored up over a lifetime to be fired off at will - is considerable, and you may be sure she will not spare you any of it.

At first I thought that it was merely my linguistic inadequacy which prevented me from being able to explain properly, but I soon learned that there *is* no language for contradicting a Polish Babcia. The least resistance and the fiercest breed of Babcia would go berserk, hurling streams of abuse that left me shaking. Five or six encounters like this in a day, not to mention being stared at like a criminal between times, and I defy any mother not to be a wreck.

I had made friends with a young American woman, living with her Polish husband and new baby nearby. Pushing Koshka in her pushchair, I was out with Genevieve, who was carrying little Lilka in a baby-sling, then still rare in Poland. She was accosted three times on the hundred yard stretch between the tram-stop and the café, our destination:

'Why are you carrying the baby like that?' one Babcia demanded. 'It's not allowed!' '*To nie wolno!*' How I'd come to hate that phrase!

'Its back will be destroyed!' a second one asserted.

'One of her ears isn't covered up properly by her hat,' another observed. 'She will get wind in her ears. Ach, what a mother!'

In the dark sanctuary of the *kawiarnia*, we collapsed into a corner over our tea and let off steam. Aside from a general twitchiness when out in public and a conviction that we were being stared at, we were both beginning to manifest symptoms of the condition I'd once seen described as 'immigrant rage'. Those who by virtue of their difference are continually failing by the standards of the society they have entered often retaliate along the lines: 'You think the way you all do things is so great, well, let me tell you…'

'I'm sick to death of the way they let their dogs shit all over the children's play-parks here,' Genevieve was saying. 'It's disgusting! What am I going to do when Lilka's older?' The dog issue was becoming one of her regular rants, while I too was developing an eye eager for double standards:

'Those same Babcias who worry so much about kids not wearing hats let the ones they're looking after run around with lollipops sticking out of their mouths. I've seen it loads of times. If one of them fell...' We tutted mournfully and shook our heads.

'Maciek's supportive, but he doesn't see what I'm complaining about. They're only showing concern, he says. He doesn't understand how I manage to do things wrong so much. His mother doesn't either. He likes the baby-sling but he thinks perhaps it isn't worth the trouble.' Genevieve looked down at her own hands around the glass of tea. 'I just want to be able to do what I think is best with my baby...' her voice wobbled.

Lilka snuffled into life and began rootling about with her nose in her mother's blouse.

'Look on the bright side,' I tried to be fair. 'Poles are never funny about breastfeeding, are they?'

'I guess not,' Genevieve adjusted the baby into the crook of her arm, lifting her blouse with the other hand.

'Are you ready to run the gauntlet?' I asked when they'd finished and Lilka had dozed off once more.

Genevieve sniffed. 'I reckon so.'

She went ahead of me, while I managed to get Koshka's pushchair stuck in the doorway. For a moment I saw her from behind, looking slight and vulnerable in a patch of sunlight in the Market Square. A group of elderly ladies had been chatting by the fountain in front of the Town Hall. They were on her like a swarm of bees.

I tried to account for the difference to Marzena, struggling to put it into Polish:

'Perhaps in Britain we just don't care - or perhaps there's a taboo about telling other people how to do their job.' Yet as far as the Babcias were concerned, I realised, the care of young children was *not* the mother's job. Far too important to be left to those flighty young working women. It wasn't insulting to set them straight in the street, just as they set their own daughters straight at home. These mothers couldn't be expected to know how to do things properly without guidance. After all, in practice, with three generations often under one roof and mothers absent during the day, who was it that minded the little ones most of the time?

It was a shock, then, to discover that many Babcias were raising children for the first time.

'I thought the whole point about grannies was their experience,' I protested when Marzena told me.

'Of course not,' she laughed. 'When we were young, my sister and I, my mother worked and we were with *her* mother, *our* Babcia, during the day. Now my mother is taking care of my sister's boy, Szymon. She thinks he is really abnormal, he runs about so much. She can't move so fast and she worries.'

154

Marzena's husband, Adam, came into their flat as we were having this conversation. Marzena had to go and change her little boy's nappy on the sofa, but Adam was happy to see me, and always enjoyed an opportunity to practice his English. Since I was a woman and standing in a kitchen, he also thought nothing of asking me to fetch him a drink:

'Not tea please, Helena. Coke. Do you think you could warm it for me a little? I am beginning a flu in my throat and the cold drinks are very dangerous for this conditions.'

A walking illustration of the effects of grand-matriarchy, if ever there was one! So *that* was how Polish men got away with their attitudes to women, their assumptions of intellectual superiority, in a society where the women seemed to run everything and do most of the work. If the men had tried to be macho, they'd have been lost, but as such a bunch of granny's boys and manifest sissies, the women let them have their supposed superiority but didn't have to take them too seriously. Many Polish men managed to retain a kind of innocence, born of being looked after by Babcias, mothers then wives and never having to take full responsibility. Adam had this appealing quality too, a sweetness, an eagerness, a sense of needing to be taken care of, which was presumably why I was bringing him his warm coke on a tray rather than tipping it over his head.

I might worry about the disenfranchised young mothers, but perhaps it wasn't such a bad deal. If they could just hold out until their own accession to Babcia-dom then absolute power at last awaited them. Most Polish households were ruled by a Babcia. The 'Dziadeks', or Grandads, were mere ciphers in comparison.

Marzena turned to Adam:

'Helenka has been creating a scandal again,' she teased me. 'She has allowed her little one to sit down in the sandpit where she will get *mokra pupcia*,' ('wet botty'). 'It's terrible!'

'No wonder I'm a social outcast!'

'When you are among the crows…'

It was easy for Marzena to say it, I thought. She was brought up here. She complied naturally. She wasn't under continuous assault for endangering her child by dressing it inadequately, for being a bad mother. Effortlessly, she knew what the requirements were, and so did not transgress half as often. Well, actually she did sometimes - which is probably why we were having this conversation at all. She had two year-old twins and, as Adam explained to me, as parents they had given up the unequal fight:

'There are two of them and two of us - but look how much energy they have? We are out-numbered really. So if they want to climb and jump and pull off their hats, I'm not going to be always fighting and always losing. Lucynka loves to swing on those bars and Lukasz is crazy for pulling off his mittens and burying them in the *piaskownica* - what do you say, the sandbox?'

'I say the sandpit, but I think Americans call it the sandbox.'

'Well, if I am trying to stop it, he thinks it is all the time a better game - much more funnier for him, and then Lucynka will join him... I am without doubt one hundred percent defeated,' he lifted up his hands. His mother was horrified whenever she came to stay, he admitted, 'but they are healthy and happy and we are not destroyed... We give it up now.'

Koshka and the twins were certainly kindred spirits, which was just as well, since it seemed that only her fellow 'delinquents' were going to be allowed to play with her. Her other two companions, Marta and Ludwika, at five and three, roamed the playground and the building site behind the flats completely unsupervised at all hours. Their parents introduced themselves one day when I took the children home after Ludwika had fallen out of a tree:

'I am Gregorz and this is Iza,' the man in the slippers and baggy cardigan raised his right eyebrow in a circumflex. 'We are, how you say, sky mechanics?'

This turned out to be a description of their profession rather than their attitude to life, though coming to know them better, the phrase would probably cover both. As birthplace of Copernicus, the town naturally boasted several fine observatories and a renowned department of astronomy for its university. It was a mixture of logic and lackadaisicality with which Grzegorz and Iza raised their children, gambling on the probability that nothing too terrible would befall them and that, this being so, they would grow up having had a hardy and unimpeded childhood, free to develop in what directions they chose. It was unclear whether a scientific rationality or sheer otherworldliness led to this approach. It was notable that both of these families had come from far away and had no Babcias of their own nearby to keep them in line.

These, then, became our daughter's friends and ours - which was just as well, since all the other mothers in the dilapidated playground (to which I took her religiously every day to help her make friends) appeared to ostracise us, dragging their reluctant children away whenever they approached Koshka in the sandpit:

'Come away, she doesn't understand.' The mothers would then gather in groups and discuss us, with regular tuts and gestures and glances, audibly and, even with my imperfect Polish, all too comprehensibly. One day I marched over to them:

'She may not understand but I do - so please talk more quietly. So much for the famous Polish hospitality!' I added as I stalked off, knowing it was the only blow beneath the belt I was capable of delivering.

They were silent for a minute and they did talk more quietly - though no less venomously - after that. The hospitality jibe probably didn't even register, I thought miserably, since cultural difference governed the definition of that virtue as it did everything else. For them, hospitality was a matter of lavish displays and generous provision of abundant and beautifully prepared food to those who qualified for it. It had nothing to do with friendliness to strangers. The concept of a foreigner in your country as a 'guest' didn't seem to have much purchase. Rob and I were forever being told that 'naturally we Poles are very hospitable' by people from whom we had never received so much as a crumb. At first we used to misread this as a preamble to an invitation, and had looked eager, got ready gratefully to accept. On the contrary, we learnt slowly, it was just a statement of fact to be acknowledged.

We had indeed experienced some wonderfully warm and generous hospitality during our time in Poland. There were some occasions, though, which seemed to be more about *demonstrating* something to the guests - and perhaps themselves - than about pleasing or getting to know them. Precisely because there were no half-measures, the very expectations Poles placed on themselves could become a burden. Together with the huge amount of effort - never mind expense - involved, it was easy to see why they might want to avoid such an undertaking altogether.

Certainly, *informal* hospitality wasn't the order of the day. The only woman from the Hostel group I had ever persuaded to come back to my flat spent the time asking leading questions about our wealth and status back in Britain and, as ever in Poland, how much we currently earned. She could hardly wait to get out and tell everyone that I'd '*only given her tea and biscuits!*' A reciprocal invitation had not been forthcoming.

Koshka begged me to teach her Polish so that she could show she did understand, so I started naming things to her around the flat in Polish and giving her little instructions. Polish is very good on imperatives, which are always juicy, enjoyable to say and to the point. Marzena helped me out, telling me the names of objects I didn't know.

I didn't want to moan to Marzena about people who might, after all, be her friends, but it was still a relief to have someone with whom to lick my Babcia-inflicted wounds from time to time.

'You can get rid of Communism,' I complained one day, 'but it'll take a hell of a lot longer to overthrow *Babciaism*, this… this *regime* of governing Babcias and their conformity police.'

'And the priests,' Adam added.

I'd taken Koshka to church only once since we'd lived in the town. The priest had delivered a sermon on the necessity of withstanding the invasion of foreign values that threatened to corrupt their country. It didn't seem to be the materialism he was worried about, but rather the licentiousness and in particular the tolerance of abortion. Since Communist states had permitted abortion as a form of birth control for years, it seemed a bit rich to define it as a Western value, but it was when he began to address the children directly that I became really uncomfortable. I didn't think the little cluster of two, three and four year-olds, including Koshka, gathered at the front for a better view were ready for the information that mummies and daddies might ever, at any time, not want a baby - never mind that they might do anything about it, or, more specifically, 'put it to death' as the priest was busy announcing. There was pressure in Poland to make abortion illegal, and though this was not yet the case, many doctors already refused to perform them as a matter of conscience.

'So girls go to Hungary instead, on buses,' Marzena informed me. 'They call them abortion tours.'

'I'd like all of you to go home today,' the priest had admonished the children, 'and say to your mummy and daddy, thank you for letting me live.'

Hotel Asystencki

Returning to Poland after two years, the most immediately visible changes - the sight of butcher's shops full of meat, people rooting in bins and the presence of beggars - were in some ways less surprising than the altered demeanour of those in positions of petty power. *Portiery*, for example. In former times, three out of four of these people, usually women, who had to be negotiated on entering most public buildings or institutions, were officious and unpleasant. Regular visitors soon got to know the one who stood out, 'the nice one.'

The Hotel Asystencki on Gagarin Street had four *portierki,* on rotating shifts, yet, of these, three were polite and helpful, happy to show where the hoover was and relay phone messages. Only one remained in the old mode, resentful and cantankerous, requiring to be shown legitimation cards and other multiply signed paperwork at every opportunity, declaring simple requests 'impossible.' The experience was repeated in various locations: now 'the grumpy one,' the bad-tempered, obstreperous one, stuck out, the conspicuous minority. The strange thing was that these were the same people as before. The personnel had not altered, simply the prevailing ethos no longer empowered or endorsed such behaviour, but it was a source of continual amazement to me that this could effect so swiftly such apparent change of heart.

Ours was a one room flat, with bars on the windows and a huge bookcase dividing the main room. It was just the right size for a two year-old and Koshka loved it. We, her parents, could never get too far away and there was no corner from which she could not see or hear both of us. There was a hatch to crawl through from the kitchen and a fold-out table over her bed enabling her to bounce while painting or eating. Getting her to sleep in such a confined space, with Rob already at the desk, was not easy. Taking her nap later and later in the day, she was still full of beans by the time we needed to start 'our' evening without her. Rob had to write a series of lectures on early American literature, a topic he confessed to knowing next-to-nothing about. Koshka's bed-time she-nanigans, which once he would have found at least partly amusing, now brought forth thunderous denunciations of the spare-the-rod variety, delivered in the style of Cotton Mather and the other New England, Puritan divines in whose company he walked.

We were granted a welcome interlude from these struggles when my brother and his American girlfriend came to stay. The flat became so impossibly crowded that daily life became fun, like camping, and Rob retired to the library to write his lectures. Perhaps, as far as Dave and Gina were concerned, the world we showed them was quaint and not quite real, but at least this gave us the chance to re-imagine the place and to see afresh how much we loved it.

The town looked exactly as I had imagined Hamelin when I was a child, nestled on the banks of the fast-flowing river, ringed with pine forests, the towers of its brick churches low against the sky. Crossing the bridge from the railway station, we pointed out the picturesque view with pride, the wide water rushing past small islands of reeds.

Our guests duly appreciated everything, strolling the streets between the two market squares, enjoying how the mellow light and the shadows fell on the honey-coloured and pale blue facades of the buildings, or the bright washing strung between the balconies of the backstreets, while we thought how lucky we were to live in such a lovely place. In front of the Ratusz, the Town Hall, the statue of a fiddler boy, who had once rid the town of a plague of frogs, stood in the centre of a stone basin, ringed by seven brass frogs spouting water from their mouths.

'The golden frogs!' shouted Koshka, who always loved to come there, cupping their smooth backs under one hand and tickling her other palm with water. We took our visitors into the nearby *Garmazeria* where our daughter's favourite, '*gulasz z makaronem*', was priced by placing the plate of spaghetti onto the scales and then adding the ladles of goulash. We drank fizzy orange sitting on high stools, hypnotised by the slow revolutions of the chickens in the rotisserie.

Adam had urged us to visit the geological exhibition currently showing at his Institute in one of the streets near the New Market square.

'It begin here but it will travel whole Poland. This exhibits will arrive to Warsaw for day of Saint Barbara,' he added. 'You know perhaps that she is special saint for all miners and geologs.'

Debating whether Saint Barbara was also, therefore, the patron of underground metro systems, we set off in search of the building. Twice, people came out of their shops to exclaim over Koshka's red hair, wanting to give her chocolate. Poles didn't worry about junk food and ruining teeth. It wasn't so long ago that there hadn't been any such snacks available and sweets had been on the ration. Perhaps I could give myself a break and not worry either. It didn't seem fair to have to be lumbered with my own cultural anxieties as well as dealing with the burden of Polish ones every day!

Koshka having dragged us round the displays of 'pretty stones' in record time, Gina and I sat down by the statue of Copernicus to wait for my brother and Rob to come out of the exhibition. Part of the cobbled street had been dug up and there were three large piles of fresh sand. Two Romanian gypsy children, about five and seven years old, were supposed to be begging in the doorway opposite, but when they saw Koshka inspecting the first heap of sand they came over and joined her. The three of them soon discovered that they could scrabble up the highest mound and fling themselves from it, landing on their bottoms in the smallest pile.

People were streaming out from evening Mass. The girls wore pink woollen tights, black shiny shoes and denim skirts edged with broderie anglaise, the boys little suit jackets and buttoned-up collars. Several of the girls had been allowed to take Barbies to keep them quiet in church and clutched one in each hand. The children's heads twisted on their necks as they passed, unable to take their eyes from the three figures flying from the sand-heaps over and over. It was not easy to tell whether their looks conveyed envy or disdain. No similar ambiguity was discernible in the gaze of their parents as they hurried them away.

Gina was interested in everything: 'Hey, Dave, come take a look at this,' while my brother was clearly very much interested in Gina. For Rob and me it was a new kind of pleasure to take them for coffee and cakes at 'Under the Apron,' to browse with them in the Mickiewicza Market or wander in the Bydgoski Park, basking in the beautiful surroundings of our life and the proximity of their recently discovered love. Holding hands behind the pushchair, we showed off our child, our existence, feeling that we inhabited the much-to-be-desired next stage in a natural and fulfilling trajectory.

I would have liked to show them my recent discovery, the Russians' Market, as well, but my brother's visit to Poland coinciding with that of the Pope made this impossible. The Russians, with their panoply of wares spread out on blankets on the bonnets of their battered cars, were deemed by the city authorities too unsightly, even from the air. The papal helicopter flew over the town, while the Russians' usual pitch sported several rows of flower-stalls with brightly coloured sunshades.

It wasn't easy to return to the reality of our 'normal life' when our guests had gone. In common with most Polish tower blocks, the hostel had its own play-area adjacent to the building. It had been vandalised the previous summer, and only the sandpit remained intact. The slide had a rail missing, the see-saw seats were cracked down the middle. The sole remaining swing had a metal spar dangling above it making it suitable only for pushing dolls to and fro. For a culture so devoted to children and anxious about their safety, it appeared a strange anomaly. All the residents continued to use it and no attempt was ever made to repair it. Koshka had dubbed it 'the Broken Playground,' and we went there every day. Like the dead animals that lay for weeks by the roadsides or next to the tram tracks, it wasn't quite anyone's responsibility to deal with these matters any more. Or at least, if it was, there was no longer the structure in place for ensuring that they did so.

Grzegorz jiggled his eyebrows up and down in the way he always did to signal ironic enjoyment of 'such anarchistic situation.' There was still a Resident's Committee, he told me, but its chairman didn't do much.

'It is Ryszard - you know him a little?'

'I was introduced to him once, when we first moved in.' I recalled a burly historian with a fluffy beard and very soft hands, a passion for the life of Napoleon and collecting antiquarian books. 'He seemed a nice man.'

'He is a nice man, but you know his name means "not taking care", what is it, careless? Or, how do you say it? Neglecting?'

'Ryszard means that?'

'No, no, his family name.'

I knew his wife, Halina, very slightly too - largely because she was too indecisive and etiolated a person to shun me properly like the others and hence lowered her eyes and gave muttered responses to my '*dzien dobry*' whenever we ran into one another. She was one of the most haunted people I've ever met, forever trying to smooth down her wispy fair hair, looking out from the dark shadows round her eyes.

'Her daughter, Kinga, is stronger than her,' Marzena confided to me once. 'Her children, she can't control them - but she has to.' As well as Kinga, Halina had a son, barely toddling.

'But those children always behave so perfectly,' I protested. Kinga always struck me as a sharp girl, with a real glint in her eye, a spirit not very successfully repressed, but always impeccably behaved. Michal too.

'Those children behave so well in public because if they don't afterwards there are reproaches and rages. Halina doesn't sleep because she is ashamed of her anger.'

Poor Halina, eaten up with remorse at her ineffectual mothering, driven to fury by trying to live up to a standard she had not shaped. The one job she was supposed to be able to do, she knew she was not very good at and she cursed herself. It looked as if Ryszard was not taking care in that department either.

'Mostly he is not there,' Marzena explained, 'and when he is, she has to keep them quiet for his work.'

'Of course,' I said grimly. I knew about *that*. Clearly, there was a price to pay for that conformity which always seemed to be so effortless to most of these Polish women. I resolved to try and help Halina out if I ever got the chance. Not that an association with me was likely to do her reputation as a mother much good!

'Yes but my children are crazy - no-one spoke to me for a long time either,' Marzena reassured me. 'In the end they will speak. I am sure of it.'

'I'm not sure I'll want to speak to *them* by that time,' I grumbled.

Zlobek

All of which left me with the necessity of finding somewhere Koshka could play with other children and pick up more Polish. I also wanted to do some part-time work if I could. Koshka was too young for Pre-School so I would have to explore the option of a Zlobek, or Nursery, even though I was assured that only bad mothers deposited their children in such places. I took that with a pinch of salt. They must mean mothers who couldn't afford to take the second eighteen months of maternity leave on half pay - supposing the government hadn't abolished that already. Or mothers who had not had the foresight to have a Babcia on hand to perform this function for them, namely working-class mothers, with Babcias too young or too strapped for cash to give up work.

I wheeled the pushchair up the cinder track from the tram-stop. The Nursery was a low, grey building with white windows, belonging to Merinotex, the adjacent textile factory. Beyond the green metal gate embossed with two burnished suns, faded wooden structures - trams, trains, rockets and aeroplanes - rose from the long wet grass. To my eyes it resembled a children's paradise, but I remembered that, due to the dangers of 'mokra pupcia' and indeed 'mokre' everything else from the damp vegetation, they would be unlikely to be permitted to play there except in the height of summer.

The impression of neglect was in marked contrast to the interior of the building. A Polish nursery is no amateur affair. Despite the white paint and stone floors characteristic of old hospitals, it reminded me most of my sixth-form college. It had its Dyrektor's office, a finance office, a medical room and several kitchens, giving out the mingled smells of soup and fruit *kompot*.

Being used to village halls, shared with numerous other groups like the Brownies and the W.I., where the playgroup has a cupboard to keep its things, I was rather overwhelmed by this establishment. Nor was it going to be that easy to gain admission, since, as the Pani Dyrektor quickly pointed out, I had none of the relevant qualifications. A heavily made-up lady, with silver nails and copper hair, she nonetheless agreed that, subject to medical approval, I could come on Tuesdays and sing English songs and play action games with the children. She handed me a list of the X-rays and tests for various parasites which would be needed. My daughter would be allowed to accompany me and to participate in the life of the Zlobek, including the meals, for that day.

'Medically approved,' therefore, we re-entered the Zlobek two weeks later. The Pani Dyrektor showed me into the classroom for Koshka's age-group and introduced me to the first of the 'Ciocias' or 'Aunties'. Ciocia Grazyna wore a blue overall and her dark hair in bunches. She had been to England once, she said, to Leeds to visit her Uncle:

'Oh, yes, I remember your country, with its very short grass.'

The room - in reality one of a suite of rooms - was beautifully appointed: bright, airy and spacious, with tables and chairs at one end for mealtimes and shelves of toys around a large floor-space covered with a huge, patterned rug. The shelves around the walls displayed tin lorries and clockwork trains, stick puppets of storks and frogs, of Red Riding Hood and Baba Jaga, plastic Russian dolls with full cheeks and blue slanted eyes, flat-faced cuddly cats in checked trouser-suits and corduroy goats in neckerchiefs and long shorts. There was a little cloakroom of pegs and wooden painted lockers, a bedroom full of neatly made camp-beds for 'lezakowanie' (the designated two-hour rest period each day), and a washroom with rows of little basins. There was even a cinema, with green wooden seats for showing slide films, its ante-room set out with larger toys: a big brown velvet rocking horse, echelons of wicker prams and wooden cradles, piles of carefully folded sets of doll's bedding in dimmed green and orange, 1950s prints.

It was still early, the children having just finished breakfast, though some had arrived before the morning shift at six. Ciocia Bogusia, a woman in her fifties with a bun on top of her head and very flat feet, was ordering them to sit in a large circle on the rug, insisting on a certain distance between each child before she would deposit in front of them their allocation of 'klotski', tipping a small heap of these wooden bricks in front of each one from a basket she carried as she moved around the circle. I told myself that her strong resemblance to the Baba Jaga puppet on the shelf - that chin approaching the nose effect - did not mean that she might not be a very nice woman.

'Now, play,' she commanded them, walking round the circle with her basket.

Each child began to build or arrange something. Talking was forbidden - 'Quiet! Now play.' - as was touching a neighbour's bricks, much less swapping or embarking on any co-operative enterprise. Sitting on a bench at the side with Ciocia Grazyna, I suppose I should not have been surprised that leftover Communist habits of authoritarianism should take this form, for it was clear that conformity and obedience were the priority and solidarity among the construction workers was to be prevented at all costs. I was quite glad that Koshka snuggled beside me and showed no sign of yet wanting to join in. Children who spoke, moved closer to each other or handled bricks not allocated to them were shouted at, then jerked to their feet and sat down hard.

As the morning went on, I was amazed at the level of irascibility and physical aggression the women managed to maintain. Cioca Jadzia was dark and thin, about forty. She had recurrent stomach problems, she told me, for which she had to drink a lot of coffee. When her stomach was not giving her trouble, she could be quite loving with the children, stroking them as she held them on her knee, but became at other times bad-tempered and unpredictable. Ciocia Grazyna appeared a softer, more compliant person generally, the only one of the three with a child of her own. She scolded the children for acts of non-conformity but rarely manhandled them.

Ciocia Bogusia, on the other hand, was relentless. She seemed to feel it her moral duty. Children were punished for stepping off the rug at any time, Kamilka for wheeling her toy pram off the approved route, Adas for making an engine noise as he pushed his lorry, Jacek for helping Damian with his puzzle, Lidka for skipping rather than walking. It wasn't just the least sign of boisterousness but the least sign of *life* that called down retribution. The flow of reprimand never stopped. Surely it couldn't be like this all the time? I hoped - God forbid - they weren't trying to impress me, to show me they ran a 'tight ship' or something. Then again, at least if they were, the regime would relax eventually. I could help that to happen.

When it was time for me to do my party-piece, I wanted the children to sit spaced out on the rug so they would have enough room to do the actions, to stand up and to dance about, but the Ciocias were having none of this. They crammed the entire class onto two low benches, with pinches and slaps for anyone who did not sit down fast or remain still enough - and for Damian, who fell off the end.

'Be quiet,' Ciocia Bogusia hissed at them. 'Auntie is going to sing you a song.'

Ciocia Jadzia walked up and down behind the benches, poking any fidgeters in the back with an extremely bony-looking forefinger. I sang 'Cockles and Mussels,' just to get them used to me and the guitar, Bogusia scolding the inattentive throughout. After that I insisted that they had to be able to move their arms and we did a fairly successful rendition of 'The Wheels on the Bus' - except for poor Damian who was jogged off the end again and pounced on, though luckily only by Grazyna.

'Now you have to let them lie down on the rug,' I told the Ciocias, and we embarked on 'See the Little Rabbits Sleeping.' I got Koshka to show them what to do, so that they knew to leap up at 'cock-a-doodle-do' in the middle and hop around for 'Hop, little rabbits, hop,hop,hop.' I had to make sure that the Ciocias as well as children had absorbed what 'hop' meant or I was pretty sure Bogusia and Jadzia would wade in among the bouncing bunnies dispensing summary justice. Luckily 'hop, hop, hop,' is close enough to 'hop sa sa' in Polish, but even with my precautions, at the crucial moment of that first cockcrow, I had to combine my singing with some serious eyebrow-work and head-nodding to reassure them that this frenzied hopping was indeed part of the plan in order to avert an imminent baton charge by the Ciocias.

By the time we moved onto 'Jingle Jangle Scarecrow' and 'Row, Row, Row Your Boat' I was beginning to enjoy myself almost as much as the children.

'Row, row, row your boat gently down the stream.

If you see a crocodile don't forget to scream - *aaaaaaaaaagh*'

I had the feeling that 'scream' would be the first English word every child in the room would learn. No wonder the Ciocias thought me a subversive influence. Taking my pedagogical responsibilities more seriously, I taught them 'Heads and Shoulders, Knees and Toes' and 'If You're Happy and You Know It Clap Your Hands', noting with satisfaction that the children mastered clap, stamp and nod without any difficulty.

At the appointed time, the children filed into the bathroom, and sat for forty-five minutes on the plastic potties or 'nocniki,' no chatting or fidgeting allowed, and woe betide any who stood up before authorised to do so. At the end, they waddled into a queue with their tights round their ankles to have them pulled up by the Ciocias. Koshka, who pulled up her own, was considered a prodigy, but when Lidka tried to emulate her she was slapped and told she'd be locked in a cupboard. Then they were taken into the *lezakowanie* room full of camp-beds, dressed in their pajamas and lulled to sleep with menaces, so the Ciocias could go for their long-awaited coffee and cigarette break.

I was left holding the fort, trying unsuccessfully to persuade Koshka that she really needed to sleep in this strange place a full two hours before she was used to. In the end I gave up and took her back into the main room and let her look at some toys. I was frustrated that she wouldn't take her nap earlier, since it meant she'd be wide awake that evening when Rob would have to start working on his lecture. More stress and Cotton Mather-like pronouncements would undoubtedly ensue.

Having decided very swiftly that I would under no circumstances leave Koshka unattended in the care of these women - I'd already seen Bogusia eyeing her and knew she'd dearly like to get her hands on my daughter and sort her out - I was left with my childcare problem unresolved. Still, Koshka had made friends with Adas and Lidka, so I thought I would come back. There were bound to be some cultural differences after all, and, having seen how the Ciocias loved any opportunity for extra breaks, I was confident I could persuade them to let me do the singing session on my own before long. I could have a little sing-along in the bathroom during the interminable *nocniki* hour too. I'd already spotted a ledge above the radiator I could perch on.

'Sing another song, please.' It was Ciocia Jadzia, who had returned alone. 'A sad one.'

I sang her 'Spancil Hill' as the first one that came into my head. I knew Jadzia did not understand a single word of English and I had reached the final verse before I saw the tears rolling down her face.

'It's an Irish song,' I answered her questions. 'My grandmother taught it to me.'

'Sing another Irish one. Are they the most sad?'

The most mournful Irish ballads I could muster had her in tears for the rest of *lezakowanie.*

'Do you sing?' I asked her. 'Will you teach me some Polish songs?'

'Not today. My stomach is too bad.' She stopped crying abruptly.

Grazyna and Bogusia were back and it was time to get the children up for 'obiad', the main meal, at the little tables. There was plenty of force-feeding and consequent gagging, threats to lock in cupboards or never be reunited with parents unless they ate their schnitzel or their sour-cabbage and beetroot salad. I was desperate to go home, to breathe on the tram, free from this atmosphere of constant oppression, but almost as soon as the meal was over, Bogusia and Jadzia knocked off. Grazyna and I combed the children's hair and waited for their parents to collect them in dribs and drabs as they came off shift.

'Who is that little boy?' I asked her. I'd noticed him particularly at *lezakowanie.* His limbs were so spindly and his hair and complexion so pale he looked almost albino, except that his eyes were a watery blue. He struck me as a walking separation trauma, tremulous, peeled and quaking, continually shivering, like a person with no outer skin. It was appalling to think of such a person away from his mother, never mind in such a harsh environment. 'Is there something wrong with him? I mean, is he ill somehow?'

'Pawelek? Yes, he's not a full boy,' Grazyna said matter-of-factly.

'Is it a condition, or was he born early or something?'

'I'm not sure exactly. I think so.'

He was one of the last to go home. I gave him another toy car, a bigger one, to play with as he sat on the floor with his spider limbs splayed out around him. The look of joy on his face was too much to bear. I had to go to the bathroom to blow my nose and recover my composure. When Grazyna wanted me to sing again, I looked at Pawelek and began 'Early One Morning,' even though I knew only one verse, simply for the lines:

'Oh, don't deceive me, oh never leave me,
How could you treat a poor maiden so?'

He appeared mesmerised by the singing, and gazed at me as if in a pleasant trance. Then he smiled. That would be Pawelek's song, I vowed. I would sing it to him every week. His mother was a small woman, hurrying in, smiling nervously. The ecstasy on Pawelek's face when he saw her occasioned another trip to the bathroom for me.

Kolegium

Pawelek's mother *had* to work, and here was me wanting to do so just because I felt like it. I resolved not to leave Koshka in any such institution on such flimsy grounds. If I didn't work till she was older, well then, it wasn't so long out of a whole life, was it? And at least I had the luxury of choosing. Then Marzena solved the problem by proposing that she and I did a swap. She'd been offered a morning's music teaching on a Wednesday, whereas she'd heard the teacher training college was looking for a native speaker of English to work similar hours on Mondays. Perfect. Koshka loved Marzena and the twins, while they seemed very much at home in our flat.

The Dyrektor of the College of Teachers of Foreign Languages introduced himself as Jerzy Komorowski.

'You must to excuse the scarves,' he said, indicating the two around his throat. 'I have a small pneumonia and have to be careful.'

I had left Koshka happily playing with Lucynka and Lukasz, having guiltily picked up the two plastic bags I'd seen lying about. These had been unheard of in Poland just a few years before, and few seemed to be aware of their dangers to children, particularly as the warnings on them were often in German. If they were kept out of the hands of children it was only because they were status symbols too precious to be wasted.

I tried to concentrate. The College had been awarded a large grant by the out-going government, Jerzy was explaining, probably because they knew they would not have to fund the project themselves beyond this year.

'And what is the project?'

'At the moment, as you know, we have problem in Poland with many teachers of Russian. Everybody had to learn this language but now nobody at all wants to do so. Our college prepares teachers of foreign languages to teach in schools. This will bring about the improvement of teaching English, French and German to our schoolchildren. Not this year but in nearest future we will also be having the plan to retrain all these teachers of Russian as the teachers of English, French and German.'

'That'll certainly kill two birds with one stone.'

'Ah yes. I always love this saying. In Polish it is to bake two loaves in one oven.'

I could teach two classes back to back, he told me, the first on British Culture, the second on British Literature: 'any kind, it is of your choice.' In my previous job at Lodz, I remembered, the 'native-speakers' had never been allowed to teach British Culture classes. Apparently, the staff knew from previous experience that we were too irreverent and our account of the subject did not square with the syllabus. Fellow native-speaker Drew had once covered for an absent colleague who accused him the following week of teaching his class 'nothing but the culture of negroes' when he should have been talking about beefeaters and the take-off times of planes at Heathrow.

There had been a meeting of all staff the previous week, Jerzy continued, to decide how to spend the budget. He spread out various brochures and catalogues on the coffee table and pointed out the items they had selected, more audio-visual hardware than I'd ever imagined in one institution.

'Don't worry,' Jerzy's English fragmented in his excitement, 'we are making sure all place is very alarming. We have spent so much money to this also. Such alarms, so complicated systems - and such insurance!' He threw up his hands. The teachers had voted to replace all the blackboards so that the classrooms could have video screens around three of the four walls. It sounded amazing, I agreed.

'You did order some books as well, though, didn't you?' I'd seen the Library and there wasn't much in it.

'Oh yes, of course, and you can order books too, as many as you like. What kind of literature are you going to teach?'

I thought of the two conscripts I saw waiting at the tram stop every day, in their khaki and puttees. Just yesterday, a biplane from the historic aircraft enthusiasts club, had flown over as one of them stood, reading his book. I'd started *Goodbye to All That*.

'We'll do twentieth-century poetry,' I offered, 'and begin with the First World War poets.'

It was all fine by Jerzy Komorowski, but was I sure I didn't want any more multi-media appliances? He noticed also that my voice sounded a little hoarse. Did my nose have a lot of mucus? He really thought I should see a doctor as soon as possible.

The first shock of my opening session of the British Literature course was to discover that my fourteen students considered the First World War - that horror of wasted life and futility, mud and death on which I had been raised - was a good thing. It was, as one put it, an 'extremely excellent historical event' because Poland had got its independence as a result. Furthermore, with the hated Germans on one side but the hated Russians on the other, it wasn't clear who the baddies and victims were. Poles had fought on both sides, due to the partition of their country at the time, so they were victims of course, but there wasn't a Polish 'side' to support. In short, an earnest girl called Malgosia explained, they 'couldn't imagine to have the sympathies for any body in this war'. I proposed maybe having sympathies for everybody - or imagining people from so many countries, often no older than themselves, caught up in it, but I could tell they weren't convinced. They had few mental images of the First War, for the Second loomed so close behind them and stood in the way. Perhaps I could get hold of some documentary footage and use some of Jerzy's wonderful multimedia equipment after all.

We moved onto the poetry itself. I handed round some 'kseroxi' and a list of authors and titles we would be studying. Darek put up his hand. He was lanky, having to fold his legs awkwardly under the desk, with a ponytail and an almost perpetual smirk he'd suddenly lost. Poles rarely mince words. He singled out the name of Isaac Rosenberg:

'Why is there a Jew on this course?'

It wasn't necessary to press this button very hard by this point to start me off - 0 to 60 in fifteen seconds, no intermediate stages.

'Because he's a fucking good poet, and he wrote his fucking good poems in the trenches.' I paused to breathe. 'Why is there an anti-Semite in my class, I might ask you, when I keep being assured that there aren't any real ones in Poland? And are there any more of you I should know about?' I glared around the class, who looked suitably mortified. Malgosia broke the silence, appearing from behind the curtain of her fringe as she always did to make a statement:

'We are very sorry and not at all meaning to be anti-Semitists - but I have one question. Was he soldier, this Rosenberg?' Her tone seemed to imply that there was something inherently unlikely about this.

'Of course he was.' I was nonplussed. 'Not before the war, but during it. Like everyone else. He died in 1915.'

Darek put up his hand: 'You don't mind if I say it. It's always so cool when British people swear, especially women. Are you a lesbian?'

Looking around at their faces, I knew it was inevitable: I would spend time with them and I would become fond of them, a thought which, just at that moment, I found considerably annoying.

We started taking regular trips with Gregorz, Iza and the childen out to their observatory at Piwnica on the other side of the forest. Crammed into their rattling 'Fiat Polski' we zoomed through the whistling pine trees until we arrived at the wrought iron gate, glimpsing the pure white building with its grey dome through the pear trees in the fading light.

There were apple orchards too, and a lake. Tessellated shapes of fragmented ice floated on its surface like an unfinished puzzle, brown fronds of reeds frozen into peculiar attitudes by the frost, the air breathing a bluish tinge from the lichen that formed fantastical shapes around the trunks of every tree. Rob and I fantasised regularly about coming to live in one of the abandoned cottages nearby.

In late November we made a bonfire, dragging the broken branches, caked with crispy lichen, that lay on the ground. The three girls between them managed the biggest of all, laughing as the lichen broke crunchily against their mittens.

Before Christmas, when the first really deep snow fell, a greater expanse of pristine, untrodden snow than I had ever seen in my life, we built a snowman to guard the door to the observatory. He was so huge we had to lift the children onto our shoulders to make the face and to put on his scarf and hat.

At the Kolegium, all the glossy Penguin classics I'd ordered had arrived, though there were still no textbooks or reference books. We were supposed to be discussing the British education system in my Culture class. The students were familiar with the basic structure of the State and private systems from photocopies I'd managed to scrounge from the British Council in Warsaw, but something more was definitely required. In desperation, I got them to interview Rob about his experiences at Prep and Public school. They were riveted by his tales of Dickensian deprivation, of little boys beaten for stealing a potato from the staff dining room and buggery in the dormitories.

'I've just committed a massive act of class betrayal,' Rob declared happily afterwards. 'I think you'd better take me for a drink, I feel a bit odd.'

'Oh for God's sake - really?'

'It's all right for you. You never had much class to betray in the first place.'

'Thanks!'

We were late getting to the Zlobek, despite our haste. For this was to be the day when Mikolaj - Saint Nicholas - would be coming to visit the children. As I folded up the pushchair, the imposing figure, his blue robe embroidered with gold, with his mitre and crook, his red boots and his long silver beard, strode towards us up the corridor with the smiling Pani Dyrektor. She gestured him into 'our' room, just as a scarlet-clad Santa walked in the front door. He looked about nineteen under the cotton wool beard, and was accompanied by a photographer in a leather jacket carrying a very flashy-looking Nikon camera.

In Poland, the man in the red suit on Western Christmas cards and carrier bags was recognised as synonymous with Mikolaj, even though Saint Nicholas does not necessarily wear red, comes on 6th and not 24th December, and despite the existence of counter or additional traditions in the East of the country of Star Man and Jack Frost who bring presents at New Year and on January 6th. The Pani Dyrektor looked mortified:

'I think I did say something,' she admitted. 'I wasn't sure the State Mikolaj would be coming as usual this year. You know how it's been. Nothing certain.' The youthful, 'importowy' Mikolaj scuffed his trainers, but the photographer looked belligerent:

'This is the first year we've tried to run this business. It's proper private enterprise. We spoke to Madam two months ago and you agreed we could have this job.' He looked around as though to waylay the rival Mikolaj, but the State representative, oblivious, had proceeded into the classroom.

'I know, I know,' the Pani Dyrektor moaned. 'Come in here, please, to my office.'

The pair complied, the older man muttering about payment and breach of contract.

The State Mikolaj was already in the classroom, selecting some lucky child for the honour of holding his crook as he set up his scales. He rummaged in his sack: Who, he inquired, was brave enough to be the first to come forward? Adas edged to the front, placing his little hand on one side of the scale to see how good he'd been that year. Mikolaj placed a present on the other side, making sure it appeared to balance.

By the time he had finished the whole class, swung his sack onto his shoulder and headed for the stairs, waving to the girls and boys as he went, the scarlet, private enterprise Mikolaj was being ushered to the front door. Not before Lidka's sharp eyes caught sight of him in the corridor. She nudged Koshka:

'Look,' she squeaked loudly. 'Two Mikolajs!'

Women were leaning over the stalls in the market poking at the heaps of wet fish. The carp were bought alive, sometimes direct from a tub of water, sometimes recently removed from it. The women would take the fish home, where it would swim in the bath for one or two days, before being killed and prepared for the many dishes of *Wigilia*, the Christmas Eve meal.

A group of carol singers ringed the statue of Copernicus in the Town Square. I wheeled Koshka's pushchair forward, but she had slumped to one side, fast asleep, her hat almost over her nose. They were singing 'Jezus Malusienki' - 'Little Wee Jesus'.

This carol must have been penned by a Babcia, I thought, listening to the words. Even the Holy Mother is under scrutiny, her efforts met with an element of reproach:

'Little wee Jesus lies among the stable creatures,
He cries from the cold.
His mother didn't give him a covering;
He cries from the cold.
His mother didn't give him a cover.'

This was a world away, in a whole different tradition from 'Once in Royal David's City', and 'Little Lord Jesus no crying he makes.' The Protestant baby Jesus is a good baby, a well-behaved baby - indeed he is differentiated from ordinary, mortal babies precisely by these qualities. He doesn't make a fuss or display symptoms of original sin such as grizzling or making demands. The Catholic baby Jesus, or certainly the Polish one, is a real baby and he *suffers* - as later he will for all of us and our sins on the cross. This is no cosy pastoral scene with soft, sweet-smelling hay and docile, comforting animals (designed for a Victorian audience who no longer had much contact with either). No, the straw is prickly and he's surrounded by scary, heavy-breathing beasts. He cries from the cold. He has no coverlet, only straw, and the cloth his mother takes from her head, but this doesn't really do the job. How he cries!

'He had no cradle,
Nor any pillow;'

the carollers sang pitifully. Even the Blessed Virgin doesn't quite cut it as a mother, so what hope is there for the rest of us? Letting his little coverlet fall off. It's cold! What is she thinking of?!

I wandered back past the diminishing piles of dark, shiny fish with their red rust-spots and the intent, headscarved women. Choosing the carp, and indeed cooking it was a female prerogative, but killing was the duty of the man of the house, as the students in the Culture class had explained. Since no-one seemed to like doing it, this was a task passed on as soon as possible to the younger generation.

'We are all hating the tastes of carps,' one of the students confided. 'My father he always is strongly not liking to do it, so this year is my second year of killing of carp.' He twisted his face.

'How do you do it, if you don't mind my asking?'

'You are seeking very hard to hold the fish and then you hit it with a... a tool for smashing of potatoes.

Darek twirled his ponytail round his finger:

172

'I couldn't face to beat this fish, so I tried with the hair tongs of my sister to electrificate it.'

'Oh my God, in the *bath*?'

'Yes. It wasn't so successful method. For the carp I mean.'

'You might have killed yourself!'

'Yes,' he confessed. 'It was very nearly.'

Wiosna - Spring

Spring came, with its usual late but sudden glory, as if the dormant earth cracked one day in May and the white blossom and purple crocuses and fresh green shoots erupted from it all at once.

The Babcia's Council on when to shed tights and jackets had evidently met, and decided that the combined factors of date and temperature at last warranted such behaviour. I realised how premature I had been when, following several days of fine weather in early March, I had dared to wear no more than a cardigan and to go without my winter tights. Not only had I been signally alone in my recklessness but I had been scolded from pillar to post all day. Since the air had been undeniably warm, the admonitory voices had been forced to resort to 'it isn't the twenty-first yet.'

Fortunately I had not taken the suicidal step of allowing Koshka to appear in public so scantily clad before the official first day of Spring or I'd doubtless have been strung up from the nearest 'trzepak'. These metal framed structures stood outside each block of flats for the purpose of hanging rugs to be beaten. At Christmas and then again at Easter the sound of relentless pounding sent comforting signals of the approaching holiday.

Each time we went into town now, one or another of our favourite shops had closed, each replaced by a 'Boutik', an emporium of imported Western goods: high-heeled fluffy mules, lycra mini-skirts and sequined tops, leather jackets and denim skirts trimmed with lace, multicoloured, synthetic sweaters of zig-zag design, or fake-angora cardigans with as many fringes and bobbles as they would hold, shampoo and coffee. All these new *boutiki* sold the same products - hardly surprising, since, as Gregorz pointed out, all were supplied by the same importing warehouse in Poznan. It seemed the West was happy to offload most of its cheapest, least saleable items which here would fetch a far better price than could be expected at home. Polish women had always been smartly dressed and made-up, but they had never looked dolled up as they did now. The effect was such that a group of women crossing the town square in the morning gave the impression that they were returning from the previous night's party, instead of making their way to work.

'My *God*,' the former British Council Representative exclaimed, making a return visit to the town after an absence of two years. 'My God! What *happened?* The Polish gals always used to be so damned pretty - elegant, you know,' he confided. 'Chic and sort of dignified. Lots of them used to make their own outfits, you know - or got a dressmaker to do it. Good quality, hard-won stuff, I tell you. Now they look like a...like a...bunch of Italian prostitutes, that's what.'

I went to the slipper-maker's to buy a pair to send to my father for his birthday. It had been only a fortnight since my last visit, but the shop had closed down, the glass case on the wall outside empty, the name-card missing, the glass besmeared and the basement windows dark. The town was flooded with black, cotton, Taiwanese slippers with plastic soles. People had not seen slippers like that before. They looked smart and somehow modern. Most people bought the Taiwanese variety only once - but Pan Twardowski's survival required his customers to buy all their slippers from him, for he sold nothing else. By the time people were complaining, with a mixture of satisfaction and reproach, that these 'Western slippers' were not so great after all, and also very expensive, especially considering that they did not last so long, for Pan Twardowski it had come too late.

With the warmer weather, we began to take picnics out to Piwnica. Iza showed the girls how to weave chaplets of dandelions for their heads. In the evenings, we sat on logs around the camp-fire, chatting, cooking sausages and drinking beer, the stars that Copernicus saw above us in the sky. Marta, Ludwika and Koshka built a tunnel in the bushes and there were periods of rustling followed by quiet, then thuds and squeals as they blundered into one another in the dark.

The stars fell like the points of silver javelins, their glittering, unseen shafts gliding through eternity towards us, raining down on us with incredible slowness. How could Copernicus have dared to say that we were not the centre of all this? It seemed so counter-intuitive. That the world is not ordered according to their wishes or concerns, nor suffused by their desires is a realisation every child has to face before long, and which, as a species, was also reserved for us until some way down the line of history. Gazing at the sky above the dome of Piwnica, for the first time I felt what an immense thing it was for humanity to be forced to recognise that the universe did not revolve as they had thought, and that we, with our gazing eye, were not anchored at its heart.

Zlobek

I still made my way the Zlobek every Tuesday. By now I was permitted to conduct my music sessions on my own - largely so that the Ciocias could have another extended coffee and cigarette break during the morning. They would disappear out onto the verandah with knowing smiles, leaving me in charge of twenty children all too aware that this was a holiday from the rules. The children danced and sang and performed actions, but invariably ran amok before too long, delighting in the unaccustomed freedom to run round and round in circles whooping, and above all in stepping off the rug at will! I wondered whether they were not a microcosm of Polish society, with its distinct antinomian streak. After all, the children, too, spent their lives obeying rules that made no sense to them, that couldn't be rationally deduced or internalised but which were rigorously enforced. I had helped out at the local playgroup back home where a reasonably authoritative tone and a slightly raised voice had been enough to quiet all but one or two in a roomful of toddlers. This lot would have required the ZOMO riot police before they'd have taken me seriously! The only authority they recognised was the pinch on the ear between the bony fingers of Ciocia Bogusia.

They were clearly having a wonderful time, though I didn't enjoy the sneering smiles of the Ciocias when they peeped in through the door and so opted for the dubious compromise of letting the children let off steam while periodically yelling at the top of my lungs to get them to undertake at least some structured activity. At least it gave them a break from the usual regime, even if my version was no more consistent. Eventually we arrived at something of a solution when I managed to unearth a whole box of musical instruments, mainly drums and tambourines. I brought along my tin whistle and we had a marching (actually a galloping) band, with hobby horses for the cavalry. This at least slowed them down, since they couldn't bang a drum and ride very fast at the same time. It also gave me an effective threat - the removal of an offender's steed - to balance the main bribe, the chance to strum my guitar, which they did with unexpected reverence.

I consoled myself with the idea that I was making things better at least some of the time. Our sing-along sessions while the children were confined to their *nocniki* had proved a great success, and most of them seemed to know several songs off by heart and to understand at least some of the main nouns and verbs contained therein. Unsurprisingly, I was soon left to supervise *nocniki* hour on my own as well. I took the opportunity to teach them all to pull up their own knickers and tights, as a surprise for the Ciocias, who were duly amazed. They took such care to keep the children passive, but then were constantly irked at these little chores they had to perform for them, judging by the number of slaps and tweaks meted out during the acts of feeding and dressing.

I worried that I was judging the Ciocias too harshly, simply imposing my own cultural practices. Besides, it was becoming clear that the Zlobek was in decline. Merinotex, in common with most Polish state-owned industry, had financial difficulties and the Zlobek was constantly threatened with closure. Jadzia was retraining as a cook in the evenings, and there was no doubt that the insecurity of their future affected the Ciocia's commitment to the place - and their humour. More than this, though, the job no longer held any interest for them. Bogusia had worked at the Zlobek for fifteen years, Jadzia for eight. They expended as little effort and took as many breaks as possible. They merely organised the children to be quiet and excused themselves. Who could blame them? *I* might find children interesting and enlivening, but not everyone does, and who's to say I would still feel the same after more than a decade. Even so, surely it took more energy to keep the children subdued than it would to engage in some activity that might actually interest their charges and thereby themselves?

One day, quite out of the blue, Ciocia Jadzia, who for some reason had stayed to watch the singing, got up from the bench and announced: 'You've heard Ciocia Helena sing you her English songs, now for some proper Polish ones.'

The Polish song session now became a regular feature following on from mine. Ciocia Grazyna soon joined in too, and the pair of them began to teach me the nursery rhymes during *leżakowanie* so that I could accompany them on the guitar, songs about storks returning after the winter and red apples carved with a cross to tell love-fortunes.

'It is a very old song, this red apple one,' Jadzia told me, 'a very old song from the east. How old is that song you sang this morning, the one about London?'

'London Bridge? Oh, it's quite old I think, because it's about a bridge that fell down in Medieval times.'

On receiving this information, Cioicia Jadzia sulked for at least ten minutes. She turned her back, stuck her nose in the air and would not speak. I'd no idea what I'd said to offend her, unless, in this atmosphere of cultural competition, it was to imply that a traditional English rhyme might vie with a Polish one in antiquity. Several Polish friends had pointed out that Western countries were too commercialised to have any inherited lore or traditions at all.

'I thought all folk songs and nursery rhymes were old - in all countries,' I offered.

'*Czerwone Jabluszko* is hundreds of years old,' Jadzia sniffed, still not mollified.

'I don't doubt it.'

She stalked into the other room, returning with a fistful of puppets, and lay down on the rug in the middle of the room. The children lay on their fronts with their chins in their hands as she told them a string of stories - one about a stork and a frog, another about a little girl with a magic doll in her pocket who goes into the woods to seek instruction from Baba Jaga - animating each tale with the puppets in her hands. Her voice rose and fell, and the children, their eyes black and huge, were forgetting to breathe. She was pulling them to and fro, holding them, manipulating them with her words, her eyes and her tone, like the puppets in her hands whose every move they followed. She had such a gift, yet I was willing to bet she had not done this for years, keeping her listeners poised at moments of tension on a raised fingertip inches from her face, spinning the stories out of her tender stomach and her own memory.

Later, when I congratulated her, she said:

'When you go home to Ireland, will you invite me, so I can get visa?'

'I don't live in Ireland, remember? But I will invite you when I go back to England, and I will take you to an Irish pub where they sing songs all the time and you can cry all evening! Only I warn you, quite a lot of songs in the Irish pub are quite cheerful.'

'I only like the sad ones,' Jadzia asserted.

'Did you ever hear the other kind? No? Well you should try it. Perhaps you will like them?'

'O.K. I will come,' she agreed.

These improvements aside, except at the end of the day - when calm descended and Ciocia Grazyna and I prepared the children to go home, distributing puzzles and paper dolls to play with as they liked while Grazyna 'did up' the girls' hair - the regime continued as before.

Some of the children at least appeared extremely difficult to subdue. Lidka, for example, was always in trouble. The Ciocias, Bogusia in particular, could not leave her alone for a minute, down on her for no other reason that I could deduce except that she was clearly as bright as ninepence and that she possessed a more than common share of the spark of life, which despite continual scoldings and regular retribution remained inextinguishable. The Ciocias on the whole preferred boys, I noted. They punished Adas, but they admired him, pinching his legs, praising their thickness, their sturdiness. What a man he would grow up to be!

Pawelek, on the other hand, was not one of life's survivors - or perhaps in his own way he was. Perhaps his tenuous hold on life was a sinew of concealed strength. He was still the occasion of frequent trips to the toilet for a good cry on my part. I wanted to whisk him off, to adopt him and bring him up - even though that was the last thing he needed, since the root cause of his pain seemed to be separation from his mother. I could never look at him without feeling that that he was a paradigm of raw human suffering, and that it shouldn't be allowed for someone to suffer so much, He was pleased with so little, and the strength of his joy when I sang 'his' song to him or when a car or puzzle he liked fell to his lot to play with was hard to bear. I don't say he would have suffered much less under a more benign regime, but the Ciocias actively picked on him, threatening him with being fed to a wolf or never going home to mummy at every misdemeanour.

'You're such a shrimp, Pawelek, hardly a boy at all. How do you expect to grow if you won't eat your dinner?' Bogusia advanced a heavily laden fork towards his mouth, jabbing it towards the back of his throat... 'If you puke that up again,' Bogusia threw down the fork, 'Mummy won't want you. She'll never come to fetch you again. You'll never go home to Mummy, you hear me?'

Agnieszka was a new addition to the class, arriving around six months after Koshka and I had started to attend the Zlobek. She came wearing her brown hair in bunches and a red pinafore. Jadzia's stomach, and consequently her temper, had been less troublesome of late, so I was startled to notice that she seemed to take an instant dislike to her. I have never seen a child retreat so fast. By the third or fourth week she was completely incommunicado. She twiddled the ends of her bunches round her fingers constantly and chewed her lower lip until she had made a permanent red mark. A rash appeared around her nose and mouth. Was she ill or was this stress-related? I tried to be gentle with her, to show her little acts of kindness, but my attempts bemused her and got her into more trouble.

I felt the strain of protecting my own child, yet unable to intervene very effectively on behalf of anyone else's. I suspected I was only tolerated because I didn't openly contradict or oppose the Ciocias, and because of all the cigarette-breaks my presence gave them. I couldn't let Koshka behave as she did at home without feeling it showed a sickening favouritism towards her. After all, she already had a much better deal than any of the others - exempt both from arbitrary punishment and *leżakowanie*. I feared this might be a disreputable trade-off. She was permitted this special status, even though the Ciocias frankly disbelieved my claim that she no longer had a daytime nap at home either, and though they would have dearly loved to get their hands on her and show her a thing or two. Many times I'd seen Bogusia eyeing her, pronouncing her an 'indywidualystka':

'Leave her with us just one morning,' Bogusia advised. 'We'd soon sort her out for you.'

Still, I *was* making things better, I told myself. I *was*.

Hotel Asystencki

Rob was definitely working too hard. We had experimented with making Koshka do without her nap during the day, as this was getting later and later, often after four in the afternoon, in which case she was wide awake till nine or ten. The needs of our sanity justified to ourselves this often brutal and sometimes downright unsuccessful tactic. Dragging around a near comatose and fretful toddler until 6.30, when we could decently put her to bed, made the last two hours of the day almost as exhausting for us as for her. By the time she finally crashed out, we were ready to sleep too, so there was still no evening and no time together. Rob had no choice but to work, which in turn exacerbated his tendency not to sleep, and he grew starey-eyed and manic, which, in combination with the diet of seventeenth-century New England sermons he had digested for his course, led to some fulminations of righteous rage of his own.

If I succeeded in staying awake, I tried to prepare for my classes, but I'd started leaving the washing up till morning. Rob called it living in squalor, whereas I thought we should relax about it and adapt to our circumstances. We had very little space, but then we had very few belongings to clutter it up. I thought I did pretty well, considering, but Rob turned out to have a point. Polish tower-blocks have chutes by which rubbish plummets to the basement, where it waits for weekly collection. Perhaps as a result of this, they also often have cockroaches - the 'karaluchy,' or, as the Poles term them, 'the comrades.' I could have sworn our 'comrades' only came out when Rob was looking, since I rarely saw them.

'Look how many crumbs you've dropped,' he challenged Koshka. 'Can't you sit still instead of wandering about when you're eating? Do you want to share your breakfast with a cockroach?'

'I don't mind,' she said happily.

I noticed that she began to leave little piles of food at the side of her plate, and guessed for whom these offerings were intended. I didn't dare draw Rob's attention to this practice. Now, at bedtimes, not content with thunderous denunciations of our recalcitrant infant, he turned on me with ominous mutterings about lack of support. I could manage to stay awake to prepare my own classes, he complained, but not to be available to discuss his, or, alternatively:

'Oh it's alright for you. You just go in and make it up as you go along, and they love it. I'm not like that. I like to do things properly.' I had an awful feeling he was right, though in my defence I objected that my students seemed to be quite enjoying themselves, that they had been really getting into *The Waste Land* the week before. 'Huh,' Rob conceded sourly, and only half jokingly, 'crowd-pleaser!'

'Go on, dazzle your students with some more of your half-knowledge of T.S. Eliot,' he called after me as I went off to class next morning. I had the vague sense that the ability to do things on the hoof, with almost no materials and very little expertise, could have been described in a more positive manner, say, as a virtue, even a gift. On the other hand, maybe I'd like to do things properly too. Fat chance at the moment.

That evening, in a pathetic attempt to reinvent myself as an intellectual and a supportive wife, I took the hefty tome of *The Norton Anthology of American Literature* and tucked into some Cotton Mather (which Rob wasn't lecturing on any more, but there was no harm in making retrospective amends for my lack of interest) and Harriet Beecher Stowe, which he was.

Living with a man who appeared to have metamorphosed into the Puritan divine naturally meant that Mather had not presented himself to me in the most favourable light. I stumbled on the words in his Diary at the death of his infant daughter, Jerusha:

'Betwixt 9h. and 10h. at Night, my lovely *Jerusha* Expired. She was two years, and about seven Months, old. Just before she died, she asked me to pray with her; which I did, with a distressed but resigning soul. The Minute that she died, she said, *That she would go to Jesus Christ.* She had lain speechless, Many hours. But in her last Moments, her speech returned a little to her. Lord, I am oppressed; Undertake for me!'

Blurrily, and in some haste, I leafed through the anthology until I found the extract from *Uncle Tom's Cabin*, only to discover that I had traded the death of Jerusha for that of little Eva.

All of which demonstrated, at least to myself, that reinvention was not possible, that I was still a post-natal wreck, liable to weep piteously at almost any depiction of children, never mind their demise. I compounded my mistake by going to gaze at my own little girl on her bed behind the bookshelves. A folded quilt lay on the floor ready for when she would roll out, never waking, as she did every night. It was not clear whether it was the power of my tearful eyebeams, or the intensity of my gratitude that she was still breathing and not languishing with tuberculosois, which woke her. She sat up, grinning, barely sleepy at all. I looked despairingly at Rob, who rolled his eyes.

My pet theory was that Rob didn't just need more peace and quiet to do his work: he needed to get out more, needed to have friends. He had always been such a sociable person, but I suspected such mumsy solutions would not go down well. He admitted that he found it hard being always the foreigner, the 'Englishman', as if he had no personal characteristics and no biography. Certainly no-one here, he claimed, had ever seemed to perceive the existence of the former or inquired about the latter. He liked Marzena and Adam, Grzegorz and Iza, but our relations

180

were very much child-centred, and I spent more time with them than he did. So when Rob started chatting with Marcin, the quiet mathematician from upstairs, then going for the occasional beer with him in the nearby student club, I was mightily relieved.

Pani Eleanora lived four floors above us with her thirty year-old son. She too had worked in the mathematics department, and the pair had lived in the Hotel Asystencki ever since it had been built, in the seventies, when Marcin was a child. Rob told me that Marcin was earnest but sometimes very funny, with the absurdist sense of humour lots of Poles have. He looked shy and not particularly worldly in his lumpy, dark suits, though I did detect a penchant for natty if unassuming waistcoats. His dark, unruly hair was thinning a bit, but carefully combed to conceal this, and he sported a neat moustache. We saw him bring flowers home for his mother every Friday, as most Polish men appeared to do for the women in their life. I pointed this out to Rob, who did it once, then started to bring home a bottle of vodka on Fridays instead, which was probably more practical.

It was a surprise when Marcin revealed that he was going to work in Germany on an engineering project to make some money. He had a favour to ask. Would one of us go and keep his mother company some evenings while he was away? She very much enjoyed having a companion while she watched 'Wiadomosci,' the evening news. Rob withdrew at once:

'You do it. You're good with Grannies.'

'Sure I am. Most of them have a price on my head.'

'Go on, it'll be good for your Polish, and I could get some work done here.'

We had never been able to get the enormous Russian TV supplied with the flat to work, and the only place to put it had been the desk. Currently it all but filled our wardrobe and we made do with the crackly radio.

Pani Eleanora's flat had the immaculate drabness of the old days I'd always liked so much, the sense of making something out of nothing, and, even in Marcin's absence, there were always fresh flowers. Two or three times a week, whenever I was fortunate enough to have got Koshka to sleep in time, I made my way upstairs. Pani Eleanora laid out apple strudel and *sernik*, the Polish cheesecake - the best kind with crunchy chocolate bits on top - and tea and wine and vodka:

'I don't know why they don't all speak Polish,' Pani Eleanora waved her hand at the footage from the Israeli Knesset on the screen. 'They all know how to, all except David Levy.'

'You all know how to speak Russian,' I pointed out, 'but I can't imagine anyone would feel very happy if your members of parliament spoke it in the Sejm.'

'*I* know how to speak Russian, but Marcin's generation, they claim they don't speak it. They must have worked pretty hard not to - nine years of Russian at least in school, *everyone*. Marcin says his teachers always made it clear that it was not a real subject, that no-one expected them to take Russian classes seriously, but there must have been exams. Mind you,' she added, 'the maths teachers in secondary school often help their students to cheat in the exams before the School Board in order to meet the standards, so perhaps Russian teachers are the same.'

'A student I taught in Lodz told me that, at her school, the two cleverest pupils did the maths matriculation papers for the whole class and the teachers let them,' I recalled.

'Yes, well I think it's terrible, teachers of Russian who don't care about the language. Naturally, I hate the Russians, but a language is a language. It shouldn't go according to ideologies - or fashions.' I was interested to see what these future students of mine at the Kolegium, the Russian Language teachers Jerzy Komorowski had promised me, would be like.

The screen showed a particularly brutal repression of a Palestinian funeral, people running, Israeli soldiers yelling, firing after them, then the bulldozers moving into the neighbourhood in reprisal. Pani Eleanora nodded with almost maternal approval.

'There, you see. *Now* they fight. They have to. They are really very good at it, don't you think? At the beginning of the War, when we were putting the sandbags around Warsaw, they didn't want to help us. They thought it was hopeless. They never wanted to be in the Polish Army. My Uncle told me a story. He lived in a small town. A Jewish family owned a big house at the end of the main square. When the Germans occupied the town, an officer came to requisition the house as a centre for radio communications. He took off his cap. He kissed the hands of the wife and the two daughters. He said he was very sorry he had to take the house and that everything would be done to try and make things convenient for them. The wife and the daughters were charmed. They had been to Vienna, these young ladies. The officer talked to them about the opera there. They were delighted to meet someone with a little culture, a little sophistication. They thought things would be better for them now, that nothing could be worse than these barbarous, peasant, Jew-hating Poles around them. Foolish, foolish Jews.'

She shook her head, contemplating the moral of the tale: Foolish, foolish Jews, with their misguided cosmopolitanism, their inability to recognise when they were well off. A Pole, of course, would never make such a mistake, for a Pole knows that a German is *always* bad news. If those Jews had been really committed to Poland, committed enough to want to fight for it, they would have known that too. She pursed her lips. It was almost as if their fate, in her eyes, had *grown out of* that deluded

182

cosmopolitan fantasy, the mistaken belief that the Germans couldn't be worse than the neighbours they knew.

Her eyes returned to the screen. More Israeli troops in action on the West Bank. 'The Jews wouldn't fight,' Pani Eleanora had repeated. Certainly no-one was going to be able to say *that* again. 'Now they understand how it is.' It was almost as if she said 'now they are grown up.' Her tone was consistently that of a parent who'd taken on an adopted child, a problem case with a difficult history. Offered it a home. Was there no gratitude? Of course you had to chastise such a child, but you loved it really. It must know that. And now it had grown up and inexplicably gone off into the world intent on slandering its childhood home and its upbringing at every opportunity, with talk of beatings and unfair treatment.

Szymon Peres was in London, giving an interview:

'I know him,' Pani Eleanora announced. 'His family's from Wisniewo near where I was born.' She sounded momentarily disappointed as if she expected him to give a sign - 'and a big hello to all my friends in Wisniewo' - as if she waited for an acknowledgement which never came. 'I tell you,' she said again, 'they all speak Polish the Israeli cabinet, all but one.'

Her plaintive voice crystallised something I had been unable to put my finger on during numerous exchanges with others on this subject. The terminology always veered between that of sibling rivalry, marital discord and parental discipline. There was much Polish outrage at recent insinuations coming out of Germany that, while Nazi Germany had undeniably instituted the Holocaust, it was Poles who had always been the real anti-Semites. The claims were greeted with incomprehension. There was no comparison. Difficulties between Poles and Jews, if such there had been, were somehow 'in the family.' Some of the worst abuses, cruelties and betrayals in the world take place within families, I thought, the hardest to forgive, the ones that don't go away. There was no doubt that Pani Eleanora's feeling was genuine, and that it was conceived as a form of love. But then, some of the worst parents love their kids, or think they do. It's just that what they do to them bears little resemblance …

We'd missed the next item, but now came a report on Walesa's visit to Canada:

'Look at the electrician,' sniffed Eleanora. 'I do wish he'd learn to speak proper Polish. God forbid he should ever become President. It would be so embarrassing.'

Lech was addressing an assembly of Canadian Jews. Always an impressive operator, he employed the colloquial informality that made the Polish intelligentsia cringe to full effect whenever he addressed an audience. He knew that the intelligentsia comprised only about fifteen percent of the electorate and that his matey oratory was his strength in the eyes of most of the population. He also had an extremely skilful translator on hand to smooth off the edges. Even I had enough Polish to observe that Lech had rarely said exactly what the translator claimed he had.

'Well you know,' Walesa confided expansively, 'it's true that we Poles and you Jews haven't always got along. I fight with my wife - I call her every name under the sun. It doesn't mean I don't love my wife!'

The translator did a valiant job of trying to make this analogy between the history of Polish-Jewish relations and a minor 'domestic' appear less crude. The camera panned to the audience, most of them elderly émigrés from Poland and therefore unfortunately able to follow Lech's reasoning in the vernacular: row after row of stony faces. Knowing the status of women in the Polish imaginative hierarchy, it wasn't even possible to nurture the illusion that being characterised as an argumentative wife rather than a troublesome, ungrateful child was a promotion to equality.

'Now, my dear,' said Pani Eleanora, 'I think its time for more cake. You need another glass of tea. Next time you must come earlier and I can offer you a proper supper. I make very good chicken soup. It is always good for everything and you look a little pale. I think you are not sleeping enough.'

Lato - Summer

Hotel Asystencki

It was a warm morning, the playground spattered with yellow dandelions, the day all three of my charges decided to run away. They fled cackling in the direction of the nearby health clinic rather than the road, but I knew I had to catch them quickly. I was minding Genevieve's baby, and had been entertaining her in the sandpit when the mass breakout occurred. Looking around at the disapproving mothers - who miraculously managed to combine staring with studiedly refusing to meet my eye - it was clear there was no point in asking any of *them* to watch her, so I heaved her onto my hip and set off in pursuit. Koshka and the twins thought the whole game hilariously funny. Sometimes I caught two out of three, and once all three of them, but with only one hand to hold them, Lukasz soon broke free, running hell for leather towards the road. I yelled with all my might, dumped the baby on Lucynka and Koshka - who fortunately decided to take the responsibility seriously - and hurled myself after him. It took a virtual rugby tackle to bring him down. I hadn't registered until that moment how hefty and unfit I'd become. This time I was taking no chances and tied his scarf round his wrists to drag him back to the others, looking only slightly chastened at my lecture on the dangers of roads. Lucynka and Koshka had only just embarked on feeding crushed dandelions to the baby.

Hyperventilating and bright crimson, I hauled the baby a few more inches up my hip, gripping the wrists of my captives still tighter as I marched them past the playground towards the block of flats. I must have looked fairly ridiculous, but the eyes of the women at the swings and by the sandpit so infuriated me that I gave a mock bow.

'*Dziękuję za pomoc* - thanks for the help,' I yelled over my shoulder, but they were already engrossed in their dissection of the incident, tutting and exclaiming among themselves.

I knew I had better tell Marzena straight away when she came to collect the children or she'd soon hear it from other sources. In fact she already knew: three women had rung her up at work that morning to tell her how the 'Angielka' took care of her children in her absence.

'I'm so sorry,' she said. 'Lucynka and Lukasz, they started this running away thing at the weekend - they never did it before. I forgot to tell you. It's my fault. I didn't know you had the baby as well. I should have warned you.'

'Not *one* of them helped,' I told her, 'they all just watched, yet *three* of them rushed to telephone you. *Three* of them!' Marzena patted my arm:

'Never mind. On Saturday the twins both ran away in the forest in different directions. It took Adam and me half an hour to find Lucynka - and there are two of us.'

'They're really not very friendly round here, are they?' I'd never said it outright before, but now I thought of the woman I'd 'only given biscuits and tea,' and the man from the other block who'd suddenly become so friendly when he wanted me to help him with the English for a bursary application he was makng to some Swedish-American foundation. He'd quizzed me about our financial position, but this was a cultural difference I was quite comfortable with by now. No, it was the way he'd almost tripped in his eagerness to get out, presumably to report this information, and had never so much as greeted me again - though I heard from Grzegorz that the application had been successful. I hadn't mentioned these things, not wanting to offend Marzena, or seem to be whinging.

Marzena studied the floor: 'I'm surprised you say it the first time now.'

'But what have we done?'

'I don't know,' said Marzena uncomfortably. 'Perhaps they are shy.'

'*Shy?*'

'I mean ashamed, for their language. They don't speak English very well or not at all.'

'But you don't speak English - and we manage. I can speak enough Polish to have a conversation. It's horrible, being ignored by this crowd.

It's like being in the playground again, who will speak to you and who won't. I don't know why I bothered to grow up, I really don't.'

'We *are* in the playground again,' Marzena giggled. 'After all these years, that is where we are.'

Zlobek

I'd no idea it was to be a day of reckoning at the Zlobek. I had continued my project of surreptitiously making the children more independent and thus less likely to arouse the Ciocias' ire. All the children at the table I supervised now ate their *obiad* unaided. I reckoned I'd even got Grazyna and Jadzia mildly interested in copying the experiment.

Agata the cook came through with the pot of soup. It was 'rosol' - chicken consommee with strands of spaghetti - which everybody liked, so hopefully there wouldn't be many scenes over the first course at least. Agata deposited her pot and stayed for a chat. She wore a large apron and the open-toed, lace-up, canvas ankle-boots usual for those working in kitchens - a big, sloppy girl of about twenty, with a loose, fat plait of glossy brown hair to one side of her head. Multiple wisps and strands escaped and stuck to her face, damp with perspiration. She hung around, glad of five minutes away from the heat of the kitchen. She was always one for a joke, but was usually too busy to stay.

She turned round just as Jadzia, annoyed by Agnieszka's dazed refusal to unwind the strand of hair from around her finger in order to accept her spoon, fetched the girl a clout on the side of the head. The look of shock on Agata's cheerful face brought a sudden stab of realisation to my insides - the realisation that, though I had winced automatically at the blow, otherwise I had barely noticed it.

'Jadzia! Don't! What are you doing?' Agata protested.

'I didn't hit her hard,' said Jadzia defensively. 'I only skimmed the side of her head.'

'No you didn't,' Agata countered. 'I saw you!' She was really angry, pink and puffing. 'Don't let her do that,' she charged the rest of us. 'And you, Jadzia, don't do it any more. She's a child. What would her mother say?' She nodded over at me. 'What will the *Angielka* think of us?'

The *Angielka* was at that moment sinking with shame and horror against the pot plants on the radiator by the windowsill. I had kidded myself that my apparent complicity was the only way my presence would be tolerated, justified by my covert attempts to ease the children's situation. In fact, all these many months, I had done nothing better than collude in a closed world of the daily abuse of children. I had protected my own child and I had tinkered around at the edges while the sealed and oppressive system, the continuous maltreatment went on, unchecked. In came big, breezy Agata, with her broad, friendly face and expansive apron, her large hands ladling out *rosol*, and applied the clarity and moral certainty I had so lacked. Brutality normalises itself, even for those who initially oppose it. Ciocia Grazyna had probably started off like me. I had not ceased to dislike the tyranny but I had attributed too many aspects of it to Polish ways of dealing with children. I had indulged in the worst kind of cultural relativism, patronising them and deluding myself. It took a Polish woman, younger than I was, to show me that I had lost all sense of what was abnormal, that I had been propping up the indefensible. Perhaps I only imagined that Agata's second bemused glance in my direction contained the implicit accusation.

'Here, sweetheart,' she rubbed Agnieszka's head behind the ear and wiped the tears that meandered down the girl's face without any visible expression or any sobs to accompany them.

I would do one thing at least, I vowed to myself. At home-time, I lurched into the cloakroom and cornered Agnieszka's mother. She was a student, not a textile worker finishing at two or two-thirty, so she was often the last.

'I want to talk to you about Agnieszka. Do you think she is happy here?'

'I don't know, I mean... what are you saying?'

'Please take her away.' I blurted out. 'Send her wherever you like, but don't leave her here. They're not nice to her.'

She stared at me in bewildered amazement. I must have looked pretty strange, wild-eyed and imploring. What could she do? She had to pursue her studies. She'd been very lucky to get Agnieszka a place here, not being an employee of the factory and all.

'Do whatever you like, but tell me you won't bring her back to this place. They're cruel to her here. Believe me. *Do* you believe me?'

She just nodded, looking for a place to sit down, as Grazyna brought Agnieszka through to put on her boots and coat, her bunches newly tied with ribbon.

Hotel Asystencki

I trailed back from the Zlobek, feeling that the axis of the world had somehow shifted and I didn't know where I was - only to see Halina fading fast in the playground by the Hostel. She was on her own with her children. It was the last thing I wanted, but she looked like I felt, at the end of her spiritual resources:

'Would you like to come to my flat for a cup of tea? The children could play...' Avoid the word 'invite' at all costs lest it trigger reciprocation anxiety. 'It will only be a cup of tea - I don't even have any *pierniki* to offer you,' (subtext again: so it doesn't need a return invitation) 'but the tea will be hot and wet. The *Anglicy* are not at all hospitable,' I burbled on. 'The only national characteristic to which we can lay claim in this respect is the ability to recognise when somebody needs a cup of tea.' It was a bit of a caricature, but it might be true nonetheless, I reflected with a flicker of national pride. I think I would have said anything to get this woman to sit down rather than fall down. She came.

'Did you study History, Halina?'

'Yes, yes, like my husband - *with* my husband.'

I produced the cafetiere of tea, pushing the tea-leaves to the bottom, and fitted the glasses into their silver holders. Kinga played schools with Koshka, instructing her from the picture books where she'd made me write the Polish words in blue pencil under the English ones. I heard her plaintive voice in my head, begging me to teach her Polish so the other children would play with her. Kinga seemed an excellent teacher, calm, decisive and not too bossy. Michal had found the tin of lego bricks. I felt glad to have helped create an oasis of peace in Halina's day, watching her sip her tea, here in my little flat. Proud. Hospitable even. So I don't know why I said it - maybe because in my unaccustomed relaxation and hers only truthfulness was possible. Maybe I couldn't think of anything else to say:

'Most of the people here, they don't like us, do they?'

It was as if she was too exhausted to lie, even it animated her slightly, the strong tea, and having some information she could give me.

'Well,' she said, with only the merest hint of apology, 'of course everyone knows that you're Jews.'

I was stunned.

'Do they?' I said dangerously, to my ears but not to hers.

'Yes,' she went on happily, relieved to have something to talk about, vaguely proud of the perspicacity of the community, 'and you are here to avoid conscription.'

'Conscription?'

'Yes, of course, the National Army Service, for your husband. Nobody wants to come to Poland, even though everybody knows you can't be earning as little as you say - no-one believes it - so naturally you are coming here not to go to the army.'

'Being Jewish.'

'Yes.'

I was fairly appalled by the fact that she didn't have to explain the logic of this. Likewise, the notion that the academic families of the Hotel Assystencki didn't want to fraternise with us, the famous Jewish draft-dodgers, seemed suddenly unsurprising. Well, no wonder I'd had so often that consciousness of being observed, discussed and shunned. At least I hadn't imagined it. Thinking this, I almost forgot to ask the most obvious question:

'And why is "everybody" so sure we are Jewish?'

She blushed prettily. 'Well, that is easy. The brother who came to visit you - his name is David, *prawda*?'

'Do you want to know something interesting, Halina? We don't have conscription in Britain.'

Kolegium

'Pani Dauff do telefonu,' came over the tannoy into the flat. It invariably made me jump, and sent me into a huge fluster because Koshka was never 'properly' dressed to be taken out into the chilly hallway and I knew that unless I rectified this - or, more likely, *even* if I rectified this to my standards - I was going to have to listen to cluckings of commiseration with the 'poor child' and mutterings of the 'Are your little feet cold, poor darling? What is mummy thinking of letting your little feet get cold?' variety throughout my phone call.

How did the Portierka manage to pronounce Rob's surname in such a way as to make it sound so semitic, I grumbled, grabbing Koshka, who was thoughtfully attired in a t-shirt and nothing else, wearing her knickers on her head. She had put her socks on the paws of her toy cat.

'Pani Dauff do telefonu. Telefon, Pani Dauff.'

I achieved some semblance of respectability with Koshka, though I couldn't find my own slippers and went out in my socks. Polish people all wear slippers, and keep spare ones for guests. They never lose them or forget to put them on. According to his latest letter, my friend Jon had just spent a whole weekend being chided and mocked by the family of his Polish girlfriend because he had a hole in his sock. Do Polish young men never have holes in their socks? No, because somebody mends them. Maybe it wasn't just conformism. Maybe life wasn't too short to worry about that. Perhaps it was thriftiness or simply a sense of looking after things properly, a habit, in difficult times when you have no control, of holding things together. I dashed out of the flat - having shouted at Koshka for her non-cooperation, and clutching her under my arm none too gently - conscious of how admirable they all were, and that I was a lousy mother and a disorganised, insufficiently respectful person of doubtful value.

It was the grumpy Portierka handing me the receiver, and Jerzy on the other end of the line. He was just letting me know that there was a slight problem at the College, he said. I was aware that the incoming government had voted institutions like ours a grant of a mere thirteen percent of last year's budget, but it wasn't that.

'In the holiday there has been a robbery here. The thieves took all the equipment.'

'What, all of it? What about the alarms?' I tried to perch Koshka on the ledge near the phone but the Portierka was not happy with that, and took her down to show her something in one of the drawers in her desk.

'Yes, they took everything. They came around the back with a big van. It was very well-planned operation, I'm sorry to say it.'

'But all that money on the alarm systems - didn't they go off? Weren't they supposed to be connected to the police station?'

I felt something at my feet. The Portierka was kneeling down trying to shove a plastic mat under them.

'Pani will be ill,' she explained, 'on this cold floor - and you have only socks' I stood on the mat obediently.

'Thank you.'

'The alarms were ringing and ringing,' Jerzy's voice was in my ear, 'but unfortunately no-one was coming.'

'But that's crazy. What about the insurance anyway?'

'There is a small problem there also,' Jerzy admitted. 'There is some thought that it may be so-called "inside job" with the people who are installing the system of alarm. The insurance company are not very agreeable to pay.'

I didn't know whether to laugh or not:

'What about the books, the library, all the new books?'

'Oh no, they didn't touch those.'

I stood on my mat. The grumpy Portierka looked at me approvingly.

'There,' she said, 'that's better. You've more colour in your cheeks already.' And she gave me a kiss on each one and one for luck to prove it.

Borderline Cases

When we were thrown off the bus, we carried our bags and our child, who was sleeping, through the snow to the border-post. The medical students, who had been kept waiting, clapped rhythmically and banged on the windows, distorting their faces by pressing them against the glass. One man in a ski-hat near the front of the bus had passed me my bag as I got down and said in English 'I am very sorry.' I tried not to look at the jeering faces because I feared I would always remember them, and concentrated on retaining all our pieces of luggage and not slipping on the ice. Rob had Koshka across his arms like a sagging roll of carpet. The burly officer with the big moustache came behind us, straightening his uniform. The two skinny conscripts had been sent ahead.

The officer showed us into a small room and left us there.

'What about the telephone?' I asked, running out into the corridor after him. 'You said we could use the telephone.'

'Not yet.' He jerked his thumb, indicating I should go back into the room, and strode off down the corridor. From behind, he had narrow hips and was curiously high-waisted. I'd a feeling he wouldn't like me noticing that. The bulk of his large rib-cage and his stomach pulled him forward, the very embodiment of overbearing.

There was a small table in the corner of the room. I took off my coat and the shawl I wore around my head and laid Koshka on these on the table, facing the wall so that she wouldn't roll off. Rob sat down on the only chair, his coat still on, wet from the snow. He put his cap on his knees and shook his hair, contemplating the rash of snow on the cap.

The very room seemed preoccupied with the notion of borders, divided by a wooden counter with a flap, the rust-coloured carpet on the far side nearer the window so much more faded as to appear a different colour altogether. On the wall above one end of the counter, a picture in surrealist style showed a red landscape with birch trees bisected by a snaking silver stream. The painting had an orange sky, whereas that through the window was a kind of muffled flint colour. Outside there was mostly snow, and in the distance birch trees, as though a winter version of the same scene.

I perched on the counter.

'Don't sit there.' The large-moustached officer was back.

'Can we have another chair then, please?' I asked before sliding down. 'We are guests, after all.' The officer looked at me as though I were a variety of madwoman which he particularly detested.

'Is it possible, another chair?' I tried again, wishing I had not already got down. He ignored the request, glanced at the sleeping child, her curved cheek pale against the black woollen shawl.

'It is not good to put the child like that. It will harm her back.' He stalked over to the door and made to leave the room.

'Probably several chairs will be even better in that case.' I mimed lining them up, laying the child across them. The mime clearly annoyed him, as if I were casting aspersions on his ability to understand Polish rather than my own to communicate in it. 'They would be...'- mind gone blank on the word 'softer' - 'more...more comfortable.'

My mind had developed a sudden tendency to do this under conditions of personal anxiety and linguistic stress ever since the soldiers had come out to the waiting bus, the burly officer holding the pile of passports which the tour guide had surrendered to him in his hands. Even at a distance through the grimy window I noted that ours were now uppermost. I felt an instant surge of the underlying fear present all the time in Poland, not just the foreigner's fear in a strange place but a version of that referred to in shorthand by many Poles themselves: the sense that matters are beyond your control, even out of control. If you want to do something, however innocent, if you have a cherished wish or desire, 'they' can stop you, can declare it '*nie wolno*' (not allowed) or '*nie możliwy*' (impossible). 'They' can make you have a bad time - and 'they' probably will.

Instantly I sought to imagine the friendly couple we had chatted to while stowing our luggage, to picture them sitting at a table next to ours in the shabby dining room of some Russian hotel, the parquet dance-floor, the chandelier. If I could conjure this vision strongly enough it was an omen that it would become real. Neither the image nor the rationale was convincing. The tour guide, or 'pilot' as he was called, got back onto the bus and the officer followed him. There was some wrangling and our names were called. Koshka, manifesting her usual ability to snooze through all forms of trauma was asleep across Rob's knees, so I went alone to the front of the bus. The medical students were already beginning to stamp their impatience.

What's going on?' one of them said as I squeezed down the aisle. 'The foreigners? Oh, for God's sake!'

'Either chuck them off or leave them on,' his friend in the seat across from him complained, 'but let's get going. To Hell with them.' Except that he used an expression sometimes substituted for this, '*do gazu*'- 'to the gas with them.'

The Pilot explained that we could not go any further. The Russians would not accept us. I protested that the head of the Russian Consulate in Gdansk had himself made out our visas. Surely he'd have been in a position to know if there was going to be a problem. The Officer snorted at the mention of the Russian Consulate, but it wasn't our visas that were at fault. It was because of the kind of border here at Braniewo, a 'sluzbowy' border. The Officer had taken over trying to impress this upon me and was growing more and more impatient with my denseness. How could borders have different natures? I thought I understood the word 'sluzbowy', more or less, but couldn't connect it as an adjective to 'border' in a way that made any sense. A 'service border'? A 'serving border'? A 'grace and favour border'? What the Hell was that when it was at home?

'Just what *does* Madam understand?' The Officer inquired witheringly.

'I understand every single word Sir is saying except this word "sluzbowy", and since this seems to be the reason why we can't cross the border - because we are "Anglicy" and it is "sluzbowy" - then not understanding this word means I might as well not understand anything at all. It is a problem, *prawda?*'

Ironically, it seemed that a sting to the pride was able to restore some linguistic capability. The Officer reverted to the tried and tested method of physical intimidation, moving up another step so that he could loom more effectively, though he was already substantially higher than I was, and using his heavy frontage to bear down. It was difficult not to take a step back. It is not comfortable feeling people in military uniform starting to take a personal dislike to you

The bus driver helped me out:

'Only Poles and Russians,' he said.

'Yes, yes,' the Pilot joined in. 'A special agreement. Only Poles and Russians can pass here at this border.'

'Then why did the Russian Consul give us visas?'

'Why don't you ring up and ask him, your *friend* at the Russian Consulate?' the Officer replied, knowing full well it was Sunday.

Further along the road, behind rolling coils of barbed wire, squatted the equivalent Russian border-post with its single watchtower. Nearer to the wire, in a long grey coat, stood a small square soldier, dwarfed by the enormous kalashnikov he held diagonally across his body, his face impassive under the fur hat. Even from the bus I caught a glimpse of his pale hair and could see that he had one of those bleached, very flat faces. Somebody's son, a proper soldier, black boots planted firmly in the snow. It was impossible to read anything from his expression, but even so I felt I would rather take our chances with him.

'You say the Russians won't let us in,' I told the Officer. 'Have you even asked them yet?'

Rob and I went with the Officer over to the Russian soldier. Koshka was slumped over Rob's shoulder, still sleeping. How did she manage always to be such an antidote to her surroundings, either in her oblivion or in her intense cheerfulness when awake? Had she been inoculated against anxiety in the womb?

The Officer presented the situation and our passports. Though they were speaking in Russian, I was soon convinced that our representative was not using his persuasive powers to the full, since his main purpose was to demonstrate the pointlessness of the whole exercise. My 'helpful' suggestions in Polish, aimed at strengthening our case, were incomprehensible to the Russian and neither welcomed nor relayed by the Pole.

'Oh, why didn't you slip a five pound note - or, better still, some dollars - into your passports?' I knew our friends back in Gdansk would reprove us with relish. 'That would have done the trick.'

The soldier looked pretty incorruptible to me. I didn't fancy making our first ever attempt at bribery on a man with such an expressionless face. Besides, this was not a breach of the rules which he could just let pass on his own authority. Ordinarily, Rob and I observed a no bribing 'policy', though this arose as much out of ineptitude as any particular virtue. We rarely had the experience of moral dilemma because we usually misread the cues and invariably missed the boat. That pause, when some petty official has declared for the second time that what you request is 'not possible...' I filled with logical, emotional, even moral reasons why it *should* be possible, when that wasn't what they were waiting for at all. We might have liked to congratulate ourselves on our uprightness, but, to be truthful, we sometimes wondered afterwards whether we weren't both a little slow-witted.

As far as I could tell, the Officer was being informed that he should telephone his opposite number in the Russian border-post. He accepted this suggestion icily, the look on his face indicating that he was not about to ask any such favours. Each saluted. I pictured the inevitable *schadenfreude* of our friends back in Gdansk, some of whom had seemed a bit miffed that we had fixed up this holiday by ourselves, without requiring their help. The implication that you could make things happen just because you wanted to, and therefore that the situation in their country might be in any way 'normal', was always a provocation. The notion detracted from their own ingenuity and sense of their own frustrations, both considerable. Now it was our turn. It wasn't pleasant to think of having to return with our tails between our legs.

We returned to the bus to retrieve our luggage. The Pilot raised his hands in a gesture of helplessness and presented us with a card with a scribbled telephone number:

'For Gromada,' he explained. The travel company would send someone to fetch us.

Wasn't *he* going to 'phone?

No, no, they had to get on. They'd lost enough time already. They mustn't miss their connection at Kaliningrad. There wouldn't be a problem. Gromada would send a car.

'*Pontius* Pilot,' muttered Rob in my ear.

Naturally, the pilot felt no responsibility, because the situation was somehow our own fault for not behaving like 'proper' Western European foreigners. Perhaps, like the Officer, he was also at some level annoyed with us for the same reason. It was not our business to go on cheap package tours to the recent Soviet Union. We might keep insisting that we were the same as everybody else, but it was not our function to be like everyone else.

As we trudged towards the border-post, the Officer grouched:

'What d'you want to go there for anyway? It's a wild country - *to dziki kraj* - primitive and crazy. Why would you want to go there?'

After all, it was a reversal of the natural order as far as he was concerned, flouting the deep conviction that Russia was a place to escape from and Poland the land to yearn for.

Behind me, I heard again the slow hand-clap of the medical students, before the engine sneezed into life, spurting a black cloud of diesel at our backs.

****

Koshka was awake now. Were we there? Were we going on the train? I explained that this was the border, that we couldn't go any further.

'Can we go back to Gedanicks?' I always found it strange that she could say 'Gdansk' perfectly well in Polish yet often mispronounced the word when speaking English, as if they were part of two completely separate language systems in her head.

'Would you like to?'

'Yes, I want to go back. What's the Border?'

Later, she would refer to 'the Border' or 'when we were at the Border' as if it were a place we'd been on holiday - which in a way it was. Rob, after an initial, heroic display of forced cheerfulness, seemed to have closed down. As there was still no indication of when it might become 'convenient' for us to use the phone - the desire to be rid of us hadn't yet outweighed the Officer's apparent need to insist on his power in every particular - I tried to take my cue from my daughter's lighter mood and led her out into the corridor for a look around.

There was a glass display cabinet on the wall full of Cepelia folk crafts, some of which we'd never seen before. Perhaps there was a special border-post range. The soldiers all kept well away from us, congregating in a room at the far end with a television set and a Christmas tree, or darting into the room next door to make tea. There were a couple more besides the two conscripts we had already seen, at least one a woman. Poles are usually so responsive to children. Perhaps I could take Koshka along so they could show her the Christmas tree. I had vague ideas of some cosy fraternisation in the midst of disaster. This was still an experience, even if not the one we had wanted or intended to have, and as such entitled to have its own character and to be memorable.

The Officer emerged at once, bent, it seemed, on pre-empting any such contact. We weren't to take a step nearer. He waved his arms to send us packing.

'Could we have something to drink?' I asked. 'We're clearly going to be here for a while because we haven't even phoned yet so a car can't be on its way ...' He scowled at this. 'So a cup of tea would be very nice,' I finished brightly, having evidently been put on this earth to annoy the hell out of this man. If it had not been for the continual feeling of desperation I might have laughed at myself and felt sorry for him, faced with my apparently endless cheek and stereotypical national obsession with tea.

'This is not a café,' he snapped. Obviously not. I hoisted Koshka onto my hip and retreated to 'our' room.

We ate the rest of the tomatoes, wiping off the juice and the pips of the squashed one in which they'd lain in the plastic bag, and some of the ham, and the bread, already stale because it was Sunday. I recalled how I'd packed them all for the long journey, for tonight's tea and tomorrow's breakfast, wrapping everything so carefully, each type of food distinct, well in advance. Having to compensate for not being naturally organised, I never enjoyed doing such things in a rush at the last minute. Now it struck me as a bit like packing to go into hospital before Koshka's birth, the preparations so measured, touched with anxiety, anticipation and hope, but between then and the realisation of the latter something so vast, so inevitable and unpredictable. It still wasn't real, that we were here and not on our way - to a future that, whatever it might have been, would now never be, and became, accordingly, somehow unimaginable. On the bus, seeing the soldiers come, I'd felt that if I could only visualise one outcome more strongly than the other . . . yet now that the outcome was so clearly decided, was already in progress, my imagination felt in limbo, unable to envisage any outcome at all.

Rob was still more or less incommunicado - which made me feel that I had to communicate all the more desperately, with Koshka, with anyone I could make a connection with, even with the intolerable Officer. This was how Rob did his feeling bad, as I should have known by now, by shutting down and not feeling anything. Later, he would blame me for being hurt about this experience and thereby reminding him of the hurt he might have felt but had refused to feel. Knowing this made me angry. It hadn't used to divide us like this.

'Yet another ejection experience courtesy of Poland,' Rob had muttered as we'd left the bus.

'Well, to be fair, it was technically the Russians who wouldn't let us in. Usually it's the Poles who won't admit us. Now they don't want to let us out. They must like us after all.' Surrounded by the oppressive atmosphere of the border post, it was hard not to feel that we'd been endeavouring to escape from Poland and had been prevented in our flight. 'Perhaps they don't trust the Russians to give us a miserable enough time. I mean, there was a real danger we might have *enjoyed* ourselves!'

'Has this whole country been on a course in how never to let people do what they want and to head off any possibility of a pleasant experience?' Rob had once raged.

'Of course they have. It's called History,' I'd tried to jolly him along. The fact that in a Polish context this counted as jollying along says quite a lot. Now, though, I could think of little consoling to say.

'Still, I'd rather *not* be in St Petersburg with you than there with anyone else.' It was true, but as I said it I had the sudden suspicion that, for the first time, this might not be reciprocal. I sensed the reproach, though he hadn't said a word: he hadn't used to be a person this sort of thing happened to. He'd once been a paid-up member of the British upperclasses, for Christ's sake.

Tolstoy says somewhere that all happy families are the same, while all unhappy ones are miserable in their own individual ways. I'd always suspected that it might be the other way round. Similarly, it struck me that all bad experiences had somehow a similar character - or perhaps it was just that all of *ours* did. The trouble with travelling on a 'humanity passport,' with giving away what power you have because you don't wish to have status on the spurious grounds of supposed class or wealth or nationality, is that you may very quickly find you have no status at all. Refusing the spoils of victory, so to speak, the accidents of birth and political happenstance, we too often found ourselves victims instead. Surely those weren't the only two options. Rob had chosen to follow this course with me, but he was going to reserve the right to blame me when the occasion demanded.

I perched cross-legged on the dividing counter and played the tin whistle while Koshka danced, shaking her ragged ginger curls and lifting her knees and arms high like a sailor climbing the rigging. I had brought the instrument, as I always did, for those situations where, talking and drinking with people, with goodwill rather than language in common, some cultural exchange might be called for and music often seems a fair currency to offer in return for whatever hospitality might be forthcoming…in those encounters which would not now take place. I could hear the notes piping down the corridor into the other parts of the border station. I knew the soldiers heard. I didn't know what I wanted them to say for me, those jigs and reels, what I wanted them to signify for all of us. I switched to 'All For Me Grog' so that Koshka could sing along. She'd always loved the song, ever since her inability to pronounce its combination of consonants used to make Rob and I laugh so much:

'All for me gog, me dolly dolly gog,
All for me beer and bobacco…'
She had always given an especially heartfelt rendition of
'I've spent all me tin on the ladies drinking gin,
Far across the Western ocean I must wander.'
Still on the alcohol theme - perhaps it wasn't tea we needed after all - I switched to 'Dicey Riley':
'Oh, poor old Dicey Riley she has taken to the sup,' the melody came out like a lament, and as I played it grew ever more mournful:
'…have another little one.
And the name of that dame is Dicey Riley.'
I was overwhelmed by a sense of loss and division, by the impossibility of transcending languages and cultures, the inevitability of misunderstanding and helplessness. I would end up a mad, drunk old lady myself if I couldn't learn to handle this stuff.

Rob was playing hand-clapping games with Koshka to give me a bit of a break, as I had definitely been the one 'on duty' so far. He seemed to be coming back to life just as the Officer re-entered the room, taking us in with one scanning, scornful glance. We could use the telephone now. It must be humiliating for Rob, who understood a lot of Polish perfectly well, to have to communicate through me in a situation like this. No wonder he felt helpless. The Officer, too, looked toward me, projecting his customary resentment. It suddenly struck me that the two were linked, that the Officer was continually irked by the fact that I was doing most of the talking. Whether or not he realised that this was because I was more comfortable in Polish than Rob, or whether or not he was conscious of it at all, he felt he should have been talking to the *man*. It demeaned him in a way to have to carry out these transactions with me. He couldn't help seeing my comparative loquacity as a facet of character, an unnatural pushiness, which Rob should have held in check. As I got up to follow him down the hall, I knew that he despised Rob, with his clapping games and his dominant wife. Koshka had climbed up on the chair to make her taller for the clapping. The Officer plucked her from her position and plumped her on the ground, managing in one look of contempt for Rob and a glare for me to convey that he was a sissy and I an incompetent mother. Of course, I thought, for if it could be established that I were a bad mother then he would be relieved even of the residual obligation to respect me in that capacity.

At the sight of the telephone on the desk in his office, I began to panic:

'I think it would be better if you phoned,' I told him. 'You'd be able to explain what happened. They might not understand me.' If this burly bastard had any authority, it might at least be used to our advantage. He could confirm our situation, increase the likelihood of our getting our money back on the holiday and, even more importantly, impress on them the urgency of getting us out of here. He wasn't about to comply and, while I could feel all too powerfully the imminence of my own linguistic collapse, I was aware that, in my urgency to communicate that he should make this call for us, my growing fluency was somewhat undermining my case. 'Really, under the circumstances, I think it's your responsibility...'

He reacted to the word as if stung by an especially malicious insect. It was never one that went down well in Poland, as I should have known. I'd had to look it up in the dictionary some time ago because I found it a concept I regularly needed to appeal to, and yet which I'd never heard uttered in all my time in the country. Since then, in my presumption, I'd lashed about me with it, on some monstrous mission to hold everyone to account.

Needless to say, I made the phone call myself. The woman at Gromada was highly flustered, and promised a car would be despatched to fetch us. It would take about three hours.

'Is the car nearly here?' Koshka asked when I got back. 'I think it's time we went home.'

****

Home. Now, there was a notion. The flat we had been allocated on first moving to the city occupied the far end of the Chemistry Building. It had bars on the windows with good reason, for it was known as 'the foreigners flat' and was completely isolated and unlit. It was therefore burgled on a regular basis, about once a month. Although unaware of this, we had been fortunate enough to move out before receiving our own initiation, as we found the flat dark and depressing, with only a strip of concrete outside the door on which Koshka rode her tricycle over shards of glass. I had put a card in the window of the post office in nearby Oliwa. The only reply came on a postcard bearing an image of the Pope.

We were interviewed at the big, old house by an elderly lady, introduced as 'Babcia', and her thin middle-aged son. Stanislaw's drooping moustache and stooping gait gave him a mournful appearance. Babcia was about eighty, in a polka dot pinny, with pursed mouth and tricksy eyes, her hair dyed a gingerish brown, which the underlying grey rendered a grainy nutmeg colour with a tinge of green. She sat with her hands clasped in her lap and kept inclining her head and smiling coquettishly, doing her best to appear sweet and biddable. Even at the time I remember suspecting that this was not the whole story, that she must have been told to be on her best behaviour. Stanislaw did most of the talking, venturing his English where he could, managing to be at once twinkling and lugubrious, extremely friendly and extremely shy. The flat in the upper part of the house belonged to his daughter and her family, currently away working in Germany, and was rented out. We would have two rooms downstairs with Babcia. She would keep the other two rooms, and we would share the kitchen and bathroom. The rent was at the upper end of what we could afford. Babcia and Koshka exchanged a few words in Polish, Babcia patted her knees and Koshka promptly went and climbed into her lap.

'There,' said Babcia, 'the little one agrees.'

Out in the hallway, the staircase which had led to the upper floors before the house was divided now ended in a whitewashed, sloping ceiling. Koshka immediately began clambering on the banisters. I waited for the inevitable '*uważaj, bo spadniesz*' (look out, you'll fall), but Babcia only clapped her hands, put her head on one side and marvelled: '*Koshka wszystko umie*' (Koshka knows how to do everything).

And so, to the evident relief of her numerous relatives, we came to live with Babcia in the sandy street lined with old chestnut and linden trees backing onto the forest. Like most of the others in the street, the house had been built early in the century in a German style, solid but slightly ornate, with heavy stone balconies and a spacious garden. It had once been Gauleiter Foerster's house, a neighbour told us later, explaining, as though by way of compensation, that the name of the street meant 'beyond quietness.'

Babcia wore trainers and clutched a string bag when she set off for the shops. She shuffled very slowly but could cover vast distances. Koshka often accompanied her on these rambles, taking in the Cathedral and the Oliwa Palace Park, though I worried about Babcia's road sense. She kept an exercise bike in her sitting room, much loved by Koshka and the many great-grandchildren who came to visit, although she herself was never seen to use it.

Babcia was in many ways infuriating. She would follow me around the kitchen, peering into saucepans, tutting in disbelief or muttering 'oj oj oj' at my culinary practices. She always refused to teach me how to make

Polish dishes, claiming that she didn't know how she did things. When I observed anyway, she was secretive about crucial moves or ingredients, implying that they were intimate feminine secrets I was too young to know - or that I should have already grasped. She would scrutinise my efforts to make *pierogi*, offering no advice until the moment when I deviated in some way from correct procedure, when she would let out a triumphant 'tsk', rolling her eyes and sighing expressively. If Rob washed up or, God forbid, cooked anything, she would dog him even more closely, stepping on his heels and inquiring whether I were sick. She regularly used our towels to clean the bathroom floor, looking guilty enough when caught in the act to confirm that these were not accidental traits but gestures of reassertion over her territory. She would frequently mislay caches of money which she had secreted around the flat, occasioning large-scale searches amid mumbled accusations. Being deaf, she would turn the T.V. in her sitting room up to such volume as to create a wall of sound reverberating through the entire flat - and promptly fall asleep. Polish T.V. news had an extremely annoying jingle which was repeated between each item.

Babcia had lost her sense of smell, so that the delicious aroma of *rosol* - the chicken consommé she made almost every day - regularly mingled with the stench of burning plastic as yet another of her kettles went into meltdown. Without her tenants as in-house smoke-detectors she would doubtless have set fire to the place many times over.

Babcia also collected bread. Being of the war generation this wasn't so surprising, and we could seldom buy little enough and certainly never waste little enough to avoid her disapproval. She would therefore preempt our scandalous squandering of this sacramental substance by intercepting it in the breadbin and purloining it for her 'collection.' She would soak the bread for several days, in buckets which she left around the kitchen and in the bath, before feeding it to the large colony of crows which had accumulated in the garden.

It took some while to dawn on us that we were already among the longer-lasting of Babcia's housemates. For the first few months, whenever we paid Babcia the substantial rent, she would stroke the notes between her hands, cock her head to one side and moan softly, almost coyly, in a kind of coquettish despair:

'*Oj oj oj, takie malo*'- so little, so little.

This sent us into agonies of insecurity. She wants us to offer her some more. We can't do that. She's going to put the rent up. She's bound to. We'll never be able to afford it, but she'll never believe that. She'll keep on putting it up. We'll have to move. But Koshka's so happy ...

Fortunately, on one occasion, this ritual was overheard. Irena was Stanislaw's wife, a kind, elegant, disappointed woman, always beautifully coiffured and highly competent. Her hair had the appearance of golden, spun sugar. Now her blue eyes snapped:

'Babcia!' she reproved her. 'It's a lot of money - and quite enough!'

Babcia subsided meekly, taking a few sidelong glances to check whether the prohibition was truly as inflexible as it appeared. Thenceforward, Irena had always arranged for the payment to be made in her presence.

Yet Babcia's closest relationship remained with Koshka, an unshakeable alliance cemented every morning around five or six o'clock when the two preferred to rise. Stumbling through to the bathroom a couple of hours later, Rob or I would find Babcia in slippers and flowered overall, Koshka still in her orange, penguin pyjamas, capering around to the tinkling tune from Babcia's Dancing Clown musical box, a scrawny black kitten weaving between their feet. Babcia's familiar had been christened Daisy Maradonna, despite being male, but was always known as Kotek, 'little cat'. He would ride with his front paws on the handlebars of Koshka's trike as she pedalled along the carpeted hallway, while Babcia clapped her hands and crowed.

'*Granda banda*,' she would exclaim at any particular feat of derring-do. '*Granda banda!*' Egging Koshka on as she jumped from ever higher steps on the stairs-that-led-nowhere, Babcia remained the glorious exception to all other Polish babcias, never modifying her opinion that Koshka was some species of prodigy who was capable of everything and thus should be permitted to attempt anything. In her dining room the dresser was completely given over to the display of around sixty clockwork dolls, clowns and bears. Bronislaw, Babcia's elder son in New York, had sent them to her over the years, to charm the great-grandchildren. From time to time, for a treat when the pair became especially excited and conspiratorial, they would wind them up and endeavour to set them all going at once, Koshka's excited squeal vying with Babcia's cackle, rising above the grinding and clicking of the twirling, full- skirted, crinolened dolls. Babcia would hop up and down, raising and lowering her arms like a gigantic, conjuring crow, while Ola, Ela and Ala, three of her great-granddaughters, giggled helplessly and Koshka impersonated the clockwork doll dance with her own less stately gyrations on the back of the sofa.

Moreover, Babcia never fully accepted that our two rooms were no longer hers, helping herself to bits of furniture, antimacassars and anything else she fancied from time to time. Among other methods of soothing her frustration on this score, using our flannels to clean out the drain in the bathroom floor was one of her favourites. With Babcia's consent, Stanislaw had given us a dozen flowerpots for Koshka to plant seeds in, an act of generosity which she apparently regretted. After two days of palpable plotting with her friend, she conducted a raid in which she carried off all the pots, tipping out the carefully nurtured seedlings and replacing them with her own tomato plants. She stood these on the windowsill in her room.

I confronted her and in no time we had embarked on one of the ding-dong rows of the kind Babcia loved. Placing the back of her hand against her brow, prima donna fashion, she declaimed in a wounded whisper:

'I am an old woman. I have had a long and hard life. No-one has ever spoken to me as you, Madam, are speaking to me.' She looked sideways out of her drooping eyelids to see whether her words were having the desired effect.

'Well perhaps somebody should have, then you wouldn't still have the idea that it was O.K. to march in and tip out a little girl's plants without even talking to anyone first about what was bothering you. How's Koshka going to feel? What am I supposed to tell her?'

'Old Helena and Young Helena,' said Stanislaw gleefully, coming upon us, seeing someone standing up to his mother and loving every minute of it, though not at the volume at which Babcia's ears were known to be effective.

'Huh,' sniffed Babcia, jerking her head in his direction. 'They can't do anything. They wait for my money.' Stanislaw stopped rubbing his hands. 'Probably they have taken most of it already. What it is to have such a family!'

I knew that the plan for Babcia and I to have a joint name-day celebration party in the Spring had originated with Babcia and Koshka., though Babcia periodically pretended that this was Irena and Stanislaw's suggestion, with which she complied out of graciousness.

With the possible exception of Stanislaw, all of Babcia's descendents were high achievers. Her grandchildren were neurosurgeons at home or scattered throughout the globe engaging in business endeavours and raking in the money in Sweden and Germany, America or Australia. Even Stanislaw had a fledgeling *Import-Eksport* company operating from the basement selling chinaware and silk ties from Hong Kong. Babcia's first husband had also been a businessman and made his fortune in Lodz during the War. We speculated mercilessly as to what nefarious enterprise that might have involved. Her second husband had been an American-ised Pole, and Babcia, it transpired, had spent almost fifteen years in the States. She claimed, however, to speak no English, a fact borne out when she would read Koshka's English books to her, renditions in which not one word was recogniseable by its pronunciation.

Her elder son, Bronislaw, had remained in the Big Apple, where his business had proved more successful than his brief marriage to a Korean woman.

'That one, only for mother,' Irena explained to me significantly, nodding at his photograph amongst the bevy of dolls on the dresser.

As well as sending her clockwork toys, Bronislaw had set up a wealthy foundation in her name. We had little notion that Babcia was a celebrity when she offered to take Koshka to see the city's Christmas tree lights switched on. Watching television that evening we saw the diminutive figure of Babcia on the platform by the overweening tree, beside Poseidon's statue in the main square. Koshka was perched on somebody's shoulders just behind. Tilting her head coyly and graciously to one side, like the Queen Mother, Babcia listened to the speeches, before rotating to give a sweet smile to all corners of the crowd and pressing the button to illuminate the whole of the Long Market to choruses of oohs and aahs.

***** **

We had come to a crisis: Koshka needed the toilet.

'Not *kupka*, only a *siu-siu*,' she assured us, in her best Poglish.

I went up the corridor to inform the relevant authority. He wasn't too happy about it, evidently, but despatched the skinniest of the young soldiers to conduct us to the black wooden hut on the other side of the road. The soldier was a bit older than I'd first supposed, so he must have been a student before doing his military service. He was tall, the fuzz of his hair tow-coloured under his cap, almost as pale as his skin. He wore the little round gold-rimmed spectacles known in honour of their most famous exponent as 'Lennonki'. He was apologetic and embarrassed as we entered the block and I realised the source of the shame which had been discernible in his commanding officer's usual resentment: it was a latrine for soldiers in the middle of nowhere, blocked and overflowing and stinking, not, to his mind, a facility to show to women and visitors. I had some difficulty persuading Koshka to use it:

'It's only *siu-siu*. Can't I go outside in the snow?' Finally, she concluded that at least it wasn't as bad as train toilets because it wasn't moving and you couldn't see the tracks and didn't have to worry about falling through onto them.

Returning, we crossed the packed ice of the roadway, eyes fixed on the frenetic activity of the rollicking clouds above passive fields of snow.

'Could we walk about a bit, just for a little while?' I asked the young soldier as we reached the border post once more. 'You know, for exercise - and to see the sights a little. It is our St Sylwester holiday, after all.' I looked straight at him, didactic as ever or simply desperate for the glimmer of human sympathy in the eyes behind the small, gold-rimmed lenses. Sure enough, he winced, though the flicker of human recognition was soon replaced with uncertainty as to the legality of my actual request. Nonetheless, he nodded us forward and we strolled a little way, inspected the views in different directions, threw a few snowballs. We gazed across the snow to the dotting of trees, then the black curtain of forest where Russia began.

'Don't worry, we won't take any holiday snaps,' I smiled at the soldier, who had now followed us. Never a good topic to mention, even in jest, in a military zone. The young man looked nervous. He had been unsettled by our overt gazing, pointing out this and that to each other. Rather, he knew that anyone watching from the building ... And there he was, the Officer, beside us. He barked several sentences at the erring conscript, and himself ushered us back into our room, treading on my heels every step of the way in case we tried to deviate again. Rob looked tired, as though he'd been waiting for us, as though he hadn't been sure we'd come back.

'What do you want to go there for, to that *dziki kraj,* on a cheap tour like that,' the Officer reiterated as he delivered us, like straying sheep to their incompetent shepherd. 'Is it not good enough for you here?'

'Because it *was* a cheap tour - so we could afford it - and because we wanted to go somewhere different...'

'You can say that again,' he interposed .

'We wanted a holiday - *like everyone else.*'

'Well, you can blame the Russians for that.' The Officer embarked on a blustering speech to the effect that the Russians could be blamed for numerous other things as well...

'*Co to zły, to nie my,*' as the Polish saying goes, I thought: 'Whatever's bad, it's not us.' The phrase at least speaks of some national self-knowledge, even self-irony, and, sure enough, victim nations, like people, can't afford self-criticism. 'But they mean it,' I fumed to myself. 'There isn't any irony - that's just an excuse, a disarming ploy. If I have to listen to this one more time I'll throw up!'

It would be the same old line. For there wasn't a social ill or unfortunate turn of events in Polish life which could not be attributed to a non-Polish source: to neighbours (Russians and Germans), to history (Russians and Germans and others), to Communists (alias Jews) or, suddenly nowadays, to the World Bank (also alias Jews). The Church favoured 'Western influences' as responsible for imminent break-down in Polish traditional family values, particularly through the medium of Hollywood (alias Guess Who?). Conveniently enough, it didn't appear necessary to have a Jewish population in order for your country to be subject to a fully-fledged Jewish conspiracy.

How many years of running their own country would it take before Polish politicians and 'Polish vices' took the rap? But Polish anti-semitism took a peculiar form: not 'you are Jewish so I don't like you' but rather 'I don't like you therefore you must be Jewish.' This meant that any hated or disreputable figure, anyone in the public eye who 'stuffed up' didn't have to be Polish at all. Perhaps few countries like to admit that their politicians, as a breed, emanate from them. But, though the political figures might have changed and the configurations had combined and re-aligned, Poland was traditional in its cast of villains: 'Lech Walesa is the agent of Gypsies, Jews and Germans,' read the graffiti on the underpass leading to Koshka's Pre-school.

I hadn't listened - and, sure enough, I hadn't thrown up. I just caught the last few phrases. At least he'd stuck to the Russians. The Gypsies, Jews and Germans had got off unusually lightly. He was consistent, I'd give him that. He didn't seem much of a 'multi-tasker'.

'But we haven't spent the day with the Russians. We've spent it here, with you.'

'Z Panem,' he corrected my unwarranted use of the familiar form, nastily.

'Alright, with Sir then - and it would have been possible for Sir to have been nice.' With great self-restraint, I thought, I had resisted reissuing the hospitality jibe. I was beginning to bore even myself on that one. 'We're people,' I ended lamely.

The Officer looked as though he seriously doubted it. People don't go around saying 'we're people,' for a start. He didn't bother to reply.

It grew dark. We'd been at the Border for seven hours. The soldiers began to prepare to go off duty. Three new ones arrived in a truck. A cleaner started work in the room at the end of the corridor. She came on a bicycle up the ice-glazed road from a nearby farm, a girl of about eighteen with a blondish ponytail. There had been no traffic through from the Russian side since we'd turned down the offer of a lift in a petrol tanker on the grounds that the man from Gromada was due to arrive any minute and it didn't seem fair to have let him come all that way for nothing. Four hours on, such consideration seemed somewhat misplaced. Another call to Gromada a while later had established that, three hours after our first conversation, a car still had not actually been despatched. It was a question of locating their driver. The woman on the other end tried to imply that he was busy on another job and succeeded only in conjuring up visions of him in shirtsleeves and chauffeur's cap slumped in the nearest vodka bar.

'For God's sake,' I said, 'we've been here all day. I've got a three year-old child ... '

More assurances were all I could get from her. Resignation was setting in, together with an obscure sense of satisfaction that, as time went by, our stranded state was becoming the Officer's problem as much as our own.

As though to confirm this, the Officer burst in. He had himself contacted Gromada and spoke through gritted teeth even more than usual. The driver had indeed been located and was on his way, though he had to stop off somewhere else first The Officer clearly did not believe a word of this claim, which he nonetheless managed to deliver in an accusatory tone, since it was our credulity and outright stupidity which had called forth this display of incompetence on the part of his compatriots. It finally dawned on me that Gromada's performance, even in a way his own performance in front of these foreigners, even such pathetic victim-foreigners unworthy to be impressed, was a source of humiliation to him and that this fuelled his anger and sharpened his contempt.

'What are we going to do, then?' I said. In this new spirit of understanding, as I thought, I was willing to let him take the 'we' as inclusive if he wanted. He marched out of the room without replying, but returned a few minutes later with the cleaner. Koshka had already befriended her while she was mopping the corridor, being allowed to dip the mop in the bucket and then wring out the water. I assumed immediately that the Officer disapproved (Koshka, having no such impression, went on trying to lift the mop bucket now that she was unsupervised until Rob went to retrieve her) but in fact he came to propose a solution. This was Marynia, he explained with such uncharacteristic cordiality it made me queasy.

'I know,' said Koshka to him in Polish, as if to spare him such unnecessary introductions. 'She's got a guinea pig at home.'

The boyfriend of Marynia would be here shortly to make a delivery. The two of them would be driving to Gdansk for this evening in Pszemek's van. They could give us a lift if we wanted. 'Better than a taxi,' the Officer finished expansively, with a positive leer which I attributed to relief at getting rid of us.

We greeted this suggestion with gratitude and delight. Were they really going to Gdansk anyway? That would be wonderful. A rusty, pale blue van growled up outside and Pszemek came in, dark and tousled in black, fur-topped boots and a checked jacket, carrying boxes into the kitchen next to the end room.

We gathered up our belongings and moved them out into the corridor. Rob picked up Koshka. The Officer had resumed his haughty expression and stood in the doorway. Thank you for having us-type jokes seemed out of place, but I never could resist pushing my luck and his stony face was too provoking not to elicit irony. For some reason he got one of the young soldiers to load our luggage into the boot, as though to make sure that every particle of our contaminating presence was removed, while at the same time keeping us shepherded in the hallway, blocked by his bulky body at the door, as if he wouldn't let us go. Overseeing operations, he nonetheless turned to look at us from time to time unpleasantly. Koshka reached across Rob to fiddle with the light switch and succeeded in plunging the corridor into darkness. Before Rob could move, the Officer had turned it back on, pointedly, as though we were incapable of performing a correct action even in this, let alone controlling our insufferable child. Delighted, Koshka reached over to try this trick again and continue the game.

'Stop it,' Rob batted her hand down. The Officer was saying something and we had to concentrate. We both felt the stress of these last moments now that we were finally leaving. Koshka reached again, the lights went out. I hissed 'don't do that' where I thought her face was in the darkness. Rob smacked her hand. Light was restored to the sound of her wails, her tearstained face a few inches from mine. Why is it that we do not betray those we love for the sake of people we admire, but for those we dislike and do not respect, for those whose respect we cannot gain whatever we do?

'Don't take it out on her,' the Officer observed coldly, and we shuffled out into the snow, wrong-footed, lousy parents to he last.

The journey back at least seemed characterised by the 'human touch' we had craved. I chatted away to Marynia about her family. Her youngest sister was just a year older than Koshka. Rob was having a conversation of sorts with Pszemek, with Koshka acting as translator. Rob claimed he'd long ago got over the humiliation factor in being helped out linguistically by a three year-old, but in retrospect it struck me that he had slowed in his efforts to learn Polish since she had been at Pre-School and overtaken him. I felt another twinge of guilt: I'd brought him to a country where he couldn't speak. It wasn't his fault that he liked to learn languages more formally than I did, nor that I'd had a year's head start. Nor yet that three year-olds are language-learning machines. Koshka was between us on the back seat, but he looked relaxed. They seemed to be discussing Pszemek's van, a topic which, since Rob didn't drive and had no interest in motor vehicles, I suspected had been dictated by either Pszemek or Koshka. She had no doubt *she* could drive, given the chance, though she would have preferred to drive a tram because she'd had more opportunities to observe that activity.

We stopped at a garage, but Marynia was adamant that they wouldn't accept any money for petrol. Rob nonetheless managed to buy a bottle of vodka from the proprietor which we attempted to foist on them as a present. In the end Marynia took it and the journey went on. Marynia and I continued our small-talk. Pszemek occasionally glanced meaningfully at Marynia, but I put this down to the annoying habit of many Polish men of deciding when their wives or girlfriends have done enough talking.

There was a brief tussle on reaching Gdansk as to where they should drop us. Marynia insisted they could drive us to our door, whereas we kept saying that we could be deposited wherever they had been planning on going and could simply get a tram, or even stop in town for a pizza. No sooner had I said it than I knew I couldn't face the likelihood of an attempted rip-off on the bill which was usual for foreign customers, even Polish-speaking ones.

'That really would be the perfect end to a perfect day,' Rob agreed. 'Koshka seems fine. I don't think she heard the P-word luckily. Let's get home.'

The luggage was unloaded and leant against the gatepost. We had hugged and kissed and thanked Pszemek and Marynia and wished them a great night on the town, yet there was a pause, a hesitation. They stood around awkwardly and did not go, so we in turn remained, facing them. Pszemek put out his hand, a little awkwardly. I thought he wanted us to shake it, which seemed a little strange after all the hugging and cheek-kissing.

'Now you pay us,' he said. We must have looked confused. 'Captain Boltromiuk said you will pay us, like a taxi, two millions.'

'But we don't have two millions. It's a whole month's wages.' It was doubtless a great deal more than a whole month of Marynia and Pszemek's wages.

'Dollars?' He said hopefully.

'We don't have dollars. We took roubles - for our holiday,' I reminded him. Pszemek looked embarrassed and put one hand in his pocket. The other dangled uncertainly. 'I'm sorry, I don't know what the Captain said. We've got a few thousand zlotys and the rest is roubles. We thought you were driving to Gdansk anyway. We thought you brought us as a favour - you know, out of kindness.'

There was a hiatus, filled with the mutual horror of realisation, the stickiness of embarrassment, of mortification and a dawning sense of being hard done-by on both sides. Marynia's feet shuffled uncomfortably in the soft sand of Zacisze Street. The wind blew through the branches of the chestnut and the linden trees, clattering a little. There was no snow here as there had been at the border, but it was still cold. Our breaths whistled slightly in our chests, making the transition from our bodies to the air. I thought of giving them what we had, the zlotys, but it was such an insultingly small sum. It wouldn't even pay for them to have a night on the town, a night to remember, to make the wasted journey worthwhile. And the gesture would deprive them and us of the last vestiges of something, I wasn't sure what. Besides, I could feel the anger rolling in, blanketing the hurt and the incomprehension. They would go back and complain to the Captain, if they weren't too ashamed to do so. There wasn't much doubt whom he would blame. The stingy foreigners, who'd either duped them out of their money, or hadn't even the grace to be rich!

The house looked dark green and sleeping in the moonlight. A big white splash of moon lay on the stone balcony to the side. The wind harried the topmost branches of the chestnut next to the gate. Marynia went round and opened the passenger door. I supposed her stricken face must reflect my own.

'Well, we're sorry,' I said.

'No, no,' she said.

'Well, thank you anyway for bringing us. We really do appreciate it.'

Pszemek's other hand went into his pocket for his key. Rob and I looked blankly at each other as they drove away. Koshka had been leaning sleepily against his leg. He let go of her hand. At the top of the steps, Kotek climbed out of the box for parcels and letters in the lower portion of the wooden front door on shaky legs, black fur sticking out all over. Babcia, being deaf, often didn't hear his cries to be let in, and when he was smaller Kotek had been able to squeeze in through the letterbox. He was too big to use it as a cat-flap now and meowed, shivering, on the doorstep.

'Poor Kotek,' said Rob, but Koshka was already halfway up the path, bellowing in Polish:

'We're home, Babcia. It's a surprise!'

Tykocin

We drove down the long, flat road to Tykocin past snowy fields flecked with clods of frozen brown earth and the grey stiffness of trees against the sky.

'Here you can see there was an ornamental lake,' Stefan was explaining, 'and here the avenue began - can you see those pollarded trees, there, behind the silver birches?'

'Is that part of the house?' my wife asked him.

'No, that was a lodge of some kind. *That's* where the house was - somewhere over there.' He took his hand off the steering wheel to gesture to the left. 'Of course the grounds had been reduced before Grandad's time, but the house was only destroyed after the war. It was ruined for quite a while - looted, by all accounts. In the end the Russians burnt it. They didn't save anything, the family. All rather sad, *I* think.'

At the corner by the synagogue we got out of the car, the snow forming soft circles about the cobblestones at our feet. Stefan leaned across the passenger seat to remind us:

'Give my love to Aunty Krysia when you get back to town. She'll make you very welcome, I'm sure. The whole family will. Tell her I'm sorry I can't come in person this time - but you know how it is.'

'Pepsi-cola calls,' my wife said. 'The new Poland and all that.'

Stefan was to attend to an important meeting in Olsztyn that evening, where representatives of the Pepsi interest - of which he was one - were to negotiate a settlement to the recent cola-wars with their multinational rival. Since the Wall had come down, Pepsi could not expect to maintain its virtual East-European monopoly - the standard four bottles of Pepsi and four of mineral water beside every place at state functions and Party meetings. The advent of true competition was upon them, and naturally Coca Cola's product had the advantage of being perceived as more 'Western.' They'd made serious inroads into Pepsi's market in several cities, but now a provisional deal had been struck, Stefan had confided.

While maintaining the appearance of a 'war', the two giants would in effect divide the country between them.

'That's not competition, that's a conspiracy,' my wife had said.

'That's Capitalism,' Stefan had agreed, happily. She's not a cynic, my Nell. Sometimes I think it would be better if she were. I never thought I would, but I occasionally find her endlessly renewable idealism tiring and in itself depressing.

'They'll rumble you, you know, Stefan,' she'd told him. 'Our neighbour told me the latest joke in the lift the other day. He said, "You know under Communism everything they told us about the Communist state, about our country, our system, it was completely false. Unfortunately we now discover that everything they told us about Capitalism was true!"'

'That's good,' chuckled Stefan, 'that's very good. Still, as I always say, History is an ongoing process.'

Our little girl was already examining a manhole cover some way away with a stick. The Synagogue was an immense cream-coloured building with a red domed roof and a Spanish look among the shuttered, single-storey wooden cottages, painted dark green and brown, which lined the main street. In the distance I could see the peeling yellow stucco of the Catholic church and the double cross of the Orthodox church behind.

'Tell Aunty Krysia, next time, O.K? Poor Aunty'll probably be a bit miffed I haven't come, especially being so close. I used to be over all the time when I first came to the country, and Ewa and the boys used to come and stay.' Stefan's usually cheerful face, with its close-cropped hair and dapper moustache, pulled itself about momentarily at these slightly troubling thoughts. 'She likes to see the boys, but I think they find it a bit stifling there - and she finds them a bit much, too boisterous for her or something - but *c'est la vie*, don't you think? And business is business. I don't think she really understands...'

'Life in the fast lane,' Nell teased him, heavily. Everything she did seemed to annoy me that day. 'It's very kind of your Aunty Krysia - and you,' she was saying.

'She'll love to have you - you're sure you've got the address, and you know where to get the bus? Greet Uncle Witold and Bronia for me, and enjoy the village,' he waved a hand at it expansively, 'land of my fathers and all that. Bye.'

The quiet, blue, Western car with its Polish plates pulled away, and we went into the synagogue, the first I'd ever entered. Warm yellow light came from the creamy walls with their ochre inscriptions. A menora, prayer books, a prayer shawl and phylacteries were set out in a case, together with a figurine of a Jewish man wearing these garments. A slight screech, and a tape recorder started up, though we had so far seen no-one to operate it. Chanted prayers and singing in Hebrew snaked between the pillars and crept up the walls like smoke in that high, empty place.

In the outer part of the building there was an exhibition of paintings, inspired by events early in the German occupation, when half the inhabitants of the town, with blankets over their heads, had been marched into the forest. Our daughter had found some steps to play on. A couple of matronly women were engaging her in conversation, exclaiming over her replies. She was by this point completely bilingual. Nell started chatting to them too. I envy her facility with languages - she seems to learn them simply by pretending to be the people she's talking to. Look at her now, her expressions, the way she moves her hands, her eyes, how she's standing, her chosen phrases. She seems to her interlocutors so sympathetic, so un-foreign, so comfortingly familiar somehow. She reminds them of someone they can't quite... She says herself she makes plenty of grammatical mistakes, but no-one seems to notice: she's not at all as they would imagine an English woman, they tell her, she seems, well, Polish - is she sure she hasn't got any 'ancestry'...? They don't realise, she's not just being Polish she's being *them*. Her assimilative energies alarm me: there seems no end to them.

Then she wonders why people *mind*, why they feel betrayed when she suddenly expresses unorthodox or unacceptable opinions in their own homespun phraseology, which felt a moment before so cosy. Having inhabited them, she feels so hurt when they 'reject' her, when they fail to throw aside the prejudices of a lifetime, when they won't make an exception for her - and her inexhaustible didacticism.

One of the women is giving our little girl something.

'Oh, kokoshka, kokoshka,' Koshka exclaims. It is a little hen, an egg cosy knitted from pink and red wool.

'For your Easter breakfast,' the woman tells her. 'Keep it safe until then.' Nell assures her that we will, thanking her. The woman is explaining that Koshka's red hair is lucky, and I think Nell is repeating the Polish saying that a woman without freckles is like the sky without stars. She's so good at this sort of thing. I don't know why I begrudge her. She's an extraordinary person - that's what I thought when I first met her - so full of warm feelings for other people. I just wish she wasn't so traumatised when they're not returned. She still has that pinched look under her cheekbones because she's in a synagogue and there are no Jews, and because of thinking about the soldiers and the people with blankets over their heads, but she is gaining new hope from this encounter, I can see. The woman is speaking of how she was a child in the war when these things happened. She and Nell are both sniffing and patting each others' arms. The second woman looks on, nodding and shaking her head by turns, bringing out some tissues before distracting Koshka by pretending to hide behind a pillar.

The bus shelter is wooden with a thatched roof. Six headscarved women are sandwiched together on the bench inside. Two elderly men stand around, hands deep in pockets, studying a poster on the wall. The women greet us noisily, moving the baskets by their feet to make room for Koshka. We protest that it isn't necessary, and ask about the bus to Bialystok, as one woman hauls Koshka onto her knee.

It seems we will just about have time to nip into the village shop over the road, as Stefan has enjoined us to do. The proprietor, in a red head-scarf and a tight, lime-green sweater, also greets us enthusiastically. She is the mother of an old Solidarity friend of Stefan's, an erstwhile union or-ganiser now in parliament. She offers Koshka a lollipop - the imported 'Western' kind you never used to see - from a stand on the end of the counter which doubles as a window display. Koshka is delighted with her 'lizak' and starts unwrapping it at once.

Rising out of the dome of lollipops is a plastic statuette of the Virgin, an Israeli flag crooked in one elbow. I suppose the village must have a fair number of Jewish visitors, a standing synagogue being a rarity in this part of the world: perhaps survivors - if there were any - or their descen-dents, or pre-war inhabitants who left in time. I deduce that this is either a very friendly or a very cynical gesture. Nell looks about to cry, so pre-sumably she thinks the former. She is prone to benign interpretations - or at least I would have said so before she got so sensitised and now she's all the more devastated when it turns out to be the opposite. And who has to deal with the fallout from that? *I* do. I know it sounds petty. I know she's entitled to feel this way, but it's so predictable. I don't want her to toughen up or pull herself together or anything like that, or I guess I do, a little. She can't go round being so *raw* all the time.

The lime-green lady is receiving our message from Stefan with evident delight. Several other customers come in and Nell is introduced, then Koshka, then me, 'the husband.' I call Nell my wife, even to myself these days. We long ago gave up trying to explain. Apart from anything else, I can't pronounce the Polish word for 'girlfriend'. Conversation is well under way, so I feel a bit stiff and foolish - as if my role is simply to look the caricature Englishman (as I do much of the time). I understand quite a lot but I can't launch into another language as Nell does - and Koshka too of course - who overtook me within weeks of starting Pre-School. I've been to classes and I know a fair bit in theory. Nonetheless, it's somewhat discouraging being outstripped by a three year-old. We barely get out in time for our bus.

The passengers on the bus are debating whether we are Jewish.

'*He* is, that's for sure,' one of the men is asserting. They're not con-vinced about Nell, though they think Koshka's red hair is suspicious. Overhearing us speak English, they assume we don't understand what they are saying. Perhaps they don't care if we do. Even I can't fail to register that sharp-sounding word 'zyd' over and over. Nell is starting to flinch. Any minute now she'll have to weigh in - pleasantly as ever but with that undertone of urgency and - can't she ever see it? - so much more to lose than they have. And she'll engage them in conversation and half win them over.... If she could just stop educating everyone for a moment, if she could just not *listen.*

It's like the lyrics of songs, surely. You don't have to hear them if you don't want to, you can simply receive the overall impression of the sound, the music. Mind you, Nell always *does* notice lyrics, even when not focussed on them, whereas I never do. Maybe it's the way her brain's wired, not a matter of sensibility at all - in which case I shouldn't blame her, but I *do.* Has she no will? Why the Hell can't she *not* listen, *not* suffer all the damn time. I know it's their fault not hers, but I am angry with her. She doesn't *have* to let them determine her life like this. She thinks you can alter the world by enlightenment, by good will and persuasiveness. She has plenty of those, so she's certainly the one to do it - if that's the case. I suppose I don't. I don't know what I think. I guess I'm tired. Lucky Koshka has crashed out with her head in Nell's lap.

There was waste-ground either side of the house in Elektryczna Street. Brown spikes of dead weeds poked up through the snow. The street had once had another name and the houses been quite grand, but now the walls of Number 8 had a charred look against the uneven white ground. It was one of only two nineteenth century mansions that still stood, converted into flats, with newer single-storey houses of concrete or wood dotted in between. The house had belonged to Aunty Krysia's husband, a doctor, Stefan had explained, and the couple and their remaining daughter currently occupied half the ground floor.

In accordance with Stefan's instructions, we rang the bell of the side door. The door stuck, and it took a while to get it open wide enough for us to enter, never mind see our hosts. The hallway was dark, and the coat-rack, thick with hats and scarves and old fur coats appeared to extend across its entire breadth. It seemed it was Bronia who had opened the door and was still behind it urging us to please, please come in. I could hear effusive greetings bobbing about beyond the swathe of black fur, and the more solemn voice of Uncle Witold.

We finally squeezed our way into the hall. Bronia emerged to help with our coats, a woman in her late thirties, very eager and very nervous, quivering with welcome. There had been dark hints from Stefan about her not having been terribly well. She certainly did not look at all healthy, with clammy, waxy skin to which her thin, dark hair seemed to stick. There was a bluish sheen around her eyes and temples and even to her large, uneven teeth. I liked her immediately - oddly enough because, despite the evasive mannerisms, she struck me as a straightforward person, as well as an intelligent one.

Wasn't it lucky, Aunty Krysia was saying, we were just in time for Supper?

She was a rather dumpy woman, with pink cheeks and grey, flyaway hair. She gave expansive hand gestures, slightly reminiscent of Stefan, and seemed to smile whenever she spoke. She disappeared into the kitchen, refusing all offers of assistance, but giving Bronia a keen look that caused her to follow a moment later, leaving us to Uncle Witold, in his shirt sleeves and braces, eager to show us his 'Radio Room'.

This was a dark cubby containing a small wooden chair submerged by stacks of books and piles of papers. Behind the invisible desk was a large wireless set with knobs and dials. The chaotic shelves were crammed with various odd-looking gadgets, only one of which, a nautical barometer, I could identify. Since only Bronia spoke any English I was somewhat at a disadvantage during this exchange, but Uncle Witold appeared extremely gracious and friendly, and, judging from Nell's responses, I gathered he was also witty. Looking at him, it was clear where Bronia got her sallow complexion, though his had the addition of a pall of grey stubble, and moist, surprisingly red lips. When he laughed - as he was inclined to do suddenly - his large pointy canines lent him a wolfish, hungry look.

The guests didn't want to be bothering with his nonsense, Aunty Krysia asserted, reappearing. She ushered us past the dining room, which seemed to be laid for a banquet, into a spacious salon with grand piano. In the manner of the East of Poland, the parquet floor was bare while the Persian carpets hung on the walls. Except for two framed photographs in a corner, there were no other pictures, though a curved ornamental sword hung over the piano. Krysia intercepted my gaze:

'We saved nothing, nothing,' she moaned, waving her hand at the interior.

We soon learned that this would be her cry almost every time she entered this room. In fact most aspects of life in the household had this ritualistic quality. We sat in that room each day before being called into the dining room for meals. Everything was slightly askew: door-frames slanted, the once-polished parquet floor was chipped and sloping, requiring the legs of the Steinway to be levelled with small blocks of wood. Even the ornamental sword hung from a bent and dangerously protruding nail. As we conversed with Uncle Witold, a chair-arm knocked by a careless elbow would detach and clatter to the floor, and the silences were broken by the occasional patter of plaster, the soft trickle of white powder from ceilings and cornices forming little conical heaps beside the skirting board.

Meanwhile, once we were conducted to the table, Aunty Krysia would emerge from the locked kitchen with braised beef cutlets, red cabbage, potatoes sprinkled with dill, and pickled green tomatoes on antique silver dishes, or bring tea in silver pots on a silver tray. No-one but Krysia was permitted to enter that kitchen - even Bronia had to wait at the locked door to receive her burden to deliver to the table. It was only by means of some assiduous spying that I got to glimpse that mysterious sanctum, our hostess stepping over the piles of dirty plates on the floor to reach the 'pantry', a kind of glass conservatory lacking several panes at the back, then rummaging for cutlery among the pyramids of encrusted pots on the table, by the sink or on the stove. The stacks of unwashed crockery formed little pillars all over the floor as if someone had excavated the ruins of a Roman under-floor heating system. Aunty Krysia wove her way tetchily but stolidly among them to conjure those immaculate, traditional meals for Uncle Witold and the guests seated at the white-clothed, mahogany table. The effect was rather of being waited on by a whole troupe of menials - with Krysia herself as both servant and grand dame. She sat at table, ate little and daintily, keeping a hawk-like eye on her guests, urging them to eat:

'Don't you like the pickled tomatoes? No, no you don't like them...,' despite protestations that we had already consumed three helpings. Bronia always went stiff when her mother entered the room with the tray, and her palms would begin to stroke her skirt downwards compulsively over her parted knees, which trembled under the table, although usually incidents were avoided. Once, Bronia, carrying in the second tea-tray behind her mother, suggested some milk for the English visitors.

'No, they don't need that,' Krysia barked contemptuously. 'Don't be foolish, Bronia.' Bronia looked as though she might drop the tray to the floor but she placed it on the table in slow motion and with audible effort and care. Aunty Krysia broke the silence, pouring tea and speaking lightly of this and that. Bronia turned to me with urgency and I willed her to be about to say something I could help her with.

'At the University you teach literature, yes?' she said in English. 'You teach some Romanticists?' It was almost a plea.

'Yes, it is my speciality, my special subject. Do you...?'

'I very like,' she said heavily, 'I very like Coleridge. And Byron. You know Coleridge his work?'

'Yes, yes I know him.' She pulled out a small leather-bound volume, which she seemed to have been secreting under her cushion, to show me. I took it with interest: it looked like an early edition.

'I very like Coleridge you know,' she said carefully, then at once appeared so overcome with emotion that she ran out of the room, leaving me with the book in my hands. The next moment we heard strains of the Grande Valse Brilliante, modulating swiftly into the Fantasy Impromptu, swelling to a barrage of declamatory sound. No-one said anything. I felt uncertain about my original impulse to follow her with the book and discuss it further on our own. Although the music in itself would have drawn me, it seemed for all its declamatory nature to be an act of entirely private communication, directed solely at its performer, or possibly its dead composer - and I could not go and stand next to her while she made her wild and anguished prayer to the soul of Chopin. While I still contemplated how intrusive this might be, I registered another change. The music was still Chopin's, but something else had entered it.

'Mama,' said our little girl, who had been amusing herself in the salon and now came running in. She dropped her voice as if she didn't quite like to mention it: 'Mama, that lady's playing the piano - like *this*' She thumped her two clenched fists up and down on the edge of the table just as the music from next door collapsed in total discord and disarray, and part of the leg supporting the table broke off to distract us.

I remembered the faded colour photograph in the salon: Bronia and her two sisters - on cello and violin - about to play on National Television. It must have been the early seventies, to judge from the swirling brown and orange hues and hexagonal designs of the studio. The older girls looked in their early teens. Bronia, aged about twelve, was seated at the piano, hands in her lap, eyeing the camera. They had been a family of prodigies then, always in demand, always playing together, touring the USSR and Bulgaria, once a big concert in Prague. Now the elder two lived abroad in the West, one in France, one in Switzerland. Only Bronia remained, giving some lessons at the Conservatoire, and occasional recitals. The cellist was married, Krysia had told us at dinner, and had a little boy.

'She didn't tell us about him until he was one year old - just fancy,' she had said.

The next day Bronia took us on a tour of the Music Academy where she worked, but she was very subdued and conversation was difficult. She apparently preferred talking to Nell in Polish and helping Koshka try out various pianos and a harp. I felt oddly estranged from Nell. Something was missing, and I realised that the sense we so often had of ourselves against the world, of our closeness and similarity among so much cultural difference had evaporated. I didn't know why and it bothered me, so no doubt I was rather morose. Bronia's nose was dripping and she didn't wipe it. She looked very vulnerable, and I reflected miserably on my luck that one of the first people I had felt I might be able to have a conversation with, a conversation that I alone could supply, was probably too barking mad to have any conversation at all. It had seemed to matter - at least briefly - that I was a man and might know something about poetry. Now I'd resumed my customary invisibility.

218

Bronia had to stay at work, so we trudged on into town over the crusty snow. Although no more had fallen since we arrived, the temperature during the day was well below freezing and kept the snow along the pavements hard and white, not slushy at all. Koshka, in her Russian fake-fur hat and coat, was in her element scrambling over the crunchy heaps, though even she began to close down somewhat under the effects of the cold. I found it simply hard-going. We had reached one of the older quarters near the centre of town. Nell read out a street name:

'Isn't that where Stefan said his Grandad lived ? You know, when he had to live in the town after the War. I'm sure that's the name he said.' Nell's memory for detail was beginning to strike me as almost as annoying as her other 'talents,' so I kept my reply non-committal as she pointed to a straggling row of low wooden houses. All I remembered was Stefan explaining that we might find Aunty Krysia a bit moody sometimes:

'She's a bit touchy you know. She's never got over Grandad's death. Didn't I tell you? About Grandad and the KGB man? It's a great story - a bit tragic really. Well, after the War, when he had to leave the estate, Grandad changed his name, got hold of a dead man's papers and went to live in Bialystok - but every few weeks he would get a visit from a KGB man, each time the same one, and this man would come, and have tea and chat about local affairs. Grandad was on the People's Reconstruction Committee (everybody had to participate in some of that stuff) and his visitor would say casually:

"You know we are still looking for that bloodsucker Gosiewicz from over Tykocin way.' Grandad would have to agree that such landowners and bloodsuckers of the people were the cause of all misery in the world. 'Come to mention it, you look a bit like him. Yes, a really striking resemblance. You're not related to him, are you? No, no, well no-one would want to be related to such a person - not a good idea at all."

He played with him like that, like a cat with a mouse. Sometimes he would not come for two months or more; other times he showed up several weeks in a row. Grandad knew he had nowhere to run to. He had to keep his nerve. They would take him in if they wanted to. The strain went on for several years - but in the end his heart couldn't stand it. He was fifty-four when he died.' Even Stefan, with his disengaged tone and his incorrigible and most un-Polish cheerfulness, had seemed momentarily saddened. Nell was all for taking a look down the street, but I found that I powerfully did not want to, and she did not press it. Once I would have assumed it was because she understood how I felt - or because we felt the same.

So we walked back past the vast white sweep of the Branicki Palace, a high school now, Bronia had told us. Not for the first time, I wondered what Stefan must have been like at eighteen, sent over from London with his bassoon to relatives he had never met, to study music and to live in this strange country he had heard about all his life. The bassoon had been stolen long ago. Mirroring his adopted country he had undergone a series of transformations. By what means had the fun-loving but earnest young man who sat around campfires in the woods and had friends in the underground made way for the sharp-suited businessman, dapper and smiling, with his little moustache and implausible skinhead haircut, his upbeat manner and his energy? And Ewa, his wife - tall, competent and very beautiful, a doctor at one of the city's hospitals - which had she chosen? When she turned to him her chiselled face and drew back her long, black hair, which incarnation did she see? Or were they in the end a continuum, in essence the same?

'He is named Michael but I call him Uncle Mis,' Bronia was explaining. 'It is diminutive for Michael but it means also 'Bear' or Teddy Bear, yes?'

It was one of the secret errands we had promised to perform for Stefan, to conduct Bronia to her disgraced aunt. Krysia had never spoken to her younger sister in the thirty years since the girl had gone and married a Ukrainian of whom her family disapproved - as if there could have been a Ukrainian of any other sort!

Uncle Mis was indeed a heavy, ursine sort of man with an impressive Dali-esque moustache and monocle, which he screwed in when he wanted to view his paintings. Perhaps the monocle was also a tribute to Dali, since it seemed an oddly aristocratic touch for a man who clearly in all other respects loved to play up the attributes of the muscular peasant which I suspected had first so attracted his wife and so horrified her family. He showed us several of his recent works, catching them up lightly in his big hands from where they stood, propped along the wall, holding them in front of us: maidens with long, tangled hair against apocalyptic orange skies, gazing into pools, or seated beneath sepulchral and twisted tree branches pierced by a purple moon, suggestive damsels on white horses... I didn't really know whether this style was catering for a new post-Communist liberal taste. He was demanding Nell's opinion. I could see she didn't like them but in her customary way trying to find something that she could say with sincerity that would still be complimentary. For the first time since I've known her, she found nothing, actually told a lie and pronounced them 'very nice'.

'Huh,' exploded Mis. 'Nice?! They're crap! I do them for the tourists, the Boche.' He opened up a cupboard in which were stacked smaller paintings, not dissimilar but in a finer Blakean vein. 'These are a bit more like it; these are mine - and this - 'he pulled out a bronze sculpture of Pilsudski in his Marshal's uniform on his horse, riding along glancing down to one side. 'Now *there* was a man,' he said. I hoped Nell wouldn't get into discussion of the activities of the supposedly benign dictator in the twenties and thirties, but she was still sufficiently embarrassed at her bad faith over the paintings and its rebuff, and did not. Also I suspect she was a little unsure of this man, who appeared to have made a career of speaking his mind - especially as she had just been caught out *not* speaking hers - afraid to find out what sort of a mind it might be.

'Zosia isn't here.' Mis enjoyed stating what was by now fairly obvious. 'Why don't you people ever tell her you're coming - though she's grateful enough, poor wretched little cow. If I was her, I'd tell the whole pack of you where to go. Now you'll have to put up with *me*.' He lumbered off to make us tea and serve up a goosesberry cheesecake that he had made, an unheard of accomplishment for a man. Nell felt almost sure enough of his benignity to comment approvingly on the fact.

'Oh, my little mushroom does not bake,' was his rejoinder. 'She does not cook - in fact it's hard to know *what* she does. She was earlier at her friends all the afternoon, gossiping and talking nonsense.' Then, of Stefan: 'Give my regards to that ridiculous, mincing midget, my nephew. Give him my big love - oh and be sure you tell him I called him that, he'll like it.'

I didn't follow the next part of the conversation he was having with Bronia until I remembered that, on the journey down from Gdansk with Stefan, there had been some reference to an older man her parents had wanted Bronia to marry before her illness last year.

'You follow your heart my little fishkin,' Uncle Mis advised her loudly across the table. 'Look where it got me! Who do those morons have in mind for her?' he turned to us: 'Some dribbling fool of a university professor, still lives with his mother. You marry your Ethiopian if you want to and damn the lot of them.' Bronia blushed:

'He's from the Sudan, and ....he's not going to marry me,' she said. 'Probably he has a wife.'

'Probably several,' put in Uncle Mis helpfully.

'Don't you know?' Nell asked, incredulous.

'It is not a thing to ask,' replied Bronia demurely.

I wondered what the hell was going on. I had definitely missed something.

'Then he's a fool!' Uncle Mis patted her thigh.

The next afternoon, following another foray into town, we returned to Elektryczna. Krysia was in the kitchen, unable to reconcile her unwillingness to open the door lest we should see inside with her need to intercept us and assure us that the guest we would find in the salon with Bronia was there with none of *her* approval.

'He is here,' she said, managing to convey a smile for us through the clenched teeth required to hiss her displeasure at events in the other room - whatever they were. 'I don't like for him to come here, of course, but he comes for Bronia. It is for Bronia. What can I do?'

Nell made a rueful face and nodded sympathetically, as did I. Did she know what the hell Krysia was talking about - because I hadn't a clue? *Who* was here? As so often when much of the interaction has taken place in a language I don't really follow a lot of the time, I might well have missed some crucial piece of information. Nell doesn't always remember to tell me: because she and Koshka understand, she tends to assume I do too. Perhaps it was the fifty-year old suitor we had heard tell of - but I thought the family was in favour of *him*. Or a psychiatrist of some kind - that would be it - Bronia seeking help after her putative nervous breakdown: the family evidently didn't want certain things to come out.

We walked into the salon and saw a tall, black man almost folded up in the small armchair across the silver tea tray from Bronia. They had the tray on a little stool between them, she in an armchair from which the caster immediately fell off as we entered the room, causing a bit of a flurry but allowing me to help her find something to prop up the chair and therefore cover some of her embarrassment. I knew at once that she had had to insist on the silver tea service, just as I knew with equal certainty that Bronia had not been permitted to receive her guest in the dining room. I thought of all Krysia's kindness and hospitality towards us - we who qualified for it by virtue of our race, nationality, status and family association - and felt sad, as if it were all invalidated. Or maybe I felt sad that it was not, that being a racist doesn't mean you are necessarily a horrible person, merely places an absolute limit on your kindness and whom it's extended to. Yeah, and Hitler was nice to his dog, Nell would say. I was still not fully dissuaded of my psychiatrist theory when Bronia introduced him as Dr Mahdi:

'Khalid, please,' he said, straightening his angular limbs like a folding ruler to rise from the chair, and standing up to shake hands. I caught sight of Bronia's face, her lips no longer pulled back over her teeth, as they often were when she was tense, her face shining at him: she could handle this social situation, as she could handle anything when he was there. I thought we shouldn't stay, since Krysia, albeit out of dislike of being in the same room as a black person, had been so good as to leave them alone, but he and Nell had begun conversing in Polish, so I ended up with Koshka doing drawings on the floor, which she would go and present to her chosen recipient at intervals. Bronia brought more tea and some cakes, and in between discussing the subjects for her pictures and assisting Koshka in several artistic decisions, I watched the scene as if from afar.

He was eating the cake with a spoon, so softly, between smiles. The way he raised his hand to his face was like a cat washing. He did not see Bronia's madness, only her vulnerability, or rather he did not mind it in the same way. Bronia was not just a sister, though there was some of that. Of course he would be a doctor and he must go back to his country. He would marry a young woman and have children.

He was a cautious man, Khalid, I thought, observing him as closely as I could. He appeared naturally reserved and I did not think he meant to lead Bronia on, but she had so little experience, I surmised, that any efforts of reticence on his part were wasted. I saw the way his smooth forearm lay on the tray with its sleeves rolled up to the elbows. It looked longer than it should have done, as though it stretched to reach further across the tray towards her. He did not make expansive movements but was comfortable with his gestures - yet with every motion forward or back of his body or his arms, every inclination of his head Bronia moved with him, his mirror image, as if she could not leave him alone. I have never seen anyone so near to tears for such a sustained period, tears of pure joy, and yet never one fell, and his image swam in the glowing irises of her eyes. I couldn't bear to watch. For all kinds of reasons, cultural misunderstanding among them, she would be crunched, it was clear. She would lose because it was now in her nature to lose - and because his apparent reciprocity might be no more than politeness, part of his grace.

I remembered the party where I first met Nell, how we'd never stood more than a few inches from each other in our conversation - which we'd thought was banter but which we could not allow to end. Just like that, that mirror image thing, that complete mutuality. Whatever our conscious minds might have thought about it, I had followed her and she me. Even when I'd had to go to the toilet she had sat outside the door, and when I came out she'd handed me a cat, which scratched me, somehow symbolically. And I'd been perfectly happy and fallen asleep next to her on the stairs as though we'd been making love for several hours - though as yet I hadn't even known her full name. How far we'd come from that!

Koshka was giving Khalid a coloured drawing, which he took, admiring, asking her to interpret various details of the design. Bronia had no will in relation to him. Were I in his position, I realised, this would frighten me far more than if she had. *Then* I would have known what to do, but she had only the residual will in fighting her mother. Without that, there would have been no connection at all - but this terrible no-will of hers, this giving herself up without condition or question, as if a man were something of which she had no experience, and to which she had no resistance, handing herself to him on that silver tray....? Nell had always seemed so robust, so feisty almost. I'd liked that from the start. I must admit I find it really irritating when she's ill, or when she's upset, as she is a lot these days. It's like she's asking for something I can't give, that wasn't part of the deal. I looked again at Khalid. I would have been afraid to be the object of such devotion, of such need.

Nell and Khalid appeared to be discussing his experiences of racism in Poland with some fervour. Bronia simply looked bemused.

'Why did you have to get him onto *that*,' I hissed at her afterwards. 'That's your preoccupation, not his. He's over here studying to be a doctor, getting opportunities, using equipment he'd never get near at home. Of course he gets this racist shit, but the pay-off's completely different, can't you see? Why can't you give people some credit?'

'He said he had to be home, to walk before it was dark. He seemed quite nervous about it. I only asked him why.'

'As if you couldn't guess …'

'He was chased by a gang last week, he said, waiting in the street outside the hostel, waiting for Arabs or Africans to beat up.' She paused for breath. I didn't concede anything. 'Look, we're talking about a country where old ladies cross themselves in the street when they see a black man, where shopkeepers serve all the white customers first … For God's sake, no-one else is going to ask him about that aspect of his stay in Poland.'

'Oh and you're going to let him express himself? Perhaps he can talk to his fellow-Africans or the Arab students back at the hostel - or maybe they don't feel as damn sorry for themselves as you think they ought to. Who's the racist here? It's *you* that thinks because he's black he has to be suffering - and he has to be suffering in the way *you* suppose, because it's the way *you* would, the way *you* do. I'm sick of it, frankly.'

Nell's attempts at sulking are usually pretty laughable - she can never resist the temptation to communicate - but she managed for the short remainder of the afternoon. I have to admit the uncharacteristic silence did begin to unnerve me.

It was to be our last evening at Elektryczna. Bronia arrived unkempt at the table. Her tufted hair would not smooth down. She had seen her guest off over an hour before and been invisible since then. For the first time I registered how defeated her posture was, the taut protruberant bulge of her belly.

'Water retention,' Nell had observed, knowledgeably, the first night, 'and hormones. She has a little row of hairs on her chin and her moustache is quite dark.' Women notice things like that. I felt momentarily mollified towards Nell. Perhaps she understands all this better than I do. 'Her body isn't processing stuff properly,' she'd said. 'Liver, or kidneys, or whatever it is. She isn't well.'

The conversations of that final meal blurred for me. It was as though an awareness of the limited time remaining propelled each of our hosts into a hyped-up, intensified version of themselves:

'Coleridge very, very beautiful poet for me is,' Bronia was stating urgently. 'I very like Coleridge, you know - and Beethoven, very, very fine,

very strong, you know, many, many very beautiful feeling is in his music..
I very like ...'

Uncle Witold had embarked on an anecdote about an encounter before the War involving a 'little Jewess from Lodz', mimicking her marked
accent and plaintive tones. I felt an odd tightening of my stomach and
glanced across at Nell, but her eyes and her expression were fixed. I tried
to imagine a world in which 'little Jewesses' from Lodz or indeed any
other Polish city were commonplace. It was clear that Uncle Witold still
inhabited it, the spittle forming at the purple corners of his red lips as he
pursed them in imitation, laughing at the punch-line, which he repeated
several times.

Aunty Krysia was explaining that only Lech Walesa could save Poland
now, because he was a worker and of peasant stock, a true son of the
Polish soil. Accustomed to the universal derision directed at this 'only
hope of the nation' by our middle-class, intelligentsia friends - how humiliating it was to have a president who didn't even speak 'proper Polish'
and so on. - this assertion came as a surprise. Perhaps Aunty Krysia ex-
emplified the old Marxian adage about the proletariat and the aristocracy
having more in common than either class with the bourgeoisie. The
thought cost me the next part of the conversation and consequent bewilderment as to how it had transformed into reminiscence of a Ball at
the Branicki Palace:

'It was the Military High School in those days,' Krysia smoothed her
flyaway hair. 'I was just a schoolgirl, and we went first to a special Mass.
Oh, but when he came and sat beside me in his uniform, in his white
gloves, I was the envy of all the other girls. That was the last time I saw
my brother,' she began to cry.

After that had come the War, then he'd been in Damascus, then London, condemned to marry an Englishwoman (nowhere near as disastrous
as a Ukrainian and at least mitigated by necessity, in Aunty Krysia's view)
and a life of exile in Crouch End. There Stefan had spent his childhood,
imbibing these stories and his peculiar detachment from them, learnt not
only that he was inscribed into these narratives of faraway places and
people but also that he was in some fortunate way exempt from them.
Yet he had said with unconcealed pride on the way to the village:

'If you get into any difficulties at all, with anyone, just mention my
name. The surname will always do the trick. They'll remember the name.'

Koshka was fast asleep in the brass cot under the embroidered shawls.
Her breath came easily through her soft lips, which formed that trape-
zium shape we had so admired when she was a baby, the sucking pad
still large enough to hide her teeth, quivering with the passage of air. Nell
was restless beside me, slapping me across the chest with the back of one
hand, muttering. I'd never heard her talk in her sleep so continuously,

assembling what almost amounted to a narrative of her dreams. Uncle Witold seemed to figure, judging by the number of times she mumbled his name: Uncle Witold in his cubby-hole room with his radio. His radio was talking, she said, or at least *he* claimed it was, ventriloquising through her mouth as she began to emit a stream of incomprehensible Polish with all the clicks and hisses of poor transmission provided by her tongue.

She was unnerving me now. She has much sharper hearing than I do, and I strained for distant sounds of Uncle Witold's radio that might be inspiring this. Uncle Witold was looking straight at her, she said. He'd turned and seen her with his white, wolfish face staring out of the dark corner with the piles of books and the radio. He was easing himself out of his chair, smiling and saying 'my dear,' but he'd picked up one, no two, or even more of Bronia's black fur coats. He had them in his arms, over his hands....

I grabbed her arms, trying to wake her, but she was thrashing and gasping for breath. She'd managed to get her head underneath a pillow and was twisting from side to side, gulping at the non-existent air. Realising that my grip had incorporated itself into her dream and was increasing her terror, I let go. He was pushing the coats down into her face. He was going to suffocate her, smiling all the while above the mountain of fur, as her tongue worked furiously to spit it out of her mouth.

In a single movement she flipped over onto her front, as decisively as if she'd been turned with a fish-slice. Rising onto her knees in front of me, she hit me backwards full in the mouth with a clenched fist. I was so angry I punched her hard in the small of the back as she twisted away and the next moment she was bolt upright, screaming into my face.

Aunty Krysia and Bronia appeared in their night-gowns in the doorway, Uncle Witold coming up behind, fully clothed. They were most concerned. We were so sorry, a bad dream, we mumbled across one another, red-faced. It was Uncle Witold who suggested - or joked - that there might have been a mouse, and they left smiling reassurances and wishing us a pleasant remainder of the night.

We glanced anxiously at Koshka, who miraculously had not stirred, then, disbelieving, at each other. I had seen it in Nell's eyes when the others were in the room, that somehow everything that had appeared merely eccentric now struck her as sinister and horrifying, that all the madness of that house and all the history of its people had come together, condensed, oppressive and unendurable. I didn't want to hear her say it. I couldn't tell her it wasn't so - and there was nothing, absolutely nothing, I could do about it. We watched each other at that moment in a way we never had before, dropping our eyes with the ebbing of our shared embarrassment, sealing our longer shame, each knowing with certainty that we had no comfort to give the other.

The Latest Persian Blue

'It is so-called Persian Blue, my cat, very rare,' Wandzia was explaining to Ray and Sally, the two Peace Corps volunteers who'd come into her office to borrow a book. She swivelled languorously in her office chair, trailing her arms and lulling the already complacent cat, whose furry grey sides lapped onto her thighs like the deflated skirts of a hovercraft. It was not a particularly fat cat, just extremely furry, with pale, smoky fur like dandelion fluff and the expression of someone trying to puzzle out a crossword clue. It could suddenly turn its translucent sea-green eyes on you, as though you alone might hold the answer, but apart from these disconcerting moments of total eye-contact would ignore everybody and everything.

'In Poland you can buy such cat only for dollars - from Russians of course. They bring these animals over in suitcase, over the border, you know. They are asleep with drugs, naturally. Often they do not survive - later they have many illnesses - but I was lucky: I received my cat from friend who bought it from one Russian man in Gdynia. This cat was already grown and it was quite healthy, but my friend could not keep it - his wife was allergic,' Wandzia gave one of her loud laughs. 'His wife is allergic to me too, so I think it is suitable, right? And I take it in my flat.'

Ray and Sally nodded, looking faintly stunned, trying to follow all this - but as ever privileged to be near such competence and worldliness and generosity as emanated from Wandzia.

'Today he is with me because he is not well, poor baby. Under all this cloud-puff he is tiny, skinny thing. I have to take him to vet. It's the big fucking expense.'

Ray and Sally took their borrowed book and slipped away, reluctantly. Others soon replaced them. I had brought Koshka to see her; Justyna had popped in with her two nieces, Ulka and Agnieszka, as she was passing. Agnieszka was one of Wandzia's many, many god-children. Maja was gleaning a few tips for her new 'Active English' courses, and Dougie, the Scotsman from the Language School with a sideline as a Dictionary Rep., was there with a special offer and a few reminiscences of the previous night's party. Wandza entertained us all, returning the cat to his wicker basket and putting out her umpteenth cigarette.

She stretched out her white arms and folded them behind her head, where they shone palely against her ginger hair. There was always a performance, and yet the performance was always authentic Wandzia. She was her own creation and there was always life where she was, and energy. If she was depressed, or otherwise bored or annoyed at something, she would fulminate frenetically and make herself and others laugh. It was a wonder she ever got any work done, but that was *how* she worked, typing like fury with a child chatting on her knee, conducting business calls in the midst of a room full of people, passing jokes back and forth. At the centre of a vast network of friends and connections, she nonetheless had attention enough to spare for everyone.

Wandzia was one of those secretaries who ran everything. Some of her 'bosses' might not like it, but that did not alter the fact. Heads of the British Council 'mission', as it was jokingly termed, might come and go, but she was the fixture. Wandzia was the one who knew everyone, who knew how things worked. She was the one to ask about this or that. She was the one to arrange matters, and a wise boss recognised and made the most of that. Celia, the current incumbent, despite occasional surges of ambivalence on this score, was mainly one of these.

'It is the latest cat, darling,' Wandzia mimicked her pet's donor. 'These actors are the worst!' She knew almost as many actors as she did artists, having been an artist's model in her time. She wore her hair outrageous colours and in outrageous styles when she felt like it. When she was dowdy she bore it with panache, like a statement, that made those around her conspire to cheer her up. Her clothes were eccentric, often gleaned from the theatrical productions with so many of whose participants she was on intimate terms. In short, she had a quality usually unforgivable in her society: she did not seem ready to conform - and the fact that she got away with it made everyone feel better. She smoked in the street in her 1950s elbow-length lace gloves and swore when she felt like it. She could hold her drink, and was tall enough to tower over many of the Polish men around. And though not exactly hefty, she certainly bore little resemblance to the stick-thin Polish girls who made up the majority:

'I am what your friend Julie calls a 'thumping quine,' she told me once delightedly. 'It is a Scottish speaking, *prawda?*'

While there was no shortage of such female powerhouses at Babcia's age - the point at which most women seemed to come into their inheritance - it was usually considered decorous to wait before revealing such strengths, since premature display of this kind might well do you out of the means of attaining that ultimate power, namely a man, a family. Of the four other women I knew who had even a shade of such lack of submissiveness as was Wandzia's defining characteristic, her independence of mind, her dangerously observed wit, all were single: one divorced and the others, even in their late twenties or early thirties already recogniseably '*stare panny*'- old maids.

Only extreme prettiness could outweigh such 'disabilities', and Wandzia was enchanting and gorgeous rather than appealing in a mainstream sense, plump and creamy, with a slightly heavy, puckish face, whose individual features she was adept at working in a droll and expressive manner. Wandzia had no husband but she had plenty of admirers. She was everybody's friend and auntie, godmother or confidante. A gay icon in a society which barely acknowledged the existence of homosexuality, a femme fatale, every woman's rival but every woman's intimate companion, almost always too close to the wives of her admirers, too fond of their children held at so many christenings, to capitalise on her apparent conquests.

The next time I saw Wandzia she looked terrible, her eyes puffy and red, cheeks yellowish and swollen with crying.

'He was putted down, my cat,' she said. 'My poor cat.'

'I didn't know he was so ill.'

'Neither did I. He had a cancer of his liver without any signs to see it. He stopped to want his food, it is all.'

I recalled the mixture of mock disdain and sardonic endearment with which I'd always seen her address the cat and realised with shock how completely she was distraught.

'Now am I really alone,' she said. I gave her a big hug and she sobbed so hard and so noisily into my neck that I found I had begun to cry too, emerging from our snuffling heap to look anxiously at Koshka, surely traumatised by the sight of two wailing adults, but she gave us a tolerant, almost cynical look. Two grown-ups crying couldn't be for real in her book, her own exuberance rendered her impervious to distress or unpleasantness and she went back to galloping the toy figures from Wandzia's desk up and down the coffee table. It didn't seem to be a defensive mechanism, just a natural cheerfulness. Perhaps it was her response to Polish pessimism, just as mine was to refuse to be anxious about all the things 'they' worried about - cold ankles and lack of headgear in children, the inevitability of poor health, the height and dangerousness of slides - while unconsciously growing more and more nervous about everything else. After all, I had reason to know that that the dangers of Poland were primarily to the psyche.

'We're going to the opera tonight,' I said. 'There are lots of complimentary tickets. I'll get Marek and Julie to get you one. Come out with us and cheer up.'

So I was there when Wandzia was introduced to Yuri. Leszek, a journalist colleague of Marek's, brought him over to meet us, a visitor from the Russian Federation, a physicist studying at the new laboratory on Chopin Street. The inherently bizarre nature of opera was accentuated by this production of *The Magic Flute* in Polish, the sublimity of the music set oddly against the possibility of understanding the banal snippets of libretto as Suzanna, in white frilly organdie dress and pantaloons, poured forth her aria from a swing that pendulumned across the stage.

Yuri was quite tall, at least by Polish standards, with a large crooked nose, and appeared to be trading without embarrassment on the yearning quality of his stereotypically 'sad Russian eyes.' He gazed at each of us, repeating our names slowly, as though being introduced to the love of his life at the very moment of learning the desperate circumstances which would divide us forever. In his grey polo-neck sweater and wide-lapelled brown jacket, despite the air of cultivated tragedy, he still communicated insolence.

'Huh,' Wandzia whispered, 'he looks like he knows he has very big dick.'

'Well, perhaps he has,' Julie and I giggled, the risqué frisson of women who don't consider themselves likely, or have much desire to make such comparisons any more.

'I know what you mean. I don't like men who fancy themselves either.'

Still, he struck me as a person so obviously on the make that he actually might not be. I don't know when or why I became cursed with the notion that the obvious is to be overridden, that what proclaims itself most powerfully to your judgement is to be rationalised away. Where on earth did I get the idea that the truth is so damned subtle? Did I imagine it or was he really scanning our hands for wedding rings, sizing up Wandzia and myself, since we had both come alone? Should I refer to Rob, who was back at the flat babysitting, or lap up a bit more of that flattering attention before he decided I was too washed out and matronly to be worth the expenditure of his energy? I really *had* lost confidence, I noted, even as I registered that he had already lighted on Wandzia.

The two of them were thick as thieves in the bar at the next interval and flirting shamelessly as I left them to retrieve our coats. I could hear Yuri's laugh and the unfamiliar sound of Wandzia speaking animated Russian. Julie and Marek had departed promptly, needing to relieve their neighbours' daughter who was minding little Tomasz. Clearly surplus to requirements, I deposited Wandzia's coat on a nearby stool and scurried after them.

Within a week there was a change in Wandzia. A frisson of excitement hung over every action she performed, as if everything she did, viewed from some imaginary, external perspective, made her more beloved. She had always had confidence, and everyone knew she did her job well. Now the wrist bone glowed beneath her skin as she reached for the telephone, the curve of her calves and motions of her fingernails as she stood before the cabinet rummaging for a file were etched differently in space. She had always been fluid and languorous but now each part of her body seemed otherwise aligned, as though so many caresses had altered their relation to the air around them. A phrase of Blake's came into my head - 'the lineaments of gratified desire' - and we, her many friends, were glad for her, and not a little envious in a way we told ourselves was nostalgia. For we too remembered the beginnings of things. How lovely it must be, we reflected, to be still in that phase of existence. Of course Yuri was a bit of an operator, but Wandzia's manifest happiness allayed our misgivings, at least for the moment.

****

His hair is very black and very sleek against his head, shaped like a seal's - or at least he tries to keep it that way, but really it is floppy hair that wants to wave - and his jaw is always a little blue from stubble. A small scar, curved like the imprint of a thumbnail, interrupts the stubble on his chin. He has little purplish shadows under his eyes from working late, with a touch of yellow, almost like bruises, hardly noticeable, just enough to draw your attention and make you want to kiss them, kiss them away with little butterfly kisses. His eyes glitter when he looks at me between his kisses. I want to tip myself right into him, to pour myself into him through their complete blackness, and he holds my face so gently between his two hands. Sure, he makes me a little crazy - but who cares? I am not a teenager - far from it - and I can look after myself. I want to make love to every part of him, I want to crawl over every inch of him doing that, trawling for the stuff of my obsession - starting with his ears under the floppy hair. Even to have him stroke my fingers makes me want him so much I can hardly bear it - he is the first man ever to stroke my fingers so I never dreamt how much I would like it.

'Clever hands,' he says, as if I were a concert pianist, not a secretary - but not as though he just means clever when I touch him, though I hope I am that too. In fact all Yuri's compliments are the more effective for being slightly awry or delivered at inappropriate moments:

'You have blindingly beautiful tits,' he tells me on the tram.

'Blindingly obvious, you mean,' I deflect him. I feel as if my insides are being drawn out of me whenever I look at him or even think of him, and that he's reeling them in, laughing. He looks at my face and laughs sometimes. I don't know what he sees there. He did that the very first time I met him, but I was so excited then and I thought: 'Let him laugh. I shall have him.'

I know what they think. I know what they say about him, that he is presumptuous and a wastrel and taking my time - and will take more than that if I let him. I know. I will give him whatever I want to. Of course I know he has a wife and a son too. He told me he is separated from them already for two years. He has to tell about them on his application form to study here - I've seen it - and for the visa. The Russian authorities want to be sure that he will come back - and the Poles too. The British do the same at their stupid Embassy when you go for your interview for a visa, ask if you sleep with your boyfriend, if you love him and so forth. If you don't have one you make one up quick, or a sick mother or anything. Do I believe about this separation? I don't care - but I do believe it - and if I didn't I wouldn't care either. I tell my friends, he needs a woman now and I need a man - it's simple as that. We need a fuck and everyone needs a hug and warm feet under the blanket. We go out and we have fun. We smoke and we kiss and we tell jokes. Who cares whether I love him or he me? In any affair between two people, no-one knows for sure. No-one ever knows. Do they think they know?

The first time with him in bed, the first few times he was quite silent. I was afraid he didn't like me. It was the first time in my life I have to wonder about this. I know I am beautiful. I know I am a sexy woman. Usually they are so grateful, usually they say the little things that make you know it is all right, that they are glad to be there. And usually it's plain that they are very glad indeed. Of course it is always a little unfamiliar in the beginning with someone you don't know very well - even though often they were my friends before, and I am proud to say they stay my friends after. But Yuri, who can rattle on all the time, about cars, about football, about music, about people he's met, who is so full of jokes and compliments, said almost nothing at all.

'You're very white, aren't you?' This was his only comment. Of course I am. One reason I dyed my hair ginger is that I have the skin for it. It didn't sound like a compliment particularly - or not, either. Just an observation. Compared to whom? I didn't like to think about it. Still, he made love like a man full of emotion, so naturally I don't complain. Some people don't speak when they feel a lot. I hoped it was that.

And before long he could not be near me without putting his hands on me and I felt I had my answer.

****

'It's obvious to everyone that this man's a complete schmuck,' blazed Justyna. 'Everyone but her.'

'Well, the wife and son thing may not be as clear-cut as all that,' I ventured, 'I mean, people have complicated arrangements for flats and such over there.' I played shamelessly on the old prejudice that Russia is a wild country, a 'dziki kraj', strange, Eastern, faintly barbarous - or often definitely barbarous - as Justyna snorted and I wished I believed my own statement.

'He's just using her,' she reiterated for about the fourth time in the conversation, and we lapsed into silence and our own rather complicated feelings, including jealousy, I suspected. In discussions such as these with Justyna and others, I didn't want to feel part of a female *schadenfreude* party, driven by the notion that it had to be impossible for people to have this much fun and be happy without a price - if not the price we had all subsequently paid then another one. It wasn't so bad, family life, but our greater or lesser degrees of contentment and our relative security didn't seem to allay our sense that we were missing out.

One of the pleasanter side-effects of feeling at times marooned in a sea of cultural difference, I reflected, was that it drew Rob and I together. We could carp about the things that infuriated or upset us, check our reality against one another's. It must be similar for Marek and Julie, I supposed, though perhaps less so, he being Polish - or at least Scots Polish, though she was the one who'd assimilated, if you asked me. It occurred to me that I seemed to perform that function for her - certainly as far as children were concerned. Julie had no time for Yuri at all, claiming that she could tell he was a person with no sense of responsibility, and as I knew this was a pet hate of hers I made no more feeble excuses for him.

Yet while Justyna ranted, Maja, who owed more to Wandzia than any of us, said hardly a word. Maja had stayed in Wandzia's flat, during her temporary separation from her philandering husband. That was after she had lost the baby, and before she started getting the money together to set up her own language school. Early on in Wandzia's affair, she had been the only one to propose explicitly warning her friend - though it was unclear what she could tell her that Wandzia did not already know - and latterly had fallen silent on the subject, as if her suspicions were too deep and too dreadful to be given voice.

****

We took the night-tram to Jelitkowo, walked from the turning circle through the gap in the bushes onto the beach. Pebbles clumped blackly on the shoreline. White undersides of seagulls gleamed in the reflected moonlight bouncing off the sea as they hung above the recurring lines of breakers. Over and over the fringes of white foam hovered before smashing down.

In the dark on the beach we found him. I don't see too clearly, and of course I won't wear my glasses.

'Is it a seagull?' I said, catching speckled movement in the gloom.

'A fish,' said Yuri, 'a fucking fish! No - a seal, a seal.'

We staggered over the shingle to where it lay, like a miniature submarine, tail flippers crossed, its mouth open in a soundless cry. Whatever it is that makes baby creatures instantly adorable he had in abundance, looking up with his soft black eyes, trying to use his flipper to scratch his nose. He had a full set of tiny teeth as he yawned again. Did that mean he was not so young, that he could catch his own food? Yet there was a fluffiness to his small, rotund body, speckled grey and white. The white patches shone oddly, accentuated by moonlight. He had a darker blotch over one eye.

233

'What do we do?'

'I only know you're supposed to leave them,' Yuri said. 'If you touch them, the mothers don't like it. Maybe they reject them after, because they have the human smell. You're supposed to leave them and the mothers come to get them.'

'Yes but where the hell _is_ she?' The wind had got up. I scanned the churning water for the dark blob of a seal's head watching the shore.

We walked away from the seal along the beach. In the far distance we could see the clustered lights of the resort of Sopot, the long sweep of Monte Casino Street and the dark sliver of the Molo, glinting like a needle, extending into the sea. Baltic swans would be sleeping under the wooden props. We wandered, but we didn't want to leave our charge and sauntered back.

The seal kept adjusting its head on a large stone as if trying to get comfortable on a pillow, closing its eyes fitfully, opening its mouth, emitting no sound that we could hear. In between its apparently determined attempts to doze off, it would switch to a continuous eye contact.

The tide was coming in. The seal continued to gaze at us as if it knew that we were of the utmost significance to one another, even to the point of survival. There was still no sign of the mother.

'We should adopt it,' Yuri suggested.

'It takes after its father, that's for sure,' I looked up at him.

'Why, no sense of direction?'

'It pulls the same face as you do when you're going to sleep.' I impersonated the seal, the way he stuck out his muzzle, resolutely closed his eyes and breathed out audibly, even over the crash of the waves. The seal showed absolutely no sign of wishing to return to the water. As the encroaching waves lapped its tail, it inched away and actually tried to pull itself further up the beach. I tried to drive it back, clapping at it to turn it back as it came towards me. It gave a few half-hearted swipes at my hands with its teeth.

'No, you crazy creature, _that_ way.'

The seal regarded the water fastidiously as if it didn't much care for its natural element. I noticed how nervous I was, how anxious about this animal. Wouldn't it be for me, ordinarily, just an absurd incident, a funny story to tell? Out here in the dark so close to the sea all my bravado was gone, and I realised I lost it some time ago. I couldn't understand it. With men, the power I had always made me feel like I had a safe place. Only with Yuri did I feel so insecure. What happened to good old 'what-you-see-is-what-you-get' Wandzia? I didn't feel like myself any more, or I felt like myself from a long time ago. Just this silly regression of being in love. That was it. And it seemed as if the sea gave us something so precious we didn't know what to do with it but stare and be afraid. Maybe we fished it up ourselves by accident somehow, like in the fairytales - but it wasn't going to give us three wishes. _We_ had to do something. It trusted us to do it, and we didn't know what.

It reassured me that Yuri was unsure too and I reached for his hand. Afterwards it occurred to me that Yuri was a proper father perhaps for the first and last time that night and he didn't know what to do. So for over an hour we stood and kissed and

234

looked at our protégé, keeping our vigil. How long could he last without his mother? For the hundredth time the creature fidgeted about to get comfortable on his bed of stones and yawned and closed his eyes.

'It's probably a protection mechanism while he waits for his mother, to conserve energy, like hibernating,' I proposed hopefully. I couldn't help thinking each time he closed his eyes that he mustn't fall asleep, that hyperthermia would claim him and he would slip away.

'With all that blubber?' Yuri teased me, but it was hard to overcome the natural impulse to want to cover the seal up, to keep him warm as you would a person. I had started to shiver, and in the end Yuri convinced me that my need was greater and gave me the extra sweater he had round his shoulders.

While I was pacing about trying to get warm I realised the seal had followed me up the beach. I grew agitated at this and turned and ran into the sea.

'Hey,' Yuri shouted, laughing at me, but he watched as the seal manoeuvred itself round and hauled itself cumbersomely after me. I was up to my knees by the time he metamorphosed into the purposeful, competent creature he became the moment he hit his first wave. There he was, riding each one, bobbing expertly. I came back to Yuri.

'Did I do the right thing? Will he be O.K. now, do you think?'

'I hope so. It should be easier. At least he is mobile - he looks much more in control, doesn't he? He can find his own way, or some other seals will find him - or his mother. Maybe he can even catch his own food. At least he can move. At least he is not only waiting.'

I hugged him, smelling his smell on the sweater I was wearing.

'You are all wet,' he said, and for once he was quicker to say it than I was: 'I love you,' kissing me his wonderful kisses.

****

With near triumph, Justyna repeated the news to me when I came in half-way through:

'The money for the new private courses - Wandzia drew half of it out on Thursday; She didn't get to the bank in time so she kept it overnight in her flat and it's gone. Celia's going mental.'

'She's lost it?'

'Don't be stupid. Only one other person knew it was there.'

'Oh how awful.'

'Isn't it just.'

I felt sick, the sensation Wandzia must have felt when she first realised the money wasn't there.

'In her knicker drawer,' Maja confirmed grimly.

****

I could see what they all thought, but there has to be some other explanation. Yuri helped me search every corner of my flat. For three solid hours we searched, but I knew it wasn't there. I knew where I had put it, and I knew I hadn't moved it. So did he. Forty million zlotys. He offered to lend me some - as if that would help. It wasn't my money.

Did I know Yuri had a new computer, Maja told me ten days later, in his room in the hostel, a brand new computer?

'Yuri is many things but he is not so stupid as that,' I informed her - so the next time I saw her she just happened to mention the three new computer programmes he's supposed to have bought, programmes for improving your English.

'He could have saved himself the trouble, I would be quite happy to talk to him in English.' Except that he hasn't been to my flat for three days. We didn't have a fight but I know he has stopped coming. I remember how the sleeves of his sky blue sweater flopped over his wrists and the backs of his hands like a pianist's fancy cuffs as he rifled through the desk, looking. He always stretched those sleeves by pulling them down to cover his hands when he was working in his chilly room in the Hostel or late at night at the laboratory. I watched the purposeless movements of his fingers in the drawer, knowing that he was not seeing what was before him for the first time.

Yuri is going to Germany, then America. He will return to Russia first to collect some items. I don't ask what these might be. There are other people present in the office when he gives this information. Apparently he has an invitation to Texas and the possibility of a research fellowship.

On the day before he is due to leave I bump into him in the Long Market. It is to be our goodbye, evidently. He kisses my hand but makes no attempt to hug me. I am frozen there and don't realise until he doesn't that I had even wanted him to, even to pretend, even that he might be sorry, that he might regret that I'm no longer any use to him, that it might have meant something when I was.

'It's been a pleasure,' I try to pull an arch face. And all the time I stand there as if I am waist deep in the sea and each breaker sour with the taste of humiliation hitting me and drenching me anew. I sense already that the humiliation is the least of it. I don't have to know yet. If he would just hold me I could look past his shoulder and not know.

It is growing dark already. Over his shoulder, above the Brama Gate, a satellite dangles, looking at first like a single star. You see them quite often now, the commercial rather than the spy variety. There always used to be plenty of those. I remember there was one outside the window when I sat on the bed, at my Grandmother's out in the village, and Waldek told me. I sat on the edge of my Grandmother's bed, staring past the soft down of Waldek's face at the stubbly field in the twilight beyond the window. He looked young even to me then - a mere seventeen myself - and the gingerish down on his upper lip reflected the light. My Grandmother lived only a few kilometres from my parents, but her more lackadaisical chaperoning always made it easier for our purposes to meet there. She had never lived in the town, where living space was in short supply and young couples suddenly needing to get married presented real problems.

Waldek, my first lover, was explaining to me that we couldn't go out any more when I went away to University. I wasn't even going to the nearest city, but to Gdansk. We were such different kinds of people, he said. I was the clever one, after all. He was going to work in the Tractor Plant like his Dad. I was too grown up. He wanted to have a good time. Perhaps he didn't want to stick with just one girl. I took things a bit too seriously. I thought of his body, lying next to me in the narrow bed, how sweet it was. Though I was as inexperienced as he, somehow I knew he was afraid of me. I would move into a world he didn't know, and grow away from him with people he had never met. He was getting in first with the rejection he diligently expected to be his. Though he was so tentative with me, sexual experience had given him a bit of a swagger. Lately he'd been sniffing around Monika Kasprzyk in a way that made me feel slightly sick.

And I hear his voice telling me these things, blurring with Yuri's voice saying God knows what, thankfully not much. He has started to chatter but has the grace not to continue. I see his lips forming the words as I once saw Waldek's, knowing he would never allow me to kiss them again. I was so tempted to enfold Waldek in my arms: I didn't believe him, or any of his reasons, just this other thing which emanated from him, this strange resolve that smelt like fear - and surely I could embrace that away. As though to forestall me, he moved quickly to squat in front of the chimney stove, poking in more kindling. If I hug Yuri it won't solve anything, won't turn or stay his course - adults are so much more fixed in their purposes than children, the children Waldek and I, at lofty seventeen, did not for one moment imagine we were.

Even saying nothing, I'd made Waldek feel stupid, as if I laughed at him. It was true that I didn't believe him and that nothing made any sense. He continued poking at the fire, unnecessarily, since it was already blazing and then took up a copy of that day's 'Dziennik' and began to roll the first page diagonally into a spindly tube, though there was plenty more kindling in the box. The anger was in his face, stiffened by shadows and the orange heat of the fire. Unable to speak, I was forcing him to serve it up 'neat', making him a bastard in his own eyes.

Didn't he know that it was all for him? What could I do differently? Had I made it all too easy for him? I had believed in love, not in all that stuff. I had never played hard to get, or only briefly in the very beginning. He had me and he didn't want me. He didn't want me at any price. Did my body not please him? Was I not the person I felt myself to be when he looked at me? How would I ever care about any of the things that I was if he didn't want them? And because I couldn't say any of this, because I couldn't conceive of the world we inhabited, the places we went, our friends without us together, wildly I came out with: ' but what will I say to …to the people we know?'

His contempt was instantaneous: 'Is that all you care about? Tell them what you fucking well like.' Later, grinding with anger and shame, I would accuse myself of playing into his hands. He had done this to me yet I was the one convicted of the utmost shallow conventionality. He, Mr Tractor Plant! Hardly the most Bohemian individual on the planet! Yet nothing took away that sense of having been tricked, *even at such a moment, into being in the wrong, into giving him the relief, so palpable, that he barely knew he sought.*

I had looked out then at the single unwavering light, and thought: why should it not be a spaceship? And I prayed harder than I had ever prayed in my life, so hard it made my insides hurt, to let this be a miraculous day in the whole of human history. Perhaps I could not bear that this should have happened to me on an ordinary day, or I longed to be overtaken by events so overwhelming they would engulf and alter everything. I looked out of the window to see them come, lit by the phosphorescence of the mother ship, rows of stick-like figures tottering across the stubble-ridged furrows of the field. I know now the Martians don't land for occasions like that. They don't ever land at all.

Yuri is gone now. I carry on down Dlugi Targ. The statue of Poseidon raises his trident ready to strike. Even the muscles of his back look like Yuri's. Now we won't make tiny babies with big noses, but that isn't the worst of it. I am not a man. I don't know what it feels like to want to make a woman pregnant when you are fucking her. Yet I do know what it means to want to hold Yuri's child inside me, for my womb to hold his child. It was never very likely - I am almost forty - nor probably a very good idea. He does not seem like a man who would respond well to stress, to pressure and obligation. Maybe it would just have been to have something of him after I'd lost him. Did I know it all along? I don't think so. I remember the breakers on the beach at Jelitkowo, row upon row, and our lost, piratical seal.

Those first few days when he seemed lost for words, was it then perhaps that there was something real, something that surprised him? I won't ever know. And whatever account I come up with for myself, to save myself, even to forgive myself, I will never be able to think of him without this sensation, as if my intestines are being ripped into strips and twisted between his hands like faggots of newspaper for the fire.

I still have his sweater from that night on the beach. For a whole week I wear it, even to bed, smelling of him. I breathe the smell and I don't have to think. Then I take it off, roll it into a ball round my hands and push it into the washing machine. I don't cry any more after that.

****

Celia attempted to adjust her bra by shunting it with her elbow under her purple sweater and pushed back her straggly, unevenly-highlighted hair one more time. It needed doing again she knew, and stretching out her legs beneath the desk she was aware that her feet inside the calf-length leather boots felt swollen and a bit sore. She was trying to drink less these days, and was managing - mostly - but she'd certainly overdone it last night at the Heveliusz. She was experiencing what her mother - a complete lush who never quite knew it - following a night of outrageous excess, huge and hideous family scenes etc., once famously described as a 'strange lassitude'. Unfortunately Celia's daughter, Charley, had phoned

238

from boarding school quite early on in the proceedings when they were still all at her flat but when she was already quite well gone. Now she'd have the daughterly disapproval to deal with next time they spoke. And if she didn't phone her back this evening, having fobbed her off - as she recalled anyway - last night, there'd be the daughterly hurt and rejection to boot.

It wasn't quite lunchtime yet but already Celia felt a distinct need for the hair of the dog. What the hell was she doing here anyway, no use to man nor beast? Wandzia could run the whole show in her sleep. She retracted her feet, heaved herself out of the chair and went over to the door joining her office to the main one. It was the usual hive of activity in there. Celia felt even more wrecked and superfluous, seeing herself momentarily through their eyes as they looked up at her framed in the doorway. She was just nipping out. Would Wandzia please cover for her, just for a while?

I was checking the order for the new library books for the University ordered by the British Council Lecturer. There seemed to be something wrong with the Romantic Poetry section of the list. I glanced across at Wandzia. How she had been in the several months since those events? In a way, that time seemed more remarkable for what did not happen. Her temper did not alter. Her face didn't harden. Nor did she devote less time or cheerfulness to her friends. Was her wit sharper, a bit more lacerating? Not really. Yuri was never mentioned by her - and naturally people tended not to refer to him in her presence. She appeared simply to have reverted to her good-natured, sardonic self. Only once, when Dougie proposed to the assembled company that they might like to offer a home to one of the litter of kittens his step-daughter's cat had just produced, Wandzia said with unexpected heat:

'No, I couldn't do that. I wouldn't have another cat.'

Market Forces

The lassie before me in the bread queue opened her wallet - her Ma's wallet it must have been, for two black-and-white snapshots of the lassie herself, some years younger, and her brother looked out through the plastic lining. She put the notes into a wee basket and pushed it under the lifted grille, taking the bread and her change back the same way.

It was drizzling now in the market - what my own Ma would have called a 'smirr o' rain' - like any dreich November day where I come from. Three spots of rain fell on the plastic of the upturned wallet, onto the serious, shadow-eyed schoolboy and schoolgirl faces, photographed slightly from the side. Away off beyond the wooden huts and kiosks of the official Polish part of the market, Russian traders pulled plastic sheets over their wares, which were laid out on blankets on the ground, on rows of raised concrete slabs or the bonnets of their battered cars. Some draped swathes of polythene over the rugs, bedspreads and flowery overalls which hung on the perimeter fence. Others, deciding no more business was to be done for a while, stowed away the neatly folded scarves, sprigged flannel night-gowns and bright-coloured children's shirts in enormous waxed-canvas bags, which they strapped onto two-wheeled trolleys. One woman stopped to shoogle the knot of her head-scarf at the back of her neck, and to smooth down the material over her forehead before joining two others, dragging their trolleys piled with the blue-and-white checked bags towards the main gate. As they passed, a grey-haired man scooped a second drowsy puppy out of its now soggy cardboard box, shovelling it gently into a suitcase.

The lassie finished putting her money away and moved aside, tucking the string bag with the bread in it under her coat against the rain. I ducked my head to bring my face close to the grille.

'I'm listening to Madam,' the dark-haired woman on the other side said automatically, then focused and gave a wee smile of recognition. I asked for my usual loaf, and five rolls. Taking the bread and my change, I thanked her and dandered off. Waiting in the queue, I had already totted up what I would have to pay - from habit, for they knew me at this bread stall and had not tried to cheat me for years.

I was awful sick of being cheated - or rather of having folk *try* to cheat me, since this was by now quite difficult to accomplish. My time in this country had certainly done wonders for my mental arithmetic if not for my stress levels and incipient paranoia. In food shops and at stalls and kiosks, cheating was anyway less common, but in cafes and restaurants, or on the rare occasions when Marek and I took a taxi, the attempted heist was fair inevitable. I dreaded the moment when the waitress would place the bill on the table, studiedly avoiding not looking at me (but nonetheless *not* looking at me), hated seeing the extra ten thousand zlotys that I knew I would see in the figure scrawled at the bottom, hated having known I would see it, hated having hoped, even for a second, that I might not.

Sometimes she would pull the pad out of her apron pocket, lean on the table, do the calculation on the back of the bill, then flip it over and write a larger sum on the front. *That* blatant, as if as well as being rich and foreign and not quite real (had my wee boy not been overheard speaking to me in English?) I was also blind, or stupid. I couldn't bear the ignominy of saying nothing yet, each time, the knowledge that I would have to challenge her, to look up into that closed but conscious face, to begin in my foreign-inflected voice, in a language not my own, 'Excuse me, but there seems to be a mistake...' produced in me a physiological aversion, a slow leaden somersault in my stomach.

She would argue it had been the cream in the coffee, or the bread roll with my *bigos*. The braw want of embarrassment had me scunnered every time. She would shrug, knock off the ten thousand (often knowing she'd sneaked in another couple of thousand on an individual item that I'd not picked up on). I cringed at the cynicism in myself that had me cantle up so quick, whispering 'check the bill' the minute a waiter or waitress called me 'kochana' - 'darling' - in a voice like two palms being rubbed together (as if I didn't *always* check the bill anyway). I hated the way I now mis-doubted wee acts of apparent kindness - the extra plate of biscuits for Tomek, the waiter patting his head, the waitress letting him help set out the table or play with a pile of napkins - knowing from experience that, in the peculiar psychology of the dishonest, such placatory (or compensatory?) gestures *invariably* preceded a particularly large addition to the bill.

Since Tomasz had been going to Pre-School, he and I found that we ordinarily spoke Polish together (though he sometimes forgot - it depended what he was thinking about). When Marek was still biding with us, he used to come home at the back of three o'clock, and over the next couple of hours we would gradually drift into English. Marek wasn't awful canty speaking Polish with us all the time, even though it was theoretically his first language. I think it made him tired.

When we went out as a family, we usually spoke English between ourselves at least part of the time. I often wished Tomek would stick to Polish and not draw attention to us, but I couldn't bring myself to tell him to do it - as if we were *hiding*, scouking about - nor to explain why. So he yammered blithely on, switching naturally and seamlessly between languages, depending on mood or association or interlocutor. He nearly always spoke English to his Da.

And I would see the glimmer in the eye of the waitress as she stroked back a strand of her grey hair, keeking at our table from her post by the kitchen door, maybe saying something to the waiter as he passed (so he could shoot a wee glance at us too). I would shiver as she hovered by our table, in that extra-attentive mode I knew so well, watching her hands as she set down the spoon she had brought for Tomek's ice-cream. I felt like Hansel in the cage as the witch clutched and groped at his finger, wishing, as Tomek blethered away to Marek and the waitress looked dotingly at him, at us all, that I had a bone to poke out through the bars and that we were not so obviously fattening nicely.

'Poles are cheated also,' our Polish friends would assure us. 'It is very awful. Workers are so corrupt.' No doubt Polish people were cheated, and to negotiate many of the transactions of their lives, which we were spared (arranging a telephone line, getting their child into secondary school, obtaining certain medicines or good treatment from a doctor), they felt obliged to pay bribes. Nonetheless, I reckoned, on any particular day, their chances were better than ours:

'There are thirty-nine million of you to choose from and only a handful of us. With us it's *every* time,' I told my friend, Justyna, once. 'It makes you feel... *hunted*, you know, like prey.' She wanted to think I was making a joke, and at once I was a wee bit ashamed at my obvious lack of proportion.

In the beginning I had been cheated also at food stalls and in shops, but cashiers in general appeared less prone to this particular vice, and it was in these situations that I had most often *falsely* suspected people of malpractice. It would be better to be duped a hundred times, I would conclude moralistically, my insides churning with shame at the wrong I had done the man in the tram-ticket kiosk, than to suspect *one* innocent creature, even in my heart. But I couldn't live by this maxim. It felt too sore. It wasn't the money. It was the feeling transmitted by the act, at the moment of the sting, the 'swick', from that other person to me - the necessary feeling, in order for them to perpetrate it at all - not contempt exactly, but a negation, an utter negation of our shared human qualities, of my claim to have a soul like theirs.

Marek said I shouldn't take it so personally. After all, waitresses and shop assistants didn't earn a great deal. Even taxi drivers, now that petrol was off the ration and the official currency exchange rate was the same as the black-market one, weren't the leather-jacketed wheeler-dealers they had once been. I snorted. Next time we had this argument he left out the taxi drivers.

'They overhear us speaking English and naturally assume that we are rich - rich, fortunate, untouchable, not-quite-real 'Westerners,' who probably don't understand the money (all those zeroes) and who'll barely notice the orra ten or twenty thousand. Where's the harm?'

'You fair take a scunner at any other British folk you hear talk that way,' I retorted: 'So tolerant, so benign, as if it isn't quite in good taste to notice. Patronising you call it, the old colonial guilt - it doesn't do to criticise other cultures, yet actually in no doubt as to the superiority of their own. That's what you said. Well hark at yourself *now*. I put on a caricature of his voice that I knew he hated, a little more pompous than he liked to think he was, his words chosen as though he were writing them down: 'What do you expect? These folk have so little. Of *course* they help themselves at the expense of those they perceive by virtue of their Western voices to be fabulously wealthy... well aren't *you* the gifted social critic?'

This was still during the relatively good-natured phase of our stooshies on this subject. Not everybody did it, anyway, I thought, and it wasn't the poorest in my experience who were most likely to. No, it was folk with privileged access - waiters, hotel-workers, taxi drivers - folk who felt *entitled*...

'Don't talk about their assumptions, I *hate* their assumptions,' I'd scraiched at him once. 'We're not visitors from Western Europe with a wallet-ful of money we barely understand, feeling like we're on holiday. We *bide* here. Every time it happens it's like a denial or something, like our life here doesn't count. And I'm sick-tired of scrimping, threaping and fretting about money so we can get by, only to be ripped off for being rich.' Marek had earned a local, not a hard currency salary, though things had got better once Tomek was old enough for Pre-School and I'd been able to start part-time at the Politechnika. Our current flat, luckily, came with my job. We could warsle through right enough, but we could not take our son home to visit his grandparents in Glasgow, except the time when Marek's parents had paid for the tickets, and we couldn't afford to be nipped for an extra ten or twenty thousand zlotys every time we bought a bowl of soup or a glass of tea. We'd stopped eating out altogether by then, our enjoyment of the meal too many times ruined by anticipation of the bill-scenario to follow. Marek felt the same, though he often chose to imply that it was *my* sensitivity that had closed off this option. We had our arguments over meals at home instead.

Yet though Marek had lost patience with me, and though I experimented with various methods of transcendence, in my heart I felt I was right. It wasn't just that it was stealing (though they didn't think so) and therefore demeaning to *them*. ('Your bloody Scottish Calvinism,' sneered Marek, 'and you from a good Catholic family, too'). It wasn't the twinge of losing a few thousand zlotys, which we could ill afford. It always came back to the same thing. To me it was an assault, a denial. For at the moment of presenting the incorrect bill the cheat has to have closed off any imaginative connection with the victim (indeed, should have taken care not to build up any such connection in the first place), has to see the victim, above all, as not *like them*. In that instant my link of humanity, of affinity with the waitress who'd exclaimed over Tomek's curly hair, the cashier who'd joked with him as she let him unload the shopping from the basket, with the taxi driver who'd blethered with me all the way, was ruptured and shown to be a sham. I felt myself rejected and all my efforts at assimilation, all my friendliness, my facility with the language set at nothing. 'Foreigner,' the act said. 'We don't want *you* - just the extra ten thousand zlotys will do, thanks.'

Perhaps it was vanity, as Marek had not failed to suggest when we started to fight about this, as about everything else. He was piqued, as he'd admitted early on (in the days when there were still concessions, when we still occasionally admired one another): even though he'd been brought up speaking Polish at home in Glasgow and attended Saturday School religiously (the only aspect of his life, apparently, against which he had never rebelled), he did not speak the language somehow as *Polishly* as I did. I really *inhabited* it, he'd said, with all the mannerisms and facial expressions, all the clichés and little slang works I'd picked up. Though later:

'You won't *be* them, you know. They won't let you.'

It was I who was Pani Julka to all the neighbours: I loved being Julka or Julia, with the y sound at the beginning, way bonnier than plain Julie.

I felt the injustice. Surely I wasn't *such* a push-over, so desperate I'd hurl my own identity out the window without a second thought. I'd noticed changes in the way I spoke ever since Tomek's first words, or even before. And it wasn't B.B.C. World Service English my language students got from me - or that polonised English it was so easy to fall into. Nobody in my Spoken English classes could ever accuse me of contributing to the illusion that Britain was a country without marked regional variations! It was almost a conscious decision at first. My wee protest against my own assimilative urges - or was it that, for Tomek, I had to stand in for an entire linguistic culture and an extended family he rarely got to experience? I'd hear myself sometimes, almost like an echo, as if I were giving him my mother through me.

'But that's about not being *English.*' Marek jabbed a finger, sure he'd rumbled me. 'Poles don't differentiate, calling us *Anglicy* all the time. That's just a reaction. *I* do *that.*'

And what did you turn out to be? I wanted to bawl at him, though it seemed a wee bit unkind, even for me. 'You've always had a get-out clause,' I charged him. 'You never have to be implicated in anything. You were never quite Scottish, or never just Scottish, and now you ...At least I try to be part of something.'

'Oh, you do that right enough.' Marek imitated my whine: 'But I *bide* here ... Listen, this is a country from which people *emigrate* to the West, they don't *immigrate to* it...'

'What do you *expect?*' I interrupted, trying to cut him off with an imitation of his continual refrain to me.

'Why are you so desperate to be loved anyway, even by anonymous people? Is it some kind of craving you have? Tell me, Mrs Zielinska, how long have you had this problem?'

'Not to be loved,' I protested, though it was a lie, I felt, saying it.

'To be accepted then. Why do you need that so much?'

'Because I love *them,*' I cried, almost horrified to discover it was true.

'Unrequited fellow-feeling is a terrible thing,' said Marek in his sarcastic journalist voice, and turned away because his face seemed to indicate more sincerity than his tone meant to betray.

What fashed me the most was that I knew fine well that this stuff bothered him *like hell* - though like everything that was associated with some form of humiliation or weakness, he refused to acknowledge or speak of it, as if he could score it out of his consciousness completely. It was not, he claimed, that he was distressed to see behaving in this way his own countrymen (of whom he'd been brought up to have a somewhat romanticised view, as I did not fail to point out). It was not the thing itself, he insisted, it was me not standing it that he couldn't stand.

'A canny move,' I yelled at him, 'shoving me between the world and your feelings about it that you can't face. How convenient. A live-in scapegoat!'

It wasn't out of consideration for me, I decided, but out of his own fear of all forms of 'weakness'. This was a man who was exasperated if I had a cold, a man who would raise his eyes to heaven and be away out the door if I so much as stubbed my toe (though this didn't prevent him dwelling in loving detail on any ailment of his own). I grew cynical about what I saw as his inconsistencies. He could lie snottering in his bed supping hot lemon, but I had to be strong always. I wasn't *allowed* to have any problem that he couldn't solve. I needed to recount the minor unpleasant incidents of my day, but he invariably cut me off. He didn't like to see me getting het up about this stuff, this *trivia,* he said. It was unworthy of me. And so I was caught in this double-bind of his false regard, unable to mention what had upset me, knowing it would make him feel bad and that he would make me feel worse.

Nonetheless, I carried on my policy of 'non-compliance' with cheating, my own pathetic battle against petty fiddling and corruption, though it taigled me out, and I didn't much like the person I had become - watchful, always ready, but never ready enough. I had no aptitude for this kind of vigilance and my own wariness exhausted me. I knew there was an unpleasant name for how I was feeling - even if they really *were* all out to get me.

'Hell,' said Marek, 'give yourself a break. Give us *all* a fucking break. You have to stop minding, hen, or you have to leave. It's masochism otherwise.'

He was right. I knew it. I would go horn daft this way.

'They're just... primitive, that's all. I mean they're just at an earlier stage in their...'

'Civilisation?' I inquired.

'In their development... It's a political thing,' he ended lamely.

Primitive. He could say it, as I could and would not. They were his people, or I supposed so, though you'd not think it to hear him lately. Marek seemed rather further from his own Polishness than he had in Glasgow when I'd first known him. When anything truly affronted him, I discovered, he would cut it off, like a superfluous limb, without a word. It seemed I had to keep testing him to the limit to see if he'd do the same to me.

So I was the one who had remained, while he went back to Glasgow for a job in local TV. Only a year, we agreed, to begin with, not to be up-rooting Tomek when he was just away to start his new class at Pre-School. We weren't separated exactly, merely apart. Yet here I was, two months into the second year, dividing my time between the Politechnika and some teaching at two newly-established and faintly cowboy language schools, not applying for jobs, here or anywhere, conspicuously not accumulating articles communicating my fascinating perspective on Eastern Europe to adorn my portfolio, or making any attempts to convince *anyone* that I should be writer on post-Communist affairs in their Glasgow office...

How long could it go on this way before something had to give? How long could the story be 'Dadda has to work in Scotland and we'll see him next month?' And Mummy? What the hell was *she* about? I missed Marek appallingly. He'd come over twice and paid for us to go back once - camping out at his parents' and in his tiny one-room flat (the only dwelling I'd ever entered whose dimensions were smaller than those of a Polish flat). Escaping into the rain and walking, soaked, into the café near the Polish bread shop on Lennox Place, we'd drunk tea and stared through the steamed up windows, overwhelmed by homesickness for two places at once.

Just once, Marek hinted that I was scared to come back, that I was on the run from my responsibilities. I cantled up at that one right enough, knowing fine well that it was true. We'd managed only one weekend visit to my Da on our trip to Marek's parents' the previous year, though it was only a couple of hours on the train and another on the bus to get there. It wasn't the house I had grown up in, but it was still awful hard to see him there, his hopeless hands, his tufted hair, a man dwarfed by the cushions on his own settee. My mother had been a woman of strong likings. Now it was hard to tell what my father's preferences were. Did he want a cup of tea? He didn't rightly know.

'I wis aye a follower,' was all he'd said on the matter. It wasn't true, I was sure of it, but I could've sworn that he followed her now. As if he'd shut down and gone after her, as surely as he used to pull down the metal grille over the shop front, click shut the padlock and swing his leg over his bike when he was on fire duty. From my bedroom window I used to watch his wobbling progress up the hill to the fire station on Tulloch Brae.

In the first years I had tried to comfort him, to say the kinds of things we had never said.

'I blame masel,' he'd said, like a textbook case, 'I should hae kent she wis sick.'

'How could you?' I said. 'She was always that cheerful, that damned *impressive.*'

I knew I should persevere, trying to bring him out, but even wee Tomek couldn't really rouse him, and my resentment grew. Berating himself over something he couldn't change, I thought, as if it were an excuse for not doing anything about being so useless now. It was easier to have my own excuse of being far away than to have to see those un-seeing eyes on my son.

Was it cowardice, then, or mere inertia that kept me swithering here, taking no steps either to stay or to go? Or was it the retentiveness of love? For I loved this place, even without Marek, loved the life that was ours in it, the days by the lakes with friends in summer, the mushroom picking in the forest, the sledging to school, stopping for my messages each day in the market, buying parsley and celeriac from the stall behind our tower block, sitting on the tram, eavesdropping, on the way to work, or listening to Tomek blether his day's doings in Polish coming back from Pre-School. Our sweet, bilingual son. Part of his personality was here, traits that exposed themselves, that existed only fully in this setting, in this language; he was more cute, less sceptical, naughtier - or differ-ently naughty. In English he liked to be outrageous to make us laugh, in English he was cheeky - but in Polish somehow 'roguish.' In English he was confident, in Polish more dependent, more easily affectionate to other adults.

How could we make him give that up? When I thought like this I would go into a swoon of love for where I was, like living in a perpetual flashback out of my own future, when all the Polish objects of my existence here, so specific and so charming, all the wee items I had picked up in the Russian Market, would adorn some other flat or house, just a talking point, a point of interest about us, to folk we did not yet know, who did not care. Marek and Julie used to bide in Poland, you know. Mementoes of a life, a whole life. I could not bear it.

****

I stayed for the Russian Market. There were days when I was fair certain of that. For there alone I was not a foreigner. To the Russians I was simply a Pole with a none too canny command of Russian, and even Poles, in that context of bilingual double-dealing, could not spot me. One woman, whose help I enlisted when a Russian trader was seeking to persuade me to buy not one but several of his lacquered trays (offering me some complicated deal I could not follow), translated for me into Polish, then scolded: 'What were you doing in your Russian classes at school, dear? Sleeping?'

As if there were not a thousand other reasons for loving it. I loved the *things,* the particularity, the otherness of each item: the wee plastic toys with their 1950's look, the wooden pull-along squirrel beating on its toadstool cymbal with its two wee beaters, the clockwork frogs and birds of gaudy tin, the children's scissors shaped like a donkey's face with the blades for its ears. I loved the striped cotton socks, the tin buckets daubed with hedgehogs and swallows, and the handkerchiefs with their stars and clowns, their cyrillic lettering and child-cossacks on rocking horses.

I would stravage about among the stalls, relishing the bright materials, the faintly old-fashioned prints and cuts of the clothes, turning over objects where the traditional and the socialist utilitarian styles often mingled in one design. The colours were different, too, I noticed, eyeing the girls' summer dresses with their puffed sleeves and aprons: a certain kind of blue, a way of juxtaposing blue, green and orange or blue, green and pink. I would finger the soft winceyette of the wee shirts and pyjamas, pink or bright yellow, or red and green, with patterns of flowers and berries, goats or dwarves, bears and cockerels, bees in headscarves and ice-skating foxes, smelling of the apricot soap they had been packed in to ward off the fumes in the belly of the buses that had transported them.

I loved the way that everything was there, everything from screwdrivers to samovars - the whole clamjamfry, as my Ma used to say. I loved the jumbling of everything together, the way that a single blanket might display car parts and shower fittings, Russian army binoculars and soap, camping stoves and cuckoo clocks, babushka dolls and slippers and wee furry jackets, saucepans and headscarves, thermos flasks decorated with bullfinches, cake tins and rifle sights, tablecloths, umbrellas, a child's bicycle, a guitar... The blissful lack of specialisation never failed to captivate me and lent to each object of merchandise a unique allure: the round-faced, blue-eyed doll in his cap, high boots and red breeks among the saw-blades, the picture-bricks showing scenes from Russian fairytales beside to the tabletop mincing machine, a laboratory microscope rising up behind a rickle of baby bonnets and children's pyjamas, neighbouring in their turn an inflatable telephone, a coffee grinder, a wind-up tin train, a set of knives with inlaid handles, some bathroom taps, a black wooden ladle painted with gold leaves and red strawberries and a musical box in the shape of a hen marked 'a present from Kiev.' Were I to light on any of these, I couldn't go somewhere else, to another stall, say, and get one like it: what I saw was here alone, and now my only chance to possess it.

The joy of rammling about among such an abundance of arbitrary objects, with never a thought of what I would find but knowing always that I would love it when I did, with no preconceptions but the certainty of delight! The thrill of searching for nothing in particular - until that moment of suddenly seeing, of recognising the very thing among the mixtermaxter of all its unlikely fellows, as if re-encountering a person known in a previous life. The physical sensation in the instant of glimpsing that flash of material or outline of something, that instant of connection between oneself and an object (registering its significance, as if I could perceive in a single moment all that its existence would mean in my life), the birl of gladness in the stomach ... This, I felt sure, was the exact counterpart, the antidote, to the leaden, intestinal arabesque that accompanied so many of my financial interactions elsewhere. The excitement as I edged towards the stall, ready to make my bid for the already beloved item, was just the braw opposite of the dread with which, in taxis and cafes, I awaited the moment of reckoning.

For each transaction here seemed designed to *confirm* humanity: there was the Kirghiz woman from whom I had bought the knitted slippers for my cousin's wee girl. She was hunkered down under one of the few stalls to have a roof and, remembering, smiled across at me, biding out the rain. Away off by the fence was the man from Riga who had sold me the colouring books for Tomek and Koshka. We knew nothing of one another's lives, yet we never doubted there was something to know. It was somehow agreed between us. We were real to one another. We were people in each other's eyes.

I haggled because it was part of the procedure, of forging the link between buyer and trader. Besides, I enjoyed the ritual and the playacting of it, the language of our faces and eyes, the few decisive words, the gestures of our hands, mine mirroring theirs as I was drawn into being more emphatic, more demonstrative, sometimes more outrageous than I would ever otherwise be. Theirs showed ostentatious disbelief at such a low offer, mine at such an unreasonable price; the pretended uncertainty as to whether they would sell for such a ridiculously small sum or whether I could afford such extravagance for such an overpriced and relatively commonplace object. I didn't drive an awful hard bargain, and neither did they (they'd no need), but both of us were satisfied. I'm sure they never sold for less than they intended at the outset, but nor did I often pay more than would retain their respect. I was not a tough opponent: I cared too much about the upcome for that. Yet in the counting out and passing between us of the agreed money and change, in the handing over of the purchased object, it felt as though we had effected a more fundamental exchange.

I bought for friends, to send back to family, to friends' children and for their new-born babies, for Marek and Tomek, at Saint Nicholas and Easter, as if I wanted everyone to share in the place's pleasures. It was acquisitiveness, I couldn't deny, though everything was so cheap that it didn't feel like it - and there were occasionally even things that I did not feel the need to possess, but was simply heart-glad to know they existed. I could recall every purchase I had ever made whenever I saw the object thereafter, could conjure up the face of the person who had sold it to me, the stall, the burroch of objects among which it had lain. Ironically, these mass-produced artefacts of a post-Marxist state - pouring no doubt from their factories by the million but here displayed in all their singularity - spoke to me as if they were the handcrafted creations of pre-industrialised labour. Here, among these Communist-bred traders and their wares, I was initiated into the pleasures of primitive capitalism - for the first time in my life an unalienated consumer.

What is more, the Russians *never* cheated me. They'd no need - the simple capitalist trick of selling something for many times more than you have paid for it was glorious scam enough for them. They came over the border in mud-spattered buses or their rattling cars, bringing goods from their still-subsidised factories to the beleaguered capitalist population of Poland. The Polish state textile and crockery factories were collapsing. The wee family-run businesses which had been permitted under Communism, the indigenous craftsmen and women in their dark workshops in back courts and down alleys, the glovers, the hatters, the brush makers, the cobblers, had been swept away before the deluge of imported goods since the Wall came down. Folk used to be always girning: 'we have money but there is nothing to buy.' Now, two years on, the situation had exactly reversed. They had spent their savings only to discover that Western products were not automatically or invariably superior. The shops had become emporia of Western goods. Some of the population were getting richer and could continue to indulge their preference for imported items. Plenty of folk again needed cheap, everyday things.

My colleagues at work, who considered themselves intelligentsia, were awful snobbish about the Russian Market. The wares were of poor quality, they said, and would soon wear out or break down. It was terribly dangerous, my students told me. No, of course they hadn't been there - they would be sure to be robbed, or worse - they would never dare go to such a place. They related tales of mafiosi or of Russians selling kalashnikovs or their wives. Still, many Poles, less well off or disinclined, could not do without the Market, and they came.

Some were grudging about it, to be sure. Just because they were reduced to buying from Russians did not mean that they had to be nice to them. I, on the other hand, went around, smiling, being welcoming and friendly to these 'neighbours' of 'ours', seeming to them a friendly Pole, doing my bit for international relations under false pretences. It would have been hard not to smile in such a lightsome, good-humoured environment, for among the traders smiles were easy and many, the huge joke of making money while providing an undeniable bargain, of the rip-off without a victim seemed to generate something of a carnival atmosphere.

The Polish stalls, selling imported clothes, further over, besides being of little interest to me and in general more than a wee bit pricey, appeared to be manned by people who considered selling an awful serious business and a market no different than a shop (which from their perspective of course it wasn't): no jokes, no reductions. The Russians, on the other hand, though far from home, working hard and biding in uncomfortable conditions, in the high spirits of their easy profits often conducted themselves as if the whole enterprise were a kind of capitalist holiday tour, bantering and sending themselves up. One man, trying to sell a picture of a horse for 1000zl, began by addressing it eloquently, praising its good looks, as a wee group gathered round. As no-one offered to buy, he insisted that the horse was like him: it had that subtle kind of appeal which could only be appreciated slowly, and by a special kind of person. Finally he fell to commiserating with it: it was just him and the horse, no-one wanted either of them. Within minutes he had sold it.

A trader once tried to rowp me an outrageous plastic tortoise with rolling eyes, one of a pair that he had.

'Pani *must* buy it,' he asserted. 'It is the tortoise you are looking for all your life.'

252

'Must I?' I replied. 'And if I don't?'

'Then beware - if Pani doesn't buy it, I will *give* you *both* of them!'

I had been in the market the previous week when a Russian was trying to sell a camera, which he swore was American, the latest in photographic technology.

'Probably stolen,' the man next to me muttered, but he asked the price. 'Huh,' he responded sourly, when told, 'Why should I give you so much money? You'll only spend it on drink.'

'Ah - *drink*,' said the Russian, as though the idea had just occurred to him. 'Buy a camera,' he exhorted those around him, 'and feed the Russian soul - drink, medicine for the Russian soul - buy this American camera and pay for Russian to have *drink.*' And he broke into a drinking song, in which most of the traders around him soon joined. Someone picked up an accordion he was selling and they were away, swaying from side to side and belting out the chorus, as though liberated into a joyful national caricature of themselves.

****

I moved slowly towards the far gate through the dripping market. I thought the rain was beginning to ease, but I knew it was almost time to collect Tomek. I passed the row of old ladies in headscarves from out of town selling churns of sour cream, bottles of dill vinegar, jars of pickled gherkins and home-made mayonnaise. I was headed for the area near the gate where local people sold their own belongings second-hand. I took a last gype backwards. Inby a concrete wall, a group of middle-aged Ukrainian women was taking shelter under an awning, down on their hunkers among their checked canvas bags. I recognised the only one that was stood up. I had bought turquoise and yellow bell-shaped Christmas tree lights from her last year. Her taut headscarf and long neck gave her a Nefertiti look. The women were easy together, taking it in turns to massage each other's shoulders and showing their gold teeth when they laughed.

A wee bit further over were the Kirghiz women in their several shawls, a couple of Mongolian men in ear-flapped hats, Siberians in padded jackets and Tadziks in turbans; folk with brown skin and almond eyes, others with straw-coloured hair and plump cheeks, a group which, to my eyes, looked Polynesian, traders from Belarus and Estonia and Uzbekistan, and the new arrivals in recent months, the Vietnamese.

A rare old ragabash, my Ma would have pronounced them with relish. I had to stand still, feeling that dirl to my guts - like when I first saw Tomek's crumpled face keeking out of that blue hospital blanket and realised in the same moment that I was looking on a sight she'd never see. She was always one for variety, with her Nigerian cushion covers

253

picked up at the Kirk Sale, her attempts to learn Italian from Victor in the village café and her experimental cooking. As for me, I was heartsick of the self-proclaimed homogeneity of Poland, which my Polish friends seemed to think so self-evidently desirable. This was what I craved, this cornucopia of humanity.

I looked across at a group of turbaned women, conferring, and at a tall man, missing several front teeth and wearing a round, black, fur hat, broad as a tractor wheel. I thought of Marco Polo, and of the eastern traders referred to throughout history. These folk have been doing this *forever.* The thought had me awash with happiness.

Reluctantly I moved on. It was less crowded in this part of the market, being mainly an area where Poles sold their belongings to raise some cash. An elderly woman sat on an up-ended crate, greeting in great gust-ing sobs. She wore a red and green floral headscarf, a raincoat with a man's tweed jacket over the top, and trainers. Under the rain-smittered polythene laid out on the ground before her were a couple of pairs of second-hand shoes, some school text-books and a tennis racquet.

At first it seemed nobody was stopping - a fact which I at once took for indifference, though, to be fair, despite the advantages of greater proximity and shared language, those nearer to her may have found the situation no easier to read than I. Several nonetheless had a head-swivellingly good gawk as they went by - the unashamed, carelessly hos-tile stare of those who recognise unorthodox behaviour when they see it and who, knowing themselves on the right side of convention, feel enti-tled to gype without awkwardness at those who are not.

'There's no empathy in this society,' I thought angrily, surprised by the fury and probable injustice of this generalisation, too redd up to bother with the provisos of recent political history which I was normally so careful to apply. 'Why do they never think it might be *them?* Because they spend their whole lives - *devote* their whole lives - to making sure it *isn't* them.'

I, on the other hand, was suffering from an excess of empathy as I felt my feet take me towards her. I had picked up on this unhappiness from a considerable distance, I noted with alarm, before even seeing her, as if I had an antenna sensitised to grief.

As I got inby, a man in a cap with his hands stuck in his trouser pock-ets was asking her something, and two women also stopped. The old woman wasn't moving, and she held her head surprisingly still - except that her shoulders were shaking as she forced out her enormous sobs. Then she began raising and lowering her outstretched arms, palms up-wards. She had on a pair of gloves too big for her - gardening gloves from the looks of it - so that these great floppy clown's hands were re-peatedly extended to the heavens then dropped in her lap, while her

254

mouth drooped in a clown-like parody of misery. The sobbing stopped and a thin rivulet of sound dribbled from the downturned corners of her mouth in a wordless, craiking moan.

Then she spoke and my heart stopped and my eyes burned. A fair swarm surrounded her now. They'd taken her money, some boys, pretending to look at what she had to sell, claiming to have found what they wanted, an exercise book and a text book - no, it wasn't *Geografika Polskiej*, you know, Madam. Making out they were going to pay, they had snatched her cash box. The aluminium box lay jack-knifed on the ground. One small brass coin still clung to its bottom like the gold piece to Ali Baba's sister-in-law's scale. The crowd looked at it. I wanted to offer to pick it up but feared the gesture might be misinterpreted. One of the boys had shoved her as he grabbed it, knocking her to one side.

'He pushed me like that, madam,' she turned to the nearest woman. 'Pushed me here,' putting her hand to her right breast as though she clutched a tumour there. Now they knew her plight, they would sympathise with her, I thought, hovering.

'They've fleeced you all right,' said one man, with the grim but evident satisfaction of one who has had his view of the world confirmed yet again.

'What did you expect in a place like this?' Another woman offered. 'So many Russians. You have to watch everyone.'

The woman barely seemed to comprehend, then she said:

'But they weren't Russian boys, they were *ours.*'

'Ours, you say,' her interlocutor rejoined. 'You see how it is. Now they watch these American movies. They are Americanised, such boys. They care nothing what they do.'

'Otherwise they would not act like that. Like gangsters. American gangsters.' Having reached this satisfactory analysis, they exchanged companionable glances with compressed lips and a sense of arrival. Me, I can't stop gawking at the woman, at her face, caught in this everlasting moment of bewildered pain. I shoogle closer.

'She wants to *tell,*' I think, furiously, 'Why won't they let her?' She tries, over and over, replaying the incident, how they came, what they said, the exercise book... but her audience feel they know this story already.

'You shouldn't be surprised in a place like this,' one man tells her, 'crawling with Russians. It isn't safe for you.'

'That's right,' another man in a short jacket joins in, waggling his shopping bag to emphasise the point. 'They have their Mafia to watch out for them - or they'd be stealing from each other, fighting and killing one another all the time.'

'You have to have a purse-belt,' another puts in. 'That's the best way.'

'That's right,' the man in the cap agrees. 'A box like that is no good. It's asking for trouble, a box like that.'

I stand there, near the front, a wee bit to the side, staring my sympathy at her for all I'm worth. Why doesn't anyone speak a word of comfort or real commiseration? Why does nobody pat her arm, call her a 'poor thing,' let her relieve herself of this experience, let her *say*?

The man who suggested the purse-belt returns to his pet theme:

'At least that way they have to kill you for your money.'

Some folk laugh at the back.

She is still greeting, shaking her head, but no longer tries to speak. I look at this broken figure and feel a dirl of hatred for the onlookers and their ghoulish satisfaction. It's not to do with her. They *want* bad things to happen to confirm their sense of reality. They *need* things like this, to validate them, and their own suffering, or as some perverse charm against it.

I should say something, but I am afraid for my voice with its unplaceable foreign cadence to be heard by all these folk, striking a note which goes contrary to such a fundamental need of their psyche. They will sense it at once, as folk always do in matters of emotional survival, and my contribution will meet with a swift rebuttal or an even more hostile reaction. I know fine well that it's cowardice, but somehow that dread of 'making a fuss in a foreign language' which I have felt so many times pervades me now.To embark, yet again, on an interaction where I am anxious about the upcome and at the same moment reveal my foreign-ness is more than I can contemplate. So many times, as the waitress has plumped my falsified bill on the table, I have trembled, knowing that I must try to make an intervention, to make a difference, to claim my humanity or to make a plea on behalf of humanity, yet known that to open my mouth only demonstrates my dehumanising otherness before all the world.

Yet look at her, how she suffers. The woman tries one more time to embark on her tale. I gaze at her as though I could suck her sorrow out of her by osmosis. I know I should speak, and I have to touch her, as if it will break a spell. But if I do she will turn to me and the words will pour out of her. What if I'm not able follow her? What if the phrases I can manage to frame in this other tongue are not adequate? What if I cannot carry the burden I have asked for? I know I should be away to fetch my son from Pre-School. I'll have to skelp to be there on time as it is.

The crowd is starting to disperse, leaving her to her despair. She begins to dotter about in a kind of stunned misery, bending over her polythene sheet as though to gather things up but not actually doing so. Her hair is all raiveled and a stiff leg has her hirpling on one side. How much does it matter that one person winced for her? She doesn't even see me.

My face forms one of the confused mass of faces that will be part of this painful memory for her. I catch sight of the lassie from the bread queue, her dark eyes wide.

I skite forward, pick up the box and put it by her crate for her, keek up at her as I rise to move back. There are tears on my face. I want her to know I am greeting too - I want her to know I feel for her, feel with her. I want to be redeemed by that moment of recognition of our shared anguish. I want all my pain to go away, to be taken away. I want her to take me in her tweed arms and let me snivel and sob on that rough material that will smell of I don't know what, but I know I will remember all my life.

She sees me.

'Poor lady,' I say, 'I regret, I really regret...' and I pat her arm (at least I manage that) and at the same time move behind her as though to walk away. 'I can't stay,' I say, as though excusing myself, barely realising that I have switched to English. Of course I can't stay. It was madness to think I could stay. I want Marek and I know I can't bide here any more. I have to fetch Tomek, I tell myself, backing away from the old woman, afraid not for once of rejection but of an acceptance that is more than I can bear - and because it's no longer clear whether I desire to comfort her or need her to comfort me.

The Elephant and the
Polish Question

Cricoland

Cricoland opened for the season with clowns and a dancing bear. The children could go and see the bear in its cage before it began its performance. Its head drooped and it wore a leather muzzle, like the bears from the Prague Circus who'd ridden on motorbikes, Koshka remembered. It was led out to the small, circular arena by four men, on a long chain. Pipe and tabor music was supplied by a dented, silver ghettoblaster. The bear danced like the shyest boys at the school disco, Rob thought, with a foot shuffle and a minimal hand-jive. Yet it was still a bear, its big, hairy beariness was still strongly present, just its soul was in abeyance and not to be viewed behind its filmy, black eyes.

The spirit of the little boy nearest them was clearly not in abeyance. His brown eyes crackled with the strain of trying to break away from his mother, who was having such obvious difficulty holding him that, in the presence of the bear, two men felt compelled to go to her assistance. The fact that his mother was exceptionally pretty - petite in a tangerine suit and matching stillettoes, and with her perfectly cut, mahogany-brown, shoulder-length hair and olive skin most resembled a visiting Latino super-model or film star - may have had something to do with it. Luckily, the boy lost interest in the bear and instead transferred his attention to Koshka, specifically her ginger hair, whose properties he explored by seizing hold of a handful to see whether, unlike other shades, it could be removed.

'Hey!' Rob was about to intervene. Perhaps due to having no older sibling, Koshka tended to react to all acts of infant aggression against her with total surprise. Yet, after her first yelp, even she seemed to recognise that this boy needed a firm hand. As the mother prized his hands away from her scalp - 'No, no, Karolek, do not do that to the little girl' - Koshka rounded on him in very robust Polish. Belatedly registering that the boy's mother had spoken to him in English, she gave him the translation as well.

In the midst of all this, Cricoland was declared officially open and the ancient, dusty-blue and orange machinery creaked into life. Music flared up suddenly from the loudspeakers at the edge of the forest, behind the roller coaster and the Klowns Loteria, alternating Russian folksongs with Polish, 50s-style crooners. Even on this, the first day, some of the more complex machinery gave out almost straight away, and there were gaps, ranging from twenty minutes to several hours, while the roller coaster or the cyclone-twister were repaired. The rides for the little ones were more reliable. Koshka and the little boy had two rides on the flying elephants, swooping and gliding to the strains of 'Kalinka, Kalinka' and 'Black Eyes'.

Rob felt sincerely sorry for the boy's mother, who had introduced herself as Dolores and appeared permanently frazzled. Her son had already thrown an enormous tantrum when it seemed that he might not get to ride in a *red* elephant, and now, as he rose into the air once more, was hanging out of the side, as he explained after, 'to make it more fun by getting more dizzy.' Karolek was more than just a sensation-seeker, Rob concluded, watching him as Dolores tried to impress her anxieties upon the child with a shrill lecture and a fair number of her own tears. Shaking the boy's arm with each urgent point, she ended by trying to pull his chin around with her long, amber-painted nails so that he would look at her, but Karolek was already scanning for new excitements. Plenty of children have an insufficient grasp of physical danger, but Karolek seemed to Rob have an active death-wish.

Next, the two children sampled the long caterpillar with the smiling yellow face, its trucks decorated with red and turquoise swirls and orange, polka-dotted lollipops. Clunking over every sleeper, it hauled itself up its rail-track hills and rumbled down the other side. Karolek insisted they had to go again so they could ride in the head of the caterpillar, a notion with which Koshka was strongly in agreement. On the crest of the steepest slope the boy stood up in the little truck, silky black hair flying back from his face, thrusting his clenched fists at the sky and whooping his greetings at his mother below, frantic with squealing and gesturing to him to sit down.

From the summits of the ride they could see 'the big cranes,' the gantries of the shipyard at Stocznia Gdanska and, further along, those of Nowy Port. Fortunately from the point of view of Karolek's long-term survival, the caterpillar's motion being rather uneven at the best of times, it teetered at the top, giving enough of a jolt on the brink of its descent to knock the boy backwards into the truck, where he banged his head and howled with rage. It wasn't clear where rage ended and grief and pain began, and he was still bellowing when he came off the ride at the end.

Dolores was beside herself, though Rob did his best to assure her that it was just a nasty bump, that there was no cut and she should just keep an eye on him for signs of concussion. Karolek continued to cry passionately for a further ten minutes until he spotted the guns of the rifle range. This time Dolores was adamant and, with Rob's help, carried him physically from the scene.

Koshka followed behind, with an expression of some awe. This was a new breed of person to her. This was a level of child behaviour, an intensity, which she had never thought to explore to anything like this extent. Her own exuberance and cheekiness seemed positively staid in comparison. Karolek was clearly someone mad, bad and dangerous to know. She liked to try her luck with the best of them, but such complete disregard for adults and for self-preservation she had not known was possible. It looked pretty amazing, though she eyed him with a certain wariness, at least for now.

Dolores was from Colombia, Rob established.

'My husband, he is from Gdansk originally - in fact still his mother live in a part of the city. He left to go to Germany when he was still much a young man, to Munich, for working. Much years he live there.'

'Is that where you met him, in Germany?'

'No, no. I meet him when he come to Colombia, to my city, for business. Karolek was borning on Colombia. Some years we are living there.'

'But now you are here.'

'Yes, we are here,' she sighed a little. 'Al has here some business. Much business. A big business,' she corrected herself. 'He is Aleksander, my husband, but nobody call him Olek, not even his mother, only Al. He prefer it.'

She seemed genuinely sweet-natured and without artifice, Rob thought, and Karolek was clearly a bit of a handful. It was pleasant to be around her because she was so beautiful, the way she touched her cheek when she talked, her plum lips quivered and her liquid eyes were so often on the verge of tears. She really did need a bit of help, of the easiest, practical, male sort.

'My wife works all day on Fridays,' he offered, 'so I look after our daughter after Przedszkole. I was thinking of taking her somewhere next week. Would you and Karolek like to come?'

Now that he did these 'Daddy Days' regularly, he actually enjoyed them. Cricoland had been their first outing of the 'season', and he definitely wanted to come again. Despite being so distinctively Eastern European in its sounds and colours, its main appeal for him lay in its international fairground flavour, the world of black-handed men, oily machinery and blaring music. Although *in* Poland, it wasn't quite Polish territory. He felt it gave him a break. Still, he could see that it might not be the safest environment for Karolek.

'We could take them swimming at the Poseidon Hotel.'

Dolores went silent. 'Karolek was drownding when he was two,' she announced. Rob was about to withdraw the suggestion, but she seemed to take heart. 'So, it is very important for him to learn swimming.'

Przedszkole

I hadn't met Alina's husband before, because she and the children lived with her parents in a small flat near Koshka's Pre-School, while Andrzej lived with his parents in another part of the city. Their son, Piotrus, had been in Pani Ola's class with Koshka the previous year, but now he had moved up to become a 'Sredniak' - a 'Middle One' - while she remained for her second year as a 'Maluch' or 'Little One'. His younger sister Magda, at three, was just starting as a 'Maluch' herself.

We often went back to Alina's parents' flat after collecting the children, for a quick coffee, before Koshka and I headed off to the market to buy food for *obiad* and returned to Babcia's, where we lived, to cook it. Magda was swaddled in blankets in her pushchair. She had a weak chest and could not walk far. Koshka and Piotrus took turns on Piotrus' bike, which had a broom-handle attached to the saddle so that Alina or I could guide it without seeming to.

Naturally, *obiad* at Alina's mother's was already well in hand, the soup had been bubbling on the stove since morning and her mother had just come in from work to add some sliced sausage to the brew. She was a stout, fair-haired woman with a very straight mouth. She was friendly enough, but perhaps it was the fact that her face seemed to be made up of too many horizontal lines - the mouth, the broad, straight chin, her dark, unbroken eyebrows and the heavy line of her blonde fringe - which gave her that constant air of disapproval. It was not me of whom she disapproved, except insofar as I was an example of the kind of person her daughter would be bound to bring home. She disapproved of her grandchildren's boisterousness, such as it was, but this was not unusual.

She corrected every single action of Alina's, particularly in relation to the children, coming along behind her in the hallway, moving the boots Alina had put away just a fraction, adjusting the folds of the coats she had hung up. This wasn't uncommon 'Babcia-behaviour' either, but there was something about the way she did it, as if each gesture came with the same price-tag. I could not understand what she wanted, for Alina appeared to me to be an exemplary daughter for such a woman: domesticated, scrupulous, conventional, a kind, slightly fussing mother, hardworking and considerate around the flat. I had an image of Alina at eight years old in a short cotton dress, a pale ribbon to one side of her hair, standing before her mother. The voiceover provided by the mother in my head pronounced: 'this child does not do as we would want'. I was a mite suspicious about that side-parting - it looked more forties than sixties. Perhaps it was Alina's *mother* I had seen, in front of *her* mother.

I didn't meet Andrzej that day either, though Alina had claimed he'd promised to be there. He was apparently to get off work early, but he didn't show up. Piotrus was growing irate with promises of 'Daddy later'. His colleague at work had a new Mercedes, Alina told me drily. Probably her dear husband had been unable to resist being 'shown' its properties. Andrzej was the chief computer whizz at the local branch of the national T.V. network. He hadn't been there long. He was still enjoying it.

Alina and I made jelly for the children while they watched cartoons on the wide-screen T.V. in the next room, and her mother tidied up every shred of kiddie-detritus from the furniture and floors. By now, we were soaking up the double dose of her disapproval which saturated the atmosphere - of her son-in law for being such an unreliable and unworthy waster, I deduced, and of her daughter for being such a sucker as ever to have expected anything better of him. Alina appeared fairly resigned, pounding pork cutlets without exceptional vigour, grinding the pepper mill over them and dipping them in egg and breadcrumbs. I gave her what I hoped was a rallying, sympathetic smile - more a grimace of solidarity.

Alina herself had a very sweet smile, gracious and trusting and all of a sudden. I remembered being surprised by it the first time, especially since I had used to think, seeing her often at collecting-time at Przedszkole, that she didn't want to know me. I usually misread shy people quite badly, because, although I have feelings of shyness and awkwardness myself, the truth is I find it far more embarrassing to ignore people or avoid talking to them than I do to talk to them - which I suppose means that, by some definitions, I cannot claim to be shy at all.

She had wiry, brown hair under her hat and wore the collar of her coat up and her scarf over her chin so that it looked as if she were sinking down into them. Perhaps she was self-conscious about her skin, for her cheeks were quite pitted with old acne scars and she had still some angry red patches here and there. I interpreted the set of her mouth as mutinous where I should have discerned a determined practicality. She appeared to be a person who so naturally complied with whatever was required that it never occurred to me she might have to concentrate. Whatever the target of her resentment, she certainly wasn't in revolt against the social conventions around her. She was like all the other exemplary mothers but perhaps even slightly more so, doggedly insistent in observing all the niceties of proper dress when it came to gloves and boots and scarves, brooking no opposition, forcing hoods over heads and tucking in each layer, ignoring howls of protest, until Piotrus and

Magda resembled two padded snowmen, unable to bend a limb. Magda, a tiny, pale child with enormous dark-ringed eyes, had then to be inserted into her pushchair - first slotted through and then wedged under the bar - where she had to remain in a rigid, mummified posture at a forty-five degree angle to the seat throughout the journey home.

It was inevitable that we would speak in the end, for Koshka had been friends with Piotrus last year and now appeared to have adopted Magda. Pani Ola had asked her to take care of the newest *Maluch* in the beginning, but Koshka, responding to Magda's frailty, continued to take her duties seriously, helping her on and off with her slippers, leading her to various activities by the hand. Magda was not physically robust but she had an extremely energetic, slightly subversive spirit and was never short of ideas for imaginative games. The two were almost never apart.

Piotrus and Koshka were giggling about the fact that, at *obiad*, when the Panis, Pani Ula and Pani Dorocia, had wished them good appetite - '*Smacznego*'- and the children had chorused 'thank you' in the sing-song, ritualistic reply: '*Dziek-u-je-my*' the *Sredniaki* had added the rhyme: '*A na obiad Pania zjemy*' (and we'll eat *you* for dinner). Alina rolled her eyes:

'I remember this joke from when I was at Przedszkole.' Alina had in fact attended the very same institution, Number 36. 'We thought it was so incredibly funny too.'

With mounting excitement, the pair were now reciting another playground favourite:

'*Spadla bomba do piwnica,*
Napisala na tablica
S.O.S.
Glupi pies!'
A bomb fell into the cellar
And it wrote on the blackboard:
S.O.S.
Stupid dog!

The ladies at Predszkole were called the 'Panis' (the Misses) as distinct from the 'Ciocias' (Aunties) of Zlobek. There were three attached to the *Maluch* class: Pani Ula, Pani Basia and Pani Dorocia.

Koshka had put down a roll of paintings while she changed out of her slippers. I unfurled them with the customary exclamations of parental appreciation and delight.

'Pani Ula told me to take them home, they're bad pictures.'

'Why did she say that? They're lovely pictures!'

''Cause I painted black on them,' Koshka confessed. I had an art teacher once who said never use full black in a picture or it deadens everything around it, that nothing in nature is true black, but I'd a feeling this was not going to be an aesthetic argument of this kind. 'Pani Ula and

Pani Dorocia say black is a bad colour and to stay away from it. They said not to paint it on my pictures or my luck will be runned out.'

'But they must have black paint, or you wouldn't have been able to put it in your painting.'

'They said don't use it, Pani Ula said.'

'And what do *you* think?'

'I think you need black for painting black things. And when you want to do black patterns. And for cats. Kotek is black,' she added, 'All over.'

Alina was an invaluable friend for an immigrant mother like myself. Poland was not a multi-cultural society, not any more, and they liked it that way, as they rarely tired of telling me. It was assumed that every parent knew when to send their little one to school in fancy dress because it was Karniwal, or with flowers for Pani Ola because it was Teacher's Day, or that they must bring their Babcia along to be serenaded with songs for Babcia's Day: 'Long live Babcia we sing, because we love our Babcia. May she live for a hundred years!' To *our* Babcia, knocking eighty-five, this might not any longer seem a particularly generous allocation, I reflected. Nonetheless, duly tipped off by Alina, she had kindly agreed to do the honours for Koshka and had sat there, listening to such perorations with the other grandmothers, inclining her head to one side with a simper of coquettish appreciation.

It was Alina who managed, in five minutes of quick thinking in the cloakroom one morning, to wrap a pink scarf round Koshka's head, a red fringed shawl round her waist and declare she was Zosia Samosia ('Sophie Do-It-Myself') from the children's poem, so she didn't have to go into class as the only child not rigged out for Karniwal. It was Alina who explained to me what was the problem with Koshka's 'Wieszak'.

These were pieces of material on hangers with pockets around the bottom for children's handkerchiefs, hair bobbles, spare knickers and socks in case of accidents. I'd had to produce one of these at very short notice on a Sunday night, the day before Koshka started at Przedszkole last year, never having clapped eyes on one in my life before. My design was a little unorthodox, to be sure, but the principle was the same. Having no other material to hand, I hung a red T-shirt over the hanger, tucked in the sleeves and sewed along the seams, and folded up the bottom of the shirt to make the six pockets. I was rather pleased with my ingenuity and Koshka was delighted, as the T-shirt was red and had a small dancing elephant logo on the front.

I couldn't understand, therefore, why it was always on the floor, or rolled up and stuffed in with her shoes, or, on several occasions rammed down behind the cupboard in the hallway. The other *wieszaki* all hung where they had been left that morning, and Koshka always denied having touched hers.

'It isn't Koshka,' Alina explained, as I picked it up from where it had been left on the floor and trodden underfoot for the umpteenth time. 'It's the Panis.'

'But *why?*' Alina looked genuinely sorry for me, not for the fact that my handiwork was crumpled and covered with footmarks apparently by someone's conscious design, but because it wasn't immediately obvious to me why this should be so.

'It is different,' she said simply.

'Yes, but it's fine - it does the job,' I protested with some outrage but, apparently, little relevance. 'Koshka likes it.'

'It is not the same as the others,' Alina stated again.

'But, dammit, why should I have to ... O.K., O.K., I'll make another one,' I fumed. Alina smiled one of her very sweet smiles.

'You can get good material for *wieszaki* in the haberdasher's next to the market in Oliwa. It's good quality and quite cheap.'

Andrzej

We finally achieved our introduction to the elusive Andrzej when Alina sent him round to Rob's office at the University to help him with his laptop, which was playing up. The laptop contained Rob's doctoral thesis, which he was in the slow and painful process of turning into a book. Rob was even more desperate to see the back of this project than I was, so any sudden bizarre behaviour on the part of his ancient but previously reliable computer filled him with alarm.

Andrzej, on the other hand, was delighted, testing out various aspects of the software, but, soon concluding that the fault had a technical origin, flipped the machine onto its back and produced a screwdriver. He communicated a continuous excitement, an exuberance combined with such manifest competence that his jokerman, little-boy-let-loose-in-a-toyshop persona was actually somehow reassuring. He had black hair, a short, black beard, and wore a shiny, turquoise jacket, a pink shirt and a patterned burgundy-and-orange silk tie. Everything about him sparkled, from his frequent jokes to the rings on his fingers, his glittering eyes and his full, shiny red lips.

His manner was a strange mixture of continuous smiling, eye-darting eagerness to please and a sense that he cared about no-one, I thought, as he held out his hand. He was restless but at the same time incredibly focussed, clearly loved to meet new people, to hear about other places and customs, and especially to travel. When he had fixed the computer, a task which took him all of fifteen minutes, he was happy to produce from his briefcase photos of a trip to Hong Kong, undertaken during his previous job working for a local businessman. These shots of himself among the faintly debauched-looking businessmen, each in different garish shades of shiny suit and relaxing in sundry exotic locations - restaurants, geisha salons, cocktail bars - evoked the pleasantest of memories. He loved best of all to go away from Poland and to live the high life, he declared. He knew he was a little manic about his passions, like cars, very expensive fast cars, but when a man drives only an old Audi he has to dream.

He prevailed on us both to come back with him to Alina's to celebrate our new friendship.

'I apologise that I can't offer to you visit in my own flat with my wife, but yet we didn't manage this,' he said. 'Come, we will go. Alina will be very surprised to see me. I try not to go to her place so often or they will to expect it,' he joked.

The usual Polish arrangement, given the shortage of housing, was for young couples with children to live with one set of grandparents, often the mother's parents. Piotrus was nearly six, yet his parents had never lived under one roof.

'Aha,' I teased Andrzej, 'this is not such a bad deal for you. You don't have to live with your mother-in-law. All the day-to-day stuff with the kids is taken care of. I bet *your* mother still does your washing!'

'Yes, of course,' he admitted cheerfully. 'I am not so stupid.'

Alina's mother had, rather pointedly I thought, gone out soon after we arrived, and her father was snoozing in an armchair. The television, as always in Polish households, was left on at full volume at all times, regardless of whether anyone was watching, like a permanent lantern-show in the corner of the room. The car chase over, the children had lost interest in the American T.V. series on the screen and Alina had set them up with a board game.

The two Dads had been a huge sensation on first entering, with the three children swarming all over them, requiring to be lifted up and swung upside-down, until Alina complained the children would be sick and were becoming overexcited and impossible. Now Andrzej had nipped out to fetch some more wine and some vodka, and Rob was having the intricacies of the board-game explained to him by the children. It involved geese as counters, and all sorts of complicated manoeuvres dictated by the colour of square and the throw of the dice. Realising that he couldn't read the instructions, and given that they couldn't either, Piotrus and Magda were making it up as they went along, with Koshka, as translator, part of the conspiracy.

'No, no, no, that can't be right,' Rob threw his hands in the air. 'You little monsters are having me on! I'm going to tickle you till you tell me the proper rules. Which of you cheeky little monkeys is first?' The three of them laughed so much they flopped all over the board, scattering the geese underneath their tummies.

Alina and I could hear the giggling and squeals from the kitchen.

'Vodka,' Andrzej trilled, hanging up his coat, and coming into the kitchen for a tray and some shot-glasses. He unscrewed the lid of the bottle. 'You know this Polish tradition?' he inquired. 'Once lid is off, it is not polite to put it back until all bottle is finished. It is point of hospitality.'

Alina smiled. Andrzej spoke to me in English, while she invariably spoke in Polish. She must understand more English than she admitted, for she never seemed to have trouble following the conversation. I could see how a child might, as the son of our friends Stefan and Ewa once told me, gain the impression that men spoke English and women Polish.

'Ah, my dear mother-in-law, what a pity she is not here for share it with us. Grandad will be very happy,' he giggled. 'She can't stand to be in same building with me,' he added. Alina said something to him in Polish which I didn't catch, though it didn't seem to be disagreement.

'It is because I am Jew,' Andrzej declared in English.

Oh no, I thought. Not again. Just this once let this not be the reason for anything! Alina turned on him in Polish:

'No, Andrzej - they don't like *you*. It doesn't matter that you are a Jew.'

'It is same thing,' said Andrzej virtuously. 'They don't like my parents,' he added.

'Who are... Jewish?' I put in, suspecting Alina's case to be fairly weak.

'No, no, my mother is Russian,' Andrzej reverted to English. 'My father is Jew.'

'Your mother is your mother. It's bad enough,' his wife informed him.

'Even you don't like me, for being Jew,' he said with some melodrama.

'You are not a Jew. Only your father is a Jew. All your life you didn't know it, and now you decide to be a Jew just to be irritating, to be annoying everyone.'

'It's true.'

'Which? That you didn't know it or that you do it to be annoying?' I sought to clarify.

'Both. Would you like some vodka? Where is Rob? We men must have some vodka. Leave the women to have silly discussions.'

Poseidon

Since becoming a Dad, I had noticed a shift in the patterns and objects of my desire. Now, I had to admit it, I fancied 'mummies' best of all - drooping eyed, engorged, breast-feeding mothers, mothers oblivious to the sick down the back of their blouses or, like Dolores, glamorous but frantic with maternal anxiety. As the chaperone for my own child, for the first time in my life I was able to have free and companionable access and, by watching them with their children, bask in their sexuality without feeling compelled to do anything about it. My enjoyment was heightened by the fact that the women felt so safe. At the same time as enjoying male company, they weren't really thinking about it. The child was the badge of their allegiance to another - even though I couldn't help noticing that the other in question was not usually in their good books at the moment. Exemplary, wife-relieving, child-carer that I was, I benefited from the comparison. The perks for someone in my position were considerable.

I liked the Poseidon Hotel for its 1970s, James Bond feel. It was situated well back from the sea, through a grove of trees, at Jelitkowo. There were modern, white concrete sculptures leading up to the door. The swimming pool was large and usually deserted, and the restaurant did cheerful, holiday food. Dolores and I started to meet there every week to take the children swimming. Dolores, not unexpectedly, looked as if she were competing in the swimsuit category at a beauty contest in her sleek, maroon costume. I didn't exactly feel like God's gift in my own ancient and rather threadbare trunks (they might even have been the ones I'd bought in my final year at boarding school) so it was just as well I wasn't into pulling anyone at the moment.

'The gentleman doth protest too much!' Nell would have said, had she heard my thought - which it rather felt as though she had.

There was no time for flirting in any event, since preventing Karolek from repeating his 'drownding' experience at two years of age was a full-on, full-time, two-person job. The boy tore around the edge of the pool, slipping on the wet tiles, flung aside his arm-bands and belly flopped into the deep end - and this with three people (including the pool attendant) watching or physically restraining him all of the time. Dolores was in a perpetual fluster or in tears, though there were periods of relative calm when I could persuade Karolek to play games with Koshka and myself, provided they involved a lot of splashing and wrestling.

Sometimes we would go into the Tea-room next to the pool and drink various Chinese teas and choose from the selection of 'galaretki', cakes with fruit imprisoned in bright green jelly. The children had jellies sprinkled with raisins in tall glasses. Although I liked Dolores very much, I could rarely recall the snippets of information we had actually exchanged. Karolek's drowning accident had occurred in Colombia, for example, and the boy had been clinically dead for two minutes, and taken ten minutes before breathing again. Or was it the other way round? Surely you couldn't be clinically dead for ten minutes and survive, but, on the other hand, what did it mean not to breathe for ten minutes - wasn't that dead? Or did she mean breathe unaided? It was clearly so traumatic for her to remember it, I didn't like to ask about it on another occasion.

Koshka's wariness of the boy had not diminished. She was not keen on his apparent determination to give her a 'drownding' experience of her own by pulling her underwater by the legs, or rearing up out of the water and landing with his whole upper body on her head. She was, however, a great devotee of cheekiness, loved all forms of outrageousness and was pretty adept at many of them herself. She couldn't decide whether she liked him. Probably she didn't - but he was definitely fun to watch.

Now, in the Tea-room, Karolek nudged Koshka with his elbow, shunted her over so he could sit on half of her stool and shoved his small teddy bear head-first into her fizzy drink. Koshka looked momentarily stunned, before fishing out the bear and dumping it wet into his lap - whereupon he started to giggle, falling backwards off the stool and throwing the soggy animal back at her.

Manhattan

On one occasion, we went back to Dolores' flat in a new block not far from the suburb of Wrzeszcz. We walked through the new shopping area, full of wooden or pre-fabricated kiosks which had been turned into barred-windowed, pricey boutiques. As not one of them was more than a single storey in height, the district had been dubbed 'Manhattan'.

The flat was minimalist in style, with gleaming, white walls, polished floors, a black and white geometric rug, black leather furniture and a glass coffee table, on which stood a metallic fruit-bowl and a vase containing the single stem of a blown-glass lily. Two things struck me as odd: the central living space bore not a single trace of the presence of a child - and of such a child, the least containable child imaginable, as it was hard to believe could have his evidences and effects confined to his own bed-room. Secondly, the few pictures on the walls were all iconic, black and white, model shots of Dolores in various sultry, semi-erotic poses, except for one - half artist's impression, half architectural elevation - of a white villa overlooking descending cascades of forest and bougainvillea and a scalloped, bright blue bay.

'That was our home, our villa,' Dolores explained. 'Al, he design, he build it, everything - perfect.'

'Such a beautiful place, you must have been very sad to leave it,' I fished. 'It must have seemed a shame after so much work ...'

Dolores looked troubled but she didn't answer.

I got only a little nearer to discovering what brought them to Poland:

'My Al, he want to build in hills, in this very nice place above all town, not far from here, in Niedwiednik. In this moment it is not so good part of town, but he want to make there beautiful apartaments, like nothing seeing in Polands before.' Dolores' face grew sorrowful. 'So many people here, they have money but they don't have opportunity to have homes, and now these mortgage companies are starting - peoples don't knows what is it, they are taking so muchos money from them. They don't understand what is it loan, what is it interest.'

Niedwiedz means Bear. At Przedszkole with Pani Ola we sing about 'Stary Niedzwiedz mocno spi', the old bear is sleeping, and we have to creep up on him on tiptoes. The bit just before the bear pounces is the most scary and the most ecziting because you know it's going to happen, you just don't know ezackly how or if it's going to be you what's grabbed in its paws. You can't run yet but it's

like a whistle inside you getting higher and higher so you might burst.

'Is Niedwiednik where the bears live?' I ask Karolek. 'Is it where the Cricoland bear lived before he was catched? Do you think he still has realatives there?'

Me and Karolek have disgust about realatives before. He has lots of grannies and cousins and uncles in another country and so do I. I have two grannies in England. One of the grannies has a grannydad but the other one doesn't. Realatives are people who really belong to you, even if you're not in the same place. It might be like that for the bear and the other bears in the forest.

Karolek says: 'If my Tata builds in this Niedwiednik, this Bear-place, he will shoot all the bears - dead - bang, bang. I'll shoot them for him. I already shooted ten bears, didn't I, Mama, at Grandpa and Uncle Pedro's in Medellin?'

It was at this point that Al returned, a rather ursine figure himself, in a padded, black leather jacket, with discreet silver jewellery. He seemed very clean, the skin on his face softened and perfumed, his short hair and large silver-grey moustache perfectly trimmed. His years in Munich seemed to have most influenced his sartorial image, and he had on a pair of extremely stylish, rectangular, German glasses - at least that was my guess, as I shook the big, warm hand held out to me.

Al was delighted to meet me, he said, had heard all about me, was extremely grateful for the help I gave Dolores with their son, who was admittedly a great deal of work. Would I like some beer? Would you mind, my darling? I know you have worked so hard today. He kissed Dolores reverentially on the forehead, saying something else in Spanish, which included the word 'balcony'. I felt vaguely as though I shouldn't be there, so that Al's worship could progress to the desire he evidently felt at the least proximity to his wife, but Al moved lightly aside.

I liked him, and his friendliness, and wanted to know more about him. I wasn't sure I really did get to know more about him, though I continued to enjoy his warmth, as he spoke passionately of the need for craftsmanship, the necessity of importing certain materials, certain practices and standards of labour and so forth, of the purity of line and beauty of interior he would achieve in these flats he was going to build, flats that would be worthy of the aspiration of those who purchased them, in a way never achieved, never even thought possible in Poland before this time.

I took care to be very straight with him. I was conscious of striving for a particular frankness in everything I said, even though we weren't discussing anything that might have required evasion, just the usual pleasantries about work and family and so forth. He was not a man to be messed with. I sensed he knew that I liked him, that I respected him, and that he in turn recognised that I was not going to make a move on his wife. I was not that stupid.

Bicycles

I had just placed my thousand złoty note in the saucer on the cloakroom counter and the old man had handed over the two squares of grey toilet paper when I got the idea about the bicycles. We could cycle in the woods and the hills behind Oliwa, or along the beach path from Jelitkowo to Sopot. We loved going out with friends to their holiday huts by the lakes in Kashubia, with beer and sausages round the campfires - but, if I'm honest, I don't like having to depend on other people so much. However nice they are and however good their intentions, it's still putting yourself in the hands of other people. You're completely at their mercy really. It would be great to be able to explore by ourselves.

'We must get bikes now it's Summer,' I said, coming back to our table in the dark café.

'I know a really good place in Sopot where we could buy one of those wickerwork child-seats for Koshka,' Nell enthused. 'Can we afford new bikes? Should we try the Russians' Market?'

In the end, we found a little shop in a row of railway worker's cottages in Oliwa. Wheeling the two bicycles through the maze of paths in the long grass by the station - the lean, pink and purple Russian Racer and the more sedate, turquoise Polish model - Rob perched Koshka on his saddle. The sound of crickets synchronised with the quiet whirr of well-oiled wheels, submerging it in one drowsy hum. The crossbar of the racer was inscribed with the word SPORT in Cyrillic lettering. The stirring leaves of the linden trees splashed the sunlight alternate green and yellow on the ground below them, while shadows played on the warm trunks. Koshka caught a ladybird on the back of her hand, calling it 'God's Cow', the nick-name she had learnt from her friends at Przedszkole, displaying it proudly as she let it crawl over her knuckles.

The grass was long and dry, almost white at the tips, so that it took a moment to realise that all around, on every side, in little depressions in the grass, lay sleeping men, perhaps a hundred of them. They slept flat on their backs or curled on one side, their hands under their cheeks, the top of one brown foot fitted snugly into the instep of the other. Their neckerchiefs were tugged loose at their throats, ragged shirts open on smooth chests, and hair flopped forwards over their faces. Breathing through their soft lips and every one of them fast asleep, Romanian Gypsy men - no women or children in sight. I recalled with amusement the number of times I'd been told how the women and children begged but the money went all to the men, who organised everything, ran cartels and syndicates, who would rob you and cut your throat without blinking, and who cut each others' throats with great ferocity and regularity in their many feuds. And yet here they were, apparently worn out with the efforts of their own depravity, stirring the grass stems with their even breaths.

Even Koshka was quiet so as not to wake them, as we pushed our gently whirring, spanking new and eminently stealable bikes through the midst of this sleeping menace, smiling at each other in the sunshine.

I like it best when it's just us, the three of us, and we're on the move, as we are now, speeding along the path by the beach on our bikes between the gorse bushes and the pines. Koshka is wedged into the bike seat behind me. I can hear snatches of her singing carried off by the rush of the wind and her raucous laughter when she whacks me on the backside when I stand up to pedal harder.

'I got you on the pupcia,' she crows by way of unnecessary explanation.

*The sun is warm and the sea is simply there, stretched out, an uncomplaining blue. Nell is cycling, sometimes just ahead, where I can watch her (talking of backsides), sometimes behind, where I can tell she's there without looking, or beside us when there's room. There are people on the path, but not any that are going to impinge on us - old people side by side, young people with their arms around each other, families holding children by the hand or hoisting them onto shoulders. People cheer up so dramatically when the summer comes. That awful, closed down 'nothing doing' demeanour that I find so hard to deal with day in and day out is just <u>gone</u>. They even nod and acknowledge one another as they pass on the path. Cycling along, I feel perfectly satisfied. This dream of family life that I've had, that I nursed in my heart ever since I was sent away to school, it's real. Like being on **Exeat** every day of your life. It's real and I have it.*

We can eat chips and ice-cream when we get to Sopot, easy, portable food. Proper, Polish, sit-down food is much nicer, but that often comes with strings, with complications. There's a kind of pub a little way back from the path called Foka, The Seal. I remember someone tipped me off that they don't cheat foreigners there. Perhaps we'll give it a try. I just don't want anyone to do or say anything that could set off a chain reaction. I'm sick of feeling embattled and helpless. I just want it to be us, the warm sun and whirring wheels, and no-one and nothing else to deal with.

Far ahead, the Molo at Sopot is shimmering, pointing out into the sea. We can wheel our bikes out along its faded planks - if bikes are allowed, that is.

It's sunny on my legs and the seat is squashy and makes a pattern on them. The sea is quite noisy. It's blue not grey now. It's grey when we feed the swans in Winter. Once the beach had snow on and the sea was frozen with the waves lifted up all stiff.

The sand is very pale on the beach. It's not yellow. The horse and cart are waiting by one of the piles of seaweed while the man scoops it up and throws it into the cart with a big fork like the one Daddy uses with the big knife for cutting chicken. All along the beach there are haystacks of black, dry, crackly seaweed the man raked up before. The wind is a pale wind like the sand. We make the wind more by riding fast.

We are going to Daddy's favourite pub called Foka. We go there lots of times. The Seal, it means. I have a little furry grey seal toy. Auntie Wandzia gave it me. It's called Foczka, or Foczek when it wants to be a boy. It's a nice shape to hold, round its neck. It just fits with its narrow place between my finger and thumb so its head sticks out and looks around. Daddy says that's what I looked like when I was being born out of Mama. Once I left my Foczka at the Seal pub, but we went back and found it when we knew it was lost.

Andrzej

I am sitting at our square coffee table, looking at my third shot of plum vodka. Andrzej is on the sofa opposite. The table is littered with plates, empty beer bottles, a few remaining slices of gooseberry cake, and, I can see now, disguised by the pattern of pears and cherries on the oilcloth, a small patch of encrusted playdough. Andrzej is telling me about his latest unsuccessful attempt to negotiate a mortgage. The bank manager was dubious, given his frequent changes of employment, he says.

Reading between the lines of his various anecdotes, I deduce that Andrzej is an enthusiastic and even a loyal employee. He has often become the right-hand man to his various bosses. Not being ambitious for the top job, he prefers to orbit freely, playing second fiddle, or more often crown prince, very happily. I suspect that when a job becomes too familiar, too easy, he probably does not conceal his restlessness, even impatience, in a way which makes his bosses uncomfortably aware that he is cleverer than they are. This quickly becomes difficult for both of them.

Not long ago, he told me, he'd absolutely had enough, and had gone through the procedure to apply for emigration to Canada. He'd had all the papers necessary from the Canadian Embassy, but Alina had refused to go. I thought about his wife. She was absolutely right, from her point of view. All Alina's virtues were Polish virtues. They might well not translate into those of another culture - though there were surely plenty of Poles in Canada, so perhaps that wouldn't be necessary. Meanwhile her husband, pouring us both another vodka, could never thrive fully in his own country. He had a kind of energy and a meticulousness which were always thwarted. He set himself high standards in an environment where these were still unusual and barely recognised. Whatever was promised in the new Poland, his time hadn't yet come, and he couldn't wait.

Maybe he felt as I did, sitting there opposite him, chatting and sipping vodka, somehow <u>unseen</u>. I liked Andrzej a lot, and it was pleasant drinking with him. Yet, apart from a joint interest in beer, and of course vodka, we had not a great deal in common. I felt that his warmth towards me did not arise out of the least sense of what I might be like. I represented foreign-ness, and he focussed on me rather than Nell, to whom he was temperamentally far more akin, because I was a bloke. It's at times like this, after a few vodkas, that I realise how lonely I feel. Not for the first time, I con-

274

clude that, on balance, I prefer the company of women. I hope I can hear Alina and Nell coming back from the kitchen, as the conversation turns to fast cars, soft porn and other such topics in which I'm assumed to have an interest.

Not long ago, I met a lecturer working for the British Council, in Wroclaw I think it was. He had been in the job two years, a man in his early fifties. For some reason it came up, and he confessed with some bewilderment, that not one of his Polish colleagues had ever asked him if he was married, or had been married, whether he had any children, not even which city he came from or where he had worked before.

'Perhaps they don't like to pry, in case my wife ran off with the chimney sweep or died a hideous death I can't bear to talk about,' he said, but he knew the truth. He was an Englishman, and that, for them, was the sum total of his life experience, just as it was his entire function in their lives. Then again, how interested <u>are</u> human beings in one another really, when it comes down to it? How interested am I in Andrzej for example? I hardly know a thing about him.

In an attempt both to rectify this and to change the subject, I ask him again about his travels. Andrzej, it transpires, has been to Israel too. In fact, his Uncle turns out to be Israeli Ambassador to Poland.

'You wouldn't consider emigrating <u>there</u>?' I ask. I could imagine all too clearly how Alina would feel about that.

'No, no. I am European man. Finally it is so. In Poland I feel Jewish because it give me something to do, but when I see real Jewish persons I know I am not. My Uncle tease me that I have not enough angst. I am carrying something but it is not the same. So I think what the hell, life is too short. Let's get drunk, let's watch pretty women on late night T.V., preferably without clothing. Of course, these are the best.'

'How come your uncle ended up in Israel but your father's still here?'

'My father was separated from his brother during War. They were both in partisans near to where they was growing up, in small shtetl in East of Poland - now it is in Soviet Union, sorry, CRS. Near to end of War, my father took papers of one Polish man who was killed. He didn't know him. They are becoming papers of my father. Always since, he is living under this title. '

'What happened to the brother?'

'He escaped to Palestine in forty-five. He was in South Poland, near to Zakopane, to mountains, where were many people returning to homes, from camps and other places. Many were congregating in Krakow and then dispersing in South. There were some pogroms then - the people, some of them, were very disappointed: 'We thought we had seen the last of you Jewish bastards' and so forth. The British were not allowing for Jews to come to Palestine. In Germany even they were collecting Jewish refugees in camps for preventing this. My Uncle organised some escapes from this South Poland region, then he flied away himself.

'My father was meet with my mother in partisans. They find they are in Poland and are coming to Gdansk because are much spaces as all Germans are fast deporting from city. It is city of strangers. It is better for them. My father never spoke about to be Jewish. We never know about it. Only we noticed, my brother and me, that when we are coming from school saying bad about Jews he didn't to like it. There was one

joke, very popular, and my brother say about it at home: "What do you have against Jews? Only Zyklon B." We see my father didn't like. Also he went to theatre every month with same three friends. These friends all were Jews but I didn't to notice it. When one my friends in school class is repeating to me something not nice his parents said about it, I was embarrassing quite strong.'

'Does he still not speak about it? How did you find out?'

'He is retired man now. My mother is still working as doctor, but in present time they are in world cruise, very happy. The compensation money was very big for them.'

I looked across at Nell, as I habitually did when I thought I might have missed something crucial, but she was over by the doorway receiving complex instructions from Alina as to the making of her delicious yeast-cake. At least I deduced that was what was going on. Alina had written out the recipe for her. Nell had the sheet of paper in her hand, but they were still ironing out the finer points.

'Compensation? For what exactly?'

'For his imprisoning. You know about 1968 in Poland, don't you?'

I nodded. I knew anti-Semitism had been invoked as part of the power-struggle within the party which had finally brought Gierek to power. Sweet, cuddly Gierek, architect of Poland's massive debt but fondly recalled by many Poles as the man who had flooded Poland with Swiss chocolate and French perfume during the 70s.

'It was necessary to mobilise workers against intellectuals,' was Andrzej's summary, 'and also to turn many students against their teachers. Many Jewish students and professors were losing their places in the university. Many Jewish people left from whole country. There was pressure for them in their jobs, for them to change their family names to ones more so-called 'good Polish names'. They were leaving and they were offered from State only visas to Israel. Many other countries in West didn't even to know about it. It is not a very popular knowledge, yes?'

I shook my head. I was thinking how inseparable history and biography are in Poland. Of course that's true everywhere, in Britain too, especially if I think about our grandparents' generation - it's just that it appears to be mediated through the social, social conditions and social attitudes: illegitimate or adopted children, absent fathers, mental illness... Of course these are historical and political too, and of course unemployment and war affected people's family stories and their life opportunities. Perhaps we just don't see it so clearly, but here the effects seem so much more direct, overt and immediate, entwined with lives even down to the present generation.

'My father also is having the visitation of one official. The man offer him visa to Israel but my father is all times very stubborn man, and he don't agree. He say he will consider for going to Denmark. He thinks it is good country, but other he won't considerate. The official went away. The next week he come back and he offer to my father the visa to Sweden - only-other it is not possible, or Israel of course. He have brother there, after all, says this man. My father is in each case and all times very stubborn and he say he will not to go. The official tell to him that he will regret very much that he refuse generosity of Party in this way.

My father was engineer, quite important in designing in shipyard. In very quick time he was trying in the court and sent in the prison during six years for spying -

something like industrial espion. All of other six persons trying in same time were Jewish, so propaganda could to say that in this time is broken very devilish Jewish circle of spies for destroying economy of Polish state. My mother explain me that my father have very sudden gone to sea. I was only the young child in this moment, eight years old. When I was twelve I make discovering and afterwards I can go to visit him. My brother knew some months before.

'So what happened after? Did he stay in jail?'

'He is releasing after maybe five years, but he cannot work like engineer, and not to work it is impossible. He begin the work to repairing cars. Now he doesn't longer work, but he still enjoys to repair the cars, and he grows a lot of things in garden. My mother interests in the herbalistical potions, for curings, you know, and in the nights he study and he study, advocating - how it is, the law, you say? And last year he represent for himself like advocate and he sue Polish government for his years of imprisoning.'

Przedszkole

It was Alina who revealed to me that my daughter was not being fed like the other children after *leżakowanie*. Koshka hadn't stayed for *leżakowanie* in the beginning, but had been collected after *obiad*. After a while, though, she had caught onto the fact that, tedious though it was to have to lie down for such a length of time, much of the social interaction, the giggling and whispering - and even more importantly the events giggled and whispered about the next morning - took place during this time of lighter supervision and supposed sleep. She began to clamour to be allowed to stay, and so I'd fixed it with the Pani Dyrektor and brought along her little sheet and pyjamas.

'You didn't pay the supplement?'

'What supplement?'

'For the extra time and the *podwieczorek*.' 'Podwieczorek' was the warm drink and snack administered once the children got up, before home-time.

'We already paid for *leżakowanie*, even when Koshka didn't use to stay,' I said. 'The Pani Dyrektor never mentioned anything else when we changed the arrangement.'

'Perhaps she didn't think about it,' Alina suggested. 'It's just that Magda said something to me, that Koshka isn't allowed *podwieczorek* like the others.'

'She used to get *podwieczorek*, I'm sure of it. She used to talk about it. She liked the fruit.' My head was starting to spin, visions of the children sitting at their little tables, fruit and biscuits on their little plates, hot milk steaming in their mugs decorated with mushrooms and squirrels - and my little girl to one side, her plate, depicting a gnome asleep under a toadstool, empty before her. Perhaps not even permitted to sit down at all, an outcast playing by herself in a far corner of the room. It had been months since she'd started staying in the afternoons. Months! And she'd never breathed a word!

At that moment, children began coming out of the *Maluch's* classroom in ones and twos. Other mothers gathered to receive them. Koshka came out dragging Magda by the arm. We quizzed them as tactfully as we could. Koshka looked a bit embarrassed, but Magda blinked her dark-ringed eyes earnestly:

'The Panis say Koshka can't have *podwieczorek*. Pani Dorocia said her mummy doesn't pay even though she's so rich and doesn't have to work.'

'Is that true? Did they say that to you?' I asked Koshka.

'Pani Ula says my mummy's such a fine, rich lady I shouldn't get *pod-wieczorek* like all the other children whose mummies work hard. I shouldn't get it for free. Is it very expensive? Or did you just forgot?'

'I don't know. I don't think so - but, sweetheart, I didn't know we had to pay any extra for *podwieczorek*. The Pani Dyrektor never asked me for any more money. Pani Ula shouldn't say those things to you. She should talk to me.'

Koshka was already busy taking off Magda's slippers. I didn't want to make a bigger deal of it in front of her than it already was. 'What's all this stuff about being rich and not working?' I asked Alina.

'They don't think that doing translations is working. It's your language so it's easy for you. You are a foreigner, of course, and if you can afford to stay at home, even to work at home, you must be wealthy. Last week,' she confided, 'I came to collect Magda early because she had been sick. Pani Basia and Pani Ula were still combing the other children's hair. I heard Ula say to Koshka,' she impersonated Pani Ula's sniff: "Since your mother has so much time, how come your hair has a knot in it? Doesn't she comb it properly?"'

'But to say it to a *child*...? Look after Koshka for me a minute.'

I went on the rampage. I barged into the Dyrektor's office. I spoke to Pani Ola, who was sympathetic. She'd had no idea, she said. She didn't supervise the meals. I confronted Pani Ula, who scowled and sniffed and tossed her head: If she had any more difficulties she could address them to me, not to my daughter! I paid the supplement. Yet from none of them did I have the sense that they saw anything fundamentally wrong in communicating in this way to a four year-old.

'Of course,' admitted the Pani Dyrektor, 'the children are before their eyes, in their hands, the mothers are not.'

One Hundred Days

Lyceum Number XV was a prestigious institution, much sought after for the standards of its English teaching, which, as everyone knew, was the way for their children to get on. In the new climate of competition, the primary school grades of prospective pupils were carefully scrutinised and the Dyrektor interviewed each set of parents. At the end of the interview, it was said, wise parents should place a small brown envelope on the table between themselves and the Dyrektor, next to their application forms. They should then get up, shake hands with the Dyrektor and head for the door.

'Are you sure you've got everything?' the Dyrektor would inquire.

'Oh yes, quite sure,' would be the judicious reply, closing the door softly behind them.

Despite his metamorphosis into a dapper businessman, Stefan still taught one English Language course at Lyceum XV as a favour for an old friend who was head of the English programme there. There was to be a 'Stodniówka', he told me, a 'hundred-day party' - to mark the fact that the students had one hundred days until their exams.

'Like a Mardi Gras, *you* know, before a fast'. Would I accompany him?

'Ewa can't go, she has a do up at the hospital. Wiesia's said she'll mind the boys.'

Their elderly neighbour must've been high on something when she agreed to that one, I thought, given the fragile state of Wiesia's nerves and the irrepressible energy of Stefan's sons.

'Come, you'll love it,' Stefan urged. 'It's all rather sweet, *I* think.'

Ewa was winding the huge knot of her black hair onto the top of her head. She wore a low-backed dress of blue and purple, swirling chiffon, fixing her grey angora stole at the shoulder with a brooch of pale opal and jet.

'It was my grandmother's,' she mused as she fastened the pin. 'She died last year, you know. She held our whole family together, always. She came from Wilno and had a weak heart. She always smelt of valerian drops, yet in the war she was deported in a cattle truck, with her younger sister, and my mother just a little child, six years old, to Gladilo in Siberia. The Russians had a penal settlement there. She worked as a lumberjack. Just think! That little tiny woman!'

Stefan quick-stepped into the room, diminutive in a soft, charcoal-grey suit, with his neat little moustache and the close-cropped, dark fuzz of his hair. His eyes rested on his wife with a mixture of admiration and complacency. He came over, adjusting his cufflinks.

In the largest room at Lyceum Number XV, students had pushed the tables back against the walls to create a dance-floor and turned out the lights. They had taken all the chairs and some tables into the room across the corridor, where they stood laden with plates of *kanapki,* cakes, fizzy drinks and bottled water. Stefan had naturally ensured that Pepsi and not Coca-cola was the drink of choice for the evening. There was crackly disco music coming through the speakers mounted at the far end of the room. Various guests and members of staff seated themselves on the tables in the corners, but of the school students themselves - even those who had greeted us at the door - there was now no sign.

'Ah,' said Stefan darkly, enjoying every minute, 'that's because they will dance the Polonaise. The music changed to a stately three-four and the crocodile of students, in pairs, their arms thrust forward, one hand on top of the other, heads inclining regally from side to side, began stepping forward into the room in a long line. The Polonaise is an incredibly aristocratic dance - a fact not immediately apparent when I'd seen it performed by the *Starszaki* (the six year-olds) at Koshka's Pre-School on Mother's Day. Even the flirting part in the middle, when the couples make windows with their arms and gaze at each other through them, is still about deference and decorum. Enacting the continuity between these young dancers, their parents, grandparents and beyond, the sight of so many teenagers performing this ritual so solemnly - without a trace of irony - was very moving. It would have been hard to imagine a bunch of British secondary school kids doing something similar, and the thought gave rise to mixed feelings. I looked at the serene, young faces, inclining this way and that. Why don't they ever *rebel?* Why don't they have a counter-culture of their own? Because they learn to do this when they're tiny, precisely because it's an expression of nationality and fulfils a need. What happens if a people has nothing which performs this function? Are British kids deprived?

I felt like I had the first time I'd ever seen the audience in the Lodz opera house stand up and sing along with the enslaved Hebrews in *Nabucco* and wanted to cry and be sick at the same time. The level of feeling and the level of conformity had been both stirring and alarming. They were expressing something they all felt, their opposition to oppression, together, in human solidarity. Yet the collective feeling was not primarily human but national, and as such was, as always, a bit scary. This was about *them,* and *no-one but them.* God help anyone, Hebrews included, who tried to muscle in, who in any way came between them and this feeling. Or who got in their way while they were having it. I'd been torn between the desire to join in - to be *able* to join in - and to run away, and had protected myself from both impulses with that no doubt very British defence, irony: the irreverent thought that there was something inherently funny about a room full of probable anti-Semites singing the Chorus of the Hebrew Slaves!

After the Polonaise, everyone went through to the room with the food and tucked in. Stefan introduced me to several of his pupils, leading to the inevitable question from each one:

'How do you like Poland? How do you find our country?'

This placed me in the usual impossible position, so, determined not to be sucked into anything, I stuck to 'I like it very much.' This met with the usual pitying response. I could neither represent the whole truth on my part nor provide satisfaction for them. Often, therefore, they provided the answer themselves or steered me in the right direction:

'Our country have many problems,' said Beata.

'Poland is very poor country. It's third world country actually.'

Between a rock and a hard place, I was meant to disparage the country or concur in disparaging it, but only and precisely in the terms acceptable to them - and even then they wouldn't like it. Everything about the place was dreadful, I was supposed to say, but the people were wonderful and beyond reproach. Whereas I actually held the heretical view that there were some fine things about Poland, which its people didn't appear to value at all, eager to throw out the baby with the bath-water, but that it might be time for its people to go in for a spot of self-examination.

'I expect everyone has been so nice to you,' Jolanta said.

'Yes, lots of people have been really kind and welcoming.' I steered an impossible course, trying to be diplomatic *and* truthful. I knew they waited for the expected compliments, which it was hard to give as they were so insufferably smug in receiving them.

'Of course we are very hospitable nation,' agreed Beata.

I'd had this conversation so many times, the phrases, the vocabulary, the underlying messages were always the same. You'd think I'd have learned to handle it by now. I despised myself because I hadn't, while the students, as ever, lurched between inferiority and superiority in their statements about their country. The subtext was clear. They, the Poles under Communism and for hundreds of years before, had lost their freedom but we in the Capitalist West had lost our souls - supposing we'd ever had any.

'In West all things are so commercialising, even all religious festivals and families holidays,' Beata was saying.

I wasn't disagreeing with her ...

'Yes, yes,' her friend Ania put in. 'That is why you are making the Christmas puddings one month before!'

'I think *that's* to do with letting the alcohol soak in, or something, but it *is* true in general, about the commercialisation. It's awful. But isn't that what you wanted, a free market, a capitalist economy? If you're not going to lose *your* souls you'll have to be really on your toes.'

They immediately grew gleeful each time I conceded or offered something negative about 'the West', notching it up, but would never concede anything, or engage in any self-criticism of their own society at all. It made me feel I'd been a bit disloyal, offering hostages so readily in return for nothing at all, even if I'd genuinely given my opinion.

They want me to say Poland is bad in the way *they* think it is - that it's backward and deprived, but they won't like it if I do, and anyway, I don't think that. So they'll poke and prod until I come up with something critical. Anything I'm likely to say that I actually do think will be too unorthodox. There'll be the immediate bristling, the disbelief, the sourness, the resistance. They'll react and I'll be drawn into trying to convince them, because now I've claimed something I'll want them to believe me. And because they're so nice and I really do think it's true, I'll give examples - which I'll care about too much - and then will come the retaliation, probably of the 'do you think *your* country so perfect?' variety. Not at all, I'll say, and one of them will come back with 'Well, my uncle was in America,' (because of course all 'Western countries' are the same and I'm supposed to defend and represent all of them), 'and he had such-and-such a bad experience, or witnessed such-and such an undesirable aspect of life there.' We'll be into the usual hopeless spiral and I'll end up feeling that I'm the person with the problem, the weird vision.

I could hear Stefan in the group behind me, holding forth among the eager young people with his usual teetotal effervescence. He never had this difficulty - but then, he was Polish, despite the childhood in Crouch End. His foreignness simply added cachet, was not an albatross around his neck. He didn't see things other people didn't want to see, or, if he did, he did not have the temerity to enlighten others about them

'Your wife is very beautiful,' one grovelling student told him.

'Thank you,' Stefan laughed, 'but it's still a hundred days to the exams. And also,' he relished the joke, 'this lady is not my wife.'

I turned round: 'His real wife *is* very beautiful,' I put in, embarrassing the poor lad still further.

'This is Krzysztof,' Stefan introduced him, abandoning me to the round of 'how do you like our country' questions all over again with this new group, as he went off in search of more Pepsi. Perhaps it was that chemical cocktail which kept him so continuously cheerful.

'How can you like to live in such place? Poland is such poor country. It's awful, really,' Krzysztof was saying.

'With days of Communism was always queueing and queueing and nothing in shops to eat and now is unemploying four millions,' said Romek.

'We suffered very much, for many years,' summarised Danuta.

As the representative of a privileged Western country, this had to be impressed on me. It would have been churlish to remind them that many of their parents had used to think that unemployment in capitalist countries was a myth put about by the Communist propaganda machine, or that the group of economists I used to teach, several of whom were now advisers to the government, had always asserted that it wasn't too high a price to pay for a free market. Or to mention the underclass anywhere else. Besides, they didn't care about the miseries of unemployment in *other* countries.

'The poorest person in your country is richer than richest Pole,' declared Romek.

'That simply isn't true. I bet your family has a *dacha*, a place in the country to go at weekends. Mine doesn't. The poorest people in Britain …' I started.

'I remember when was no food in shops and the long queues, was awful,' Romek returned to surer ground. 'We was poorest in all Europe, while in West even poor persons was having the swimming pool. Was terrible life for us.'

I knew they believed this account of themselves, and as a general claim it had a lot of truth to it … but - hang on a minute - they had been *children*. They hadn't queued for anything, I'd have been willing to bet, except cassette tapes of the latest music and trendy clothes, with all the thrill of knowing where to get hold of the scarce and much-desired object and then of obtaining it. It was their mothers and grandmothers who had queued for *food*. I knew because I'd queued with them. These favoured only-children came from families far too savvy and wired into the right networks to have suffered much real deprivation. I too recalled the empty shelves of the shops but I also remembered the full fridges of my Polish friends, and conjured a sudden image of my pregnant self tramping the streets, scouring the empty shops and the wooden vegetable stalls, returning in triumph with a bag of carrots. I couldn't suppress the insoucient notion that perhaps the only person present who'd actually *lived* the Communist nightmare was myself!

I looked at the group. I wasn't being fair. They had grown up under oppression, while I had been merely inconvenienced. And even such temporary exposure to that situation had marked me, so of course they were right to stress its effects on them. They're such sweet people and so young, I thought dotingly, even though they were scarcely ten years younger than I was. They think this because it's what they've always been told - and because it's what they and their parents genuinely feel. That's why they always use the same phrases when they talk about it. I could feel it coming on again, the old didactic temptation, the desire to persuade that always drew me in. I turned down another drink. It was all a bit more complicated than that, I began.

The students were not happy. I had expressed sympathy and acknowledged hardship, but I had not commiserated *enough* for their taste, or not in the terms that would assuage their need at this moment. They were going to punish me by hitting where they thought it would hurt, by taking another jibe at *my* country.

'My cousin was in London,' Krzysztof observed, 'where you have all of those negroes running around.'

It did hurt, though not for the reasons they supposed. I knew now the conversation was doomed. The racism was always my undoing. I had never succeeded in convincing anyone on this subject, but equally had never learnt to let it pass. I would feel sick if I didn't speak, and ashamed of myself if I did.

'They're not running around. They live there - like everyone else. You talk as though black people should be kept on a lead - like dogs, or dangerous animals. You wouldn't say that if you knew people as neighbours and friends. I reckon Poland needs more difference, not less.'

'I am not racist, but I think asphalt should stay on the ground,' said Joanna primly.

'We have already these Arabic students everywhere. They are coming here, Arabish men, buying Polish girls.'

'Such girls are whores,' Krzysztof contributed. 'I say it to them, even if were my own sister.'

'It's funny, you never have anything good to say about Poland the way it is, but the people are sacrosanct, not allowed to be criticised at all,' I said. 'Yet I've noticed you don't mind admitting Poland isn't a tolerant place. It's the only admission of a fault in your society that I've ever heard any Polish people confess to - except for things that can be blamed on the Germans or the Russians or the Communists or the Jews. You know why? It's because you don't really think it's a fault at all. You think that countries with different populations in them end up like Yugoslavia, that it's inevitable. You don't like what was done to the minority populations in Poland. It wasn't pretty. You don't like killing people. You wouldn't do it yourselves, but you don't really mind that someone did it for you. You like the result don't you - 99% of the population Polish Catholic or whatever it is? Don't you think that compromises you just a little?'

That's right, tone it down, make it palatable, why don't you? Was I *so* bent on convincing the Polish population, one by one if necessary, that their country was a cesspool of prejudices - even if it was?

'Do you think your country is so good example? Romek said huffily.

'Of course not. There are terrible racists in Britain. It's not about saying another country is *better*. It's just that, because there are lots of different kinds of people living there, that's an ideal, living together - at least for some people.'

284

I was physically uncomfortable, a burning in my stomach, knowing I had more at stake than just my credibility. Now I would be caught up in trying to make them see what I was seeing, and I would feel rejected when I couldn't get them to believe me, couldn't alter anything, couldn't make my description prevail. What am I asking them to do? By what monstrous piece of presumption and sense of superiority had this become my mission? I looked at their eyes and saw the resistance, the disbelief, a kind of horror - and I couldn't blame them for that. They didn't like me and they thought I was more than a little crazy. But I was still angry, I was still a teacher to my core and I was on my soap-box by now:

'The trouble with having a tragic history is it makes people experience themselves only as victims. The hardest thing for you will be to see that you are perpetrators as *well* as victims.'

'But we are Poles. We have more tragical history than anyone,' Joanna countered simply. 'We suffer more, we suffer worse, always.'

'That's just it. You don't care about anyone *else*'s tragic history. You can't even conceive of other countries, or other groups within countries as *having* a tragic history. Or if you do, you get all competitive about it. The trouble with nationalism,' I launched into my pet theory, 'is that it uses up all people's imagination on being themselves, on conceiving their own identity, on their own wrongs and sufferings. There isn't any left over for anyone else. I don't think you Poles really believe anyone else *exists!*'

It was half belligerent flourish, half desperate plea to be believed, even as it dawned on me that I had a similar tendency to dwell on my own slights and injuries, and perhaps was somewhat of the same persuasion. Maybe that was why I could recognise the syndrome.

'But of course,' Romek agreed readily. 'Have you not heard the joke about the elephant and the Polish question?'

'I've a feeling you're about to tell me.' I grouched, with an obscure sense it might be a racist joke about elephants.

'A professor in some so-called international college give to his students the essay on subject of 'The Elephant'. The Englishman write 'The Elephant and How To Hunt Him'. The Frenchman he title his work 'The Love-Life of the Elephant'. The German he is doing much of research and finally he produce 'An Introduction to Preliminary Study of Gastronomic Possibilities of the Elephant'. The Russian he smoke many cigarettes in big anguishment before he arrive to his title: 'The Elephant - Does It Exist?' And the Pole…'

'Yes?'

'He write simply 'The Elephant and the Polish Question'.'

We all laughed, even they, who must have heard it a hundred times.

'It's a great joke,' I congratulated Romek, 'but if you know this about yourselves why doesn't it change? Or is the joke just to disarm everybody so you don't have to?'

'That is extreme cynical interpretations,' said Romek, genuinely shocked.

'I guess so.' I was a little shocked myself. 'I think I'll have that other drink after all.'

It all ended amicably enough with the students, with lots of good wishes for the coming exams, but I felt exhausted, that I'd gone overboard, that I had no self-restraint. Yet again I'd acted out a ritual, which all my careful foreknowledge had been unable to prevent.

I came back to Rob, buzzing with his own virtue at having selflessly stayed in to baby-sit so that I could go out and enjoy myself.

'How was it?' he called out. 'Have a good time?'

I burst into tears, as full of shame as if I'd got drunk and disgraced myself:

'I can't do this any more. I want to go home.'

Cat

'Everyone in my class's favourite colour is red. It useded to be mine too, but now I think that yellow's nicest. Today I looked at yellow when I was painting a balloon picture. It's even nicer, I think, so I wonder why isn't it my favouritest colour. I'm going to change my favourite colour to yellow. It's my really favourite colour now.'

'That sounds like a good idea,' Mama said. 'Lots of people's first favourite colour is red, but afterwards you can have different ones. I liked yellow, then I liked green, then blue, I remember. Then everyone liked pink, all the girls, when we were older than you are, about eight, and I remember thinking: I don't really like pink, but it started to look a lot nicer when everyone else liked it so much, and I wondered whether I'd be able to help liking it, even though I didn't really. I could just see what was nice about it then.'

'Red's much nicer than pink,' I said, 'but pink's nice for flowers sometimes. What's nice about pink is the flowery part of it.'

'When I said my favourite colour was yellow,' Koshka informed me, 'Robert Fibich laughed at me and Marta Wisniowska said I was a stupid dog - red is much better. Today when Tereska said what's your favourite colour at the table, I didn't want to say yellow. I nearly said red, but yellow is my favourite, so I said it really quietly - and everyone said theirs was too, even Robert and Marta!'

'Well, there you are then. Perhaps they were ready for a change,' I said, actually relieved and unable to resist pushing home the moral: 'You just think what you think and don't be afraid about saying it and you'll be fine. Often the people you worry will be nasty to you will change their mind.'

Koshka gave me one of those inscrutable looks that never fail to give parents the uncomfortable consciousness that they are happy to teach a lesson they haven't managed to learn themselves.

I could give her these easy, liberal principles, but she would either reject them as she grew older in order to fit in, or she would have an uncomfortable - perhaps richer but certainly no less uneasy - relation to the place herself. What would we say when she came home with the school textbook I'd seen with the picture of a little black child in a loincloth nappy squatting opposite a monkey, in mirror image, each peeling a banana? How would we respond when she too brought home the Zyklon B joke, without being contemptuous of the society that was her world? Perhaps only her children would be completely assimilated, the third generation. I saw Rob and I, then, the immigrant grandparents, never losing the accent or assumptions of the old country, strange misfits of whom any right-minded child would be tempted to be ashamed. Everything we would give to our daughter would lay up trouble for her - or get her into trouble there and then. That's why being an immigrant is such a big deal. Why would you do that if you had a choice? We'd have to wait for our grandchildren to find us quaint, secure enough in their own belonging to start to ask us questions, for our crazy opinions to pass as wisdom. Probably we really would be crazy by then.

'You know that cat? I asked Mama when we were looking left and right to cross over the tram tracks. Mama didn't know what cat I meant.

'What cat,' she kept saying, 'when?'

'The cat we sawed on the way to Przedszkole, the one lying down.'

'On the pavement, when it was frosty? That was ages ago, last winter. Is that the one?'

I saw it before Mama did. I took her chin and tried to turn her head away so she wouldn't see because I knew she'd start to tell about it. Mama esplained the cat had been hitted by a tram and that someone must of moved it to the side of the road so that the people whose cat it was could find it. It was curled up and looked sort of hard. It was there every time we walked past it.

'That cat,' I said to her again.

'What about it? I explained to you, didn't I? It was...'

'That cat,' I had to tell her quickly, 'it was sleeping.'

Julie

I would get the tram over to the Grosz supermarket in Zaspa, I decided, and call in on Julie while I was about it. Her job had finished last Friday, and Tomek, like Koshka, would still be at Przedszkole. If she'd started packing, she'd probably welcome a break.

Grosz was new in Zaspa, occupying an old aircraft hangar painted sky-blue and bearing the inscription SUPERSAM in yellow letters. Like many places in Poland, it was situated in the middle of a wasteland, in this case consisting of an overgrown runway and some scruffy sand-dunes. Grosz was pleasant to visit because there was a choice of every-thing, but only a choice between two products in each case. This seemed just about right to me, who had long ago decided that I was clearly un-suited to Western consumerist living: the average British supermarket sent me into a zomboid daze after just a few aisles, or induced an over-powering desire to flee, convinced that I didn't need to buy any food after all. In Grosz, the sensation of choice was thrilling, but manageable: it stimulated but did not overwhelm.

I ran into Julie at the checkout, where she was scrounging boxes.

'I can't believe how little time I have left,' she said, as we carried our bags back to her flat, littered with other, half-filled boxes, the table scat-tered with children's drawings unpinned from the walls. My eye kept returning to the garish painted and crayoned designs, Tomek's name neatly in the corner of the Predszkole creations, in others the names of my daughter and her son marching proudly through the middle of the picture, evidence of their longstanding artistic collaboration. Evidence also of many hours Julie and I had spent drinking, eating and chatting in her flat. Tomek would be with his Dad as well as his Mum soon. That couldn't be bad. They'd come to Poland all together, the three of them, because of Marek's Polish roots, but Marek had found the frustrations of life here too much to bear, and had returned to his native Glasgow over a year ago. I didn't know how I'd manage without Julie.

She'd been ripped off by the woman in the post office that morning, but she was unusually philosophical, though she did use the word accep-tance rather a lot for someone turning the other cheek.

'It's taken a fair bit of getting used to, the way Polish folk always bandy the word foreigner about. I always bridle, whether they do it in Polish or English, but maybe I'm just reacting to it in a British sense. I mean, in Britain, not many call folk foreigners to their faces, but maybe that's because it's truly a dirty word, everyone knows it's an excluding word, and that those it's applied to are excluded. Folk are only so con-siderate because they feel sorry for them, those who have the misfortune not to be British. Here it could just be a statement of fact. So maybe I needn't get so redd up when someone I think I'm close to talks about a

Swede in one breath, a Canadian in another and the next minute is away to ask me whether 'foreigners' think or do or are such and such, as if we're all the same. I take it as a slap in the face, but I probably shouldn't.'

'Isn't that the definition of a foreigner in most cultures, really, though? Those other people who are not like us and all the same? It's like with Justyna's mother. I really like her, and I know she's fond of me too. Last time I saw her, she said, 'Oh, Helenka, you're so nice, not like an English person at all. You seem, well, *Polish* really. Am you *sure* you don't have any "ancestry"?'

'Yeah, but you've been lucky with Justyna's Ma. I know you genuinely like her, but you've never had to challenge any of her cherished beliefs. Why? Because you've barely spent any time with her. I'm fair sick of always clamouring for acceptance - but the minute I get a whiff of it, I start fighting for it to be on terms I can stomach. I can't help noticing that whenever I'm offered it, I catch on awful quick that the price is too high. Anybody can fit in anywhere if they don't question what the folk themselves don't question, if they can assimilate themselves into the prejudices as well. Or if they could assimilate themselves out of seeing things differently. I could have acceptance often enough if I could just keep my big mouth shut. You know fine well you're the same. You can belong or you can *live*.'

'You're giving up then?' I said tetchily, because what she said was probably true.

'You only see it like that because you're still fighting. I've felt more at home here than anywhere else in my life. I like Glasgow fine, but it's not home. Neither is the North-East any more, though I grew up there. I'm going where we can be a family, me and Marek and Tomek, and we'll *make* a home. I thought that would be here, but it's no.'

'We always said, me and Rob, that we'd never go back while the Tories were still in power. It's unhealthy, being in opposition all the time. It's as if something heavy has lain on you and left its imprint.'

'Have you not finished up the same way here? And is it not exactly that imprint of oppression you're always blaming the Poles for having?'

I tried to protest but she was on a roll. 'And if I may say so, hen, back in the old country, they don't seem to be managing awful well to get rid of the giant people-squasher without you. Now *there's* a mission for you, if you're after one.'

I noticed that Julie often said 'hen', Marek-style, when delivering some pithy home truth. She'd used to say 'quine' or 'quinie', in the North-East way when she was teasing me. I remembered because she'd had to explain the term to me - whereas the Glaswegian 'hen' was self- explanatory. It was as if she had to represent Marek, to *be* him, when he wasn't here. Perhaps it was the same impulse that made Koshka insist on being known by the names of children she liked after they, or we, had moved away, even those met on holiday if they'd had a particular bond. It went on for weeks, even months. When she was two, she'd refused for ages to answer to anything but 'Dudek' (her pronunciation of Wojtek) after a 13 year-old she'd admired. It had been embarrassing having to explain all the time, not least because a *dudek* is a goofy kind of bird and also means 'fool'. Was I going to have to address her as Tomek for the foreseeable future?

'Will you let us give you a leaving party? We've been meaning to have a get-together for ages. Your flat's too small, but Babcia's is perfect - if she'll co-operate.'

Dog

We were in town, getting the last few things for the party. There had been two days of summer storms. People wore coats and carried umbrellas, hoping to dodge the downpours. The sky went dark as evening. There was virtual gridlock, and the air stank with fumes and reverberated with the sound of revving engines, enough to make you nostalgic for the days of petrol rationing. I had Koshka on my shoulders - or rather she had me in an armlock under the chin. I complained that she was throttling me, that she didn't need to cling on so tight when I was holding her by her red furry boots. She just laughed and held onto my hair instead, before trying to use my ears as reins.

A thin brown dog wandered through the traffic. The first phalanx started forwards as the lights changed and the engines roared as they moved across the intersection. The car which hit the dog, a dirty white Polonez, seemed to bump over its leg as it lay on the ground, and continued forward. The other cars hesitated at least for a moment, but the Polonez continued round the corner. Several pedestrians stared, while others appeared not to notice. The dog hauled itself on three legs onto the opposite pavement and into the nearest shop doorway where it lay, howling.

*The lights changed again and we crossed over. It seemed to be mainly the leg, which lay at an implausible angle to its body, but it was hard to asses whether there was anything internal to worry about. The howling was unbearable, rhythmic and low, rising to an inevitable cadence at the end of each phrase, going on and on. A woman stopped and tutted, and then a man. They agreed with Nell that it was terrible and that the beast needed a vet. Did they know where the nearest one might be? Would the vet come and collect an injured animal or would it have to be taken there? Sensing that her train of thought might involve them having to actually do something, the two soon took their leave. They didn't know the whereabouts of any vets, they said. The man bent down to stroke the dog's head before he put his hands in his pockets and walked off, with his head down. The dog's dirge, lower now, went on and on, throbbing like that refrain from the Russian Orthodox service Nell's choir sings - '**Hospodi pomiloj, hospodi pomiloj**', 'Lord have mercy, Lord have mercy ...'*

I am an atheist and I have always disliked dogs, but I couldn't stand this sound, above the endless roar of the traffic. I almost wanted the wretched hound to die so it

290

would stop. I had to take Koshka off my shoulders. I knew Nell wouldn't want her to be upset - and of course I didn't want the dog to die in front of her - but she was just too heavy with that hideous keening of canine suffering in my ears. I felt so hopeless not being able say anything to anyone.

'Where's the nearest phone box? There's a vet's surgery in Oliwa, I've seen it, but I don't know the number,' Nell says.

She looks around in appeal to those on the pavement. Some stop briefly, others look with distress or sympathy, but no-one looks fully, and those who stop are careful not to step within the half circle that will draw them into direct involvement with the dog. One or two mutter that it's a disgrace - though whether that such dogs are victims of heartless hit-and-run drivers or that they are permitted to wander the streets at all is unclear - and a much smaller number expresses the opinion that the dog needs a vet.

There is a famous photograph of people walking past an elderly man lying on a Warsaw pavement. One arm with its star armband reaches upwards. It must be early in the war because he isn't in the Ghetto. There is something familiar now about the faces of the people and the semicircular space before the recumbent figure, an arc within which no-one will step.

There were powerful reasons then, but what the fuck is the excuse now? Force of habit? Nell's face is looking pinched with the effort of working out what to do, and she's starting to cry, but trying not to, so our little girl won't see and think this situation is even worse than it is. Nell has crouched down beside the dog's head. He still howls, his wet, serrated, black retriever jaws are floppy and trembling. His brown eyes are cloudy and bloodshot, and with them he just looks and looks, his voice coming loud out of his quivering stomach, shiny with sweat, a voice that hits a pitch, like a baby's cry does to its mother, which enters the body directly into your very guts, the cry of suffering, suffering that must be stopped, that won't stop.

Koshka is squatting by the dog's head too, stroking his ears.

'His ears are hot,' she observes. 'Poor doggy.'

'He needs a blanket,' Nell insists. 'I'm going into the shop to get him one, and I'm going to use their phone to call a vet. They've probably got a phone book. You look after the doggy, there's a sweetheart, you and Daddy, and we'll get this sorted out.'

I can tell she's relieved to be able to give our child the impression that these things can be brought under control, that you can do the right thing and bring about the proper outcome, relieved to have something she can do - and, yes, to be able to move away from that appalling sound. God, it's a strain when you've got kids, always having to be exemplary. For the first time it occurs to me that no-one in the shop has come out to see what the matter is, even though the yowling is so loud it must be almost as intolerable for the three women I can see moving back and forth behind the counter.

There are rolls of cloth on the shelves behind them, stacks of brightly coloured towels and the kind of soft, fluffy blankets used for baby's prams and pushchairs. Christ, it's even a shop that <u>sells</u> blankets! The two customers who have been inside the shop up to now, leave, stepping over the inconvenient hound. I am full of rage and hatred for the whole damn lot of them, and with Nell for bringing us to this God-forsaken, miserable, war-scarred, retrogressive country where no-one in their right mind would *ever willingly go, with the self-obsessed, heartless, pathetic, irresponsible, uncivilised bastards. I hate myself because I can't speak Polish and tell them what they are. The dog still howls. Can't it subside to a whimper, for Christ's sake, even though that might mean it was getting worse? I hate the dog too.*

I peer in through the door. I can hear Nell even though she has her back to me. Perhaps she's shouting. I wouldn't blame her. The woman behind the counter is fussing around with bales of cloth, trying to make out she's carrying on as normal, her expression awkward and unresponsive at the same time. There are another two customers in the shop - and this dog in the doorway and this little scene are a bit embarrassing.

I am surprised to find that I understand pretty much everything. Perhaps it's because I already know what will be said.

No, the woman says, she doesn't know the number of a vet, and no, she isn't planning to phone one. It has nothing to do with her. She didn't run over the dog.

'Of course you didn't run over the dog, but the person who did has driven away. The dog is in your doorway. It's hurt, can't you hear it? It isn't your fault, but it is your responsibility.' (She never messes around, my Nell, never lets tact and diplomacy get in the way of a clear moral point, I'll say that.) 'If you'll lend me your phone book and let me use your phone, I'll try...'

'Responsibilty? Responsibility!' The woman explodes. 'I don't know what you're talking about! You take the stupid dog to the vet's if you care so much about it. Is it your dog?'

'It isn't my dog, and I don't have a car to take it anywhere. If you would please let me phone to a vet, perhaps they would come to take it.'

'It's nothing to do with me,' the woman growls, thumping a roll of cloth on its end behind the counter. 'I don't have a dog.'

At this, I see my dear wife go berserk, rounding on everyone in the shop, waving her arms. The combination of this wall of resistance and the incessant agonising contribution from the dog has goaded her beyond endurance.

'Oh yes you do,' she yells. 'You have a dog! It's your dog! And yours! And yours! This is your dog! Listen to it! It's your dog because it's a creature and it's suffering and it chose your doorway to die in! It'll always be your dog! If you let it die, its ghost will still be your dog and it'll haunt you! Your dog, your resp-ons-ib-il-ity! Understand?'

This diatribe, surprisingly to me, appeared to have some effect, for the woman retreated through the curtain at the back, and Nell turned to mime picking up a receiver and dialling through the window. In no time though, Nell came flying out through the door, breathlessly.

'She said she did it, but she came back far too quickly. I'm sure she did no such thing. She just wanted to be rid of me.'

Nell darted out among the traffic, stopping cars. The phrase 'barking' came to mind, but seemed a little unfortunate under the circumstances. And, in the end, it was a sympathetic pedestrian who responded, a smiling lady in a big coat wearing a leopard-skin hat with a small veil. She took off her gloves to pat the dog. She assumed at first that it was our dog. She had one herself, she said, very like it, who had died. Of course Ronni had been quite old and had had a tumour. She was quite familiar with vets. She would go home to her husband and he would drive back with the car. I was afraid she would change her tune when she discovered that the dog was not ours, but in fact her eagerness did not diminish in the least.

'What about money?' Nell asked. 'Is it free if you bring in an injured stray like this?'

The answer to this never became clear, lost in Pani Danka's effusive efforts to ward off the notion of accepting any form of contribution from us.

'I know you English are famous for your love of pets, especially for your dogs,' she finished.

Nell thought this was hilarious, since I normally detest the species, and our amusement got us through the ten minutes or so until Pani Danka's return. Together with Pani Danka's husband, and using a car rug, we lifted the dog, still howling, into the back of their Fiat. Nell and Pani Danka exchanged phone numbers, mutual thanks and kisses.

'I bet that's what they all thought in that shop - stupid Englishwoman, crazy about dogs,' said Nell, half amused, half humiliated.

I wanted to say the right thing, though probably nothing I said would be the right thing anyway. I wanted to tell her that she'd done the only decent thing in there, that I admired her, that the outcome had been great, but I didn't dare in case all that came out was my anger, even though it had subsided a little. Against them. Against her. For putting herself in that position, for being at their mercy, for feeling so hurt, for making me have to feel it through her. If I could only communicate properly, I knew what I would say. I knew I could make them feel small and ashamed, backward and inferior and all the things they hate to feel. Then she'd make excuses for them, say they felt inferior already, and that was the problem. It wasn't <u>their</u> fault the public part of life was destroyed in their country. She could give an account of all the political and psychological dynamics at work, analyse it till the cows came home. All very rational no doubt, but the way she actually tackled people was too emotional. She would never make it stick, and she would always get done over in the process.

We still hadn't got everything we needed for the party. Koshka was already chirping on. Couldn't we get a dog? It could be a friend to Kotek.

'Yeah, we could call it Dogek.'

Koshka almost fell off my shoulders laughing. Buoyed up by my success with the four year-old, I ventured a few 'right things to say' with the wife, but she was still subdued.

'When I was yelling in the shop and running out in the road, I didn't just look like a madwoman. I <u>was</u> a madwoman.'

'It's not your fault, it's them, it's the place, it's the culture,' I consoled her.

'I don't want to spend my whole time making horrible judgements. It's not that people aren't quite capable of walking by on the other side in other places. It's just that it has a particular quality here. I think what I said in there was absolutely right, but it's just too much. I couldn't help it then, because of the dog and the howling and

everything - but it's a recipe for a life of misery, demanding that people see what they don't want to see, take responsibility for things they don't even recognise. Who the hell do I think I am? Sure, I'm glad it turned out alright, but, if it's so bloody justified, why am I always left feeling ashamed?'

Party

'Since it's to be my leaving party and all, the least I can do is give you a bittie help with the *kanapki* and suchlike,' insisted Julie, arriving early. 'Anyway, I 'm awful glad to be away out of the flat. Packing - who'd do it? Tomek's driving me dottled.'

Having Jon and Iwona camping out on her sofa couldn't be making life any easier. We had Adam and Marzena, our old friends from Torun, staying with us, and the twins, together with Tomek and Koshka, were at this moment clambering on the hammock between the sour cherry trees in the garden, under the supposed supervision of Adam.

Rob was lining up bottles on the kitchen table, lovingly. Marzena was slicing ham and peppers, so I set Julie to sorting out plates and folding *serwetki*. Babcia seemed miraculously to have chosen this moment to take an afternoon nap rather than patrolling the kitchen. I hoped she'd re-member she was invited when she woke up.

I thought I had everything under control, but the moment the guests started to arrive I was snowed under by greetings and coats and bou-quets of flowers, for which I'd forgotten to put out vases. Stefan and Ewa were among the first, he dapper and she glamorous as usual. The boys yelled 'yehaaa' and raced for the garden. Wiesia, their elderly land-lady, who had accompanied them, pursed her lips into a big frog pout at the noise, kneaded the handbag she clutched over her stomach and put her other hand to the white beehive of her hair. Not a good day for Wi-esia then, but at least she was up. She rarely rose before two or three, so this was still before mid-day according to her body-clock. Beside her, Bronek, her small, neat, nautical husband with his trimmed white beard, patted her shoulder before kissing my hand. Wiesia gave me Polish les-sons occasionally, when she was feeling energetic. Now, she waltzed forward, firing off some Polish tongue-twisting riddle about a flea, de-manding the answer at once.

'How the hell should I know? Come in, Wiesieczku, and sit down. Can I get you a drink, or some cake?'

'My dear, my dear,' Wiesia went into her ritual lament. 'Your accent is quite good, but, my dear, how many times do I have to tell you, you speak Polish like a shop-girl? All these diminutives are most unmannerly. And what is all this waving your arms about? Are you an Italian? Well-bred Poles do not wave their arms in the air - it is a spoken language, not semaphore - and neither do Englishmen. They are all well-bred - by nature.'

Dougie arrived in his kilt, clutching a couple of six-packs of *Okocim* beer and his guitar. He brought Paulina, rooting in her handbag, laughing and adjusting her big glasses. She was always such a soothing, comfortable person, the only one I could imagine with the intelligence, presence and energy to deal with the man she'd taken on. They were both stouter these days, he eating better and she consuming more beer now they were together. Dougie's beard was spruced and trimmed, giving the ruddy brown the upper hand over the grey. He looked so much happier, booming out jokes and greetings, plumping down his beer and scanning the scene with enthusiasm.

Wandzia was there, wearing a late forties, silk, blue and white polka-dot number, legs crossed, swinging back on her chair, smoking a cigarette in a holder and relating some anecdote that had those around her laughing uproariously. A small, black, velvet hat was curled up on her marmalade hair. Maja, looking less pinched than she used to, was talking to Leszek the journalist and his wife. Giedymin, the jeweller from Sopot, was chatting to Mariusz Szymor from the English Literature Department. Szymor was relating his recent success in interesting Prince Charles in a project to resurrect the Renaissance theatre Shakespeare had once visited on its original site in the city, now a car park.

Justyna had come with her husband, Jacek, the two of them sparring slightly when together, watching each other jealously when apart. Julie was speaking to them, introducing Adam and Marzena. Jacek's attention was wandering, but Julie coaxed him to talk about the Business Dictionary in English he was compiling, quaffing gallons of coffee and staying up all night to finish the various entries in time for the publisher's deadlines. It was funny the way Justyna and Jacek always gave completely the opposite account of any event or circumstance, whether consulted separately or together, Julie had once pointed out. Since then, I'd started noticing how each one's opening gambit was always to contradict the other. The impulse appeared to be wholly instinctive, and oddly enough, the edginess discernible between them didn't seem to reside in this as they rarely seemed to object.

It wasn't so much a balance of contraries as a balance of contrariness somehow, I thought, drifting past with a tray of *kanapki*. Both seemed dissatisfied, but each was relieved of the obligation to provide the other with something they weren't receiving themselves. I couldn't for the life of me have said what exactly. Of course, you never know what really goes on between couples. Perhaps it was reassuring to see that relationships could still work even when they apparently went about everything back to front.

As though by way of example, their five year-old son Sebastian came and tugged at my skirt, asking to be shown the toilet. Jacek had been born and brought up in Manchester, to a French mother and Polish father, whereas Justyna spoke fluent but accented English. At home, Jacek tended to speak in Polish, arguably his third language, while the boy's mother preferred to use English, aware that it would give her son certain advantages. Sebastian, their bilingual son, had therefore managed to gain his Polish from his father and his English from his mother, and didn't sound entirely plausible in either. His Polish was the weaker of the two, yet, in English, he produced a strange but very appealing accent with a sing-song delivery, which Koshka often adopted when they were together.

Koshka, Tomek and the twins soon joined the invasion, having exhausted the possibilities of the sandpit and all fallen out of the hammock, both by turns and *en masse*. Lukasz had a rope burn on his wrist and Lucynka and Koshka had evidently been eating sand. They were lobbying for a go on Babcia's exercise bike, but Babcia had yet to make her appearance.

'She is just getting up. I will take her to the bathroom,' her daughter-in-law Irena assured me. 'They can go in the sitting room, but ask them to stay out of the bedroom,' she instructed her husband, Stanislaw, who stroked his drooping moustache and winked at the children:

'Come, come,' he made a gangly pied piper, leading the procession of children through the groups of standing adults into the hallway.

'Do you want to go too?' I asked Leszek's daughter, Patrycja. At ten, she was much the oldest child there and I couldn't blame her for wanting to remain aloof. Apart from Irena and Stanislaw, none of Babcia's usual entourage had yet appeared, so Aga, the eldest of the great-grandchildren was not available, as I had hoped, as a companion for Patrycja. She sat on the sofa, with her mother on the arm beside her stroking her hair.

Leszek's wife was called Monika, but Rob always referred to her as Puss in Boots, since she invariably wore fluffy jackets, tiny skirts and suede thigh-boots. It was very common to have only one child, but the level of continuous adoration of their daughter by Monika and Leszek struck me as a mite unusual, at least in the form it took. Neither of them could keep their hands off her, perpetually stroking, caressing, grooming. Whenever we had been to their flat, Monika was always disappearing to wash her daughter's back in the bath or help her to dress. It didn't seem to be simply physical affection or appreciation, which would have been perfectly lovely. The parents orbited around her, in a way that made her seem somehow less than alive, as if she provided them with something necessary between them, and was only animated between their hands. Shouts of glee and clamourings for a turn could be heard coming from the sitting room. Patrycja shook her head, then reached back and unrav-

296

elled her single plait, inclining towards her mother, who began to run her fingers through the stream of hair.

I ushered Piotrus and Magda through into the room with the other children. I'd barely registered Alina and Andrzej's arrival, except to deduce from Alina's compressed lips and set jaw that probably it was some fecklessness of Andrzej's which had made them late. Alina would have wanted to come early and help out in the kitchen. She'd brought one of her wonderful yeast cakes.

I hadn't known it was possible to fit quite so many children on an exercise bike until I peeped round the door. Stanislaw waved me thankfully away, insisting it was all under control. Mercifully for the harmony of the group, Dolores and Al, who had just arrived, had left Karolek with his grandmother.

'My parents came back from their cruise,' Andrzej sauntered up to me, clutching a beer. 'They say to tell you a thank you for your invitation but my father is now again too busy for coming to you for party.'

'Why, what's he doing?'

'He was passing book stall, one near tram stop by university, you know, and he see there the book of Jaruzelski - his autobiograph, about old years in Poland. My father open that book and he is looking, and he see on one certain page that it is writing 'the spy Sprzyszak and his associates'. It was quite famous case in 60s. Jaruzelski probably he didn't make trouble for check it - or his redactor either - perhaps he still believe... but it is, how you say, a slandering. He will pay.'

'Your Dad will sue Jaruzelski?'

'But of course. My father is very happy. He very like to build better house, with bigger garden for my mother's herbalistics planting.'

Perhaps he will lend you and Alina some of it, to help you get a flat of your own.'

'Most definitely yes. I am talking to this big, bear, Germanish-like man.' He pointed at Al. 'At least, I am when I can stop my eyes from sitting on his most beautiful wife!' he giggled. 'His project is very interesting for us I think.'

'Guess what?' Rob collared me in the kitchen as I tried to lever more slices of *sernik* from the baking tray and onto a plate without disintegration - theirs not mine. I was having that party-hostess sensation of ministering madly to everyone without ever meeting their eye or having a proper conversation with any of the guests. It was quite satisfying in its way, for the less real interaction on my part, the more I had the sense of a successful party. All talking to each other, while I was orchestrating and supplying cake.

'Hang on a minute, I've just got to take this through...' I came back: 'What is it?'

'I've just been talking to Dolores. You know the week I have to go to Warsaw for the British Council Conference? Well, she's meeting her sister there the same day. We'll be on the same flight.'

'Oh well, that'll be good. You'll have someone to talk to on the way.'

'No, you dope. Don't you see?'

'See what?'

'Well, it isn't going to play too well with old Al seeing the bloke who spends one day a week hanging out with his wife disappearing with her through the departure gate for a week in Warsaw is it?'

'Now you mention it…' I sniggered. 'It might just ruffle Big Al's unshakeable conviction that a little half-pint like yourself would never dare mess with his moll. Does he know yet? Did you tell her?'

'I haven't been sent a horse's head, so I presume he doesn't.' Rob rolled his eyes, his mock terror shading into genuine unease. 'What'll I do?'

'He'll probably kill you,' I said unsympathetically. 'If you're lucky, he'll do it quickly - have you gunned down between the kiosks and the tram terminus in Manhattan. Or he might reserve something especially slow and painful for those who have the temerity …'

'You don't have to be quite so gleeful about it. It *is* a problem,' said Rob grouchily.

'You'd better tell him,' I advised. 'It'll be much worse if he only twigs when he sees you at the airport.'

'I can't,' Rob moaned. 'Now I've thought of it like that I can't say anything without it sounding really nefarious. Anything that comes out of my mouth'll have that suspicious ring. I wouldn't even convince myself. I'm wracked with guilt already. I'll probably laugh, which'll be even worse!'

Waldek the librarian was nursing his drink alone by the door to the bedroom, reaching up to scratch his head through his curly hair. Hostess-alert. Swiftly I steered him past the bed heaped high with coats out onto the balcony and introduced him to Iwona and Jon. Andrzej, Adam, and Oleg from Riga - whom I'd first met selling children's socks in the Russian's Market - had commandeered Dougie's guitar and were singing Russian folk songs.

Heading back to the kitchen I saw that Babcia was chatting away to Waldek's grandmother, who was reminiscing about the Pope's last visit, which her daughter had procured for her on video. She shook her head, tears of pride starting in her eyes as she remembered the scene. Marzena and Dolores were discussing astrology.

'Do you have your flight booked?' Alina was asking Julie.

'Yes, good old Lot Airways,' Julie winked at me as I went by. We both knew exactly how the conversation would go from this point.

'Oh dear, poor you,' Alina commiserated. 'I hope very much it will be alright. The planes are very bad, you know. Very old Russian planes.'

'But very good Polish pilots,' Julie countered dutifully, to save Alina the trouble. They flew spitfires in the War, she added mentally, having had identical exchanges numerous times.

'Oh yes,' Alina responded eagerly. 'Polish pilots are very good, the best. They flew Spitfires.'

'Very old pilots then,' Julie couldn't resist saying, but wished she hadn't, seeing Alina's face. Lot Airways functioned as an allegory: its ancient, dud, dangerous aircraft palmed off by the Russians but miraculously flown without as many disasters as the donors no doubt intended by the dexterity of the Poles, with their war-time experience and ill-repaid Western allegiance. 'No, seriously, I'll be awful glad to hear that slow hand-clap of the Polish passengers when we land at Heathrow.'

Wiesia had appeared somewhat droopy thus far, slumped on the sofa, barely bothering to captivate Irena, who was beside her. Stefania arrived at the door, not intending to come to the party, which she thought was next week, but just on a chance visit. She had brought two tabby kittens with her in a cardboard box to play with Kotek. Stefania sang in the same choir as Ewa and I at the University. The choir specialised in Russian Church music and its supposed Western equivalent, negro spirituals. My translations of such phrases as 'I want to go over into camp-ground' were frequently demanded but rarely considered satisfactory. Stefania had been a great help to me, as I did not read Cyrillic. Thanks to her, I was now a dab hand at recognising Russian phrases as long as they contained the words of the Lord's prayer, 'Lord have mercy,' 'bless my soul o my Lord or 'and bless my people Israel'.

Choirs are cliquey at the best of times, but I had noticed that people exchanged looks and did not remain long in conversation with Stefania. I found her Polish harder to follow than anyone else's, mainly because it was impossible to guess what was going to come next. I was never quite sure how her statements fitted together, but I was usually too busy trying to comprehend the grammatical nuances I supposed I had missed for her marked eccentricity to dawn on me. Surely she'd be just the person to cheer up Wiesia, a kindred spirit, but Wiesia had moved across the room and was tugging at Ewa's sleeve, then conferring with her husband.

'I'll just have to nip home for something,' Ewa told me. I had not met Wiesia first through Stefan and Ewa but at a translators' conference. She had just published the third of her volumes of Lorca, and was somewhat the toast of the event on that occasion. Ewa was not a doctor who took bribes, but she liked to help out her family and friends, and kept Wiesia supplied with the array of uppers and downers needed to get her through each day.

'She has still many problems connected with her father,' Ewa had once explained. 'He was a doctor like me. One day the Germans simply shot all the doctors in that town. Her father was associated also with the Underground University, but probably his death was simply due to being a doctor. Wiesia was a little girl then, but she remembers him quite well.'

Giedymin the jeweller engrossed Dolores with a small catalogue he had been compiling. Oleg and Andrzej, making for the kitchen in search of more beer, had become embroiled with Mariusz Szymor and his theatre project. The fund-raising was just beginning but so far it had been going very well, and now with the involvement of the Prince...

'Unfortunately, the car park is situated on the site of the former synagogue,' Mariusz was explaining, 'so there may be some Jews, some crazy rabbis in America protesting - but we think we can buy them off with a plaque and some money. Hopefully just the plaque,' he added, laughing.

I wasn't even part of this conversation, sailing past with a pile of plates for the kitchen, but by now it was like an allergy, a sickness in the stomach and an instantaneous flare up on the skin, which the tiniest exposure to the allergen would trigger. I dumped the plates in the sink and began running water over them. He talks as though they do it just to be irritating, I ranted in my head. Why is it Polish people can never speak respectfully on this subject? They'll never give anyone else or their suffering their due while they still feel they're competing over the same psychological and cultural space, that great Carpark of the Soul!

Andrzej's eyes glittered: 'Perhaps they will want to rebuild the synagogue,' he was suggesting as I went by once more.

'What is the point of that?' Szymor snapped. 'Who will go to it? That is not the issue.'

Stay out of it. Stay out of it, said the voice in my head, as I set down the last plate of cheesecake and Pani Marynia's mince pies on the square coffee table.

'That's hardly a neutral fact, is it, that there isn't anyone left to go to it?' I put in, turning swiftly aside to offer Dolores and Giedymin another glass of wine. Stay out of it.

Back in the kitchen, Dougie was surveying the wreckage of the drinks table in the kitchen. 'A wee bit of clearing up is in order here,' he rubbed his hands and set about emptying the contents of any abandoned bottles into his glass. Paulina, who had followed him, steered him back into the company. From across the room I could hear the edge and assertion enter his voice, speaking to Szymor and Andzrej, the tone of a drinking man who feels he's not being sufficiently regarded.

Babcia was helping Pani Marynia through the door. I'd got to know Pani Marynia, Waldek's granny, when Babcia had asked me to translate the instructions on the new packet of pills her friend had been given. The instructions, in English and Spanish, had said that the pills were intended for the heart condition from which Pani Marynia suffered, but were not to be taken if the patient was diabetic, which she was.

I had grown fond of her. She seemed a much softer character than her rather fearsome daughter, Waldek's mother. There was something in the tone with which that woman called out her son's name - 'Waldemar' - with the little up-down cadence in the middle that always made my blood run cold. That apparently unsure little quaver of total control that presupposed absolute obedience. Of course she'd had to be in control, poor thing, Pani Marynia had confided, as Waldek's father had not stayed around for long after his birth. Some people had even been cruel enough to say that absent fathers ran in the family, even though everyone knew her own dear Edek had been shot with the other Polish officers at Katyn. The Russians hadn't admitted it in those days, so it wasn't something you could acknowledge in public, but people knew. Some just chose not to.

'My neighbour's terribly worried,' Pani Marynia was telling Babcia. 'Her daughter's named her new baby Daniel...' She paused as though the problem were self-evident.

'My nephew's called Daniel,' I said brightly. 'It's a very popular name in Britain at the moment.'

'Isn't it rather...*biblical*?' she persisted. Ah. I knew full well what '*biblijny*' was shorthand for.

'Anyway,' Pani Marynia finished, 'I told her not to be silly. Didn't she know there was a *Saint* Daniel?'

There *is?*

'I brought some of those English cakes, like the ones you made me at Christmas. You left me some of the filling, so I made a tray of them this morning. The whole family thinks they are very nice. Waldek should have put them in the kitchen. You know, his mother and I are so glad he is settling down at last. Ela is a wonderful girl, a little heavy perhaps, and quite a thick moustache, but he has left it so late he couldn't be choosy. It's a pity she couldn't come today. They are making plans for a Christmas wedding - only a few months away.'

Rob had spent a fair amount of time with Waldek when the two of them had embarked on reorganising and cataloguing the English Philology Department Library last Spring. Previously the books had been shelved according to date of acquisition. I felt I hardly knew him, always friendly and polite but so self-contained that time spent in his company did not much seem to advance relations. I said something to this effect to Wandzia, who, unusually, was on her own, returning from the bathroom.

'*Jesus Maria*, you don't know anything,' she screeched, herding me into a corner. 'I lent him my flat once, when I was in Warsaw. I had left him plenty of food, even a chicken from the rotisserie in the fridge. When I came back he had gone but he had not cleaned up - and that chicken! It was like he killed it himself, with his teeth. Had he chased it around the floor on his hands and knees? I tell you there is something voracious about that man. I didn't want him to use my toothbrush, I tell you. I threw it in trash in case he had!'

I offered her one of Pani Marynia's pies and ate one myself. They were delicious and, notwithstanding the authentic British mincemeat, they tasted completely Polish. The pastry had a totally different texture and she had put a swirl of sweet cream on top instead of a lid. Isn't it wonderful, I thought, a genuine piece of translation. I looked across at Alina, who was hearing all about Stefania's interest in the teachings of Sai Baba with an expression of fixed alarm.

I knew better than to offer Alina a pie, even in this form. Last Christmas it seemed we'd actually reached the limits of our friendship over it, or, as I thought, the limits of Alina's tolerance. Alina had stared at the pie on her plate suspiciously. It was as if she couldn't bring herself to take a bite. The combination of strange, foreign food with claims to tradition or cultural significance was fatal. That cultural competition thing again. It might as well have had union jack emblazoned on its little pastry crust as far as Alina was concerned. If I'd lifted the lid I wouldn't have been surprised if it had ground out a tinkly rendition of 'Land of Hope and Glory'.

And there'd been me thinking it would be nice to bake something for Alina and Andrzej, something different. We'd consumed so many of Alina's cakes and she'd given me so many recipes, checking that I'd understood every instruction. I'd supposed it would be nice to repay a little, that they'd like it, find it interesting. I'd forgotten that Poles are so much better at giving than receiving, that they prefer to be in credit, or, ideally, under-repaid. Alina's generosity with the recipes was about bestowing the unquestionable benefits of Polish cooking on me. It counted in my favour that I had the good taste to want to receive them, but the idea of reciprocity didn't come into it.

Andrzej was devouring the pies with relish, but his enthusiasm wasn't helping:

'These are great,' he said, his mouth full of crumbs. 'Can I have another? You should learn to make these, Alinko.'

Alina glowered.

'What's in it?' she demanded.

I gave a preliminary list, but she wasn't satisfied.

302

'Oh, and something from cows. Little bits of white stuff. To bind the mixture together. It's called suet in English, but I don't know what it is in Polish.' I tried various descriptions but nothing would do and the dictionary had to be fetched. 'Loj,' I announced.

'*Loj?*' Alina looked disgusted. I couldn't blame her, thinking about it.

'It doesn't sound good, does it, but there's not very much. You really can't taste it. In fact, I think some mincemeat doesn't have it. For vegetarians.'

It was no use. Alina had refused to take so much as a bite. She had found her justification.

Ewa was back, presumably with the necessary tablets, but Wiesia and Stefania had found one another without my assistance, and were talking with animation, though no arm-waving. Andrzej, I noted, was deep in conversation with Al. Dougie had retrieved his guitar and was singing 'Goodnight Irene'. He was a fine singer, Dougie, but 'Goodnight Irene' normally signalled that he had gone past his best.

'Sometimes I stay in the country,
Sometimes I stay in the town;
Sometimes I take me a notion
Gonna jump in the *Wisla* and drown.'

Szymor and Rob were discussing the historical evidence for the visit of Shakespeare and the Lord Chamberlain's Men to the old theatre. I still felt that if I didn't give Szymor a wide berth, I might hit him or I might cry or probably both. He's a nice man. Let him be.

'It's not to do with putting a plaque on a wall, is it?' I interrupted. 'There's something you have to do in your heart. You want to resurresct the Renaissance splendour of Polish culture, you want to rebuild Western connections, that old European, Western-looking vision, without giving proper recognition to those whose places of worship lie flattened under concrete and whose bones are under the forest floors, dusted with pine needles, and the furrowed fields. You'll never be able to build anything worth having unless you can acknowledge that and say you had a part in it.'

You didn't run the dog over, the rant went on in my head, but it did die howling in your doorway. Some people stopped and helped a little, some people risked everything to help a lot, and some people didn't stop at all. And quite a lot were glad when the howling stopped and said that they'd never liked dogs much anyway.

'Many Poles died,' Szymor protested. 'Killed like dogs, by Germans and Russians. Millions of us.'

'Of course. You died *and* they died. You *both* died. No-one died any *less* because of the others.' It felt so strange to be saying this. Szymor muttered something. 'You can't pick and choose your history. You can't have Chopin and Mickiewicz and heroic Polish resistance to oppression and not have this, this appalling thing too - because it happened here. And you can't have just the story of Polish suffering in the War and not face Jewish suffering, Gypsy ...'

'Hitler hated Poles,' Szymor pointed out. 'Hated us almost as much as he hated Jews...'

'Sure he did. He despised you. He didn't visit the biggest crime in human history on your country just because you were a bunch of anti-Semites who wouldn't object too much, or because you've got lots of big forests and railway lines that conveniently go to the back of beyond. Hitler dumped this shit on you because he thought you *deserved* it - and if you keep on refusing to look at it, if you keep on burying it (whether it's under a car-park or under a theatre) at some level, *so do you*.'

'It's a pity you don't have more national pride,' Szymor observed stiffly. 'You don't seem to want Shakespeare's legacy to be honoured. It is a good thing Prince Charles does not share such strange view.' He bowed briefly and left.

'Nice one, hen,' Julie came up behind me and dragged me off to the kitchen. 'Quick, before you insult any more guests. Here, have a bosey,' she gave me a big hug. 'There's these pots needing washed,' she pointed out, handing me a tea-towel and feeling about for the plug under the plates in the sink.

'Some hostess I am!' I moaned. 'I could give courses on how to lose all your friends! I'm out of control. I might be right and everything I say might be true, but I can't stop saying it, even though they can't hear it. Probably it's not even my place to say it. It doesn't do any good. It's not my country, but I love it. I care about it. I want it to turn out O.K. Is that so incomprehensible? It seems like such an important time... but I guess that's not the point. It doesn't want to be loved by me...' I snivelled.

'Maybe you've to let folk do things at their own pace.'

'But there are neo-Nazi movements starting, ultra-nationalists...' I swallowed: 'You're right. It *is* just arrogance on my part. These things just take time. It'll all be so different in ten years.'

'It strikes me, hen, you're awful good at seeing where other folk's responsibility lies, but maybe none so hot when it comes to spotting where yours ends.'

'Very tactfully put, dear,' I deposited my cloth, slumped down on the stool next to the table and looked at her. 'Since when were *you* so laid back?'

'Since I decided to leave,' said Julie simply. 'You know you said once that countries are like people, that they have biographies and psychologies just like individual people,' she went on. 'With Poland, it's like being

304

in love with an incredibly screwed up, insecure person. You know, dark things in the childhood, a damaged, self-obsessed, neurotic person, continually requiring reassurance. You try awful hard to be honest with them because you care about them, but they're forever greeting: "You don't love me or you wouldn't say such things…" Can you imagine what it might be like to be in love with someone with such a personality? And that's supposing you're such a wonderful model of sanity, without any baggage, yourself!

In the end you have to decide whether you really want a relationship like that? You expend all your energy trying to convince them that you're not criticising, that you do love them, pouring in everything you can - but there isn't a bottom. Their self-esteem, or whatever it is, doesn't supply one. So you just keep pouring and it just goes straight through, while you're perpetually in the wrong and reproached for hurting their feelings. Eventually you have to recognise it's a bottomless pit. At least for you. At least for now.'

'Isn't that what most men think *all* women are like?' I said cynically, thinking of Rob on a bad day. Well, on most days, really.

'Marek had a girlfriend who really was like that once, for two years, at Uni in Glasgow before he met me.'

'Was she Polish?'

'No, actually, now you mention it, she was Jewish.'

People were starting to say their goodbyes. Marzena, Irena and Iwona had the clearing up well in hand, so I could help to retrieve coats from the heap on the bed and see the guests to the door. Alina had wrapped Piotrus and Magda warmly against the night air and had to dive back into the room to find Andrzej once more.

'It is the done deal,' he announced to me happily. 'I arranged all with this Al. It is a lot of money to pay in beginning, but it is best way, so that flats can to be built. I will meet with him on Thursday.'

Alina apparently knew nothing of this and her disapproval did not thaw.

'I will take the tram with the kids, or we can walk. It is not far. You shouldn't drive back to your mother's. You've been drinking. He drives like a maniac even when he's sober,' she added for my benefit. Poland's drink-driving laws were strict: No alcohol in the bloodstream while behind the wheel. Andrzej was normally conscientious on this point.

'It is middle of month,' he told me, leaning over. 'It will be no problem to bribe police. Their pay-checks will be finish. They will be quite happy. They will even be waiting.'

'Exactly,' said Alina grimly, shepherding him out the door.

Hardly anyone was left. Babcia had retired to her room. Paulina was persuading Dougie to pack up his guitar. Marzena had taken the twins through to the kitchen to calm them down and warm up some juice for them. Koshka and Tomek were taking turns to ride her tricycle up and down the hall. Jon came through from the balcony with a haunted expression:

'That bloke with the curly hair - Waldek,' he said, ushering me aside. 'He just told me he's in love with me. He begged me to kiss him. Said he'd never felt this way before. I had to agree to meet with him, he said, or he'd go mad. He couldn't bear it. He loved me...'

'Has he left?'

'Yes, he went with a whole load of others. His Granny called him. What have I done? Why me? That's the second time someone's done this in six months. What *is* it about me? We were just *chatting*.'

Koshka and Tomek brought proceedings to a close by driving the tricycle smack into the wall, dislodging Babcia's long wall mirror close by. An almighty crash came from the hallway, with the high pitched whistle of spiralling shards of glass. The heavy, gilt frame had slid to the ground, the pane of the mirror ballooning outwards. Koshka still sat on the tricycle seat, with Tomek standing on the spar behind her, their eyes closed, bodies frozen, receiving the shower. Though their t-shirts were slashed in several places, the fragments still stuck in the material, the children had only one small cut apiece. Koshka had a bleeding knee and Tomek a splinter of glass in the back of his hand.

Home-Thoughts

Rob had taken to dropping in at the British Council Reading Room in town and leafing through the Times Higher Education Supplement. We still hadn't discussed leaving so much as admitted it as a possibility, without really saying anything, for the first time. I turned down a translation because the work would run into next year. We'd been to Prague on the train the previous Spring and now talked more urgently about fitting in a trip to Budapest as well. After all, we'd never be so close again.

I began to have images in my head of a primary school for Koshka, a small, rural school with mums and pushchairs at the gates, somewhere in the North-West of England, perhaps, with friendly people, green countryside and dry stone walls. I felt liberated and defeated at the same time.

I told myself it was a fantasy, that there would be tensions and questions of belonging wherever we went, but I didn't believe my own words of caution. My heart was attached to the fantasy whatever I might tell it. I needed to live where it was at least a remote possibility that being cheerful could be construed as a virtue rather than a provocation.

Daily life was lovely here, I reminded myself, buying our *rogaliki*, the poppy-seed rolls shaped like ram's horns, hot from the baker at the bottom of the street for breakfast each morning, cycling through the forest with Koshka, stopping for vegetables in the market at Oliwa. Yet I dreamed of an existence where I would no longer feel bowed down by the burden of history, where the definition of a pessimist was not 'an informed optimist', where I didn't have to keep pointing to the bodies like some kind of demented sniffer dog. I didn't want to have to work so hard. Perhaps I wouldn't have to, if I could just get off my high horse - but every time I fell off I got right back on. I wanted a holiday, a rest from cultural difference and existential tragedy. Julie had said almost exactly the same before she left. Metaphorically - or perhaps even literally - I too wanted to shuffle round to the corner shop in my dressing gown and slippers.

Of course it wouldn't be as simple as that. Julie had written in her last letter:

'Part of me feels that it's reality I've left behind. That I like this fine well, it's awful pleasant, but that I'm on the edge, a Western outpost, like some poor wee Roman centurian, that the truth, the centre, *my* centre, the heart of everything is elsewhere, back where I was, in Poland. I was that desperate to get away by the end, I forgot I'd be having to miss it forever.'

This started Rob and I on a series of 'what would you miss?' conversations in the evenings, vying with one another to come up with more and wilder generalisations:

'I'll miss Polish ideas of friendship, the way once you're friends with people that's the way it stays, you don't have to keep earning it. It's just understood that you'll do whatever's necessary for each other.'

'Yeah, like with some of our friends back home, it's as if you have to keep reminding them why they like you, why you're worth the trouble. Or the expense even. And a lot of British people have that 'take you or leave you' attitude, which doesn't quite go away, or keeps coming back every now and then, as if you might be up for review.'

'Absolutely, and if they do something for you, there's no question who's doing who a favour - whereas Poles know that being able to do something for a friend is the big treat, and that the person who puts them in that position is actually doing *them* a service (and denying themselves in doing that). And yet they're quite happy to accept when you do stuff for them, because that's what friends do for each other. They'll even *ask* - which Brits 'll never do - since it's no shame to give someone the opportunity to have the satisfaction of helping out!'

'I'll miss the way the men are so open.' Rob said.

'I'll miss the way men take their trousers off in front of you without being embarrassed.'

'I didn't mean that kind of open.'

'No, *you know* - the way Poles aren't funny about bodies and undressing. When the choir gives a concert, the men and women all get changed

307

together, and stand around chatting half dressed and no-one bats an eye-lid.'

'I'll miss the way people touch you so much more, and kiss you, and use endearments more readily - and diminutives for everything - it's cosy.'

These probably weren't the things people would want to hear when we found ourselves, in this imagined future, unable to resist 'boring folk daft blethering on about it compulsively' as Julie claimed:

'When folk come out with that inevitable and seemingly innocent question: "oh did you really? And what was Poland like?" they have a quite specific - and of course *brief* - answer in mind, just like the Poles and their "what do you think of our country?" They want to hear that this place they've never had the least desire to visit themselves might, after all, be a wee bit nicer than the rather dreich and dreary images they have of it in their heads. Not so fine that they need to feel that they've missed out on anything - nor so bad they've to feel awkward about it's existence, their own privileges etc. They want you to speak about it like a place you might go on holiday - you know, kindly folk, pleasant scenery. Above all, don't get onto anything you might actually have feelings about, anything problematic, anything complicated, like politics, or psychology, or religion (especially not here in Glasgow) and, whatever you do, don't speak with urgency on any topic - that's in awful poor taste.'

I knew for a fact when I read this that I'd be standing at that fictional school gate with those friendly, cheerful mummies injecting into the light conversation those unwelcome doses of Central European pathos, complexity and despair. In my Western outpost, with the rain sheeting across the dales, I'd have to supply that, because otherwise it wouldn't be there. I'd sense the inappropriateness, the unease, but I wouldn't be able to help myself, because although I yearned for the absence of the burden, actually, without it, nothing would feel quite real, quite alive.

Do we *all* have that instinct to represent the missing, the ones who are not there? Or are there just habits we pick up along the way? Julie certainly thought so:

'I notice folk keeking at me a wee bit disapproving and I realise I've been talking specific sums of money in a conversation in a way that's not quite the thing,' she'd written. I never say "it cost a fortune" or "it was a rare bargain" - it's as if I always waggle the exact price tag under their nose - or I always want to know exactly how much or little they paid before I'll be impressed. Last week - would you credit it? - I even caught myself asking someone how much they earned?!'

O.K. so we'd be social misfits, but surely one of the things Britain had going for it, at least in our rosy expatriate view, was its tolerance. We'd be alright. It became clearer and clearer that we couldn't stay here. It often appeared that Poles coveted all the stuff about Britain that we despised, had tried to get away from, and disliked the only things we were proud of - the very things which had been under assault for so long by the 'regime'. We'd run away out of self-preservation, not to stand by and watch the destruction we were unable to prevent - but now that seemed like a cop-out. Tories or no Tories, it was time to go back.

Or perhaps we'd just die of boredom. Julie was only half joking when she complained that she felt half asleep most of the time, as though part of her brain had shut down, dozed off:

'When you're speaking Polish, even when content of what folk are saying is perfectly ordinary you can appreciate it *linguistically*. You get a wee rush just from the work your brain puts in to follow those constructions, recognise that vocabulary. Here, I'm just left with what folk are actually saying - and half the time, I can't believe they bother! I mean, why trouble yourself to put together a string of words to express such a commonplace thought? It sounds awful arrogant, I know, but it applies to myself too. Yet if they'd said it in Polish, I'd have *enjoyed* it, have relished putting together my equally banal but hopefully perfectly grammatically constructed reply. In fact, the more clichéd the better, since in that case I'd have known I'd said the authentic Polish thing in the circumstances. I think it's about liking to have certain wee nodes in your brain light up - but maybe I just like my communication to take place in a haze of self-congratulation.'

I read Julie's letter several times, carried it about in my bag. It was good to hear her voice. She was more forthcoming on her experience of reintegration into Glasgow life than she was on her job prospects or the state of play between her and Marek. She and Marek had a lot of stuff to work out, naturally, but there'd been a note in her voice I'd rarely heard before. Was it relaxation, or a worrying detachment? It might even have been happiness. I wasn't sure I'd be too hot at recognising that any more.

Flight

Dolores wasn't at the airport. I was quite relieved. I didn't dare let on to Nell that I was half listening out for the click of stiletto heels, half expecting to catch the black leather sheen of Big Al's jacket out of the corner of my eye. Last time that I'd mentioned to Nell that I was fretting, she'd still thought it a huge joke. It would have been nice to have Dolores to talk to on the flight.

My plane was delayed on the way back from Warsaw. I'd told Nell not to meet me. Koshka would be asleep. I took a taxi home, a plastic tea-set in my bag. I wished I didn't have to wait till the morning to give it to her.

Andrzej was sitting on the sofa when I walked in. He held a small, L-shaped newspaper cutting in his hand for Nell, who'd pulled up her chair, to look at. They

309

were so transfixed, the two of them, that they barely acknowledged me. Nell translated it slowly, out loud, as if its contents might be hard to fathom.

The clipping told a sorry tale of unfinished flats, missing pipes and tiles, of innocent Poles cheated of thousands of dollars while the mysterious foreigners who had promised so much had simply vanished, probably to South America. Al (of whom there was a heavy, villainous-looking photo) had skipped the country along with his wife (of whom there was an altogether more fetching shot in a swimsuit).

'I want to believe is very big foreigners' scam,' Andrzej was saying, 'but I heard also very many the rumours...'

'Like what?' Nell asked him.

'That in factuality scam was by workers on sites, who stole so much the materials whole project was become impossible. Others are saying that was corruption in city council, who was wanting so many and so big bribings that ...' he tailed off.

'Who knows?' Nell shook her head. 'I'm sorry to say, it could be any of these - but they've still gone. At least it looks like it.'

'You didn't give him any money, did you?' I asked Andrzej, as my head cleared.

'Luckily I didn't make such mistake.'

'But you met with him?'

'Oh yes, on Thursday. I was to be beginning to give money - very big money - on the next week.'

'You seem very calm about it.' I was feeling considerably less calm about absorbing the information that our friends might have been deliberate con-artists. Did it explain something uncomfortable about them, or did nothing make any sense at all?

'It's Poland,' Andrzej said simply. 'Such crazy stuffs happen here. It's normal.'

'You can't just accept that,' Nell started, and my heart sank. 'That's part of the problem, the passivity, the cynicism. It's a kind of collusion. You know it is. It was under the Communists and it is now.'

'Of course. Many don't accept it. Many leave. But this changing from within, it is not our style. Even it is a little suspicious, a little communistic. Always things are done to us from outside. Inside we conserve what we have and we believe and we in same time refuse to believe some very special things. And we resist what is done to us from outside, and we don't help in it any way, even if it prevent the normal life conditions. We are very good at it. Even we are specialists I might say. If what is inside was outside, even we would resist that as well. And as things are now, well, maybe we like it. Maybe it allow us something, some surreal sorts of life.'

'And no responsibility.'

'Of course not. That is the best. Now, I know you don't have any of vodka left after your party, so I brought you very special from Finland bottle'. He retrieved his briefcase from the floor by the sofa and pulled from it a bottle decorated with a menorah and a larger-than-life looking rabbinical figure. 'It is so-called kosher vodka. You can buy also here in Poland but nowadays it is so extreme popular that you can't easy to buy it. It annoy Alina because when I have beard I am resembling so much to this man.'

'But you always have a beard,'

310

'Of course. I said it annoy Alina…' He laughed as he poured vodka into the shot glasses I had fetched from the kitchen. 'Actually, when I was first beginning with Alinka, I used to have no beard in summer time, only in winter for warmth. So part of year she had me like she want me and other half I was having her not very satisfied. It was like pact. Alina was half a year in Hades with me, no?'

We raised our glasses. 'Now,' said Andrzej solemnly, gesturing with the still, clear liquid between his finger and thumb towards the newspaper clipping lying on the table, ' to be using the phrase from this most respected so-called organ of opinions of people, let us drink to "vanishing foreigners."'

'Vanishing foreigners!'

'Na zdrowie!'

Acknowledgement

The Elephant and the Polish Question has its origins a long time ago, and I have accumulated many debts along the way. It's a pure pleasure at last to be able to thank the following:

Martin Walsh, for his patience, help and collaboration, as well as Jane Nichols, and Grace Banks for reading some or all of these stories, and for their encouragement and many useful suggestions. Thanks also to Sarah Hoskin who, in the olden days, when I didn't have a computer and couldn't even type, prepared the first typescripts.

Jolanta Litwinowicz, for providing me with much-needed information and for being ever-responsive to seemingly random demands for factual details, Krystyna Kietlinska, Joanna Madalinska, Dorota Fong, and Krzysztof Zanussi: their conversations have animated the process of writing and enabled me to see Poland differently.

For support in the aspiration of writing, Rodie Sudbery, Stanley Robertson and Faith Eckersall; also Kenneth Stephen, who, as Aberdeen City writer in residence provided essential advice and direction, and Chip Martin, who first urged me to write a purely Polish collection.

Friends in Poland and Scotland for sharing their knowledge, their humour and their experiences, adding much to my understanding and enjoyment of their country - as well as for many instances of genuine and unstinting hospitality: Beata and Tomek Bolanowscy, Ela and Michael Clegg, Zofia Goljanek and Ewa Goljanek-Ritchie, Adam and Ania Gosiewscy, Dorota Gudaniec, Bozena and Janusz Hordynscy, Pia and Mirek Jascinscy, Grazyna Jefferies, Dorota and Adam Kierat, Iwona Lamb, Helena Lembryck, Justyna Limon, Stanislawa Litwinowicz, Andrzej and Zusia Niedzielscy, Jardine Simpson, Stefan and Ada

Strychaccy, Boguska and Jacek Szelozynscy, Joanna and Ryszard Witt, Ruda Zawisza, Jennifer Zielinska, and Robert Zielinski.

My long-suffering Polish teachers, Malgorzata Cieslak, Irena Bogucka and Jan Deregowski - the last of whom bears no resemblance to the professor of that name in this book, not least for never having been known to engage in fatuous praise of women! Nonetheless, his scrupulous attention to the MSS eradicated many inaccuracies and errors, and those that remain are my own.

Derek and Kathy Knott, for kindness long ago, and Celia Barrett, Rita de Bunsen, and Sybil Hollins, for instruction and forbearance. Sheila Milne of Pennan for excellent food and shelter and a perfect place to write, and Diana Grell for enlightenment and a change of heart.

For financial support, the original and the present line-up of Danse McCabre Ceilidh Band: Koshka Duff, Erin Smith and Lauren Steel, Anne Taylor, Claire White, and Frances Wilkins - who helped me to realise the brilliant plan of going to other people's parties and getting paid - and for ensuring that I got out a lot more and learnt to make people dance.

Liam O'Sullivan, who is no longer alive to read these, but who shaped the consciousness of the person who wrote them, and without whom I cannot imagine having begun; David Yahuda, from whom I learnt a great deal more than I expected, providing the impetus to finish the collection.

Koshka Duff, who is in no way responsible for the sickeningly sweet portrayal of her infant self in some of these pages, but for actually being that amazing in life, such that it wasn't possible to depict her in any other way. Also for her enthusiastic but always incisive commentary on the stories themselves. Miriam Duff, whose excellent sleeping habits allowed me to start writing all that time ago, and who nowadays rolls her eyes less at this than at most of my other activities. And for being so unhesitatingly who she is. I thank David Duff for the immense assistance he has given. This book exists both in spite and because of him: 'Opposition is true friendship'.

Anthony Delgrado and Fiona Jordan at Bluechrome, and editor Sam Bevan, for turning this into such a beautiful book, and especially to Fiona for the wonderful cover. SlingInk, Pushing Out The Boat, and Cinnamon Press for permission to reprint 'New Era, New Perspective'

Finally, Alan Spence, whose friendship and consideration have helped sustain me through the stressful process of publication, and Vladimir Brljak, gentleman scholar and sinister scenester extraordinaire, for the welcome distraction of some fascinating things to read.

About the Author

Helen Lynch has two daughters and lives in Aberdeen, where she teaches Medieval Literature at the University and performs with all-female ceilidh band Danse McCabre. Between 1987 and 1993 she lived and worked in various cities in Poland. She has previously published short stories in anthologies and literary magazines, as well as interactive web-resources for children: *Beowulf for Beginners* and *The Knight with the Lion*.